THE CALLIGRAPHY
OF DREAMS

Juan Marsé

THE CALLIGRAPHY
OF DREAMS

Translated from the Spanish by
Nick Caistor

MACLEHOSE PRESS
QUERCUS · LONDON

First published in the Spanish language as *Caligrafía de los sueños*
by Lumen, Barcelona, in 2011
First published in Great Britain in 2014 by MacLehose Press
This paperback edition published in 2015 by

MacLehose Press
an imprint of Quercus Publishing Ltd
Carmelite House
50 Victoria Embankment
London EC4Y 0DZ

An Hachette UK Company

Copyright © Juan Marsé, 2011
English translation copyright © 2014 by Nick Caistor

Este libro ha recibido una ayuda a la traducción
del Ministerio de Educación, Cultura y Deporte

The moral right of Juan Marsé to be
identified as the author of this work has been
asserted in accordance with the Copyright,
Designs and Patents Act, 1988.

Nick Caistor asserts his moral right to be identified as
the translator of the work.

A CIP catalogue record for this book is available
from the British Library.

ISBN (PB) 978 1 78206 488 6
ISBN (Ebook) 978 1 78206 487 9

The face of the angel of history is turned toward the past. Where we perceived a chain of events, he sees a single catastrophe which keeps piling wreckage and hurls it in front of his feet. The angel would like to stay, awaken the dead, and make whole what has been smashed.

WALTER BENJAMIN, 1940

1

SEÑORA MIR AND THE DISUSED TRACKS

Torrente de las Flores. He never thought that a street whose name meant a river of flowers could be the backdrop to a tragedy. From the top of Travesera de Dalt, the street slopes steeply downwards, levelling out where it meets Travesera de Gràcia. It has forty-six corners, is seven and a half metres wide, is lined with low-rise buildings, and boasts three taverns. In summer, during the perfumed days of the patron saint's fiesta, drowsy beneath an ornamental bower of paper bunting and multi-coloured garlands, the street takes on a sound like reeds rustling in the breeze, and a quavering, underwater glow that makes it seem other-worldly. After supper on nights of stifling heat, it becomes an extension of everyone's home.

These events happened many years ago, when the city was less believable than now, but more real. One July Sunday, shortly before two in the afternoon, the blazing sun and a sudden shower mingle for a few minutes, and the air is filled with a shimmering light, a wavering, deceptive transparency that envelops the whole street. This is turning out to be a very hot summer, and by this time of day the blackish road surface has become so heated that the drizzle evaporates even before it hits the ground. When the shower ends, on the pavement outside the Rosales bar-cum-wine cellar a block of ice delivered by a truck and loosely wrapped in a cloth is melting in the remorseless sunlight. It's not long before tubby Agustín, the bar owner, emerges with bucket and ice pick, squats down, and starts chipping pieces off it.

On the stroke of half-past two, a little higher up than the bar and across the street, where the optical illusion is at its strongest, Señora Mir comes running out of the doorway of number 117. She is clearly in distress, as if she is fleeing a fire or an apparition. She stands in the middle of the road in her slippers, her white nurse's uniform only half done up, apparently unconcerned that she is revealing what she shouldn't. For a few seconds she doesn't seem to know where she is; she twists round, clawing the air with both hands until she stops spinning and, head sunk on her chest, lets out a long, hoarse cry that seems to come from the pit of her stomach, a scream that slowly subsides into sighs and then tails off like a kitten's mewling. She takes a few stumbling steps up the street, comes to a halt. She turns as if searching for support, and then, closing her eyes and crossing her arms over her chest, she kneels down, slowly folding her body into itself as if this offered her some relief or respite, and lies on her back on the tram tracks embedded into what remains of the old cobbled surface.

Her neighbours and the few weary passers-by toiling along the upper end of the street at this time of day can scarcely believe their eyes. What can have got into this woman? Stretched out full length (not that this is saying much, in her case) her chubby knees, tanned from the Barceloneta beach, peeking out of her half-open housecoat, her feet in their satin slippers with grubby pompoms pressed tightly together: what the devil is she up to? Can it really be she intends to end her life under the wheels of a tram?

"Victoria!" yells a woman from the pavement. "What are you doing, poor thing?"

There's no response. Not even the blink of an eye. A small group of curious onlookers quickly gathers round the prone figure, most of them fearing they are the butt of some cruel hoax. An elderly man goes over and prods the woman's ample hip several times with the tip of his cane, as if unsure she is alive.

"Hey you, what nonsense is this?" he mutters, poking her. "What on earth do you think you're doing?"

Making tongues wag, as always, more than one of her woman neighbours must have been thinking: what wouldn't that slut do to get her man's attention? A blonde forty-something with flashing blue eyes, sociable by nature and very popular in the neighbourhood, the plump Señora Mir, who had been a Registered Nurse trained in the Falange College and now worked as a therapist and professional kinesiologist (as stated on her business cards) has forever given rise to gossip thanks to her daring hands, which give massages and soothe a variety of pains. Her ambiguous talents have encouraged many an amorous adventure, especially since her husband, a bullying, loud-mouthed former local councillor, has been shut away in the San Andrés sanatorium since the end of the previous year. In Bar Rosales, Señora Mir's manual dexterity has always provoked mocking delight, if not cruel sarcasm, and yet to see her now, flat on her back in the middle of the street in a parody of suicide – or perhaps actually meaning it, led to this extremity by some mental disturbance, and looking so firm and resolute in her decision – to see her lying there in the stream, with her round, pale-complexioned face edged with curls and her bewildered lips smeared as ever with lipstick, was beyond their wildest dreams. She appeared so sure of her imminent, ghastly demise beneath the wheel that was coming to slice off her head that it was hard to credit that such determination, such a desperate urge could be based on a complete miscalculation. Something terrible but at the same time laughable was obviously going on beneath those peroxide curls because, although the initial reaction of the passers-by when they saw her prone on the tram rails was one of stupefaction and pity, now that they could assess the dramatic scene unfolding before their eyes more coolly, it became risible: nobody in their right mind could imagine anything so absurd, a more impossible way to be run over and killed. Years earlier, a prostrate body like hers would have caused much greater alarm, even horrified protests, and could possibly have had fatal consequences

9

(although, on second thoughts, the tram would have been going so slowly on this stretch of the street that it would have been highly unlikely) but the fact is that nowadays there is no way anything like that could happen, because Señora Mir appears to have overlooked one vital detail: the rail on which her little head is so anxiously seeking the dream of death, as well as its parallel counterpart where her ample knees are resting, is all that remains of the former tramway system – two bars of laminated steel barely a metre long, rusting now and almost buried in a block of cobblestones. The whole street was asphalted over a long time previously, but for some unknown reason this short, three metre-long section of cobbles was spared, together with the two worn bits of rail. In the last few feet of its downhill trajectory, the disused tracks begin a gentle turn to the right as they approach the next corner: silent witnesses to an abolished, forgotten route. No-one in the neighbourhood could have explained why they were not torn up along with all the rest of the track, what reasoning or lack of it had left them to grow rusty and sink further each day into the brief stretch of the now vanished cobblestones, but the more pertinent question that several of the women neighbours find themselves asking is: does that scatterbrain Victoria Mir really think a tram is going to come along and kill her? Has she gone nuts like her husband? She only has to open her eyes to see there's no electric cable up there for a tramcar pole to connect to.

"Sweet Jesus! Just look at this, for the love of God!" cries an old lady standing on the kerb, a black mantilla covering her head and a rosary between her fingers. "Just look at that poor creature!"

The would-be suicide lies motionless on the tracks, hands folded across her chest, mouthing heaven knows what fervent prayer through fleshy lips, or begging for grace from the azure sky; the tremendous expressivity of her closed, pleading eyes lends her face the gravity of a death mask. A passer-by in his Sunday best bends over her with a pitying look.

"This isn't right, Señora," he says. "What are you thinking of, putting your life in danger like this?"

"What's wrong with you, Vicky?" shouts a woman in housecoat and slippers who comes running up. "What are you doing lying in the street like that? Is this a joke? You ought to be ashamed of yourself!"

Señora Mir doesn't deign to reply, but suddenly her body jerks and she puts her ear to the rail, as if she can hear tram wheels grinding round the bend, see it bearing down on her with a screech of iron: she opens her eyes and her pupils reflect a sudden terror. She turns her head in the opposite direction and, peering upwards, casts furtive glances at the balcony to her apartment, in the first row of windows giving on to the street. Her gaze becomes searching and harsh, as if she is trying to return an insult to whoever might be peering down to watch her being run over by the tram. But no-one is on the balcony, so she settles her head back on the rail again and closes her eyes once more. Somebody comments that the man she is going with at the moment is or once was a tram driver.

"She always gets these hare-brained ideas," mutters Rufina the hair-dresser, who claims to know her well. "Something not right in your head, Vicky? What are you trying to prove? Do us all a favour! That's enough now!" She grasps her under the arms, but is unable to lift her. "Listen, if you really want the tram to run you over, you can sit up properly to wait for it, sweetheart!" She closes her eyes with a resigned sigh and whispers to the woman standing next to her: "I'll bet anything this is thanks to that good-for-nothing who wormed his way into her place . . ."

"Hmm."

"Leave her where she is, if that's what she wants," another old lady says dolefully. "What's the point? Life is for youngsters anyway."

"Is your daughter home, Vicky? Somebody should go and tell her . . ."

"No!" Señora Mir immediately protests. "She's not at home . . . Violeta went to the beach with her friend Merche . . ."

A boy aged about fifteen, in shirtsleeves and carrying a book, comes to a halt and glances as if casually at the supine woman's breasts. They're peeping out of her white coat, with no sign she is wearing a bra; their rough, reddish tinge reminds him of Violeta's ugly, freckled face. A skinny, dirty mongrel ambles up and sniffs at the pompoms on the faded slippers and the folded hands reeking of embrocation, then saunters round the gathered group, whose comments are still raining down on Señora Mir, apparently to no avail. Two next-door neighbours, Señoras Grau and Trías, exchange sly smiles as they try to lift her from the riverbed.

"What's the matter, Victoria?" Señora Grau murmurs in her ear. "Won't you tell me? You've been crying . . . Has that lame devil beat you?"

"Why are you staring up at the balcony so often?" asks Señora Trías. "Is he in there now? Do you still allow a rogue like him in? Didn't you say you were going to leave him?"

"If you're not trying to teach him a lesson."

"Oh, Vicky, when will you come back down to earth?"

"That bastard husband of hers would love to see her the way she is now," jokes the owner of the corner store, protected by the circle of women. "Waiting for the tram flat on her back like this. I'm sure that jackass of a councillor would be proud, if he hasn't lost all his many marbles."

"Be quiet, won't you?" the others scold him. "Can't you see she's had some sort of fit?"

"Come on, get up, make the effort," says the man who first approached her. "Don't you realise where you are?" he says, pointing to the rail her head is resting on and gazing sternly down at her. He seems determined to make her see sense, to suggest what's only right and proper, to tell her for example listen, these tracks are no good for what you want to do, Señora, no trams have come down here in years. But all he adds is: "Don't tempt fate, Señora. Believe me, it's not worth it."

"Watch out, it's coming!" guffaws the storekeeper.

"Get her away from there, what are you waiting for?" somebody says.

"You're only making things worse for yourself, Vicky," Señora Grau whispers to her. "I'm telling you. Who could ever have imagined such a shameful, dreadful thing!"

The elderly lady with the mantilla nods forlornly and scolds her:

"Don't you know that suicide is a mortal sin, even on tram tracks like this?"

"Quite a show you're putting on, Señora Mir!" a male voice says sarcastically. "Aren't you ashamed of yourself?"

"Watch out, the tram really is coming," some wit mocks from a balcony. The warning is greeted with laughter and applause, but nonetheless startles several of the onlookers standing near the lengths of track.

"Be reasonable and get up," one woman begs her, adding persuasively: "Shall I tell you something? There won't be a tram coming through here for an hour at least."

"Are you sure?" says another woman standing next to her. "What if they've changed the timetable?"

"I don't think they have."

"Whenever did those layabouts change anything?" a bad-tempered fellow interjects. "Since when has City Hall ever given a damn about the needs of us pedestrians?"

"You're right there. This neighbourhood has always been left to its own devices."

By now the young lad is quite close, and could swear he too has heard it. Slightly perplexed, with the dog-eared book tucked under his arm, his white shirt smelling faintly of thyme, for a moment he thinks he can hear the metallic grating sound of the tram as it turns the corner, and so on a sudden impulse, securing the book under his armpit and with the tied-up bunch of thyme dangling from his shoulder, he draws closer to the group and listens closely, almost as if hypnotised. Are they saying these things just to play along with the poor crazy woman, claiming, to encourage her to stand up, that she's in real and imminent danger if she persists in her ludicrous performance, or is it because somehow they also can sense the danger? He has noticed that several of the people surrounding the desperate suicide, feigning extreme anguish and horror, and playing out the comedy of getting her away from the tracks to save her from a senseless death, cannot avoid a certain unease and are glancing nervously towards the street corner. All at once their pretence and play-acting, this most trite and farcical though well-meaning performance – everything that until now had seemed phantasmagorical and absurd – has suddenly become not only real, but natural and convincing: the disused tracks appear live and in use; the tram-car that was never going to arrive is on the verge of turning the corner and crushing them all, with terrible, inevitable consequences not merely for Señora Mir, but for many of those crowded around her. Some of them, giving up in the face of her stubborn refusal to move, have chosen to leave the road and climb on to the pavement. Jostling each other in a tight scrum, and still insisting on the farcical pretence, they cannot avoid casting furtive glances at the street corner.

Go on, you poor lunatic, put your neck under the wheel, make them see it, show them it can happen, he hears himself muttering. Possibly this is the very first time that the boy intuits, in however vague and fleeting a manner, that what is invented can carry more weight and truthfulness than what is real, more life of its own, be more meaningful, and consequently have more chance of triumphing over oblivion.

Struggling upright on the rails, Victoria Mir seems to hear only one voice among the many bombarding her with queries and reproaches. A good-looking, smartly dressed fellow with a pleasant voice and graceful, feline gestures bends down and offers her his arm: take heart, Señora, are you feeling alright? Leaning on him to rise to her feet, she smiles gratefully, then recalls some massages (or perhaps more than massages) she has given him, and suddenly blurts out: "And how are those handsome legs with that blond fuzz of theirs, Señor Reich? Is your circulation any better?" and refuses help from anyone else. Unsteady but erect, she adjusts the uniform across her chest with numb fingers that smell of essence of turpentine, and immediately those same fingers flick at the curls on her forehead with a characteristically coquettish gesture. Despite being moist and with a pained look to them, her big, wide-set eyes, slightly crossed and with thin eyelashes, are completely unfocused. She stares round about her as if she does not recognise anyone. She glances rapidly at the boy.

"You, my lad," she whispers, "you can read music, so you understand me."

The boy is a slightly reserved-looking adolescent with a sulky expression. He is wearing tyre-soled sandals, has a pencil behind one ear, and a mop of curly hair that hangs down over his brow. Taken by surprise by Señora Mir, he takes a step back, and the book slides from under his arm. He manages to catch it before it hits the ground. Witches simply know that kind of thing, he tells himself. As happens so often in his dreams, he perceives a mixture of truth and absurdity in everything taking place in front of his eyes. Watching the nurse casting about her with a trembling hand, trying to regain her balance in the centre of the crowd, she suddenly seems like an impostor, someone who has taken over another person's mental disarray, despair, and dreams. A few minutes earlier he had thought that her passionate surrender to the fatal tram tracks was utterly sincere, but now he no longer knows what to think. Apparently the good woman is as mad as a hatter and was determined to kill herself, and yet he is learning not to trust appearances. As he considers the truncated rails and the pantomime she has just put on for the benefit of the onlookers now climbing rather apprehensively back on to the pavement, he senses that another reality is slipping through his fingers. Would he someday be able to seize that other reality, would it be offered to him complete, without distortions, naked, free from mirages or lures?

As though this were some kind of promise he is making himself, he squeezes the battered volume tight under his arm to feel the life beating within it, secretly summoning close to his heart the dry, frozen skeleton of the leopard lying on the snow.

Oblivious to the comments and advice from her neighbours – "You shouldn't go anywhere on your own in that state, run straight home and stop this nonsense, Victoria, just imagine if the tram cut off your legs, go to Las Ánimas and confess, that'll make you feel better, somebody should tell your daughter, and while she's on her way have a nice cup of lime blossom tea" – ignoring all their suggestions, Señora Mir looks

15

askance at the grey cobbles and bits of rail like someone staring at an indecipherable sign. The boy too is gazing surreptitiously at the tracks. Chopped off, turning towards nowhere, parallel to the end and rotting half-buried in the road, passively enduring the rays of a punishing sun high in the blue sky, what attraction do these useless, forgotten scraps of iron exert? What is the meaning of the miscalculation or deceit they have inspired? Did the idea of death really touch her during those brief minutes she was stretched out on that delusion?

A generous hand brushes her elbow, and for an instant Señora Mir thinks she is being supported. She does not seem to hear any of the comments or to feel lost. She stares insistently at the rails and their truncated destiny, their strange call to her from the riverbed, and finally she looks away, refuses the help of a neighbour wanting to accompany her, and slowly sets off on her own, head down, back to her apartment. Instead, though, she walks past it, crosses the road, and continues on the opposite pavement as far as Bar Rosales. The stray mongrel that had sniffed her slippers follows at a distance. Eventually it comes to a halt and sits on its hind quarters looking in her direction and scratching its ear, while all of a sudden it gets an erection. From the bar doorway, treading without realising it in the small puddle from the block of ice, the frustrated suicide turns to exchange glances with the dog, her head tilted in exactly the same way, then disappears inside.

You don't have to be a clairvoyant to know that Señora Mir will order a small glass of brandy, with a siphon of soda she will hardly touch.

2

A PLAGUE OF BLUE RATS

"The devil take this country!"

In his underwear, the boy's father flicks the torch on and off three times to show it doesn't work, and for the third time curses his bad luck. It is as though the lack of contact of a poorly fitting battery in an old torch represents to him a degrading metaphor for the wretched country he so profoundly loathes. Alternatively, it might also seem as though he were sending a coded message to somebody hidden in the shadows, were it not for the fact that he is all alone in the bedroom, with the shutters closed. This possibility arises because, even sitting on the edge of the bed in his underpants and with socks and suspenders on his hairy legs like this, dishevelled and half-asleep, there is something of the man of action about him, refusal to accept everyday routine or grow accustomed to defeat. His alert features seem to sniff out adversity and, ready to confront it once again, he suddenly rises to his feet, puffs out his cheeks, puts the torch away in the small suitcase beside him, and starts getting dressed.

That case must already contain the revolver, the poison and the bait, thinks his son, peering through the half-open door. The boy hesitates a moment, then enters the bedroom, fists stuffed in his trouser pockets, trying to look tough.

"I want to go with you, Father. I'll help you kill them."

"No chance."

He allows a few seconds to elapse, then pleads: "Please, I'd really like to."

"No. You wouldn't like it. You're not old enough for that kind of work."

"I could keep an eye out at the exit. There's always some sneaky rat that tries to escape. I'm not frightened of them anymore, you know?"

"The answer's still no, my boy. Besides, they're already dead. We just have to pick them up."

"Are you sure they're all dead? There's always one or two that get away."

"Am I speaking Chinese? I said no."

It's a Saturday afternoon, and the boy doesn't have school. He has an hour of music theory and piano, but although reading music and practising his scales is what he most enjoys in the world, for once he would be willing to skip his lesson.

"Why don't you want me to go?" he whines.

"You'd faint as soon as you got inside."

"Nonsense! I could hold the torch while you finish them off . . ."

His father is sitting on the bed again, his shirt half on. He scratches the palm of his hand with long, grubby nails. As he is doing this, he stares into space with such a lost, empty look that all at once he looks like a completely different person.

"Is something wrong, father?"

He reacts immediately, and stands up.

"What is wrong is that I've had it up to here with just about everything. I said no, and that means no."

Glancing down at his watch, he mutters under his breath: "I overslept, godammit."

"You promised. You said you'd teach me to hunt blue rats."

His father is the head of a team from the Municipal Cleansing and Pest Control Service. They work in public places: cinemas, theatres, restaurants, markets, shops. When the boy first learnt this on his eighth birthday, his mother warned him not to tell his friends at school or in the parish, because they might laugh at him for having a rat-catcher father. Back in those days, he imagined him wearing a gas mask, club in hand, chasing huge rats among the seats of a cinema. That image had stayed with him for a year or two, but nowadays he suspects that the exterminator uses more rapid and drastic methods alongside the poisoned bait and pesticides, especially with the blue rats. He often hears him curse and blaspheme against the terrible, disgusting plague of blue rodents infesting the city, from the port and Montjuich right up to Tibidabo, although he himself has never come face-to-face with a blue rat, alive or dead.

In his mind's eye he sees once more his father at the counter of Bar Rosales, slowly turning towards him. He is very stiff and tipsy, clutching the glass of wine against his chest as if afraid somebody might snatch it from him, and muttering as he sees him pushing the door open:

"Here comes my dearly beloved son." A sly smile. "You like Barcelona don't you, my boy? You feel very safe in the big city, together with your second mother who saved you from the orphanage, don't you? Your mother who loves you so much and cares for you. Isn't that right?"

He ignores the reference to the orphanage and the second mother. He's still on the threshold, holding the door open but not coming in.

"Mother's waiting for you."

"You prefer to live here, don't you? Here, in this beautiful, damned capital of Catalonia. And all because I happened to see that taxi going by in the rain . . ."

"Mother says to come home, supper's ready."

"Don't interrupt me! We live in the arsehole of the world, in the furthest, shittiest corner of our Catholic realm, and yet you're as happy as can be. This is the city that saw you born almost by a miracle, and here you are, alive and kicking, and I'm pleased for you, my boy, but just so you remember, I was the one who spotted that taxi . . . Yes, this is where you'll become a useful member of society, a famous pianist admired by all upstanding citizens: that's what you think, isn't it? Well, not exactly, pumpkin head! Your fine city is nothing more than a stinking sewer riddled with blue rats! You need to know that, because you grand piano virtuosos tend to be over-sensitive."

With that he turned back to the counter, holding his glass out for Señora Paquita to fill for the umpteenth time. I'm not keeping count, he says, the tally of the glasses I've drunk is being kept by the Judeomasonic conspiracy. Oh yes, the intrepid Rat-catcher often says outrageous things like this, or even worse, while the bartender and the other customers laugh and exchange knowing winks, and the boy wonders why they laugh at the jokes, why they encourage him.

"I've never seen a blue rat, father," he says now in the bedroom. "One day in the sacristy at Las Ánimas I saw a big, fat rat on its hind legs chewing a cassock hanging from a peg. But it was grey, almost black."

"Yes, rats and cassocks, pests the lot of them!" his father grunts as he puts on his work overall. "But it's not the same, Son. Have you ever seen a fat, shiny rat writhing with poison? They crawl along squealing like condemned souls, vomiting blood from the mouth and arse. You wouldn't be able to bear the sight."

"Yes I would."

"No, you wouldn't. You'd wet your pants, I'm sure of it."

In recent months he has grown exasperated that his father still considers him a child. He peers at the case on the bed, wondering about the mysteries it contains. His father shakes his head violently as though to rid himself of a bad dream. His unruly hair, with a greenish tinge that lends it a furious look, gives off a strong aroma of roasted coffee, and that is another mystery. A secret, he was told, yet another one. Sometimes he comes to the conclusion that the poverty and other ills his family suffer are due to all these secrets in his father's life.

"Stay home and practise for your music lesson," his father advises him. "*Do-re-mi-fa-sol*, that's what you like best. Aren't you always saying you want to be a musician when you grow up? Well then, get studying. Besides, your mother will be back soon from the clinic."

"Oh, shit," the boy moans to himself, then stretches out his hand to stroke the case with his fingertips, imagining its lethal contents. "Can I at least carry the poison case for you?"

Pulling on his rubber boots, his father snorts impatiently.

"Oh alright, you pain in the neck. But don't get your hopes up, you're to wait for me in the street."

"All the time?"

"All the time. You're not to come in. So take your music scores with you and do something useful."

"Can I hold your revolver a moment?"

"What revolver? D'you think we're in a gangster movie? Take a look at the world-famous pianist!"

The cloud-cast shadow slowly climbing the façade of the Selecto cinema appears to him like a theatre curtain rising when, alone and resigned to having to wait, he bends one knee on the pavement to tie his shoelaces. It's a sunny but windy April afternoon. There's not much traffic and the people going up or down Calle Salmerón don't seem to detect the smell of poison he thinks must even now be spreading silently like a deadly green gas beneath the sealed-off entrance to the cinema and out of the projection room. He sees the men from the rat-catching brigade go in one by one through a small side door. They arrive at half-minute intervals; there are three of them, two in work clothes and one in ordinary attire. They walk by quickly without noticing him, although he knows the first two. The one in ordinary clothes is called Luis. He often comes to breakfast with his father when the latter is spending any length of time at home. The other is Manuel, and he arrives on a bike, and the boy includes the third man in the team because he approaches with the same stealthy walk as the other two, hands in the pockets of his faded overall and head sunk on his shoulders as though he were publicly ashamed of his rat-killing abilities. Some years earlier, when he was only a small boy, he had imagined the rat-catchers moving like squat robots, with green flashing eyes and knife-like fingers.

He whiles the time away by singing in his nasal, droning voice: "I'm King Rat the First, and I'm the Second, and I'm the Third", parodying the zarzuela comic opera tune his music teacher is so fond of and sings whenever he sits at the piano. Before long he's bored sick, and so devotes himself to obsessively imagining what is going on inside the cinema: he imagines his nose pricking at the smell of the pesticides floating over the stalls, he sees blue rats kicking the bucket, their bellies swollen, vomiting bloody froth from their mouths, crawling around under the seats and at the bottom of the screen, and also in the aisles, the toilets and the artistes' dressing rooms. He sees his father holding one by the tail, a big, jowly rat with a snow-white lock of hair over its bloodshot eye, driven out of its mind by the poison. He sees all this from out in the street, and lives it intensely without missing a single detail, just as if he were listening to one of Fatty Cazorla's tall tales.

He is hopping outside the cinema, scrupulously respecting the maze traced by the pavement tiles, aiming for a manhole cover with a worn, blurred maker's name on it. Once he reaches it he turns round, still on one leg, and repeats his hops time and again. At each new turn he expects to see his father at the cinema entrance beckoning to him to join the hunt and extermination of the blue rats. His father doesn't appear, but among the multi-coloured billboards announcing the acts of the variety artistes scheduled to appear, his attention is drawn to a poster about two metres high propped against the front of the building that shows a slender, smiling dancer in a figure-hugging black costume.

CHEN-LI, PUSS IN BOOTS
EXOTIC AND ACROBATIC DANCER

This Puss in Boots has pretty legs painted in golden glitter. She is portrayed as if crouching in mid-air, or rather falling backwards towards the ground, her body arched at an incredible angle, one leg stretched out straight, the other doubled beneath her buttocks. She is wearing a black skullcap with a mask and cat's ears, red patent calf-length boots, and her pert rear culminates in a bright red tail. The Selecto also puts on second-rate variety acts, with singers, jugglers and comedians who once enjoyed a fame of sorts in the popular musical reviews at the Paralelo theatre, but whose glory days have long since passed. Minors are forbidden entry to these shows, as he is well aware. Pinned to another board are blown-up stills from the two films being shown that week: "Seventh Heaven" with Simone Signoret, and "The Cat and the Canary" with Paulette Goddard. He is crazy about both these cat-like stars: their charms have often left him hot and bothered between the sheets. Now, though, he only has eyes for Puss in Boots. Why does her stomach fold in so softly above her groin? The curve of her thighs and buttocks seems to him strangely immaculate and poignant, far more beautiful than anything he has ever seen before on movie posters or the handbills he collects. Slowly, he traces the outline of her thigh, then strokes her golden skin and senses the inner tautness that propels her leap high into the air. Reflected in a window on the far side of the street, the sun's rays make the glitter sparkle for an instant, but do not spoil or lessen the urgent tension of her inner thigh, a generously delicate muscular promise he finds profoundly disturbing.

"What are you doing, my lad? What are you staring at?"

He turns round. A small, stooped man with slumped shoulders is standing on the manhole cover, blocking his path. He tries his magic trick – blinking his eyes twice – but the little man is still there, peering sternly at him.

"Me?"

"Yes, you. What are you looking at, if I might ask?"

"Me? Nothing."

"Nothing, you say. But you're fascinated by the way that little Chinese girl moves."

Ringo looks at the poster again.

"But she isn't moving . . ."

"She isn't? Can't you spot it? Those exotic dancers are never still, lad. Especially if they're Chinese and from the Paralelo."

He blinks again, and it's true, her thighs do move. The little man is scarcely taller than he is, and is clasping a leash in the fingers of a bony hand with a delicate, casual gesture as if holding a cigarette. At the other end, something is growling softly at his feet: a small, emaciated dog with a rat-like muzzle and ragged tail. It has one leg missing.

"What's that sticking out of your pocket?"

"My music book."

"Oh, my. So I can see you're a sensitive boy," says the stranger almost inaudibly. "You are sensitive, aren't you?"

"I don't know."

"And someday soon you'll be a nice, good-looking and respectful young man. I'm sure of it."

"No, sir. I'll be a pianist."

"Oh, that's very good. A pianist." The dog raises its head and stares at its master with yellow, rheumy eyes. "And what are you doing here?"

"Waiting for my father."

"Thinking dirty thoughts, that's what you're doing. Come on, don't deny it." A sound like a rasping file or fingernails scratching iron is coming from beneath the manhole cover. Alerted by something, the little man suddenly turns round, and his bird-like silhouette stands out against the grey solitude of the entrance to Plaza Trilla on the far side of the street. "Mind you, I'm not blaming you, you scamp. But listen carefully to what I say," he goes on, drawing closer, a sharper edge to his voice. "I bet you she can do things you couldn't even imagine, not if you stood here looking at her for a thousand years."

"You don't say! My goodness! A thousand years! Are you serious?" the boy asks, his voice deepening. "I could be here looking at her for a thousand years? And she could be dancing here for a thousand years, dancing the dance of the seven veils like Salome? Could she really?"

This is how some see him: a lively, observant youth alert to certain absurdities, endowed with a keen perception of other people's most extravagant, unlikely illusions, and ready to launch himself into whatever deception or intrigue the world lays before him. That's how he will be remembered: diligent, polite, steeped in the future. He does not blush, hesitate or muddle his words: he knows what he means to say at all times and why, and yet he is only too pleased to step resolutely over the threshold of the improbable or imperceptible. He stands quite still, facing the stranger on guard, noting the bony eyes with sparse lashes in a long, hollow-cheeked face, the small, pursed mouth, the shirt's crumpled collar and the black suit with shiny knees in trousers that are too wide and too big and sag over a sad, tame-looking pair of house slippers. He looks down at the crippled dog, and adopts an expression and voice to fit the melodramatic aspect of what he can see before him: "She's my stepsister, you know."

He wonders whether to add that the dancer's real name is Diana Palmer, once Edmund Dantés' other true love, and then the secret love of Winnetou, and now is linked to the villain Rupert de Hentzau, and that she could have been his half sister, but with a Chinese mother, and that she ran away from home to be a dancer because she wanted to see the world and was ashamed of having a father who was a rat-catcher and whose great paws always stink of disinfectant or sulphur or worse. But instead he only thinks all this, and the only thing he adds is: "My poor eldest stepsister. I have five more . . ."

The little man raises his hand to silence him. There is a sudden gleam in his ravaged eyes.

"So we're a little liar, are we?" Offended, he stamps on the manhole cover three times, as though giving a prearranged sign to the rats that live in the pestilential shadows beneath. Then, pointing to the poster, the stranger adds in his fluty voice: "Well anyway, let's concentrate on what's important. Besides being an exotic dancer, this lovely girl is a contortionist. Do you know what that means?"

"Of course."

"That she knows how to move in a special way."

"Of course."

"And she's really pretty, isn't she? So pretty it hurts to look at her, doesn't it?"

"Excuse me, sir, your dog has only got three legs but it stays on its feet very well, doesn't it? What's it called?"

"Tula. It's a little bitch. And what's your name, my boy?"

"Ringo. I won't shake hands because I've touched rat poison. Ringo Kid, that's my name."

He kneels down to look at the little dog, feigning a sudden interest. It has almond-shaped eyes and stiff ears. On one of them he sees a tick as round and shiny as a pearl. It's so fat you would need a pair of pliers to pull it off, he thinks.

"That's some ti—"

"Keep away from toxic products that aren't edible," the little man cuts in. "That's my advice to you. And as for that Chinese girl . . ." he hesitates a moment, gazing sorrowfully, his skinny finger pointing at the dancer in the poster, "stay away from her too. You should know that this week's programme is not suitable for minors. How old are you?"

"Eleven, almost twelve, sir."

"Besides, they've fumigated the building, so for now it's closed and sealed off."

"I know."

"So what are you doing here all on your own?"

"I've just told you, I'm waiting for my father."

"And where is your father?"

"In the cinema, catching rats."

"That's good. Rats bring the black plague."

"The plague these days isn't black, Señor, it's blue. My father said so."

Right now he and his team are inspecting the poisoned bait they laid a few days ago, he says, when they sprinkled the place with pesticides and closed it down on orders from City Hall. My father knows all the official regulations, he's an authority, he knows how to combat the rat menace. No, they don't use traps and a piece of cheese anymore, they don't have cats or brooms to chase them with, no Señor. Not even the Nogat powders – Nogat: Terror of the Rats – they're old-fashioned; my father has a Colt

45. When he grows up, he says, he will also devote himself to getting rid of all kinds of pests: rats, bugs, fleas, cockroaches and green lice.

The little dog is standing patiently on the pavement, listing slightly to one side. Its owner keeps looking furtively around him; the boy can see he is also precariously balanced, and the dandruff on his shoulders is like a layer of ash. The man nods, he's well aware of what happened in the cinema. In the middle of the magician Fu-Ching's performance, he says, a pair of rodents appeared on stage out of nowhere. Many in the public thought it was part of the act, and applauded, but not him. He was in the front row and immediately knew what was going on: they were two enormous, disgustingly real rats, the size of rabbits. They stood defiantly in front of the footlights baring their fangs, and soon panic and confusion spread among the audience.

"Do you realise how blind and stupid people have become, my boy?" the little man mutters, looking round him as though in search of visual support. "When did you ever see such a thing? Just imagine, the audience could clearly see they were rats – they were right in front of them, hairy and repulsive, and yet they all wanted to think it was a magic trick! No-one dares see things for what they are these days!"

Ringo shuts his eyes, trying to imagine the uproar and fear of people stampeding through the stalls of the cinema that night, but the golden thighs of Chen-Li the Puss in Boots are still glowing beneath his eyelids, and for now there is no room for anything else.

"That's because they're blue rats, Señor. My father explained to me that blue rats suck your blood. And when they die," he goes on, frowning, "they go up and guard the evening stars."

"Your father. I see, I see."

"You may not have seen them, but they're a plague. And something else. When the magician Fu-Ching pulls a rabbit out of his hat, it's because it was already there, isn't it?"

"Ah, who knows? But I'll tell you one thing. This beautiful Chen-Li is about as Chinese as I am Japanese. Take my word for it."

"Please, Señor, tell me the truth."

"The truth, the truth! Not worth a fig these days."

With stiff fingers he shakes the dandruff blooming on his black, shabby shoulders. He stands pensively staring at the nothing in front of his eyes, grimacing oddly as if about to sneeze, then bends down and strokes the back of his scrawny little three-legged dog. He thinks some more, until finally he loses his self-control and lets out a deep sigh. It's a momentary show of emotion that lasts less than a second, then he recovers his composure, straightens up, tugs gently on the lead, and whispers something to his pet. Another rapid flash of sunlight bounces off a window and falls, more gently this time, on the proud, glittering thighs of the Puss in Boots as she leaps in mid-air.

The boy has turned again to look at her when he hears the little man's resigned voice:

"Farewell, my lad, behave yourself. Next week," he adds as he starts moving away, "they're showing films I'm sure you'd like, if you could get in. If there are no more rats, they're putting on 'Topper' and 'The Scarlet Claw'."

"I've already seen 'The Scarlet Claw'. The murderer is the village postman."

Fog and marshes, Sherlock Holmes' hook nose, a bloody metal claw and mutilated corpses gnawed at by rats: he can remember the dark film very clearly as he watches the little man walk off down the street limping slightly, falling in step with his dog's lopsided gait, occasionally stretching down to give its head a pat, both of them leaning over and treading cautiously as if to avoid invisible obstacles. He turns back to again admire Chen-Li the Cat suspended in mid-air. Everything about her soaring body is fleeting and volatile, beyond reach. She has been caught at the moment she is rising, hoping never to fall, to stay forever fixed in this instant in memory and desire. Ringo peers at her inner thigh, that delicate, taut region that troubles him so. He spots something he had not seen before: it looks like a small tear in the skin, but peering more closely, he realises it is a caterpillar stuck to the glitter. The caterpillar has a greenish back with purple dots. It could have been attracted to the glitter by mistake, thinking it was honey, and yet it is odd to see it there. If it climbed a little higher, it would reach the groin beneath the satin shorts and it wouldn't take it long to reach the pelvis and then it could even slip inside the dancer's muff itself. Dark, moist, and sweet. But the insect is not moving. Ringo touches it cautiously, then pushes at it with his fingernail. The caterpillar falls to the ground, stiff as a board.

The Rat-catcher's poison has even got as far as this, he thinks.

He is sitting on the tram with the case on his lap. His father is standing beside him, in the middle of the aisle. It's a crowded number 24, and is going up Calle Salmerón where it crosses Calle Carolinas. An apologetic, mild-looking priest is shouldering his way through the crowded rear platform, uttering snatches of prayer from thick pink lips. He reaches the aisle, but there are no free seats; lots of passengers are having to stand. The reverend is thickset, with a ruddy complexion, heavy jowls, and a proud head of snowy-white tousled hair. Just the sort of hearty, plain-talking clergyman that my father eats for breakfast every day, the boy groans inwardly, dreading the imminent drama and how ashamed he's going to feel. His mind is still dazzled by the image of the honeyed thighs of Puss in Boots as he watches the priest advance determinedly along the aisle. He gives a magic blink to shoo him away, but he keeps on coming, and now to make things even worse is staring at him with a smile on his face, as though taking it for granted that this good, well-brought-up young boy is bound to get up and offer him his seat.

His father remains standing beside him, his hand pressing lightly but persistently on his shoulder in a gesture the boy sees as one of possession and authority that embarrasses him in public. His father's hand is large, with prominent nerves and cracked, greenish skin like a lizard's. Even when, as now, the hand is resting in a friendly way on his shoulder, or when it is clutching the neck of a wine bottle, or sweeping up crumbs on a tablecloth, or dangling over the edge of the table or the arm of a chair – even when it is cupped very still and peaceful on his mother's accommodating knee – the boy has always noted a latent fury in the knuckles, a permanent tension. It is so close to his face now that he catches a whiff of rat poison ingrained beneath his father's fingernails, the same acrid stench impregnated on his rubber boots, his blue overalls and a very strange tool dangling from his belt next to a electric torch that he must use to blind and immobilise the rats before finishing them off. Even stranger and more incongruous is the effect produced by the striped navy-blue jacket he is wearing over his work clothes, a fitted sports jacket in good condition: it is as if from the waist up his father were coming from a posh party, whereas from the waist down he had just emerged from a stinking sewer full of dead rats. For some unknown reason, the boy is suddenly reminded of the little man tapping his foot on the man-hole cover with his three-legged dog beside him.

One of the buttons on the chest of the priest's cassock has come undone, doubtless due to the pushing and shoving on the platform. His bushy eyebrows curl in every direction, and are as white as his impressive mane of hair. By now he is close by and continues to stare at Ringo. The good-mannered boy is thinking he ought to stand up and offer him his seat: at school he has been taught to be polite to women, especially if they are elderly or pregnant, but also to nuns and priests. That is what is expected of the well-educated boys who attend catechism classes. The calloused reptilian hand lifts from his shoulder, which he interprets as a sign of approval and so starts to get up, but no sooner has his backside left the seat than the hand drops on to his shoulder again with such force he is obliged to stay seated.

"Don't move," he hears his father say loudly and clearly. "He isn't a an old woman and he isn't pregnant."

The cleric smiles beatifically at the boy.

"Thank you for the thought, my son," he says, half closing his eyes. Then to his father: "The boy is well brought up."

"We try our best, Reverend."

"His intentions were good."

"That's right. But I take care of his good intentions."

"Of course you do."

The priest nods and blinks affably. Raising his hands and turning his head to one side like a father confessor, he appears to have sunk into a sympathetic meditation, when he hears the other man say:

"I also take care of handing out the beatings if he deserves them."

"Of course. You are concerned for your son. That's good."

"You see, Reverend Father, my beatings have more God, a lot more God in them, than anything you or Bishop Modrego hand out at Mass."

The nearby passengers forced to witness the scene start to look away. It's not so much that they don't want to hear, but that they wish they were a long way away. After a brief pause, the intrepid Rat-catcher resumes the charge.

"The wine you lot use for consecration is useless."

"Is that so?"

"Yes. It's not worth shit."

"My word. Well anyway," the priest intones, with an unexpected saintly calm, "we're not going to argue over that, are we? Although believe me, you make me very sad, my man, very sad."

"You know where you can stick your sadness."

"I've no idea what your intentions are, but I must ask you not to set such a bad example for your son. I'm asking you as a favour."

"A bad example? Me, a bad example? Listen, in your schools they teach something called the Formation of the National Spirit, a piece of crap blessed by the Church that almost left my boy a gibbering idiot. So don't talk to me about bad examples, Reverend."

I wish the earth would swallow me up, he thought. He's got rat poison under his fingernails, in his voice, his eyes, and in everything he says, and there's no-one who can stop him now.

"In my Church we teach other things as well," the cleric points out.

"The thing is, I don't believe in the Church as the saviour of souls and all that stuff."

"Aha."

"My wife does. She's a believer."

"You don't say? *Laus Deo*."

"Yes, she's friendly with priests. But she doesn't want anything to do with the bishop. We keep our scorn for canons, bishops and the hierarchy."

"Well, well. But there's no need to get so worked up."

"My wife only goes to church to pray. You know, *Kyrie Eleison* and such like."

"From what I can see, my son, you're fortunate to have the wife you do . . ."

"I don't believe," the Rat-catcher butted in, "that you lot help us get to heaven. I really don't." Then in an insolent imitation of a nasal, clerical voice, he adds: "Alll theese cassocks in the streets! Alll theese cassocks? Where will it end with alll theese cassocks?"

"Oh my Lord, my Lord!" the priest shakes his head wearily, then blows out his cheeks, his snorts sending his white, bushy eyebrows into even greater confusion. He stares at the boy's father and for a moment it appears he is about to rebuke him. But, filling his lungs with air and patience, and lowering his eyes mildly, he adds: "Look, I'm sure that deep down you are a good Christian. The problem is you don't know it."

The great Rat-catcher throws his head back, as if trying to avoid the cleric's hypocritical halitosis, and steals a look at the pale, podgy hands folded across his prominent belly. Now he's laughing to himself, thinks the boy.

"That's possible, Reverend, that's possible. Will you believe me if I say that sometimes in dreams I see myself falling to my knees at the feet of your bishop, exclaiming: Your Most Holy Eminence, I'm lost! Lost without hope, Your Eminence!" He pauses, then changes his tone, "Well, my humblest genuflection, Reverend Father. The truth is, I don't know if I am a good Christian. What I'm not, and that you can be sure of, is the servant of a Church that parades the Sentinel of the West with such great pomp."

There it is, he's come out with it, the boy groans, closing his eyes tightly as he hears the guffaw that follows this hoary anti-clerical rant, the stupidly sacrilegious boast, not just foolhardy but extremely risky, as his mother is constantly reproaching him. Fortunately she's not here to see the scene.

"You're not looking for trouble, are you?" the priest can be heard muttering. But the incorrigible loudmouth has said his piece and now stands there proudly, laughing on the inside. Let's hope he doesn't insist, thinks the boy, let's hope this doesn't end up at the police station. He can feel the huge paw circling round his shoulders once more, and so decides to concentrate on reading the adverts over the tram windows: Cerebrino Mandri for headaches and neuralgia, it never fails and blah blah blah. Tobías Fabregat Raincoats, elegance and comfort in instalments or in cash, and blah, blah, blah. Luis Griera's Bridal Bouquets and blah, blah, blah. C. Borja, buttons lined while you wait. NO BLASPHEMING OR SWEARING. Youth, beauty and vigour with Bella Aurora every day, and blah, blah, blah, an advert that always makes him think of a friend of his mother's, Señora Mir, and the shiny, bronze fish-tail she wears in her cleavage.

When he turns back he sees the priest's sly glance as he raises a finger to his lips as if to say: best not to pay him any attention, my boy. Although the cleric's huge head has something rugged and wild about it, as though an invisible wind were ruffling his white hair and eyebrows, the expression on his face does not reveal the slightest annoyance or offence, but rather a cheerful, stubborn benevolence, a calmness that arouses a certain sympathy in the boy. At the end of one of the priest's eyebrows he spots an incredibly long white hair that curls dramatically upwards; the tram wheels grate as it turns into Plaza Lesseps and then clanks its way on to the tracks of Travesera de Dalt. The nearest passengers have long since turned to statues, offering only their backs and the napes of their necks.

His father's histrionic, reckless behaviour with the priest is nothing new to him. Nor is the fact that he decides to get off the tram a stop early. When he gets the signal, the boy stands up and follows him, case in hand, to the rear platform, from where they both prepare to jump down to the pavement as the tram slows for a bend. The boy leans out first, and gets ready to jump carefully, hanging onto the rail with his left hand and feeling ostentatiously for the ground with his foot. As a result, his father has to suddenly alter his trajectory in order to avoid knocking him over, and in doing so slightly twists his ankle. When he starts to walk on it, the ankle becomes painful, so he curses and lets out a few very theatrical "ow!"s. They have quite a way to go to reach home; he has the case slung over his shoulder and his father limping alongside him. Even so, the Rat-catcher strides out impetuously and there is something comical about the way his arms swing so wildly to the squelching rhythm of his rubber boots.

"I know what you're thinking," he pants, limping and stifling his groans. "That heaven has punished me by messing up my ankle. That's right, isn't it?"

"It was just bad luck, Father."

"My eye! It was you, jumping off in your sleep. Well anyway, no harm done." He smiles and ruffles the boy's hair. "Don't forget: rats as black as cassocks, cassocks as black as rats."

"Fine, but let's see . . ." his voice fails him. He is reluctant to go on as he stares angrily at the limping figure's huge, crushing feet. "You know things like that always make Mother cry . . . Why? Why do you always have to make her cry?"

"Well, you know what our Alberta the light of my life is like. She suffers over everything and everyone. Always. But she understands me . . . What's wrong, lad?"

"Nothing."

"Come on, Mingo, don't be angry with me . . ."

"My name is Ringo!"

"Alright. Come here."

The hand with its greenish-black nails feels for his shoulder, as so often seeking not just support for his physical weakness but also comradeship and complicity. The rough, poisonous hand slides from shoulder to averted cheek to give it a friendly pinch, but he rejects the contact and hurries on several metres, head down and distraught. What he most hates is the fact that his father will not yet treat him as an adult. He walks faster and faster, the case bouncing on his back and the rolled-up music theory notebook and sheet music poking out of his trouser pocket. All of a sudden he cannot contain his tears, and breaks into a run. He does so keeping a tight hold on the case with one hand and the music books with the other, and does not stop running or crying until he reaches home.

"*Benedictus Domine*, my son," he hears his father's tobacco-inflected voice in the distance. "A curse on them."

—*What is music?*
The art of sounds.
—*How is music written down?*
By means of symbols, some of them known as principals, and others as secondaries.
—*Which are the principal symbols?*
There are four of them: the notes, the clefs, the rests and the accidentals.
—*Where are they written?*
On the stave.

3

APACHES GALLOPING ACROSS THE BEACHES OF ARIZONA

"You arrive at a gallop and start shooting, still on horseback. You have a revolver in each hand and are clasping the reins between your teeth. You're a rider from the prairies who's come from afar to avenge his sister's honour. Got it? The war is over, but the sun didn't start to shine again, the spring didn't bring laughter, or anything of the kind. So you're galloping across the Arizona desert in search of revenge, you gallop, gallop, gallop . . . Got it?"

The storyteller points to the smaller of the two Cazorla brothers. He goes on:

"And you are Bill's co-pilot in his airplane. You look down, and what do you see? A furious, terrible tornado sweeping across the desert, devastating everything in its path, and then suddenly, in the midst of this incredible whirlwind, a piano. The Red Indians from the reservation have stolen it from some Dodge City saloon, or from a pioneer caravan on its way out West, or from an orchestra playing at our neighbourhood fiesta, maybe the Gene Kim Orchestra, who knows . . . Anyway, the piano is shiny, brand new: it's a Steinway and Sons, so nice you just want to take it home, but how could you manage that? There's an arrow bristling in the keyboard. The Apaches' smoke signals are rising into the sky, bullets and arrows whistle past, and then, all of a sudden, a rain of fire falls on the Valley of Death, on the prairies and the rivers and the creeks and the sea, on everything on the far side of the Black Hills of Dakota."

"The plane piloted by Bill Barnes, Air Adventurer, swoops over the desert," adds Ringo after a strategic pause, "and you catch an occasional glimpse of the piano in the midst of the sandstorm, like a shiny black beetle, or better still, like a flashing black star fallen to earth and lashed by the storm . . ." This improvised and clumsily lyrical addition is not at all to the liking of his audience. One of them asks where Arizona lies on the map, but this question does not seem to interest anyone either. They are sitting in a circle like Red Indian braves on the southern side of the Montaña Pelada, eyes peeled and ears pricked: *Chato* Morales, Roger, the Cazorla brothers, Quique *Pegamil*, Julito, and Ringo himself. Apart from Julito Bayo, they're all much poorer than him: they use bits of rope instead of belts, wear moth-eaten jerseys, short, patched trousers and rubber-tyre sandals. Several of them have shaven heads, a famished colouring, filthy knees and, in winter, raw chilblains on their fingers and ears. Their feet are always freezing, like an icy fever or a crushing Malay boot. Julito is the only one who goes to school, and although they are legally underage, they work whenever they can as errand boys, altar servers, or in grocers' stores and inns. Today they have splashed each other with water from the Atzavara fountain on Calle Camelias, begged a glass of milk that was their only snack at the nearby social aid office; later, in the Camino de la Legua, they played football against the wall of the San Estanislao Kostka Centre, and finally, climbing up their street and the Carmelo main road from Plaza Sanllehy, covered in dust and kicking a bursting rag ball, they have fetched up on the southern slope of the bald hill, close to the north entrance to Parque Güell.

"Got it?" He points to Quique. "You gallop and gallop."

"And what am I doing all this time?" asks Julito impatiently. "I ask Winnetou for help, is that all? Are you going to leave me out again?"

He has been waiting for ages to take the lead in some spectacular action, but the narrator seems to have forgotten him. The distribution of roles is not always to the satisfaction of Ringo's audience. Julito Bayo has greased wavy hair, is wearing checked socks, and a scapular under his vest; on Sundays and feast days he wears knickerbockers. His mother has a dry cleaner's on Calle Rabassa, his father does removals in a van with the slogan BAYO AND SON MAKE MOVING FUN in blue lettering on the sides. He is a pupil at Palacio de la Cultura, a posh school on Traversera de Dalt, which has a garden and a tall, scraggy eucalyptus that rises like a stop sign above the school wall: five branches that look like a gigantic hand spread to prevent any of the bleary-eyed boys from Carmelo or Guinardó from getting in.

"Your revolver has run out of bullets, so you have to wait for help to arrive," the narrator explains. He turns to Quique *Pegamil*: "Where were we? . . . Oh, yes. We come out of the sandstorm. The Apaches are riding bareback across the beach. Got it? We have to save Violeta. Wungo-Lowgha has her bound hand and foot to a stake in the centre of their camp. They paint her face and chest with war paint, then they light a bonfire to burn her alive."

"Have they scalped her?"

"No, they have to kill her before they do that."

"What about her dress?" asks *Pegamil*. "Have they torn her dress off?"

"No, not yet."

"But they've ripped it quite a bit, haven't they?" Quique insists, with his crooked, gap-toothed smile. "A little, for Chrissake. That means you can see her tits, doesn't it?"

"And what do I do?" asks Sito, the younger of the Cazorla brothers. "Do I have to guard the piano the whole time? What use is a piano to us if we haven't got any bullets?"

A tiny, delicate grasshopper, translucent green in colour, has settled on his ring-wormed knee. The narrator shuts his eyes so that he does not have to see it immediately squashed by an equally ring-wormed hand. He carries on speaking from the shadows, pointing to Quique to confirm it's his turn to take the lead:

"You're galloping at the foot of the cliff, without taking your eyes off the beach, you're galloping non-stop. *Clip-clop clip-clop.*" He repeats his imitation of the horse's hooves for a while to gain time so he can think how to continue: "You arrive close to the girl, you're reaching the bonfire . . . Got it?"

"Yes, but tell me something," insists Quique *Pegamil*, "is their prisoner naked?"

"Barefoot. And her ankle is bandaged."

"Yes, O.K., a bandage, but is the girl naked, or not yet?"

"I told you she wasn't."

"No? Why haven't the Red Indian women torn off her dress?"

"Not this time."

"But listen, they always do it!" Quique protests. "In revenge for Winnetou's dead sister."

"Nooo!"

"But now they have ripped her dress, haven't they? At least the skirt."

Chato interrupts to explain that the Indian women from the Apache reservation don't do things like that to white women, they're not such savages – that's what the Comanche squaws do. The storyteller doesn't seem particularly interested, and does not clarify the question; instead, he informs them that Violeta, still tied to the stake, could have a poisoned arrow sticking in her breast. You don't know this yet, he adds, because you and Roger are in the plane with Bill Barnes. It's flying high in the sky, so you can't see the arrow. From up there all you can spot is the black smoke drifting over the Apache camp. Saying goodbye to Bill, you dive into the sea and swim to the shore of Arizona, where you take the best horses and start to gallop. Then as you're riding, Ringo appears with his saddle slung over his shoulder and twirling his rifle. At this point Rafa Cazorla interrupts him to enquire about something he's been puzzling over:

"If her ankle's bandaged, that means the girl's on her bad week."

"Nonsense, you dummy," says Julito. "A girl wearing a bandage round her ankle has nothing to do with her bad week. Donkey."

"Okay," Quique cuts in, dragging his backside enthusiastically across the ground to get closer to Ringo. "So the first thing I do when I reach her is pull out the arrow and suck out the poison. And of course, in order to suck it..."

"Come off it! He's not asking much, is he?" explodes *Chato*.

"Oh, I see," Roger protests, "the same old story with the poisoned arrow and Quique dangling from her tit."

"So what? I'm the one who does it because I'm the first to get there!"

"Listen, who do you think about when you're tossing off, Ringo?" asks *Chato*.

"What I want to know," says sharp-tongued Julito Bayo, "is this. What's a piano doing in the middle of the desert?"

Ringo was expecting this question and responds at once.

"It's like a mirage. Have you never seen a mirage?"

"Oh please, of course I have. It's just that now you've got it into your head to learn music, you bring a piano into all your stories. And there's something else. Why does the prisoner have to be Violeta, when she's so ugly?"

"You don't get it, do you? The Red Indians have no idea that she's ugly."

"You always put her in your stories because you always imagine her when you're tossing off, don't deny it. But she's really ugly and clumsy. And deaf too."

"No she's not," says Roger. "If you take a good look, the girl has got something."

"She's a bit slovenly," *Chato* adds.

"What does that mean?"

"Mucky. Her armpits stink."

"She is a bit deaf," Roger says. "But I've seen her dancing close. And my oh my, kid: she lets them do it!"

"Why don't the Apaches capture Virginia instead of Violeta?" says Julito. "For Chrissake, have you seen her in that yellow sweater of hers?"

"Why not Jane Parker, Tarzan's girl?" *Chato* suggests.

"I'd choose Diana Palmer, the Phantom's girlfriend," says the younger of the Cazorlas.

"For me it'd be June Duprez," says Rafa. "Or Esmeralda the Zingara."

"I'm happy to stick with Violeta," says Quique *Pegamil*, gap-toothed and with his Woody Woodpecker tuft of hair. "She's the one we started with, isn't she? Besides, the person telling the story is the one who decides."

Quique has always had a soft spot for Señora Mir's daughter. One Sunday last summer he happened to meet her on the crowded platform of a number 39, and manoeuvred his way round until he was right behind her. With the two of them squashed like sardines and unable to move, as he told it later, he stuck his cock between her buttocks, and she had let him do so for a good while. Later on the beach she hadn't even looked at him, and from that day on had called him *Pegamil*, the Glue-stick.

Alright, so Violeta is still tied to the post with the arrow sticking out from her chest, the narrator concedes, but not exactly in the middle of her breast, not in the nipple, because if that happened the poisoned blood could get mixed up with her milk and she would die on the spot. It's pierced her a bit higher up, almost on her shoulder. We're lying flat on the stagecoach roof, surrounded by Apaches on horseback. I'm Ringo Kid and I'm firing my rifle at Wungo-Lowgha . . . He pauses to sum up: We don't know whether they tore Violeta's dress when they seized her, nor what they're going to do to her, we'll soon see, he says, and refuses to add any more about this vital detail that some of them find so fascinating. All we know for sure is that Geronimo's Apaches have kidnapped her and nobody could stop them, not Winnetou, or Wild Bill Hickok, or Destry, or Ringo Kid, or you, he says to *Chato*, nor you two either, he warns the long-suffering Cazorla brothers, and not you either, Julito, he adds, glancing sternly at the pupil from the Palacio de la Cultura. Then he adds in a voice full of mystery:

"Something extraordinary is about to happen. End of Part One."

"Crap!" Julito exclaims, not at all happy. "You know what I think? I think I'll punch Winnetou and get out of there."

"No you don't! Winnetou is our friend and ally."

"I could reach the girl and save her!" *Pegamil* offers.

"No. Your horse has broken a leg."

"But I can jump off quickly and untie her from the stake. She runs down the beach, tears off her clothes, and plunges into the sea to wash off the war paint, but then a huge wave comes and I save her . . ."

"No, Quique, no," Ringo restrains him. "Nothing like that happens. You have to wait."

He recapitulates once more: thanks to Bill and his plane they have followed the Indians' tracks and then, once they've swum ashore on the Arizona coast, they all ride white horses bareback across the wide beach of the Indian reservation, until all of a sudden Quique gets left behind. Yellow clouds roll down from Gold Mountain, says Ringo, staring at the clumps of yellow broom high above them. This is May, and the bushes ring the hill with gold. In the distance below the haze, beyond Padre Alegre's Cottolengo, Barcelona stretches out to the sea like a muddy, dirty puddle, while above their heads in the pale whitish sky a heavy red kite with yellow ribbons floats and flaps in the wind with crystalline delight, swooping every so often towards the ground because the line is being held by inexpert hands on the summit of Montaña Pelada.

"Got it?" the storyteller asks again. "As it jumps from the cliff down to the beach, your horse breaks a leg. And as you know, that means you have to kill it. Sooo theeen—"

"That's not fair, Ringo." Quique protests. "Why does it have to be my horse? Why not yours, or *Chato*'s?"

"Good Lord! That's not right, it isn't!" snorts Julito Bayo, shaking his impeccable quiff. "Lots of things here don't make any sense, *nen*."

This is the second time he has objected to how one of the tall stories is developing: up to now, he has hardly taken part, he has not been given any heroic role, and he doesn't like it. The fact is that the stories Berta's boy tells aren't much appreciated by his audience. They're not usually how most of them like adventures to be: full of dangers and furious struggles with destiny or chance, tremendous catastrophes, whirlwinds and tornados, gigantic waves and shipwrecks on the high seas, treacherous shifting sands or refined Chinese tortures, all of which they have to continuously confront, putting their lives at risk to save the girl at the very last minute. But in Ringo's labyrinthine inventions, they are hardly ever threatened by grandiose feats or challenges, facing dangers on the edge of vertiginous ravines or cliffs, or finding themselves caught up in devastating earthquakes like the one in San Francisco, terrible fires like the one in Chicago, or furious hurricanes like the one that hit Suez, scenes they have so often enjoyed in the cinema. There is some of this in Ringo's stories, but he's always adding strange extras like a piano in the middle of a desert storm, a talking bird, blue rats scurrying between his father's legs, Señor Sucre and Capitán Blay drinking their coffees with a slug of brandy on the deck of *The Bounty* or in the Las Ánimas parish garden, or even Ringo himself fleeing down the corridors of the luxury Ritz Hotel pursued by diamond thieves as he is about to hand invaluable jewels to a rich and beautiful guest. Secret, insidious and long-lasting links regularly spoil his stories, with incidents that are too closely based on reality and are always inappropriate and extravagant, unrelated to the logic of the adventure, leaving them strewn with loose ends and characters who have dissolved into phantoms. The more real and recognisable they are, the more ghostly they become.

"So then," Ringo continues, staring straight at the sceptical Julito, "you jump off your father's van, which is carrying a load of Winchester rifles, and find Winnetou. And Winnetou says: 'Old Shatterhand and his silver mount are waiting for us to join them in the big battle on Gold Mountain. For the Apaches, it's a sacred mountain . . .'"

"We already know it's sacred," complains Julito.

". . . and Old Shatterhand, which in the Indian tongue means strong fist . . ."

"We know that too," says Julito, increasingly irate. "Go on. What do I do then?"

"You rush off firing your Winchester, with your dagger in your belt."

"Between my teeth, *nen*. I always carry my dagger between my teeth."

"Alright, between your teeth. But you don't ride along the beach to join us."

"I don't? Why not?"

"Because you ride day and night to Fort Apache to ask for help. Sooo theeen . . ." he goes on, shutting his eyes again and hesitating because he can't see how to continue, "sooo then, a great horricane wind arises . . ."

"The word is hurricane."

"It lifts the piano lid, and the piano starts playing all on its own. There is no-one at the keyboard, but you can hear 'The Warsaw Concerto', and there's a big black spider crawling across the top. So then Winnetou grabs his tomahawk, because the evil Wungo-Lowgha's final hour has arrived. Winnetou! The devil take him!" Ringo exclaims. "Only the great Apache chief is able to follow *Pegamil* along the beach without him realising it."

Quique *Pegamil* listens warily. Clutching his knees, he draws even closer, shuffling the seat of his trousers across the grey earth. Am I going to be the traitor, he asks himself in alarm, and suggests a change:

"Listen, Ringo, how about if I ride very close to the sea where the wet sand is firmer. Then my horse wouldn't break a leg . . ."

"O.K., fine, that's a good idea."

" For the love of God, the broken leg is neither here nor there!" protests Julito. He turns to the narrator with a mocking smile: "As far as I can tell, it's something else that doesn't fit."

"What's that?"

"One of your howlers."

"Howler? What howler?" says Ringo, on his guard and dropping his hand to his hip.

"The Apaches can't be camped by the sea."

"Ah. No? And why not, clever clogs?"

"Because Arizona doesn't have a sea or a coast. I've seen it on the map."

Ringo's eyes flash at him, and he stays silent for a few seconds. All of a sudden, Ringo feels robbed, usurped. Yet again Julito Bayo, who has always fancied himself as a leader, is trying to discredit him in the eyes of the other boys. What can he do? Hidden in a barrel of apples, Jim Hawkins sticks his head out and smiles at him: Don't let that idiot ruin your story! Ringo takes a penknife out of his pocket and draws five mysterious parallel lines in the no-man's land in the centre of their circle.

"So what?" he says eventually. "I can have a beach wherever I want one."

"You can't, *nen*"

"Yes I can."

"No, you can't." Julito stares at him. "How many legs does a horse have?"

"A horse? Why?"

"Answer me."

"Four."

"Exactly. It's got four legs. And you can't make it have five. Do you see that?"

"Alright, and so?"

"What do you mean, and so? My God, you've made a howler, *nen*! If there's no sea, then there's no beach, so the Apache reservation can't be where you say it is, *capisce*? And you can't have the girl tied to a stake in the sand, because there's no sand, *capisce*? So there can't be a cliff either, we can't swim through the waves, or gallop on the shore, or anything like that, for Chrissake!" Julito pauses, with a sneering, triumphant smile. "Have you never seen a map, or do you think we're all as dumb as you, who doesn't even know where America is?"

Ringo feels as though reality has burst into his world like a shockwave after an explosion (even if it is a very distant, inaudible one) and has torn something from his hands. Putting the penknife away, he stares at the lines in the dust. No-one in the group apart from him knows that a stave has five lines. He says nothing, and closes his eyes. But he's not thinking of some urgent readjustment to the landscape of his adventure – there's no time for that; he's thinking about this stuck-up know-all from the

Palacio de la Cultura opposite him, this kid with the fancy hairstyle and posh way of speaking. He can just see him staring open-mouthed at the coloured map on his classroom wall. He knows the toffee-nosed kid is about to define the real world to impress the others, and quietly resigns himself to the fact.

"Arizona borders to the south with Mexico, to the north with Utah, the east with New Mexico, and to the West with California," Julito Bayo proudly recites, then adds the finishing touch: "And the capital is Phoenix. It's true there is a desert and lots of tornados and sandstorms, but look, we'll have to go on with your story, because the way you're telling it makes no sense, *nen*, you keep putting your foot in it." Then to the others, his chin lifted in triumph: "Come on, don't be silly. Ringo has no idea what he's talking about."

The others shrug their shoulders. They couldn't care less whether Arizona has a coast or not, in the end the Wild West is a cinema world they have made their own, and where they can do whatever they like. Who cares, they gesture, what does it matter if the coast is on the map or not? They suspect Julito is getting revenge because he's been sent to the fort in search of help, and also probably because at the end, after they've fought the Apaches and rescued Violeta, he's the one who will be discovered to be the traitor. There is always one – but the only thing that really interests them is finding out who is chosen to rescue the prisoner tied to the stake.

"You'll have to take the girl somewhere else, it's no good where she is, there's no beach," Julito insists.

"I don't feel like it."

"Well then, this crappy story is over. We'll have to start another one."

Quique encourages Ringo to carry on, but he is already standing up and dusting his trousers. The circle closes again, leaving him outside.

"Fine, you all stay there then."

Hands in his pockets and a look of cool disdain on his face, the story-teller quits the group and takes one of the little paths up the hill, though he does not go far. He'll be back, but first he needs to feel excluded and spurned for a while, he wants to be misunderstood and to see himself as exiled, all alone, savouring an untouchable independence that is a mixture of rage and melancholy as he looks down on his friends without being seen. He is scornful of the show-off heir to "Bayo and Son Make Moving Fun", who deserves to be taught a lesson and who he would gladly give one to right there and then, but towards the others, these candid, illiterate sons of migrant workers who aren't afraid of defying the real geography of the world either in his tall stories or in life itself, he feels a secret affinity.

Situated between leafy Parque Güell and the miserable foothills of Monte Carmelo, this hill they call Montaña Pelada is a gloomy promontory with little vegetation and no trees, dotted here and there with small caves occasionally inhabited by tramps. Its inhospitable, bare slopes make it seem as if it has been swept to one side and punished, as if it was nothing more than a submissive wasteland on the edge of the picturesque and famous outlines of its near neighbour, Parque Güell. In the month of May its slopes are covered with lavender and broom, and June brings a few clumps of thyme and rosemary, but the rest of the year it's a dusty expanse shunned even by lizards. The gang doesn't do it anymore, but as recently as the previous year they searched for seashells and molluscs embedded in the rocks, because Julito Bayo had sworn that his History teacher told him the mountain was littered with fossils, tortoise shells and mammoth remains. Some of the caves really are prehistoric, Julito told them, showing off his knowledge. A soft, warm breeze carries the acrid smell of burning rubber up to Ringo. Most likely it is coming from the cloud of smoke hanging over the cluster of shacks that he can see not far away, below the last bend in the road up to Carmelo. He thinks of youngsters with shaven heads and fierce looks burning lorry tyres and rotten mattresses. He gives a magic blink and the smoke spreads, black as soot, to envelop the circle he has been cast out of.

As he continues to climb, the ground becomes increasingly ashen and bare. There's no-one in sight. Halfway up the hill, where the incline becomes steeper, on the smooth back of a chalky boulder that is half buried and almost indistinguishable from the ground, are three hand-carved steps. Man-made.

"Hello there, mystery."

A lavender bush is sprouting next to the topmost step. Perfectly symmetrical, a little more than two handspans wide and worn away by the rains and the gang's feet, the three steps appear without warning out of nothing and climb the hill towards nothing, for nothing. Every time he comes across them, he stops, sensing he is on the threshold of a labyrinth that could lead to a tomb. Something ceased to exist not far from here, something whose secret lies buried beneath the quiet symmetry of these lonely steps, as stark as headstones. The Cazorla brothers' father, who is a labourer and years earlier worked in the quarries at the foot of the Carmelo used to say half jokingly that a long time ago he had heard of a young peasant recently arrived from a village in Andalusia to work in the same quarry (disused nowadays) who had suddenly taken it into his head to chisel out the first steps of a staircase meant to lead to the little house he intended one day to build for himself and his family, but that he had been forced to stop to go to war. A couple of Christmases when he was on leave he came back from the front to continue the work in uniform, but just as he had finished the third step, the enemy arrived at the gates of the city, and the young stonemason was shot right there, hammer still in hand.

The whole gang spent an entire afternoon searching for gun cartridges and bloodstains on the three steps and surrounding rocks, but either the stains had been washed away or they were unable to spot them. Another day, as he was pulling up a thyme bush, the elder Cazorla brother dug up the sole of a shoe or a perished boot, and a pair of buttons. They dug around for a long while, but couldn't find anything more. Some time later the younger Cazorla announced he had found a broken hammer beneath some rocks. Of course, he could be buried somewhere here, Ringo suggested, but Julito protested: Who's going to believe a story like that, *nen*? While an excited Quique shouted: Where could the body be, Ringo? Here, underneath my feet? Yes, under your feet, right here!

Now he leaves them behind and goes to sit a little higher up. He clasps his knees and stares down at the boys' shaven heads and Julito Bayo's smart, wavy mop. They are listening to him in silence. No doubt Julito has begun his tall tale with some stupidly menacing music from a horror film like "Hold That Ghost", he thinks. And doubtless it's a stormy night with thunder and lightning, and a sinister dacoit brandishing a dagger is stealing into Virginia Franch's bedroom in her villa on Calle de las Camelias, while Quique hides behind a curtain in wait for him. Julito himself climbs the front of the house in pursuit of the Perfidious Oriental, and the Cazorla brothers are also close at hand. Then of course the telephone rings and Virginia wakes up in her bed just as the shadow of the evil Chinaman with the dagger looms behind her. She sits up and screams . . . and I'll bet an arm and a leg that Quique asks if the girl is wearing a transparent nightie.

He looks down at the city stretching out to the sea under a slight haze. He grits his teeth: up here he is at war with the world, not just evil dacoits or Apache warriors. For a moment, peering at the blurred line of the horizon rising above the buildings, it appears as though he is viewing an underwater city, more remote and improbable than a beach in Arizona. In the bright blue sky above his head, the red kite with yellow ribbons is losing height and keeps swooping round, its tail fluttering wildly as it threatens to plummet to the ground. Held by an invisible hand that seems unable to control it, the long flying line tautens or slackens following the vagaries of the wind. A young girl's hands, he decides, and at that very moment he looks down and sees Señora Mir toiling up the path in her tight printed skirt, her black sleeveless blouse with the plunging neckline, and her palm-leaf basket. She is wearing flat shoes, a green headscarf and dark glasses with white frames. She's making slow progress, and stops every now and then to catch her breath, hands on hips. Two small white butterflies are chasing each other round her thick pink ankles. She passes by Ringo without looking and carries on up the hill.

"Hello there, Señora Mir."

She either does not hear or does not want to acknowledge his greeting. Near the summit, she disappears, after stopping to cut a branch of broom. When Ringo follows her a short while later, she is nowhere to be seen. She could be on the other side of the hill, where there is oregano and clumps of thyme that has just come into bloom, but she would have had to walk very quickly to reach it, so it's more likely she is in some cave with the man waiting for her. There is no-one else in sight. From this slope he can see Vallcarca and the suicide bridge; then all at once, to his surprise he also notices that the cord of the kite he saw from down below is not being held by anyone: instead, it is tied to a large boulder at one edge of the small sun-filled bowl at the top of the hill. There is no-one around. Above his head in the sky he can hear the crackling of the paper kite, as if the strong wind had set it on fire. Taking out his penknife, he cuts the line. Freed, the kite turns a somersault and plunges headfirst to earth.

As he runs back down the hill, he pieces it all together. He bursts in on Julito's tale and demands they all listen to him.

"Are you blind or what?" He stands opposite his rival, arms akimbo. "Didn't you see Violeta's mother go past? She's in the Mianet cave right now with a man . . . Guess how they manage to meet in secret without anyone finding out?" He pauses and sits down, making room for himself between the Cazorla brothers and crossing his legs. "It's simple. He flies a red-and-yellow kite, and once it's climbed high in the sky he ties the line to a stone, then goes into the cave to wait."

"To wait for what?" asks Julito, his nose out of joint.

"Guess."

"What do I have to guess?"

"When Señora Mir sees the red-and-yellow kite in the sky, she knows he's waiting for her, and comes as quickly as she can. The kite is the signal, kids! Of course, she also picks herbs for her back rubs and so on, but that's only an excuse. She's really coming to meet her secret lover."

"Crikey!" Quique exclaims. "And what are they doing now in the cave?"

"What d'you think? They're at it, kid. I saw them with my own eyes."

"Seriously?"

"Bah, everyone knows she's a slut, and besides, she's off her trolley," Julito Bayo says scornfully, knowing he's been bested.

"And who's the guy?" Roger asks. "Do we know him?"

"It could be that stonemason who carved those steps," suggests Ringo.

"Hang on," Julito cuts in. "Didn't you say he was buried up there? Don't listen to him, you lot, he's making it all up . . . Anyway, what's so new about that? Don't you remember the day we went up to look at the anti-aircraft batteries on Turó de la Rovira and saw her smooching with a fellow behind the wall . . . ?"

"Yes, but let Ringo speak," Roger butts in.

"Yes, yes . . . What happened in the cave?" Chato wants to know.

"Well, I don't know if it's right for me to tell you what I saw . . ."

"Did you see her bush and her tits? Was she naked?"

"A lot more than that. A lot more. But I don't know whether you'll believe me . . ."

"I won't," Julito says hastily. "Not a word."

"Well, I will," Quique responds. "We believe you, Ringo. Tell us!"

The others share Quique's curiosity, and are suddenly all ears. However, although they strain to imagine some of the details the storyteller only hints at, because it's about a grown-up, plump woman like Señora Mir, whose backside and provocative swaying gait only make them laugh, the scene he describes does not really arouse them, and Ringo's account soon tails off. Even so, the credit Julito had denied him has now been re-established.

Shortly afterwards, Roger suggests they go and visit the ruins of Can Xirot a little higher up, next to Parque Güell.

"Last one there's a sissy!"

Inside the abandoned old farmhouse, surrounded by the silence of tumbledown walls and rotten wooden beams, overgrown with brambles and dusty weeds, the gang gathers beside a tall bank of earth covered in an inhospitable tangle, and conjures up dangers, confused emotions and secret pacts with the future. They take their cruel revenge on lizards and grasshoppers, and scheme as to how before long they are going to bring a girlfriend up here who will let them touch her. A little higher up, next to the collapsed stable walls, a lime tree in full blossom leaning out over the city glows as bright as a lamp as it is caught by the rays of the setting sun. The boys have sometimes seen Señora Mir sitting under this tree, sorting out the sprigs of herbs in her basket, and no doubt waiting for someone. Now that it is July, the branches of the tree resound with the constant, powerful buzzing of thousands of bees and other insects drawn to the blossoms, and they do not go near it. A wild bay tree is growing in what was once the farmhouse kitchen: Ringo cuts off a small branch for his mother, and hangs it from his belt.

At sunset they descend again to the Carmelo road. As they linger a while longer playing football with what's left of their rag ball on the esplanade outside the north entrance to Parque Güell, they catch sight of the plump nurse high on the hill. She is sitting on the three steps leading nowhere, the flowering thyme poking out of the palm basket alongside her. Peering into a hand mirror, she is busy applying lipstick. Then she fluffs up her hair, removes something sticking to it, covers her head with the green scarf, shakes her skirt, and starts on the way down, taking care over where she is putting her feet.

Shortly afterwards, as she passes by them on the way to Plaza Sanllely, Roger's looping kick at the unravelling ball crashes into her ample backside. Good shot, kid, shouts Quique, and they all burst out laughing. But Señora Mir doesn't even deign to look in their direction; she merely pauses for a moment and responds with a contemptuous sway of the hips. Ringo takes aim and kicks the ball again at the generous posterior. This time she does come to a halt, removes her sunglasses, looks at the boys with unsteady, wavering eyes that have been moist with tears since she began her descent. Shaking her head gently, and with a sad smile, she scolds them for their bad manners, while Ringo pretends to be far away, staring at the clouds.

4

A PINK ENVELOPE

For several days the story does the rounds of the neighbourhood. Can that woman have been so despairing, so unbearable her heartache, that she lost all sense of reality on those useless lengths of track? The absurdity seemed all too evident. To pretend that she wanted to commit suicide so publicly does not mean she really intended to kick the bucket, say the wagging tongues in Bar Rosales. At least, not in such a grotesque manner. Considering that in affairs of the heart Señora Mir completely lacked any sense of the ridiculous, it was agreed that what happened was simply another of her melodramatic performances aimed at reining in her fancy man by making him jealous and bringing him back into the fold. She had made a public display of anger at being scorned, a theatrical, very conspicuous gesture, but there was nothing to be alarmed about. She must have felt deeply offended and hurt, and everything appeared to indicate that she herself was certain that the fellow would not return, but even so, however desperate she might have been, and however great her disenchantment and bewilderment following their argument, it was hard to believe she really thought even for a moment that she was going to be run down by a tram in this street where none had gone by for years. They also said she must have been so confused when she left her flat that she had lost all sense of direction and gone up the street rather than down it to the nearby

Plaza Rovira, where there were trams numbers 30, 38 and 39. Whatever the truth, her misguided ruse could have had only one objective: to convey to her lover, wherever he might be – according to some of her women neighbours, still in the flat where they had just quarrelled, which explained why the crafty woman kept looking up at the balcony, even though afterwards it was generally agreed she had already thrown him out – a dramatic warning of what she was genuinely thinking of doing some day. In other words, there was no way she wanted to be run over by a tram: she simply had an overpowering need to let him know what she was capable of.

None of this is of any great interest to Ringo. In fact, these days are so full of unexpected events that he has not had the time or the desire to stop and think of that woman's ridiculous love affairs. Other people's lives – unless they are in novels or films – scarcely merit a glance over his shoulder, a bored, fleeting consideration. Instead, he has spent a lot of time reflecting on the crushed finger of fate, the finger that was lost. He's sitting at a table in Bar Rosales, his right arm in a sling and his hand bandaged, head deep in a novel he's just opened on top of his music book, which is also open. He has ordered a beer, and is drinking it without taking his eyes off the page. At this time of day, three in the afternoon, there's no-one else in the bar apart from Francis Macomber, Wilson and Margot, who are arguing next to him, throats dry, and sweating profusely as they drink gimlets, their wraith-like voices and unmentionable desires mingling with the sounds of the jungle.

The bar owner's sister, Señora Paquita, a bustling, middle-aged spinster with a masculine face and lively eyes, is busy behind the counter washing anchovies under the tap. From time to time she lifts her head to study her only customer. A strange boy, she is thinking, not very sociable or polite, possibly quite shy, who never is to be seen with the other lads of his age when they come in during the early evening to play table football or dominoes. Whenever she sees him, aged fifteen and looking so serious, sitting at the table by the window absorbed in a book, she imagines he must be reading because he's bored or because he feels lonely, and feels obliged to make conversation.

"So, how are things? How's your mother?"

"Fine," he replies, burying his head even deeper in his book.

"Working hard, I'll be bound. What other choice does she have, poor woman? And in the meantime, what's that rogue of your father doing? What's that piece of work up to?" she insists brightly, looking askance at him. "Is he at home, or still catching rats and making mischief? He's a fine one alright! Although I have to admit he's a likeable rogue."

Ringo prefers to say nothing, but to push on deeper into the distant, wild plains of Africa.

Thirty-five yards into the grass the big lion lay flattened out along the ground. His ears were back and his only movement was a slight twitching up and down of his long, black-tufted tail. He had turned at bay as soon as he had reached this cover . . .

Bar Rosales is one of the oldest taverns in the neighbourhood. It has a battered, uneven floor of black and white tiles, and an old brick counter whose edges and top are imitation rough pine trunks made of mortar and painted brown, with very convincing knots and grain. The counter was rebuilt with his own hands by the bar owner Señor Agustín, who had once been a labourer and fancied himself as a decorator. In its day, the counter was highly praised by the regulars because it looked so lifelike, but Señora Paquita detests the trunks because the tree-bark that was so much admired collects dust and dirt, and she is utterly fed up with having to scrub it with bleach. To one side of the bar stand five big barrels of wine, three on the bottom and two on top, and a few kegs of spirits also sold on tap. On the other side are three rectangular marble tables with wrought-iron legs. They are pushed back against a wall decorated up to halfway with tiles, in which a window with a faded old blind opens on to Calle Torrente de las Flores. At the back, the bar narrows and becomes gloomier near a table football game standing beneath a lamp with a green shade that until two years ago lit a billiard table here. The business is based on sales from the barrel rather than what is served in the bar, and the regular customers who drop in for a drink are few and far between, especially on weekdays. Anyone glancing into the dark tavern from the street would likely as not see the predatory, hunched outline of a silhouette at the bar, the wavering shadow of a solitary, patient drinker with a glass of wine in his hand, and yet apart from the four or five locals addicted to dominoes or card games on weekend afternoons, the same ones who on summer nights take their stools and a cold beer and sit out on the pavement, or the gang of young boys who gather noisily around the table football before moving on to a dance at La Lealtad or the Verdi, the bar is an odorous cave of shadows and silence.

When Señora Mir enters, Ringo buries his head still deeper into his book, and finishes the paragraph about the wounded lion:

All of him, pain, sickness, hatred and all of his remaining strength, was tightening into an absolute concentration for a rush.

"Hello there, Vicky, how's things?" says the woman behind the bar.

"So-so."

"Good heavens, I haven't seen you for days! And if you only knew what I have to tell you!"

"This soda siphon you gave my daughter doesn't work."

"I've got a surprise for you, Vicky. I was waiting for you . . ."

"You press it but nothing comes out, look!"

"I'm sure it wasn't me who gave it her. I always test them first."

"Then it must have been your brother, but what's the difference?"

"Okay, I'll give you another one. But listen . . ."

"And fill this bottle with a litre of white, would you?"

"Of course!" Then, dropping her voice to a syrupy whisper: "But first there's something I have to tell you, something that'll interest you, sweetheart, and how!"

Señora Mir does not appear to hear her. All of a sudden she has thrown back her head, arched her back and twisted round in a contrived gesture of coquettish abandon. She is putting on this acrobatic display simply to examine her calf, stick out her tongue, moisten the middle finger and rub off a stain on the firm skin below her knee. She does it with such a fatigued, rehearsed gesture, blinking her eyes as she does so, that Ringo finds it hilarious. A woman like her shouldn't do these things, he thinks: she's stumpy, ugly, has folds on the back of her neck, too big a backside and too much hair in her armpits, too much lipstick. Not to mention her impossible eyelashes with all that sticky gunk on them, that buxom delight she shows when she is whistled at in the street, and the hint of frustration and disappointment that appears in her eyes the harder she tries to please. A week has gone by since she played dead on tracks dating back to the year dot, and she's still living in the year dot and making herself look ridiculous.

As she straightens up, she discovers the young lad bent over his book.

"You're Berta's son, aren't you?" A friendly fluttering of her eyelashes precedes a kind of apology. "Well, I mean Berta's adopted son . . . you were studying to be a musician and had to abandon the idea, I know." Her rough voice contrasts strangely with her smiling plump doll's face. Noticing the sling and the bandage, she adds: "What's that? What happened to you?"

He closes his eyes and the book, leaving the fate of the wounded lion for a more suitable moment. Disgruntled, he starts playing notes on the marble tabletop with the fingers of his left hand.

"Huh!" he pants. "My finger got caught in a rolling mill."

"Good gracious! How did it happen? Where?"

A blink of his eyes, not magical this time, and the slow twisting of the plated gold traps his finger once more, then the two steel rollers swallow it.

"At the workshop," he reluctantly replies.

"Oh, how terrible! I'm really sorry, my lad. But you're feeling better now, aren't you?"

This time he says nothing. He intends to make it clear he wants nothing to do with this vulgar, unpleasant kind of thing, still less with the romantic heroine playacting Señora Mir goes in for.

57

"Vicky," the woman behind the bar interrupts. "Do you want to hear what I've got to say, or not?"

"Of course, I'll be right with you." She stares down at the boy's fingers playing rapidly on the tabletop next to the beer glass. "You ought to be drinking barley water. How old are you?"

"I'm going to be sixteen."

"Is your mother alright? She's such a good, kind woman. Say hello to her from me. And tell her that if she needs me for anything at all, she only has to ask."

Raising her arms to adjust a profusion of noisy bracelets, she finally spins round towards her friend so quickly she almost stumbles, but recovers instantly and, without losing her poise or the musical, festive spring in her step, that odd way she has of standing at the counter as if she were resting her fat backside on an invisible, tall stool at some elegant bar. She thinks she's living in a movie, he reflects, and yet again lists what he most dislikes about this monument to affectation and kitsch; he doesn't like her dyed yellow curls, or her puckered mouth, her throaty voice, her rounded, weary shoulders. He does not like the way she clutches the bottle under her arm, or her fluttering, ever-present hands, or that broad white belt that emphasises her haunches and lifts her breasts, or her tarty shoes with their gold straps that reveal her purple toenails . . .

"Are you feeling alright, Vicky?" asks Señora Paquita, seeing her so distracted.

"Oh, yes. What were you saying?"

"It's something you can't even imagine!" She has finished rinsing the anchovies and lines them up carefully on small dishes. Glancing slyly at the adolescent pretending to read over by the window, and wishing he weren't so close, she says in a hollow voice: "Something you're going to be pleased to hear . . ."

"Really?"

"He was here yesterday!"

"Who?"

"What d'you mean, who?" She lowers her voice still further: "Your man. He sat at that table at the back and didn't say a word for quite a while. He looked really down."

"You don't say." Señora Mir looks thoughtful: she has not yet decided whether to be impressed by the news or not. "He swore we would never see him again."

"Well, he was here. It was a little after half past three in the afternoon. Agustín had gone for a nap and I was sorting out the refrigerator when I saw him come in through that door. And listen to me, Vicky: he didn't look the same man. He was in such low spirits. He said hello, sat down, ordered his aperitif and a glass of water, then sat for more than half an hour head in hands. He really made me feel sorry for him. He asked me if I'd seen you go by, or if your daughter had been in, and I said no. He told me he had been knocking on the door of your apartment for an hour, but that you didn't want to let him in."

"That's nothing but a lie. I haven't been out all day and I didn't hear a thing, so he's lying. The thing is, he doesn't dare show his face . . ."

"Yes, that's probably it. Because I told him to try again, that you were bound to be home, but he didn't even listen. He took a fountain pen out of his pocket and asked me if I had any writing paper and an envelope. I said I did, but that he might not like them, because they were pink. It's the only little whim I allow myself, I told him when I saw him pull a face . . . Well, the thing is I went up to my room and came back down with half a dozen sheets of paper and an envelope. Then he goes and asks me if I would do him the favour of handing you the letter myself . . ."

Señora Mir betrays no emotion.

"Why on earth would he do that? And where is the letter?"

"Well, look, when he had almost finished writing a page – after stopping to think dozens of times – he picked it up, screwed it into a ball, and put it in his pocket. He struggled to write two more pages, then also crumpled them up and put them away. It was obvious that the letter wasn't coming out as he wanted, because of his handwriting or whatever. I didn't move from here, but I could see everything. He didn't even taste the aperitif, maybe even forgot he'd ordered it, because in the end he came to the counter, asked for a brandy, and said to me I can't do it, Paquita, I can't do it, I'll write it at home. I can't find the words. He drank the brandy, and guess what he said before he left?"

"How am I supposed to know?"

"That he'd send someone with the letter, and could I do him the favour of handing it over personally."

"He said that?"

"Yes, those were his exact words. I had to promise him I wouldn't tell you a thing, not even that he'd been here. But there are no secrets between us two, are there, sweetheart?" Señora Mir nods with a complicit little smile. "After that he left, taking with him the envelope and the three or four remaining sheets . . ."

"Oh, yes? And who was the letter for?"

"You're kidding me! For you, of course, you silly thing! Who else? Of course, I asked him, but there was no need for him to say a word. I think he said something like 'the name will be on the envelope'. The rogue wanted it kept quiet, which is only normal, isn't it? And by the way, the brandy he ordered is the one you like. He's never asked for that brandy from the keg before!"

Señora Mir blinks. She is confused, and strokes the lobe of her ear.

"Yes, I think I remember he said something of the sort . . . . After that dreadful row at home, when I asked him never to speak to me again, do you know what he said? Well, he said calm as you like that he was going far away but that one day he'd explain everything. At that moment I didn't believe him."

"Why not? Give him the chance to ask for forgiveness, sweetheart."

"No man deserves to be forgiven for what he did."

"And what was that exactly, Vicky?"

Wrapped up in her thoughts, looking at herself as always in a self-indulgent mirror, Señora Mir is not listening.

"Yes, now I remember . . . There was a huge argument, you see. I started shouting and my daughter shut herself in the bathroom with a towel wrapped around her head, she was so scared . . . I saw him put on his jacket and pick his things up from the dining-room table, his tobacco, sunglasses, his tube of Ephedrine for his asthma, the shirts and socks for his boys' football team – we used to wash them and mend them each week, see how good we were to him . . . That was when he said: I'd better go, farewell, I'll write to you. Yes, that's what he said. I was in the middle of the corridor, so frightened I couldn't even move, and I couldn't breathe, and thought I was going to faint . . . So then I opened the door and ran down the stairs!"

"But what was the argument about? What did he do to you, Vicky?"

There is a gleam of curiosity in Señora Paquita's big black eyes, but she waits in vain for a reply, while the boy lowers his own gaze with bored resignation, hearing without listening. He stares down at the imaginary keyboard and plays *doh*, *mi* and *sol* with his thumb, middle and little fingers, finding it hard to manage all three at once, because now in his mind's eye he can see Señor Alonso's dark, knotted hand fleetingly touching Señora Paquita's bottom one rainy night the previous winter when the two of them were standing in the doorway. He was carrying the umbrella she had lent him so that he would not get wet crossing the road to Señora Mir's place, and had opened it behind his back before saying goodbye, partly concealing them both, although not completely.

"What's clear is that he did you a lot of harm," Señora Paquita says. "You deserved something better, my girl."

"Yes, of course," Señora Mir sighs. "I deserved better luck, that's for sure. But happiness is worth fighting for, Paqui, however much it costs . . . It was my fault, you know. I told him: the door's over there. It was me who threw him out. It was my fault. I should never have allowed him to take such liberties in my home . . ."

"Can I ask you a question, dear? Don't be angry, but I don't quite get it. Who has to forgive who? You him, or him you?"

"Oh, Paqui, I would have forgiven him, I really would. May God forgive me, but if only he'd given me time . . . You have to believe me! I made a mistake, one of those great blunders of mine! What I need is for him to know that, and to pardon me for insulting him and slapping him like that!"

"You slapped his face? My, my, that must have been some scene!"

"Oh, yes, it was, it was!"

"That's such terrible luck, sweetheart! And now it's all over, what do you think now about what happened, Vicky?"

"Nothing."

"Nothing?"

"Well, I've just told you. I messed up. When I came home that day my back was crucifying me. I'd just had to deal with poor María Terol – you know, with her hundred and ten kilos, her cellulitis, and that bad temper of hers. Anyway, I was exhausted and I lost the plot. And then those damned tram tracks! Why on earth did they leave them there like that to confuse me still further! They should be dug up, and the cobblestones along with them!"

"I'm not talking about that, Vicky." Señora Paquita hesitates before saying it: "I could swear there's another woman involved . . . am I right?"

"There's always another woman."

"How did you find out? Did he admit it?"

Señora Mir shakes her head.

"Of course not. But a married woman knows when these things are happening. Especially if she's well past the forty mark."

"Ha! You're not the only one there, sweetheart. But what's worse would be if it was something serious, I mean . . . something long-lasting. If it was just a fling . . . ."

"The thing is, apparently there was nothing to it. I've already told you, I imagined things . . . and he took it very badly. Anyway, what can you do? Everyone knows there's no true love without suffering, don't they, sweetheart?"

"That's a load of nonsense, Vicky. Complete nonsense. At your age."

"Maybe he thought our relationship was going nowhere . . . . It could be, you never know with men . . . Anyway, I made it easy for him, and he took off!"

"I can't believe it! You're lying. You must be lying . . ."

"No I'm not, Paquita, I swear! I should never have slapped him like that!"

Señora Paquita stared at her, still suspicious.

"Well, that's your business. But let me tell you one thing: you ought to go and find him as quickly as you can."

"But where, for heaven's sake? He never told me where he lived. Did he ever tell you or your brother?"

"He never said a word to me."

"Well, he didn't tell me either," sighs Señora Mir.

"Really? He was a strange fellow, wasn't he?"

"Stranger than a white blackbird, sweetheart."

Yes, a strange fellow indeed. Señora Paquita recalls that when he first began to drop in he was very chatty and likeable, as well as being a bit forward. Especially with her, although there was never any way of knowing whether he was being serious or not. One day he told her with a perfectly straight face that he was intrigued by the effect of the passage of time on potatoes. No, he wasn't from the countryside, he wasn't interested in the evolution of vegetables: he explained that he had once been the trainer of a youth football team in El Carmelo, and used to massage the boys' legs with an ointment made from oil and crushed wrinkled potatoes. He was unsure how long it took potatoes to go soft and start to wrinkle, and apparently one day he heard about Señora Mir, a masseuse who was expert in that kind of thing. Someone gave him her card, but he had lost it, which was why he had come into the bar to ask if they knew where she lived.

"And there was another thing yesterday that took me by surprise. Just as he was leaving . . ." Señora Paquita falls silent as a fat, very flustered-looking man comes in and slumps at the bar, calling urgently for a cold beer from the barrel. Señora Mir takes advantage of the pause to ask for a small glass of brandy from the keg, and another with soda water. The customer is not a local, and so Señora Paquita avoids striking up a conversation with him. She serves the beer in a mug, then pours her friend's brandy and soda water. She turns on the tap of a barrel of wine and uses a funnel to fill Señora Mir's bottle. She goes back behind the counter, places the bottle on it, pushes the cork in, and forces it down. The man noisily gulps down the beer, dries the sweat from the back of his neck with a handkerchief, and casts a sideways glance at the plump woman next to him. She is staring at the picture on a calendar hanging from the wall behind the counter. The picture is a reproduction of an old sepia photograph showing a football team from the past posing on a pitch before a game. Shaking her head slightly, Señora Mir says under her breath:

"He would be better on his knees."

Somewhat bewildered by this, the customer finishes his beer, pays, and goes out.

Crouching at his table, Ringo goes over the instructions for five-finger exercises in the notebook he has just opened on top of his book of stories. The musical stave still attracts him more than fiction, and will go on doing so throughout that summer and well into the autumn. For the moment though he finds it hard to concentrate, because the two women have struck up their conversation again:

"And just as he was leaving," Señora Paquita resumes without any kind of pre-amble, picking up the beer mug and wiping the counter with a cloth, "I was about to ask him why he didn't just post the letter rather than bringing it here. I thought it was odd he wanted to entrust it to me . . ."

"It's because of the girl," Señora Mir cuts her short, and her moon face puckers as though she is on the verge of tears. "I'm sure it's because he was thinking of the girl. Because let me tell you, Paqui, if that man talks about what I'm afraid he might talk about in the letter, there's no way he would want it to fall into my daughter's hands. There are some things a young girl shouldn't know about . . . That's why he doesn't want to send it by post. So when he comes back with the letter, keep it safe and give it to me directly. And not a word to Violeta."

"Don't worry."

Señora Mir downs the brandy, then moistens her lips with a sip of soda. She pays, tucks the wine bottle under her arm, and makes to leave the bar, the soda siphon dangling from one finger.

"Above all, Paqui, whatever you do, if the letter arrives, make sure you don't give it to Violeta. I'll come and get it."

"Of course, darling. Don't give it another thought."

Exercise One: Place your forearms and your extended fingers on the surface of a table you are sitting at. Then, first with the right hand and then the left, and finally with both together, lift your fingers in the order indicated. Make sure you lower the finger you have raised before lifting the next one, and repeat each sequence several times: 1-2-3. 3-2-1. 1-4-2.1-2.4.2-1-3 . . .

He practises this for a while with his left hand on the marble tabletop, then stops and stares out of the window. A blink of his eyes, the trick he has often employed to enter the world of desire and fantasy with the rest of his gang, and on the scarred wall on the far side of the street a poster suddenly appears, announcing in red letters the debut concert of the GREAT NINE-FINGERED PIANIST. That would make a good advertisement, wouldn't it? Who knows what the finger of fate holds in store for you, even when that finger has been tossed into the limbo of unborn pianists? A few men pass by the poster, walking briskly or wearily from their homes to other bars and taverns. Some of them stay close to the walls, and all of a sudden one of them comes to a halt, head down and staring at the ground as if a chasm has suddenly opened beneath his feet. A little higher up the same street, in the middle of the tiny island of melancholy, moss-covered cobbles, the lengths of tram tracks emerging from an abolished yesterday stubbornly abide. Ringo feels a sudden, throbbing pain in the nail that is no longer part of his finger, nor the finger part of his hand. He closes the music lesson and returns to the book of short stories.

The lion is still alive; it will fight to the death. Señora Mir and Señora Paquita are standing in the doorway, chatting away. Ringo leans his elbow on the table and covers his ear with his free hand so that he can escape to the protective undergrowth, the wild fragrance of the tall grasses on the Kenyan savannah, where the wounded lion lies flattened against the ground, ears pinned back, waiting for the chance to pounce.

5

THE FINGER OF FATE

In the summer of 1948 the boy turns fifteen. He has loose change in his pocket, and a phantom finger on his right hand. In the workshop one grey, muggy morning that was weighing heavily on him, he was caught daydreaming at the electric rolling mill, trying to hum the first notes of a simple tune he could not remember properly, when in a flash the machine swallowed his index finger.

The fatal distraction, the unfortunate musical teaser that led to the accident were due above all, he thinks, to the sense of frustration that has been at the back of his mind ever since, three years earlier, he had to give up his classes in music theory and piano (his mother was forced to remind him that they were poor) and to his increasing distaste for the workshop and the jewellery trade, for gold, platinum, diamonds and their sparkle. He remembers that on that fateful morning as he left the apartment very early, his lunch tucked under his arm wrapped in a sheet of newspaper, he felt particularly bitter as he went over, as usual, the questions and answers from his favourite theory book from the Municipal Conservatoire. Half an hour later, standing at the rolling mill and persistently trying to recall the song, something in English that began with the words "Long ago and far away" that he had heard in a Technicolor film two days earlier, annoyed because he couldn't quite get it, and carelessly not paying attention to what he was doing, he brought disaster on himself. But his musical obsession was only partly to blame. Even though he might not care to admit it, the fatal slip that cost him his finger was mostly due to the fact that he had not the slightest interest in his prospects in the workshop, to a secret abandonment that had long been building up inside him. After spending two years sweeping the floor until he completed his time as apprentice and message boy, he had been working for three months on the craftsmen's bench using the blowtorch, the files and the saw, and trying hard to do things properly, but his initial enthusiasm for the trade had dimmed. Deep down inside, he had begun to doubt whether he was suited to becoming a goldsmith. To make things worse, all he is given to do now are simple, boring tasks like repairs, soldering little chains, making the occasional plain wedding ring, melting and preparing alloys for welding. He cannot say he hates the job, but something isn't as it should be. He feels he is capable of creating delicate, highly artistic pieces, and those simple tasks bore him so much he finishes them as quickly as he can without paying them any great attention. Besides, it's no life having to spend all these hours shut up in the workshop: from nine in the morning to one in the afternoon, and then from three to seven: eight hours a day altogether from Monday to Friday, plus five hours on Saturday morning, five times eight hours makes forty, plus five on a Saturday gives forty-five, and then there are four hours each Saturday afternoon when as an apprentice he had to sweep the floor and clean the workmen's benches: altogether that comes to forty-nine hours a week. No, dammit, that's not a life.

He is working standing up at the electric rolling mill, alternating these gloomy thoughts with questions and answers he has learnt by heart from his old theory book . . .

—*What is the musical stave?*

A guideline comprising five parallel and equidistant horizontal lines.

—*How are the lines of the stave counted?*

From the bottom up.

. . . while at the same time reliving the scene where Gene Kelly sings as he stacks chairs on the tables of his bar, but he can't get the start of the tune right, it stubbornly slips away from him in the workshop's busy thrum, the buzz of saws and files, beating hammers, the hiss of welding torches. At the outset, the block of gold he is rolling is the size and shape of a half-used bar of soap. All he has to do is start up the machine and push the gold between the two steel rollers so that it gradually grows thinner and thinner, taking it out on the far side and carefully pushing it back in once more, making sure to keep his fingers well away from the machine, because the thinner the bar becomes, the more dangerous it is. Ringo knows this, he knows the way the gold starts to coil and snake and lash out as it is swallowed by the rollers, but now his mind is elsewhere, and his finger has gone to sleep, as if it is resting on the bottom line of the stave.

Just a few seconds before the drama occurs, Sparry has joined him in his musical daydreaming. For some time now Ringo has had the feeling that the blasted bird he killed years before with an airgun is lurking nearby; first he hears him chirping inside the jukebox of his head and closes his eyes, and then, as he gazes back through the looking-glass of time, still blurred from the rain falling on his grandfather's vegetable patch, he imagines he can see him beneath the workbench, pecking at the greasy sheet of newspaper in which he wrapped his lunchtime roll of tinned anchovies. After five years buried in the earth, the sparrow's leaden eye has grown even darker, but the bird is not illuminated by any spotlight, surrounded by any glow or fake shining halo: this is not a hallucination, it is simply there, trotting like a little clockwork bird with a live worm in its mouth. Ringo has his finger on the trigger once more. Isn't it a relief that it is guzzling a worm? thinks the repentant hunter: the sparrow also hunts and kills, so it's a case of everyone for themselves . . . Yes, but you don't keep your promises, my lad, you swore you'd come and visit me in my humble grave, but I'm still waiting.

"He's talking to himself," someone comments behind his back. "He's always on another planet, that boy. Wake up, *nano*!"

Too late. For the workmen, the rollers swallow Ringo's stupid finger because he is always talking to himself at the machine, and because the stupid finger is right where it shouldn't be, recklessly poised on the gold bar as it slides through the rollers, a bar that has become increasingly bent, twisting uncontrollably up and down on itself, transformed all of a sudden into a lethal snare. Ringo has always preferred to believe it happened because the finger, obeying the secret suicidal impulse of a depressive music-lover, simply did not wish to lift off in time. I'll be the *doh* and *soh* on the ivory keyboard of fame or I'll be nothing in this life, he imagined the finger whispering to him before it sacrificed itself, a verbal fantasy born of the musical stave, but which he sees as being more real even than the workshop itself, with everything it contains, more real even than his own home and the church and the gang who love to tell their tall tales in the Las Ánimas garden or on the slopes of Montaña Pelada. The suicidal act occurred far from the keyboard and sheet music, far from the piano and the lesson book – everything that, cursing his fate, he was forced to give up because there was no money to pay for any more classes. Distracted by this feeling of resentment and by his musical daydreaming, he scarcely notices the tug at the metacarpus of his index finger or the subsequent crushing of the three knuckles as they are flattened by the rollers, together with the gold bar.

The blood does not spurt immediately, but starts to flow a few seconds after the finger has been snapped up. No-one in the workshop hears him cry out or moan, partly because, to his surprise, it doesn't hurt. He switches the machine off, and doesn't want, or doesn't dare, look down at his hand yet. Raising it to his eyes, he doesn't want to see it; when he can finally bring himself to do so, he stares at it as if it were alien to him, a fleshy appendage not part of his body. He turns slowly, hand held aloft, towards the nearest craftsman, who is horrified when he sees the blood gushing. Ringo himself has still not felt anything apart from a slight tickling sensation, but as soon as he realises he has lost a finger, he feels dizzy, his legs give way, and he starts to pour with sweat. Shouts and curses all round him; a race to the first aid box. Wrapped in an improvised bandage, and with his arm held high in the air, he is rushed to the emergency department at the Hospital Clínico, from where he is later discharged.

Where do pianists' dead fingers go? he wonders bitterly. He asks out loud:

"Why is it that the finger I don't have hurts so much, mother?"

"If you keep still a moment, I'll explain," she replies, cutting open the end of the bandage round the wound with her left hand. "Goodness me, just look at this. How did you let it get infected? What have you been doing?"

"I haven't done anything."

"But look at it. Hasn't it been hurting?"

"Well, now you mention it, I do feel a bit feverish."

"There you go again. It's almost as if you want to have a fever."

"What really hurts is my fingernail. Why does that hurt, if I haven't got one?"

"And look at this scarf, all covered with blood. I'll have to throw it away."

"Couldn't you make me a sling with one of your headscarves? One of those pretty ones you have."

His hand is a mass of bloody gauze, and his mother changes his bandage as often as she can because the wound is suppurating. But the long hours she works at the old people's home means she cannot do all her tasks at home, and so she leaves his lunch prepared for him – boiled rice with sweet potato, or an onion or bean tortilla – which her son eats on his own, listening to music on the radio and with a novel open beside his plate. He has finished *La peau de chagrin* and started *Hunger*. In the evening he waits for his mother so they can have supper together, and sometimes peels potatoes or sweet potatoes, or shucks beans or peas while he is waiting, even though she tells him off because he could get the wound infected. It is a week since the accident in the workshop, and two since the Cleansing Brigade left to fumigate some warehouses down by the River Oñar, in Gerona. This is what his mother has told him, and that there was so much to be done in the area that it would be some time before his father got back from the trip.

Occasionally, the missing finger is unbelievably painful. Especially the nail, wherever it is now. The loss of his index finger has left Ringo in a permanent state of bemusement and melancholy, often made worse by an anxious concern over what life holds in store for him. He thinks that with his finger amputated, there is very little he will be able to do in the jeweller's workshop; beyond that, he feels his life has changed decisively. What work could he do after the amputation? How would four fingers cope, for example, with handling a saw in a delicate, complex operation on a pendant with enamel and precious stones? He would no longer be able to hold the file or the pliers properly: he might not even be able to grip a pair of pincers, or a borax brush. Files, pliers, a drill and its bits, anvil, dies, blowtorch, saw, doming block, buff – words that until now had stood for the tools of his trade no longer demanded his attention, and were beginning to settle into the past of his artisan memory, becoming as rusty as the two useless lengths of track half-buried in the old cobblestones of the street.

Then there is the other painful consequence of the accident, one that for him is much more important than work: he imagines his right hand scuttling up and down the piano keyboard like a grotesque, maimed spider, the hand that retains a memory of the very first notes and rhythms, of the five-finger exercises and the beginning of some simple pieces that had taken him so much effort to learn, such as "Für Elise" or the "Vals de las olas". *Dooo-re-me-soh-dooo, ti-doh-re-doh-ti-do-mi-soh-tiii* . . . He had always hoped that one day he would be able to renew his theory and piano lessons, and now, in spite of what has happened, with only nine fingers and all the odds against him, he still clings to this hope. He has no intention of giving up the chords or the rapid two-handed scales he used to play on the old, yellowing keyboard at maestro Emery's – cigarette burns on the lowest keys, squawking bird sounds from the highest. Emery, a pianist who had played in popular orchestras but satisfied his love of classical music by giving lessons twice a week for twelve pesetas a month in the filthy, gloomy dining room of a tiny flat on Calle Tres Señoras. Something tells Ringo that the old maestro, with his shiny bald head and tiny grey eyes like slits behind metal-framed glasses, with his seagull's nose in unshaven cheeks, his quiet, translucent hands spotted with age, his incisive profile above the black outline of the piano and the poverty of his domestic setting, has only vanished temporarily from his life. He has had to bid farewell to the finger swallowed by the rolling mill, but not to the musical stave or the keyboard, which he hopes to recover some day along with the lessons. In the meantime, where do pianists' dead fingers go? he notes in tiny handwriting in his secret black-backed notebook.

His relationship with music has always been an intuitive one, and is far from being selective. He hums with just as much respect and pleasure a Cole Porter tune or the soundtrack of films he has enjoyed – he knows by heart the stirring music from "Stagecoach" or "The Thief of Baghdad", or the waltz from "Jezebel" – as he does a few bars from a Mozart sonata. He thinks of the musical scores he has stored away, and the dreams he had invested in them until the day of the accident, and waits for better days. Destiny has decided that the finger to be sacrificed would be his index finger, the fickle finger of fate, the one that also pulled the trigger in his grandfather's vegetable garden five years earlier, the one that plays the *re* in the five-finger exercises he misses so badly. He didn't have time to learn much, it had been barely ten months, one hour each on Mondays and Thursdays caressing the keys and reading music out loud at a three-four rhythm, but he considers what little he did learn as a treasure, a rare privilege. "Raise your head, don't look down at the keyboard so much," the maestro's smoke-filled voice still floats in the air: "The music isn't in the keys, it's in the memory of your fingers and in your heart."

His fingers' memory. He would find it hard to explain, but he could have sworn that sitting at that battered, nicotine-stained keyboard, he had learnt lessons that would help him to live. It wasn't that Emery ever gave him explicit advice about anything – except on one occasion, when he had made fun of a companion whom he was way ahead of, and the maestro told him that to be good at the piano you had to be a good person – and yet, simply by the way he stilled Ringo's hands, obliging him to leave them resting on the keyboard, calm and docile but alert, their tips barely touching the warped ivory and the black varnish of the semitones, refusing to allow him to press down until he had sung the whole score from memory, he had allowed him to absorb a knowledge that went far beyond these rudimentary lessons in music theory and piano, a certain way of understanding and accepting everything that was happening to him. He remembers that it was from this whirlwind of notes dancing on the stave and in his mind that one day he suddenly sniffed the scent of a new and strange discipline that he was more than willing to adopt in the future. Habits as simple as raising his arm as he started a bar, catching the notes in mid-air as if they were butterflies of light dancing in the darkness, or the routine of keeping his hands still but alert on the keys, anticipating the miracle of playing a harmonious chord: as the days went by, these habits somehow tended to turn into tiny moral precepts. As each lesson was ending, after a series of repeated, rapid scales, the maestro would always allow his pupil to close the piano, and every time Ringo, hands still on fire, carefully lowered the heavy lid on to the keyboard, he would let it drop the last few inches, and from the depths of the ancient piano he would be rewarded with an echoing boom that sounded both like a friendly farewell and a future promise. It was as if, during those happy days, music was the only thread in the loom of life, and in among the five lines of the musical stave he could glimpse the secret of the beauty the world had to offer. In his precarious adolescence, memorising a piece of music became something much more than a task to educate his ear; even though he could not know it at the time, the spirit and rhythm hidden in the stave would get into his bloodstream and make the readings of his favourite authors all the more memorable.

Is all that a thing of the past? he asks himself now. Is the nine-fingered pianist condemned to be nothing more than a fairground attraction? Perhaps he couldn't even hope for that much, because at home there was still no money to pay for any more classes – always supposing that the maestro Emery would one day agree to take back the nine-fingered pupil – let alone rent a piano, still less buy one. We'll see if it's possible in the future, his mother had said when she cancelled the lessons. The bad times can't last forever, Son, and for now if you're so interested in music, why don't you amuse yourself playing the harmonica?

Those were her exact words, Sparry. Would you believe it!

Don't judge your mother.

She isn't my mother.

Never say that, you ungrateful wretch!

If she recommended a harmonica back then, what would she say now? That I try the flute?

The sparrow is in the washbasin, glancing sideways at him with his dead eye while still busily pecking at some insects crawling out of the plughole. This is how Ringo likes to imagine him, wherever and whenever he can, predatory, talkative, and vengeful, pecking shamelessly at whatever he can. Ringo, meanwhile, is sitting on a stool opposite the basin, staring at himself in the mirror while he patiently allows his mother to remove the bandage. Red stars of iodine splash the white porcelain and finally drive away the little brown bird.

"What are you muttering?" asks his mother, standing next to him, a safety pin in her mouth. "Raise your arm. Afterwards I'll wash your hair, you should see how it looks."

"I can't have showers."

"Of course you can, if you keep your arm out."

"I could fall."

"You could stop talking nonsense."

She has thrown the dirty bandage into a waste bin under the basin. She uses a piece of gauze to press down on the yellowish areas of pus around the stitches on the stump of his finger, then washes the wound with peroxide, keeping the safety pin in her mouth the whole time. She's becoming more and more like grandma, thinks Ringo, staring at the pin. The image of domesticity, grandmother Tecla, whether she is sweeping or sewing or shelling broad beans, always has a safety pin in the corner of her mouth.

"Did it hurt? One of the stitches was infected."

"No, it didn't hurt," he lies. "What hurts is the nail. Why does it bother me like that? How can it possibly hurt, if I don't have one anymore?"

"Well, as you know, what we don't have is what hurts. You've always believed in ghosts, and you talk to them as well, don't you? So I don't know why you think it's so odd. The nail hurts because it's no longer there."

"It's just that sometimes it's really painful. And this shoulder too."

"I believe you, Son."

She examines the puffiness around the knuckles and puts more iodine on the stitches. Ringo wrinkles his nose at the sight of the bruised, limp-looking hand – it's as if it had been crushed and then pumped up with air – and then watches his mother's reddened hands hovering delicately above his missing finger.

"How long have you been left-handed, Mother?"

"Ever since I was born, I suppose. Don't move."

"Jack the Ripper and Saint Paul were left-handed too."

"Well, I must say, that's not much comfort," she smiles, searching for the boy's face in the bathroom mirror, "but it will amuse your father to know that."

The Rat-catcher has been away for some time now, and Ringo has absolutely no desire to ask when he will be back. A short time ago he was in the Panadés region with Uncle Luis and the Cleansing Brigade, carrying out work in the wine cellars and warehouses, as well as some farmhouses. According to his mother, there had been a plague of voles in the crops, and Ringo suspects that these are not official jobs, but individual requests that have not been authorised, and are probably therefore more lucrative. He also knows that the Rat-catcher often works on his own. He has begun to wonder about this, harbouring suspicions he cannot yet define, and has had the same dream two nights running: dressed up like the magician Fu Ching, his father puts a smoking gun into his top hat, and then pulls out a dead rat that's still got green froth round its mouth . . . Be that as it may,

Ringo does not expect or want his mother to clarify his suspicions, because he vaguely intuits (although he could not say how) that to bring this up would make her cry. He's waiting for the day when he hears her say: You'll never see me cry again, not for that reason or any other.

"The Bioscas have got a piano. They're good neighbours, aren't they, Mother?"

"Yes, they are."

"So do you think they would let me practise scales a few minutes every day if you asked them?"

"No. Are you forgetting they've got poor Rosita very sick at home? What you should do," his mother says as she wraps a clean gauze round the stump of his finger, "is to be more careful with this hand of yours. Try not to use it, or at least not until the wound has healed."

"Don't say that," he begs her. "I need to keep practising. It's good to do finger exercises, even if it's only on the table. We could also buy a keyboard. Maestro Emery says they're not expensive."

His mother shakes her head, at a loss.

"I don't understand. Can you tell me why you always take your music theory book with you, wherever you go?" She searches for the right words before adding as gently as she can: "Why are you still studying those scores, my love? Do you really think you'll be able to play the piano again one day, with that hand of yours?"

"Of course I will. I'll be a nine-fingered pianist. Why is that so extraordinary?"

Roll up, roll up, ladies and gentlemen. DOMINGO KID, THE GREAT NINE-FINGERED PIANIST. He can already see the posters announcing him in concert halls: HUNGARIAN RHAPSODY NUMBER 2 FOR NINE FINGERS. Why shouldn't it be a good selling point? He can picture himself on the platform after he has performed his favourite sonata – No.14 by Mozart. The young virtuoso acknowledging the applause, the grand piano open beside him like a gigantic black dahlia, bowing his head over and over again, tousled hair flopping over his face, wild-eyed, almost in a trance, receiving the ovation with the celebrated maimed hand folded across his chest. And who knows whether there might be a sonata especially composed for the left hand?

For now, his mother takes the celebrated hand and rubs the numb fingers with her thumb to help the circulation.

"Victoria Mir taught me this." She gently massages the four fingers, one by one. After a while, she adds: "Is it true what they say, Son? That she came out of her apartment half-naked and wanted to throw herself under a tram?"

Taken by surprise, he clicks his tongue.

"What tram? There was no tram anywhere near."

"So she wasn't serious?"

"Of course not. It was a sham, a joke. But she didn't fool me. She even dozed off on the rails, and was snoring . . ."

"You don't say!" She is pensive for a while. "Poor Victoria, people have always criticised her so . . . and what did her daughter do? She must have come and helped her."

"She'd gone to the beach with a friend. Well, that's what her mother said then. Because some time later, in the bar, I heard her tell Señora Paqui that Violeta was at home that Sunday. . . in other words, the poor woman can't get it straight, she's off her rocker, she's lost it."

"You're the one who's lost it! And what did people say when they saw her stretched out in the street like that?"

"I don't really know, I was busy reading," he replies reluctantly, with no interest in the matter. He sees himself there again, among the crowd of onlookers, but with his thoughts far off, and feeling a cold wind on his face, his favourite book tucked under his arm, a burning question in his mind: what was the leopard looking for up on the mountain top? He senses that this question, raising the enigma of the animal in the distant snows, is somehow much closer and more important to him than the grotesque spectacle of Señora Mir collapsing on the remnants of the tram tracks.

"So it's not true she fainted," his mother says.

"Of course not. She knew what she was doing! But there was one odd thing . . . Mother, did you ever tell Señora Mir that I studied music?"

"I don't think so. Why?"

"Because that witch knows. She told me so, right there, out of the blue."

"What's so odd about that? Aren't you always dragging those scores around with you?" She is thoughtful once more. "But goodness me, to throw yourself into the street like that . . . What could have made her do it?"

"Because she's crazy, Mother. Mad as a hatter."

"There's no need to insult anyone, do you hear me? Besides, it's not true. Poor Victoria, it's true she hasn't managed to keep her life her own affair, but who can these days? She's been through a lot, that's for sure. Several times she's been on the verge of leaving her husband and going to live in Badalona with her mother-in-law, who has always taken her side against her own son. And in France she has a brother she's very close to, who had to leave because they were going to kill him as a Red. Ramiro, he's called. I knew him, he's a good sort. But Victoria couldn't even mention his name in her house. Now she occasionally gets news of him through friends, your father knows him . . ."

"I knew it!" Ringo glances keenly at his mother. "That Ramiro must be the one who sells Father the French poison, which is better and cheaper than the stuff the brigade has. Isn't that so?"

Surprised but unconcerned, she shrugs.

"I've no idea, Son, your father never talks to me about work . . . What I was going to say is that Victoria's husband used to treat her very badly. And that, even if she didn't actually see him waving his pistol outside church the day that brute suffered his terrible attack, I wouldn't be surprised if it hadn't unhinged her in some way."

"That was the day of the snake, wasn't it? There was a poisonous snake behind the altar that fed on mice—"

"Don't talk nonsense. There was no snake—"

"Of course there was! That's why he was there. Why would he have

79

gone, otherwise? He would never have entered a church if there hadn't been mice and a snake inside."

Ringo recalls that the day before all this happened his father had come back from Canfranc with the most powerful poison, three bottles of French cognac, several cartons of Virginia tobacco, a bag of lighter flints and a bottle of perfume for Alberta the light of his life. And that when he was called to the Mass, he had told the two of them: it seems that a little snake has scared the nuns.

"Yes, you're right about that," his mother concedes. "But we'll never know what really happened, because your father has his own way of telling things . . . you know how he likes to make fun of these official ceremonies."

Imperial absurdities, blue claptrap, ridiculous genuflections and hallelujahs, the bilious barrack-room rites of mindless buffoons in cahoots with the clergy, had been the Rat-catcher's opening salvo. The masseuse's husband, the neatest combed Falangist you've ever seen, one Sunday last winter took up position at the foot of the church staircase with pistol in hand to wait for the faithful to come out of the twelve o'clock Mass because, apparently, a voice inside his head had ordered him to shoot at them . . . This was the beginning of a tragic story that the boy had heard twice, ending on both occasions the way his mother was describing: a blasphemous and devious tale shamelessly manipulated by his father deliberately to make his audience laugh and win the support of listeners who shared his views, but also with a secret inner fury that he sometimes found hard to contain. He found it impossible to tell the story without a vengeful, angry disdain that made his voice hoarse.

The first time Ringo heard about Councillor Mir's tragicomic exploits was in the tavern; the second during a merry supper with Uncle Luis and three other friends from the brigade, invited to a homemade paella that he would not let Alberta the light of my life help with in any way, very nearly burning the rice. That evening, Capitán Rat-catcher told them, in his most sarcastic, high-flown manner – although occasionally behind this mocking tone Ringo thought he could detect a different tone that he recalled with fear and sadness, a confidential voice tinged with bitterness, choked with hatred, despair and misfortune – told them, as he scraped the rice stuck to the bottom of the dish, swearing it was the best part of the paella, that the year before, our neighbourhood councillor, when he still appeared to be in good health, used to attend the twelve o'clock Mass in the San José de la Montaña convent, a little further up from Travesera de Dalt. He always went alone, decked out in all his Falange finery, with blue shirt and red beret folded at his shoulder, black gloves and shiny leather straps, his service revolver in its holster at his belt. Sewn into his shirt were the German eagle and the badge of the Blue Division. Also hanging from his chest was his old pair of field glasses, as if he had come directly from spotting Bolsheviks on the Russian steppe under the banners of the Third Reich, on the threatened front at Lake Ilmen, between Novgorod and the River Weresha. Have you never seen an ex-Wehrmacht soldier with field glasses slung round his neck and a huge pistol at his belt? Shit, it's well worth it! said the unrepentant fantasist, smiling as he called for the wine jug. Just like Grandma Tecla back in her village, he sprayed his open mouth with a stream of red wine and then went on, his voice more lubricated and jocular than ever.

In fact, there was no reason for all this paraphernalia, because our volunteer Altamirano never fired a single shot in the entire Russian campaign: he enlisted as a kitchen assistant, and returned in the same capacity. But only his wife and a few others were aware of this. Now let's see what happened that dark, gloomy late November day during the twelve o'clock Mass at the San José convent. There was black crêpe all round the church, in the sky, and in the eyes of the congregation; the pious flock seemed to be living a month-long Day of the Dead. Our imperial comrade was prostrate in his front-row pew, but as soon as the Mass began he was seen to stand up, genuflect towards the altar and then leave the church, contrite, his eyes moist. This was no great novelty anyway. According various accounts collected *in situ* by yours truly shortly afterwards – because by chance I was sent to the church by our most excellent city council at the request of the nuns to inspect a side chapel where the day before an old biddy had fainted from shock when she saw an enormous rat, or sleeping serpent, she wasn't sure which – Comrade Mir had behaved in exactly the same fashion the previous Sunday. Just at the moment of "confectioner God" – is that what they say? When the faithful respond *mea culpa, mea máxima* and biggest culpa, is that right? The pious ex-combatant left his pew and the Mass, descended one of the two staircases leading down to the promenade, and stood to attention at the bottom, self-absorbed and haughty-looking. Tall, handsome, funereal and dark, with a kind of glowing darkness, singing who knows what Falangist stupidity under his breath until the Mass was over and he could see the congregation emerging. Then the ex-soldier confronted them, muttering confused snatches of prayer, and took out his pistol. He pushed it against his temple, shouted *Viva Cristo Rey*! and exclaimed bang! bang!, smiling as he revealed a mouth full of gold teeth, his upper lip adorned with the pencil moustache of an acting lieutenant and confirmed cadaver. This at least was the sarcastic version of events told by Ringo's father, aimed at drawing guffaws from his audience, embellishing a story that became well known in the neighbourhood. Ringo seemed to remember that in the very first version offered in Bar Rosales as Señor Agustín filled his wine glass for the umpteenth time, there had been no mention of the moustache or gold teeth.

The screams of some of the women in the congregation could be heard as far away as the Tibidabo. There were more than enough reasons to suspect that our friend was losing his marbles, but the good people who had just washed themselves of their sins preferred to look discreetly the other way, and neither the district council nor the local Falangist headquarters, which Señor Mir often visited due to the position he held, seemed to want to know either. He was already a bit strange when he came back from Russia, his wife later declared: after he cut back his moustache still further he launched himself into everything he did with extraordinary vehemence and determination, and yet, the Rat-catcher would argue, we have seen and continue to see every day far more extravagant and extraordinary behaviour from members of that battle-hardened militia, because that is the way they are, my friends, that is how these blue scoundrels behave, that is what these days of infamy and sacristies are like. He even thought it probable that the convent authorities, as well as the congregation, would see this display by the dapper ex-combatant as a manly, martial offering in times of peace, a rite or military custom possibly inspired by a pious vow, a secret desire for expiation. This man is paying for a sin, some of them must have thought. And possibly that was why he shaved his moustache.

Whatever the truth, somebody considered his conduct both inappropriate and offensive, and reported him. So Comrade Ramón Mir Altamirano was summoned to the local Falange delegation in Plaza Lesseps to explain himself to the chief, who was a friend of his. In the Falange office, he merely shrugged his shoulders, clutched the front of his trousers in both hands, and, face to the sun, swore that it was a question of honour, a personal act of homage to a brave female friend who was risking her life for a good cause. Now is no longer the time for epic struggle, comrades, it's a time for intimate expiation, it is said he said. That was his style and he had no intention of saying sorry and anyway, damn it all, comrades, he was as loyal as ever to the cause, and was not going to add anything more. What damned expiation was he talking about? The devil only knows! He was given a serious reprimand and warned not to go around in public wearing his uniform and scaring people. If he did not comply, the next time he would have to report to the movement's provincial headquarters, and could be expelled from the party and stripped of his position as neighbourhood councillor.

Despite all this, the spectacular pantomime was repeated the very next Sunday, with an explosive variation that took everyone by surprise. Pale-faced and solemn as before, Altamirano left the church at the start of the collective *mea culpa*. Once outside, he descended the staircase again, and stood to attention at the bottom. Those who from the porch saw him standing there in his funereal uniform, straight-backed, wild-eyed, his jutting chin raised in defiance like a black, imperturbable herald announcing leaden years devoted to an urgent, inescapable cause, said that he remained motionless for at least half an hour while the Mass was being said. And that for one brief instant – so brief that very few of those present managed to see it – he fell to his knees and prayed so fervently and trembled so violently that he looked like someone kneeling in the snowy wastes of the Russian steppe; they could have sworn that at that moment, as he was entrusting himself to God and the Father and, he thought that the snow of Novgorod was crunching beneath his knees. A short while later, somebody asked him if he felt ill. He asked politely: would you mind repeating the question, *kyrsji*? Then almost at once, seeing the congregation leaving Mass and coming down the stairs, he drew the pistol with his left hand, shouted *Viva Cristo Rey*! placed the barrel to the side of his head, and pulled the trigger. This time, however, he had no chance to exclaim bang! The word got stuck in his throat as his head jerked violently to one side, because this time the gun fired a real bullet.

The rest of the story is an anti-climax, concludes the Rat-catcher. They sent for his wife, but do you know who came on her behalf to take care of that blue dummy who had blown off his own ear and part of his brains? The fellow she was seeing, that lame guy, a prickly sort. He went with him in the ambulance. Mir's skin was saved after I don't know how many operations on his nut, but when he came out of hospital he had less brains than a cockroach. The bullet shot away the left lobe of his brain, and left him gaga. He talked drivel, went round drunk all day, and kept falling down in the street. His mother, a war widow who lives on her own in Badalona and never forgave him for joining the Falange, refused even to see him. Perhaps he himself went in search of that bullet; perhaps it was always in the chamber, waiting for him, even when he used the butt to hammer in the Sacred Heart plaque on his door. Whatever the case, I bet that blue riffraff are asking themselves questions now . . . Was it his hand that loaded the bullet into the chamber? It's always said that's the Devil's work, but Holy Mother of God! Does he also load the weapons of our heroic crusaders? Does the Evil One also load our guns, blessed by the bishops?

"It wasn't his service revolver," adds the Rat-catcher. "It was a 6.35mm Walther he brought back from Germany. But the finger that squeezed the trigger was not his, it was ours."

"Now you're talking complete nonsense," Alberta the light of my life protests as she serves more rice to the youngest member of the brigade. "Just eat and pay him no attention, Manuel."

"I don't know, when it comes to Comrade Altamirano . . ."

"The most neatly combed Falangist you've ever seen, *nano*!"

"Uncle Luis says that somebody told him that Altamirano was in Málaga during the war and took part in the reprisals with General Queipo's Falange troops."

"Anything is possible where he's concerned," says Manuel. He recalls the arrogant figure with his puffed-out chest, black, oiled hair and jutting chin. By now he had shaved off his moustache, but when he spoke, and above all when he shouted, it was as if he still had one. "I haven't seen that bastard since I ran into him on the street about a year ago. He was with a spectacular-looking woman, a Chinese girl. They were about to go into the police station on Travesera Dalt, and the woman stopped on the pavement to put some lipstick on. That annoyed him so much he grabbed the lipstick from her and almost made her swallow it . . ."

"That woman you're talking about," cut in the Rat-catcher, "is about as Chinese as Columbus. She's a whore who works with the police. I've already told you about her – she's dangerous."

"Yes, we know," says Uncle Luis. Then he adds slyly: "But what about the snake? Didn't you tell us you went to the church because a snake had slipped in and scared the life out of an old biddy? I seem to remember there are gardens and a pond beside that convent . . ."

"It was a plaster snake. Just plaster painted green. But it looked real, the son of a bitch. It was behind the confessional. It had fallen off an image of the Immaculate Conception, a relic so old it was falling to pieces. It was only a lump of plaster – you know, the snake curled up beneath the feet of the Virgin. When I saw it on the floor it was just lying there, curled up and still, with the Virgin's big toe on one of its coils. That's what the whole fuss was about: a piece of broken plaster on the floor. The nuns thought they might be able to stick it back on, but no chance . . . Pass me the wine, will you? Don't you want some dessert? Go on, try this peach. Cut it into slices and put them in your glass. The best desserts are those that allow you to go on drinking, the rest are a load of rubbish. Shit, you really need to learn how to eat properly!"

"Now, let's see. We were talking about poor Victoria."

"Señora Mir is a bit nuts, Mother, everyone knows that."

"Why are you so hard on her, Son? She can be a bit extreme sometimes, but she's a good person. You shouldn't believe all that's said about her."

Not everything, of course, he thinks, because he's heard some unbelievable things; for example, one Sunday evening a regular in Bar Rosales said she had lost a marble and found a pussy, and this brought loud laughter from all those keen on coarse jokes. He's not going to tell his mother any of that sort of thing, especially since it seems she and Señora Mir had been good friends. Yet he's heard sordid stories about her involvement with some disreputable characters, none of them local men, for example a travelling salesman who had no recollection of what he was meant to be selling, a drunken good-for-nothing who liked to think he was a proud, masculine type and theatrically refused (but only for a while) to have her pay for his drink in Bar Rosales. According to a comment he overheard Señora Mir herself make to Paquita, he was a dirty pig who never cleaned his teeth and whose kisses were full of tomato seeds. And there was another one, an old acquaintance, a retired nurse who was diabetic: a poor devil who didn't last long because he died on her. And there was talk of others, each one more defeated and boastful than the last, men like shadows who seemed to be looking for a bar where they could hide from the world.

It's not that Ringo pays much attention to the neighbourhood gossip, or takes part in the low banter in the bar, but although the pretence at humour and smuttiness in these slanders might not be in the least bit funny, and be very unfair and rude, he still prefers it to the hypocritical tittle-tattle and the envious whispers going round concerning the risible, moth-eaten romances of the queen of back-rubs, that show-off who is turning into an old wreck and behaves like one, a woman who goes round painted like a doll, behaves like a tart and gives off a whiff of rancid, fleeting and improbable passions: a character that seems to him so stale, so vulgar and so ridiculous it cannot be true. It doesn't interest him, he doesn't believe it. He bursts out laughing just to see her crossing the street and stopping to straighten her stocking. She turns on herself so slowly, with a studied air of helplessness and complacency, and takes so long waving her arms about, that as if by magic the seam rights itself before she can even touch the stocking. And when he then sees her walking to the bar swaying her hips above her ridiculous high-heeled shoes, wiggling her backside for all to see, it is almost more than he can take. It is precisely because she is so real, so close and so ordinary, that he grows irritated and perturbed: to him she is too closely linked to the drabness of the neighbourhood, the tiny deceptions, ruses and low tricks that are its unavoidable daily commerce.

What nastiness are they peddling now, what's the gossip, Son, what are the comments in Bar Rosales, his mother asks as she examines Ringo's fingernails. Well, I don't know, it seems that the fit of madness she had in the street was because a married man, much older than her, someone called Alonso, had broken off his romance with her. Apparently during a massage session she had a terrific argument with that man, who had come to her because he had dreadful pain in his bad leg. There were shouts and slaps, although it's not clear if it was her or him, and he decided to leave her on the spot. You can keep your silvery hands, your creams and your jealousy, you stuck-up blonde! they say he said: I'm not making anything up. And that now she is waiting for a letter, there isn't a day goes by when she doesn't drop into the bar to ask if it has arrived; at least, that's what

Señora Paquita tells anyone who'll listen. Apart from that, not much is known about her fancy man; they say he didn't live in the neighbourhood, and that he was or had been a footballer and tram-driver. He used to wear a ring he himself had made from bone, and so Señor Agustín said he was someone who had been in prison . . .

"Oh my, and you claim you don't hear anything," his mother says. I know nothing about this man, but I do know that he has been very kind and considerate with Vicky."

"Oh yes, of course," Ringo recalls with a smile. "He used to take her roses."

"Roses?"

"Yes, paper ones. Blue ones. He could be seen every Sunday in the bar with his blue rose, marking time until he went across to see Señora Mir. . . I'm not making anything up."

"Perhaps not, but you're talking utter rot. How could they have been paper roses? Nobody gives paper roses."

"They don't? Have you seen 'The Thief of Baghdad', Mama? Don't you know that anyone who smells the Blue Rose of Forgetfulness cannot remember anything about his past life . . . ?"

'That's enough of your films. And stay still or I'll hurt you." She starts cutting his nails and then bandages his hand again, before adding thoughtfully, as if to herself: "And how can anyone know that Victoria slapped that man – who saw her? And besides, just because he says he's going to leave her, why does that mean she has to go and sit on those tracks and cause a scandal in the middle of the street? Victoria has always been a bit odd, but to go to such lengths . . ."

She doesn't trust appearances. There must be something more, she says, or she wouldn't have exposed herself to such an absurd situation, one that was bound to make a mockery of her in the neighbourhood. Or perhaps she really did intend to commit suicide, even if the tracks were no longer in use? Familiar as she is with medical terms, she suggests the possibility that her former work colleague might have suffered some kind of psychopathic attack, a temporary personality disorder.

Ringo shows no interest in resolving his mother's doubts. As far as Señor Alonso was concerned, all he could say was that he was a strange sort who did not say a lot, and no longer came into the bar. Grudgingly, he recalls him: he used to sit at a table in the back with his sports jacket round his shoulders, drink an aperitif or coffee with a slug of aniseed, and sometimes play patience or turn his hostile gaze on the rowdy adolescents who, before deciding whether to go on to dance at the Verdi or La Lealtad, relieved the boredom of a Sunday afternoon round the table football. So what was the gentleman in question really like? Hmm, it would take the smartest regular in the bar a million words to explain something that he could convey with a single glance. Yes, but at first sight he seemed more like a poor fellow, lame in one leg, getting on in years, ugly-looking, tall, thin and slightly knock-kneed. He could add that he had light-coloured eyes, a big, aquiline nose in a wrinkled face, a ridiculous fish mouth and a thick head of white hair combed back off his forehead, but his mother has already had enough.

"My oh my, nobody could say you didn't pay attention."

"Well, he was the sort of fellow who drew attention to himself. He was always joking with Señora Paquita . . . I'm not making anything up."

He doesn't want to be more explicit: the lame guy's stale gallantry with women leaves him cold. But deep inside he saw him as one of those men who are worth listening to when they talk about women. Someone who did not say much but whose eyes spoke volumes, slow in speech and gesture even when he smiled, which was possibly the slowest and most appealing feature he had. He often wore a flower in his buttonhole. He was usually to be seen on Sunday afternoons: he came in fifteen or twenty minutes before six, and always sat at the same table. When it struck six he would get up, hand the pack of cards back at the bar, exchange a few words with Agustín or his sister in a low voice, especially with the sister, who would listen to him with a flustered smile on her face, then pay for his aperitif and head for the blonde's apartment for her massage of his back, his bad leg, his groin, or who knows what: the rumours abounded. Sometimes he also came in during the week.

This had been the case for almost a year, ever since one rainy Sunday in May when they saw him coming into the bar for the first time, a soaking newspaper over his head, to ask where a nurse or masseuse lived, someone who had been strongly recommended to him, by the name of Doña Victoria López Ayala, originally from a village outside Segovia, married to someone called Ramón Mir, who didn't have a telephone. He knew all this about her, and seemed to know even more, and from the very first attracted attention. He looked about fifty, but close to it was plain he was considerably older. Even so, there was a youthful, taunting look in his eye. The light-blue jacket he wore was of excellent quality but worn and shapeless, with baggy pockets, and for all his natural elegance and neatness, he had a slightly marginal air about him. I was given that lady's business card and I haven't the slightest idea where I put it, I only know she lives on this street, he grunted as he searched his pockets. Señora Paquita came out from behind the bar and pointed out the house, twenty metres further up on the far side of the road, look, you can see it from here, it's number 117.

The man threw the wet newspaper into a basket where some of the customers left their umbrellas. He went on searching for the card in his pockets, gave up, asked for a coffee and murmured with a smile:

"The name suits it."

"What's that?" asked Señora Paquita.

"The street. We're in Torrente de las Flores, aren't we? But the name of the tavern – Rosales, doesn't fit at all."

"Oh, because there are no roses, you mean?" she said, flattered. "It's because our name is Rosales."

That first day he drank down his coffee scalding hot, his face devoid of expression, then went out again into the rain and crossed the road to number 117. Señora Mir's card appeared later on, behind the basket with the umbrellas.

His mother keeps an identical one together with an image of the Virgin, in a book by Apel-les Mestres with illustrations of lovely fairies and water nymphs.

VICTORIA MIR
KINESIOLOGIST AND CHIRO-MASSEUSE
Expert in lumbar and back pains.
Treatment of muscular, nervous and emotional neurasthenias.
BY APPOINTMENT ONLY

This is the text on her extravagant card, which she herself designed. It's a homemade affair, a small piece of cardboard handwritten in green ink in a neat, cramped writing. His mother thinks that the word chiro-masseuse is a bit obscure and pretentious, but then again, who doesn't make exaggerated claims these days just to get by. The good woman claims to have been a pupil of Doctor Ferrándiz, the naturalist who founded the School of Quiropractice; she claims she is a psychologist and practises scraps of what she has learnt of a therapy based on touch. Ringo remembers that even the Rat-catcher, some time earlier, had considered turning to her to alleviate a persistent pain in his neck. His mother comments that she likes to talk while she is pummelling muscles and tendons, and she could swear she dabbles in folk healing, but that does no-one any harm. Apparently in fact she does more than cure a simple backache. They say she can detect tumours before they grow, especially in women. The two women met on night shifts in the Clínica Nuestra Señora del Remedio when Victoria Mir was still working as a nurse. She was awarded her nurse's certificate thanks to her husband's Falange connections, but there was no doubt she was very good at dealing with patients.

"Doctor Goday used to say that her back-rubs and herbal treatments were not to be dismissed lightly. One day she gave me a head massage that left me like new," she says, starting to wind the bandage round his arm. "By the way, didn't you go out with her daughter?"

"Violeta? You must be joking. She's a lot older than me."

"Only two years, I'm sure. She can't be more than seventeen."

"O.K., but she's a real pain." Closing his eyes, he can see her in the tavern, standing there waiting as if in a daze while her bottle is being filled, or to be given the soda siphon. A long neck, wide gums that flash pink when she smiles, reddish hair, tiny breasts and a pert backside. He will never admit that this apparent lack of harmony, this mismatch between her arse and her tits is precisely what attracts him. "Besides, she's a bit deaf. A dead loss."

"Is that so? Just look at Mister Cool. Well, I heard that last summer during the fiesta you asked her to dance more than once."

"But I don't like her, Mother. Yuk!"

No, he doesn't like the girl, of course not. She's odd, unfriendly, she looks weird, and yet not a day goes by without him thinking of her buttocks swaying as she crosses the street or tautening as she turns behind the counter of the stationer's shop she works in. Again and again in the hottest depths of his dreams, he conjures up that summer night when she sought refuge in his arms, head lowered and without a word, resigned to the furtive pushing at her thighs and pelvis. She raised her indolent eyes, too close to a nose whose dilating nostrils are the only thing in her face that seem alive, while he, on hearing the opening bars of the orchestra, and merely brushing her wasp waist with his hand, found himself unable to think of anything else but the saucy buttocks that Quique *Pegamil* had so close to him that day on the crowded tram platform.

"Every Sunday," Ringo adds unenthusiastically, "winter or summer, and even when it's raining, her mother goes with her to the dance at the Verdi. Sometimes they go on to Salón Cibeles or the Cooperativa La Leal-tad. They always leave their place arm-in-arm, made up like clowns. You have to laugh when you see them like that in the street, done up to the nines, clinging to one another as if they were cold or afraid of falling down . . ."

"You're the one who makes me laugh."

"Violeta Pricktease. That's what the lads in the bar call her . . . Ow!"

He's rewarded with a slap to the back of his head and a telling-off.

"Don't let me ever hear you repeating such filthy language. Poor girl."

No girl is ugly, his mother often insists: when you're young, you can't be ugly. How wrong can you be, he thinks, even though he still cannot explain to himself why, whenever he sees Violeta, he feels irresistibly attracted by that combination of ugly face and pretty legs, why he finds that odd mismatch so arousing.

"Can you wind the bandage up to the middle of my arm, please, Mama."

"You don't need so much, it's fine as it is."

"Will you lend me your silk scarf, the one Don Victor gave you? To make the sling, instead of the ordinary scarf. That's how Bill Barnes, Air Adventurer, would wear it, if his plane had been shot down . . ."

"Vain as well as silly," says his mother. She remembers how he wore a sling for days and days when he was only ten, after he had scraped his wrist jumping down from the glass-topped wall at Clínica del Remedio. "If you want a snack, there's a tin of condensed milk and some quince left. What are you going to do today? Are you going to read up at Parque Güell, or will you spend the afternoon sitting in that bar?"

"I don't know yet."

"If you go up to the park, see if you can find some oregano. And bring me a small branch of bay."

"I really don't know yet, Mother. If my finger hurts a lot I feel dizzy, and I prefer to stay in the Rosales, because it's close by. It's the finger of fate, you know."

"What do you do all those hours you spend shut up in that dreadful bar?" she asks for the umpteenth time. "You can't play table football with your hand in that state."

"I don't like table football."

He watches as his mother struggles to cut off the end of the bandage, having trouble pushing her fingers into the ends of a pair of scissors not designed for left-handed people.

"When I'm older, I'm going to be rich, Mother."

93

"Oh, are you? That's good."

"I won't be a goldsmith by then. I probably won't be able to work with gold or platinum or diamonds or anything like that, but I'll be rich all the same."

"Goodness. And how do reckon you'll become rich?"

"Besides being a pianist, I'll be a scissors manufacturer."

"Scissors?"

"I'll invent scissors for left-handed people. Yes, I'll sell them and get rich."

His mother makes him a fresh sling with the light-green silk headscarf she was given by Don Víctor Rahola. She ties it behind his head, leaving the hand high up on Ringo's chest to lessen the blood pressure.

"You're done," she says. "Now make sure you're careful, or it'll get infected again. And remember, keep your hand up high and it will hurt less."

And so he is on his own for most of the day, with no obligations or worries apart from his crushed finger and finding enough money to rent novels from the second-hand bookshop on Calle Asturias. He secretly cultivates a nostalgia for the future, and a growing hostility towards his surroundings. He has the time and the freedom to live intensely every word of the books he reads, to come and goes from his home to the tavern or the Parque Güell, his novel tucked under his arm in its sling, with a cool but gloomy look and with romantic lines under his eyes, untidily dressed, his hair tousled, and yet always with an unshakeable inner courtesy, a fervent politeness that before long turns into a feeling of rootlessness and loneliness. No longer a child, he knows that the time of the tall tales has never stood still, never held up the blind onward march of the world, but he feels as though he is living an interval, a parenthesis between the workshop he has left behind for good, and the longed-for piano. By freeing him from work, his longer than expected convalescence leads him to the most idiosyncratic, diverse and uneven choice of books. From Karl May to Balzac and Dostoevsky, from Jules Verne to Edgar Wallace and Papini, Zane Grey, Curzio Malaparte, Stefan Zweig and Knut Hamsun. On the long table of bargains at the Calle Asturias bookshop, in the jumble of dog-eared, battered books his hand (still with five fingers) had begun to sift through the year before in search of treasure, where he had come across by chance one afternoon *The Snows of Kilimanjaro* – a small, oblong book of short stories with a white cover and three fly droppings on the front – he also suddenly discovered *A Tale of Two Cities* (*It was the best of times, it was the worst of times, it was the age of wisdom, it was the age of foolishness, it was the epoch of belief, it was the epoch of incredulity . . .*) and above all, *Hunger*.

During the day he wrote with his hands wrapped in rags, he reads avidly, and underlines the paragraph with his pencil. Not so much preoccupied as with a pleasant feeling of relief, for the first time he seriously entertains the possibility that he will be forced to earn his living in some other way, no longer from jewels or precious stones, but still hopeful that his future will be rich in emotions, clinging to the tattered ideal of the tormented, renowned concert pianist who travels the world winning plaudits and having beautiful women fall in love with him, triumphing over adversity. He still occasionally hears the harmonious echo of maestro Emery's piano as the lid falls shut, a sustained, resonant and mournful sound, as though the panoply of wires and hammers in the depths of the ancient Steinway were also lamenting its forced but temporary distancing from music. However this may be, it's almost certain he is not going be a salaried craftsman in some dark jeweller's workshop, resigned forever to the blowtorch and the zinc-lined toolbox on his knees: in fact, his parents are already considering other possibilities for when his hand is better.

Could fate have shown itself in another, less cruel and painful way? It could, he thinks, but perhaps it was better like this, all at once and unannounced.

6

SPARROW IN THE RAIN

The boy's life is far from exemplary.

To begin with, when he spends the summer holidays of 1943 with his paternal grandparents in the village of San Jaime de los Domenys in Tarragona province, his favourite pastime, the one to which he devotes most time and enthusiasm (apart from the joyous bathing in the irrigation ponds and escapades with the village children through the wheat fields in the radiant July sunshine) is to shoot at birds with an air rifle in his grandfather's vegetable garden. He has never managed to kill one, but he doesn't give up trying. He crouches and spies on the leafy fig tree, waiting for hours for the slightest beating of wings or disturbance in its branches. He fires at any excuse. He is little more than ten years old, and the bangs of the airgun sound to him just as festive as the pop of champagne corks in his father's hand at the Barcelona flat whenever they celebrate discreet, extra-special anniversaries whose significance he is unaware of, but whose exciting atmosphere of clandestinity and danger he can always sense.

He is also unaware that his very next shot will enter his ear like a tiny poisonous snake and nest there for ever. The sky has been leaden the whole afternoon, and now the first random, fat raindrops have begun to fall. A poor day for hunting, Ringo tells himself. He is on the prowl close to the fig tree with loaded gun when the rain comes on more heavily. Usually he enjoys feeling the rain on his face – it seems like a promise for the future – but today he wants to hunt, and so he seeks shelter beneath the fig tree. Raindrops patter on the rough leaves. A short time later, a sparrow flutters down from the dripping foliage and settles on the ground, dusting off its feathers. Leaning against the tree trunk, Ringo raises the gun. The damp smell of the leaves and the noise of the rain urge him on; the solid feel of the butt on his cheek excites him. A magic blink of the eye and, lying flat on the roof of the stagecoach, Ringo Kid fires his rifle at the Apaches galloping after him across the prairie. He closes one eye and aims, gently squeezing the trigger. Less than two metres from his sights, the sparrow is hopping and pecking at the ground. It stops, raises its head and looks at him, hops again, stops once more, looks at him again. It has a tiny worm in its mouth, which is still wriggling. The sound of rain on the fig leaves has always brought joy to his heart, but now Ringo is the hunter, his gaze implacable, his aim unerring, and he has no heart. This coldness and the unexpected resistance of the trigger are things he will not forget for many days. He has to fire a second time, because although the first pellet strikes home, the bird does not fall over, and merely crumples, its feathers fluffing up, and turns its head very slowly in the direction of its executioner. Between the first shot and the second, while the hunter is hurriedly loading another pellet into the air rifle, the sparrow stares at him with its beady little eye, already veiled by death, and drops the worm.

When it is all over, he turns his back on the sparrow, waits until the rain has stopped, and immediately, without once looking back at the dead bird (he knows that the magic blink of the eye will have no effect this time) emerges from under the fig tree with the airgun as heavy as lead in his hands. He heads for the house, chin sunk on his chest. Halfway there he stops and looks up at the sky, where a mass of reddish clouds appear to be swallowing each other up, chasing one another in a compulsive rush to a horizon of fire and emerald. In reality though they are as still as the ones in the outlandish backdrop at the little theatre in Las Ánimas where each Christmas they put on the Nativity play. A strange anxiety keeps him rooted to the spot, unable to take his eyes from the clouds.

A few minutes later, as he is hiding the airgun in the wardrobe where Grandma Tecla stores aromatic quinces, his eyes start to brim with tears. At first he weeps out of a confused feeling of self-pity, but this soon turns to a profound sadness. He is still weeping when he goes back to the vegetable garden, and when he picks up the bird. By now it is nothing more than a bundle of feathers, spongy to the touch. He wraps it in a handkerchief and buries it under the almond tree, placing on the grave a small cross made from pieces of cane, on which he has written the name Sparry. He feels the tears welling up from the deepest, blackest corner of his ruthless, murderous soul, and makes a secret vow. Every year in February when the almond tree is in bloom, I'll come to visit you. He only calms down two hours later, when he sees Grandma Tecla tickling a white rabbit she is holding by the rear legs, and whispering in its ear in an affectionate, sing-song voice, before breaking its neck with a single, deadly chop of her hand. Wow, that's some jujitsu blow granny's learnt! Later on he sees her with that same hand on her backside as she raises the wine jug to take a swig behind his grandfather's back, and the stream of wine splashing against her teeth impresses him still further. But that night in bed when he closes his eyes, the feelings of remorse return; he peers into the dark corners of his dreams and sinks beneath the garden soil to recover the sparrow's tiny corpse, which is already being devoured by worms and almond-tree roots. As he imagines the pellets buried in its diminutive body, and above all when he thinks that one of them could have lodged in the bird's living spirit, however ephemeral and fleeting that might have been at the moment of death, he can again feel the bird's little head in his hands, flopping from side to side as if it were made of lead, and the image turns into a nightmare.

He will never pick up the gun again except with the intention of getting rid of it, and since then not a single day of his life has gone by when he hasn't remembered that bird. Its beady eye, staring at him from the threshold of death, will accompany him to the end of his days.

"Today you'll have to go up to the vines on your own, Mingo," his grandmother tells him the next day. "Take your cowboy comics and be off with you. You're not frightened of going on your own, are you?"

"Of course not. And I don't need my air rifle."

"Fine, goodbye airguns then. And when you go back to Barcelona, you can take it with you."

He knows every inch of the old cart track leading from the village to the vines. It twists and turns up beyond the farmhouse with the mysterious name of La Carroña, the place of carrion. He loves to submerge himself in the white dust of this lonely path, deafened by the sound of cicadas. It is a bright, breezy July day. The track is barely three kilometres, but time and dreams expand along it to cover more than forty years. Wherever he goes in the future after this morning as he sets out along the path, all alone but accompanied first by Mowgli and then Winnetou, carrying the lunch basket for his grandfather who is spraying the vines, wherever life takes him in the years to come, his feet will always be treading this track, and the dust smelling of esparto grass, dung and crushed grapes will always fill his nostrils. Something of this germinal dust will stay with him for ever. Even today he is convinced that there is not and never could be any other track in the world like this one, nor one he has set off along so often in his memory.

Chewing a green almond or a sprig of fennel, he pauses beside the fields to survey the majestic stems of wheat waving in the sunshine, the placid to and fro of the ears in a golden sea stretching from one plot to another as far as the wooded areas at the foot of the distant hills of Castellví de la Marca, beyond the fallow fields, the expanse of vineyards, the gentle slopes of almond and carob trees. Sometimes at evening when he is on his way back to the village, a burst of pink light from the setting sun slowly rides the rippling wheat towards the dark horizon. Beneath a sky streaked with clouds, when he hears the wind whistling in the electric cables and the silence hovering over the ploughed fields, and observes the symmetrical languor and endless rows of furrows in shadow, the fine red dust hanging in the air round the shire horses, he believes he can grasp the fleeting nature of time, and ponders the mystery and certainty of death.

His errand fulfilled and back by now in the village, close to the Sant Pau wood he meets up again with Winnetou and Old Shatterhand. Together they decide to take another route across the endless windswept prairie, until at length they reach the house where his grandmother is waiting, looking very serious, urging him to eat as quickly as possible so that she can take him to the school to meet Señor Benito, the teacher. It's time to put a stop to your spending the whole day roaming around without doing anything useful, says his grandmother, time to stop the running wild with your friend Ramón Bartra's gang, bathing naked in the ponds, stealing peaches and watermelons, hiding in the wheat fields with your faces painted and feathers in your hair: all that's finished.

"For as long as you're here with me, you're going to school, like it or not. I'll feel a lot happier."

Grandma Tecla is a short, stocky and resolute old woman. She is black-eyed, with thick eyebrows and a snub nose above the faint outline of a moustache like a Mexican bandit's, a threatening shadow that the boy is fascinated by. Besides the moustache and the black velvet of her eyes, many other things about his grandmother often clamour for his attention, like the slow, stiff way in which she lifts the wine-jug high and keeps the red stream splashing against her small, brilliant white teeth without spilling a drop, her head flung back and the other hand on her backside, as though to prevent the liquid leaking out through there. That's what she is doing now, standing in front of the big kitchen hearth where the wind is moaning, before she takes the boy by the hand and goes out into the square with him.

It was written that this radiant, windy afternoon, so well-suited to daydreaming and adventures, here in Panadés just as much on the Arizona prairies where Old Shatterhand rides in search of Winnetou, is the one when the best-kept secret is finally revealed, a secret withheld for many years, though he had occasionally seen it surface in his mother's sad gaze after he had heard her scold her father or somebody else for an indiscreet comment. And the first hint of this secret slips out thanks to a gossipy old peasant woman who suddenly appears like a ghost out of the thick dust cloud the wind is raising as grandmother and grandson are crossing the square hand-in-hand, the boy rubbing his eyes.

"What a good-looking child, Tecla!" the old woman exclaims with a sly smile. "Who does he take after? Because it's only natural he doesn't look like Pep or Berta. It's obvious just seeing him that he isn't theirs. I mean it's natural he doesn't look like them, as it's natural that, well . . ."

"Why don't you scratch your arse rather than gab on so, Domitila?" is his grandmother's furious retort, as she tugs at the boy's hand to drag him away.

That name, Domitila, sounds to him so mysterious and funny, as if it came out of a comic with Hipo, Monito and Fifi, although it's not as resonant as Tecla, the word for the keyboard of the longed-for piano that one day he has no doubt will be his. But for now he has no wish to think of that, or of the even deeper mystery of old Domitila's arse, but rather her bewildering words.

"What did that lady mean, Grandma? Why did she say . . . what she said?"

"Because that Domitila is a donkey!"

"But what did she mean?"

"Nothing. She doesn't know what she's saying. Don't listen to her, my love."

One day, long before this, his grandmother had told him that on his tenth birthday his mother would tell him a great secret. She said it with a smile, although her black eyelashes were moist, and he has never forgotten it, although for some inexplicable reason he has never reminded her or his mother of this promise.

The school is a large, airy building on the outskirts of the village by the main road out to Llorens and El Vendrell. It is closed for the holidays. The teacher, Señor Benito Ruiz y Montalvo, has come in to check whether the carpenter has carried out the work he asked him to do, replacing some boards on the teacher's platform and repairing a window. Ringo's grand-mother could have gone to find him at the chemist's any day after lunch, because he and the chemist Granota always play chess at the back of the shop, or after Mass on Sunday, but she doesn't want anyone else to hear what she has to say to him. Although it's a long time until the start of term, she wants to ask for the boy to be enrolled as soon as possible – only for three or four months, she tells him, I'll be looking after him this winter, his parents are having a hard time in Barcelona . . .

"Who isn't, my dear Tecla," the teacher sympathises, testing the platform with his foot. "Who isn't, at times like these."

"Please can you seat him with the other children, Señor Benito? It's not good for him to be out on his own at all hours."

"No, you're right, Tecla, it's not good." He looks at the boy with mock severity. "We know he's a fine boy, we've been keeping an eye on him. Hmm, a child with a rich interior life, isn't he?"

His grandmother responds with a grunt. "A rich interior life", what nonsense this man talks. The boy is staring at the big blackboard, the wood stove with its black, twisted flue, the map of Spain, the ink-stained desks, Señor Benito's blue shirt with the red spider sewn on its pocket, and on the wall the portraits of the Caudillo and José Antonio flanking a crucifix whose figure of Christ has a foot missing.

"Well, there's just one problem," says the teacher. "As far as I am aware, this youngster has not yet been legally adopted. Therefore . . ."

"It's been impossible to do it before now," his grandmother says in a low voice. "The war was to blame."

"So we will have to enrol him under his real names . . ."

"Shhh!" his grandmother interrupts him. Señor Benito bites his tongue, but it's too late. And his immediate excuse, voiced out loud, only makes things worse: he thought the child must have been aware by now of his real family origins. Shhh! the grandmother insists, and orders her grandson to go out and play. He clings to her black skirts and refuses to budge. Why does he have a foot missing? he asks, staring at the crucifix. Then the teacher, jabbing at him with a huge, imperious finger that is ink-stained but has a pink, clean and well-trimmed nail, points to a desk at the back of the room and orders him to go and sit there. He takes the grand-mother by the arm and the two move off into a corner, although this does not make much difference. However quietly they speak, their voices echo through the empty classroom, and besides, Winnetou can understand the language of the blue man just by reading his lips. Nothing simpler.

"We'll tell him everything when he's ten," his grandmother whispers. "That's what his mother wanted. If she were here, she would have explained it to him already, but she wasn't able to come."

"What does 'interior life' mean, Grandma?" Ringo asks from his back-row desk. "Where's his other foot?"

"Be quiet, child, don't cause trouble."

"So you haven't told the poor boy anything yet," Señor Benito grumbles. "A big mistake, Tecla, a big mistake! And, in addition, he's not yet been legally adopted. For whatever reason, and that is something that does not concern me of course, the proper procedure was not followed at the correct time, and as a result to all effects and purposes this child still has the surnames of his biological parents ..."

"What does biological mean, Grandma?"

"Will you be quiet a moment, for pity's sake!"

"In consequence we will have to enrol him under his real surnames," the teacher continues. "I'm sorry, but there's nothing else I can do. And frankly, Tecla, I'm amazed that Pep and Berta haven't yet told the boy the truth."

"What are biological parents?"

"Never you mind! Señor Benito is telling me about the books you're going to need ..."

"That's right," says the teacher, adopting a professorial tone. "We're talking about biogenesis, my boy, a difficult subject you're too young to study as yet, if you follow me."

Señor Benito has a thin mouth, the delicate jaws of a ruminant, and the vacant gaze of Zampabollos the Glutton. In that second, he falls backwards stiff as a board with his eyes rolled up, while Ringo blows the smoke from the barrel of his revolver and twirls it back into its holster. Crouching in the back row, he clutches the edges of the desk with both hands as if it was about to take off, and studies the school teacher's wry grimace with the wise eyes of Old Shatterhand. Any moment now and I'll be off again out on to the plains with the faithful Winnetou and his four braves . . .

"Are you telling me that to come to your school my grandson has to change surnames?" says his grandmother, her voice deepening. "That when they do the register he's going to have to hear different family names? Family names he's never heard before, or his friends . . . ?"

"What I'm telling you, Tecla, is that I, to my great regret, am obliged to enrol him with his real family surnames. That's the only way I can accept him into the school, it is a *sine qua non*."

"But couldn't you turn a blind eye for three months, Señor Benito? Who's going to take you to task for it, with all those important Falangist friends of yours?"

"Oh, Tecla, these days we need all the friends we can get! I'd like to help you, but do you realise what you're asking? I can't shut my eyes to something so irregular that I bear so much responsibility for. What happens if there's an inspection? Because it's a matter of how shall I put it, of a blood anomaly . . ."

"What on earth are you saying? It's not as if it's an illness, or something against the regime!"

"Of course not, woman. I mean that the relationship is not a blood one, and therefore it is anomalous, and that has to be pointed out . . . Those in charge now keep a very tight control, as you know. Besides, who is to blame for this situation?" He glances out of the corner of his eye at the boy, who is crouching in his desk like a wild beast about to pounce, and lowers his voice still further. "After all this time, how is it that his stepfather still hasn't officially requested the adoption?"

"What does 'stepfather' mean, Grandma?" Ringo demands to know, stamping his feet on the floor.

"His feet are cold," she says, to excuse his behaviour. "The boy is always going round with cold feet. I have to light a fire for him in mid-afternoon." She turns and gives him a stern look. "Behave now, or I'll be seriously angry! Don't cause trouble or pretend you're a Red Indian."

She knows when Winnetou is with her grandson. How does she know? Every time she hears the boy muttering as he walks alongside her, in a world of his own and with his eyes half-closed, coming or going from the vines along the white track, or while he is helping her silently to bring in firewood, collect grass for the rabbits, or has his head down shelling almonds in the kitchen; whenever to escape routine or boredom a strange babble she can't understand emerges from his lips, she knows he is mouthing the words of Red Indians he has come across in the comics his mother brings him from Barcelona.

"The adoption formalities are very expensive, and his family can't afford them at the moment, Señor Benito," his grandmother is saying. "They'll do it as soon as possible."

The teacher looks worried, and Ringo does not take his eyes off him. Every so often he sees him take a deep breath, puffing out his chest with fake concern, and whenever he does that, the red spider grows huge and threatens to start moving its legs, as if it were about to climb the blue shirt. He's never seen anything like it, this spider crawling up the teacher's shirt! Señor Benito explains wearily that this morning he has had to put on the uniform and attend a Falangist meeting in El Vendrell. The red beret folded on his shoulder looks a little faded and stiff, but apart from that he is dressed extremely carefully, wearing black patent leather shoes, his hair oiled. He is smoking a very thin, bent, aromatic roll-up cigarette.

"It's a difficult matter," he concludes. "As long as he has not been formally adopted, here in class he will have to be called – I'm sorry to have to say this, Tecla – but he will have to be called by his biological patronymics . . ."

"Do you have to use such . . . ugly, strange words in front of the boy?"

"Let's see if you understand me. I'm talking about fulfilling a simple bureaucratic formality. And besides, I'm not sure, but I suspect somebody is trying to get away with something here . . . I'm afraid that from what I'm hearing there's been a clear breach of the father–son relationship, a dereliction, an abdication of identity, shall we say . . ."

"You're just trying to confuse me with your big words! The boy has had no problem with his family names at school in Barcelona!" She snorts, but then controls herself and speaks more softly. "Well, I don't know, there must be a way . . . what can we do, Señor?"

"It's up to you to decide, Tecla. Go home and think it over calmly."

She has made up her mind before she gets home: this child cannot spend three or four months running wild, he has to go to school no matter what, using his real family names or those he's been given. But how is she going to explain to him that he has four surnames rather than two, and why?

Sitting in a chair by the hearth staring into the flames, the grandmother silently evokes the family demons that have led to so many mishaps: if twelve years earlier her son and Berta hadn't preferred the city and the reckless joys of the Republic to the peace and tranquillity of this tiny village; if in Barcelona Pep had not got mixed up in politics; if poor Berta had not lost her child at birth, if she had not taken that taxi as she left the La Maternidad hospital in floods of tears, if the doctor had waited another day to tell her she could not have any more children . . . Chance had intervened at almost every turn, and it was happening again: if she hadn't been kept in Barcelona because of her job, Berta would now be explaining to the boy, with great tact and sweetness (from the start, waiting to see him reach puberty, she had carefully chosen the moment and exactly what she would say) who it was who brought him into the world ten years earlier, what mysterious design led that taxi to the door of the hospital just as . . . But Berta is not here, and the boy is asking questions, and the moment to tell him has arrived. A short while before, when she heard him moving about upstairs in his bedroom, helping his grandfather store the winter melons under the bed, she had quickly lit the fire in the hearth despite the heat. This is not just to cook cabbage and potatoes in the blackened pot, but because she knows her grandson likes above all to stare into the flames as dusk falls, in winter or summer. By the time he comes down and sits on the kitchen floor she has already decided what she is going to say to him.

"Today, if you promise not to tell anyone, I'm going to let you into a secret. You were going to be told anyway sooner or later. Don't be frightened, it's nothing bad. Now listen."

Despite the magnetic effect of the Mexican moustache, the words his grandmother speaks in a voice that is now softer, more affectionate, and strangely childlike, are a ghost story that is not in the least bit frightening, a tale full of twists and turns, told with all kinds of hesitations and evasions. For the very first time a confused series of vignettes is paraded in front of his eyes: a taxi roaming the streets of Barcelona in the rain, a doctor and a nun attending a young woman in labour in a ward in La Maternidad, a shack in a Sarriá shanty-town where another young mother is also about to give birth, one boy who comes into the world arse first, and another who leaves it headfirst, the first mother delivering a dead baby, the second mother dying as she brings forth the newborn the wrong way round. Now for a moment we're going to imagine, adds the grandmother, just for a moment (he can already see it: in an explosion of light and blood, first the feet appear, small and wrinkled as currants, then the legs, and finally the little arse) that the boy who came backwards into the world . . . is you. Don't you sometimes imagine you're a Red Indian with one of your mother's garters round your head and with your face painted? Well now we're going to imagine that you are the boy who came arse-first into this world, and that, at the moment you are born, your mother dies, because that is what destiny has ordained . . . And that taxi which has been going up and down the streets of Barcelona in the rain without anyone hailing it, is that also because destiny has so ordained it? In the entrance to La Maternidad, a nun and a nurse are saying goodbye and giving some final words of advice to the mother who is going home after losing her baby. Her husband, who is shielding her from the rain under an umbrella, sees the taxi going past, and raises his arm to stop it . . . She has always said he saw it first because even though it was daytime it had its headlights on, and that caught his attention. Well, the long and short of it is that they got into the taxi. And who do you think the driver was? As chance would have it, it was the husband of the lady who had died in childbirth a week earlier. And what happens as he is taking the unhappy couple home, with her weeping in her husband's arms because not only has she lost her child, but she has been told by the doctors that she cannot have any more? What happens is that the taxi driver, hearing her crying and bemoaning her loss, cannot help but comment on his own misfortune. The sad coincidences of life! she said he said, and then he told her that he too had suffered the loss of a loved one because of a tragic birth, except that in his case the opposite had happened, and it was his wife who died, leaving him with a baby . . . And as Berta herself has told it a thousand times, she went and asked him: why don't you take me to see the child? Please, I beg you, and so the driver feels sorry for her and changes his route and takes the couple to see the baby, who is being looked after by some relatives, although they are very sorry and cannot keep him. And once they are there, Berta lifts the baby from the cot and holds him in her arms for the very first time . . . ?

"And that was that, there was no way she would let go of you," his grandmother concludes. "They agreed that Berta would keep you only for a while. As a wet nurse . . . Do you know what that means? Well, a year went by, and then another, and another, and the situation dragged on, and that's how things stand now. So as you can see, the fact is you have two mothers. My word, but you're a lucky thing, aren't you? Don't you know it's a blessing to have a mother in heaven? You're a blessed child, that's what you are, a child who's been blessed! Because that man could not have raised you, and you would have ended up in the foundlings' hospital for sure, so the best thing you can do is give thanks to the heavens for being such a blessed child . . . " She studies his face, and adds: "Or are you still not convinced? How about if tomorrow I sew you a football from a pair of your grandfather's old corduroy trousers? Come on, let me see your face . . . It's alright, if you feel like crying, let it out."

He doesn't feel like crying, or anything of the kind. Not even a snivel, even though he doesn't in any way feel blessed. All that's going through his mind is a wish to play down everything he's just heard. He feels the immediate need, in order to guard against any new, unexpected revelations, surreptitiously to convince himself that deep in his heart he always knew what he has just heard. Together with an observation of his grandmother's, which over the course of time makes him smile: if that taxi with its headlights on had passed by just a minute before, in all likelihood he would not be here now staring at the flames in the hearth, he would never have come to this village or entered this house, there would be no airgun hidden in a wardrobe, nor any bird buried out in the vegetable garden with two pellets in its body . . . So it was all the result of a stroke of luck, a tremendous stroke of luck, and as a consequence, from this moment on the least stable and questioning part of himself will enjoy frequently venturing into the most incredible part of this story, in which a pair of taxi headlights shine brightly through the lashing rain.

"And be careful with what the schoolteacher is so fond of repeating," his grandmother admonishes him in conclusion. "About a rich interior life! Interior life! Be very careful. Don't go looking for trouble."

"Of course not, Grandma. And listen," he says, to confuse her and change the subject, "if we stuff the ball with corduroy as well, it will last longer. And it will look real."

Now that he thinks about it, weren't even the cloth balls his grandmother sewed for him so skilfully little more than well-intentioned lies? Down the tunnel of time, he sees her face pressed close to his, a cheery gleam in her moist eyes, squinting slightly because she is so near to him and because of the ambiguous itch of a conviction that she would not be able to put into words even if she wanted to: that life can be so unfair, unpredictable and precarious, so profoundly marked by loss and abandonment, that sometimes there is a need for compensation in the form of a stroke of luck or a soothing white lie.

That night he sleeps lulled by the perfume of the yellow winter melons under his bed. In the early hours, Sparry silently lands on one of the melons, grasps the silky rind in its claws, gathers its body and from its arse shoots its tiny machine gun: dark little droppings intended for Ringo as it peers defiantly at him through the slats of the bed and the mattress. It is about to fly off again when Ringo says:

Don't go yet. Stay a while.

What for? So that you can shoot another pellet in my body?

No, so we can talk as friends.

Me, talk to you? What rubbish, *nano*! How can anybody imagine I want to talk to you as a friend, when you're my murderer?

That morning his grandmother makes him another ball with the big needle she uses to sew sacks, one more that ends up with its innards hanging out between the feet of the boys playing in the square. Yet from that day on, Ringo prefers to spend many afternoons alone, reading in the vegetable garden. His grandmother has told him that when his mother comes she'll tell him the whole story, because there are lots of things not even I know, things they haven't wanted to tell me yet. But the oft-mentioned "bad patch" the Rat-catcher and Berta are going through down in the city, occasionally relieved by the grandmother's trips with a basket of eggs, oil, a rabbit or hen, means that it is a long time before his mother reappears, and throughout that winter he spends many hours on his own in the garden, or in the improvised swing under the almond tree, or at school.

When spring arrives, his mother brings him from Barcelona *Geneviève de Brabant*, *Treasure Island* and the new adventures of Winnetou and Old Shatterhand, and chooses the right moment to talk to him. Bright-eyed, she delicately and knowingly brings together the random strands of the story until she has constructed a verbal artefact containing, she swears, the truth and nothing but the truth. When the boy insists, she finds herself forced to admit that it was her and not his father who saw the taxi headlights in the distance through the rainstorm.

"Why are you so interested in that anyway?"

"I thought Grandma had invented it. Because taxis don't have their headlights on during the day, do they?"

"Well, this one did. Perhaps because of the rain, or because the driver had forgotten . . . You see, there's an explanation for everything. But that's not what is important for me. What's important is that you believe me. You do, don't you, Son?"

Her face and tender mouth so close to him, the faint aroma from the cherry-red lipstick, the dimples in her cheeks when she smiles, the quick flutter of her rough, reddened hands, the rain and the cab's headlights, the gift of so eagerly anticipated new books, comics and annuals (better and more numerous than on previous occasions) to be read by the fire in the hearth on rainy days. He gives a silent nod, to avoid shouting it out loud: Yes, I believe you.

Later on, when she sees him lying out under the almond tree with his books and comics, she reminds him what a good idea it is to cover them – that way they'll always be new, and again mentions how lucky he is.

"Just as well they weren't burnt with all the rest, isn't it?" she says, and adds with a smile: "*Just in case, because of the flies.* Do you remember, Son?"

And the memory of a big bonfire in the middle of the night, with the tallest, fiercest flames he has ever seen, takes him back for an instant to a ghostly scene in his own neighbourhood two years earlier, to a small, shadow-filled private garden where a pile of books, notebooks, photographs and documents splutter and burn, just in case.

7

HEROES ON THE BONFIRE

"Just in case, because of the flies!" his father says as he tosses books on the fire, one after the other with barely a glance, without checking the title or the name of the author and making jokes the whole time to encourage all those present. "Just in case there are any flies around, isn't that so, Son? We're not doing this because we like it."

He could do it better and more quickly if he had a spade, thinks Ringo, and remembers Harpo Marx shovelling books onto a fire in a comedy movie. But he can't see anything here to make him laugh. Some of the men are staring into the bonfire with grim, solemn expressions, and the glow is printed on their faces like a plaster mask.

So Señor Gaspar Huguet is burning part of his library "just in case, because of the flies", the boy deduces from the grown-ups' comments. His father has made a makeshift bonfire from dry branches and splintered trunks in Señor Huguet's own garden, behind the shed that is a lumber room by day and by night is used for clandestine coffee roasting. This bonfire is nothing like the festive ones on Saint John's Eve: Ringo knows that no children are going to come and jump over these flames or throw firecrackers. This is a tedious ceremony presided over by grown-ups who for some reason are extremely downcast. And as though the boredom were not enough, if he moves away from the fire it's freezing. He also knows that his father works with Señor Huguet roasting coffee in this shed three or four nights a week, from two to five in the morning, hidden from everyone, especially from the local nightwatchman. He can tell when his father has been here, because the next day his woollen jersey and his scarf smell of sugary roast coffee. Now Señor Huguet, seeing Ringo so close to the flames and almost hypnotised by them, comes over and, trying but failing to lend his voice a jovial tone, asks if he'd like to burn something of his own. He says yes he would, thinking of his detested school arithmetic book and also of Fu-Manchu's daughter and of the blue rats, a mass of writhing blue rats in the flames.

"Stand back or you'll singe your nose," his father warns him. "Go and find a dry branch somewhere."

But the best spot is close to the fire, the warm heart of an inhospitable night full of reddish glows and the long faces of worried people talking in whispers. The faces pucker and say things he doesn't understand: they talk in low voices about a surprise police raid on Señor Oriol's house, of the large number of books impounded, a disgraceful abuse, Berta, and with what excuse, eh, what crime is he accused of? Good God, you can imagine. Nor can Ringo understand when someone hidden in the darkness intones "Who lights the fires where none were lit before?" and flames leap out of the roaring bonfire like long-fingered hands calling for and greedily receiving still more books. The thick, swirling smoke reminds him of the genie Djinn springing from the bottle after the sea waves have thrown it up onto the beach, the black smoke against the sky that suddenly turns into a giant, whose booming laughter astonishes the tiny Sabu.

This is during the dying days of a long Barcelona winter, his scarf wrapped round his ears, and his feet always cold, in the street and in the cinema, at school and in the parish choir, under the greenery of Parque Güell and on the slopes of Montaña Pelada. He has just turned eight, his nose is red, curly hair, good big ears, slightly bow-legged like a cowboy, and with his eternally cold feet. Not tonight though, in the dark, overgrown garden where the fire curls books and notebooks, diaries and photos, all kinds of documents and postcards and the identity cards of his father, Señor Huguet, and of some neighbours who have also joined in the burning. He watches forlornly as the flames devour a next-to-new spiralbound notebook with squared-off paper and a cream-coloured cover where someone has written *C.N.T. Membership Dues* – the anarchist union. He has always wanted to have a book like that. A week before he had seen his father at the dining-room table with this notebook open in front of him, patiently using a razor blade to scratch out names and figures from its pages, until at length he grew tired and furiously threw the blade into his glass of wine, shouting: All on the bonfire, it's safer that way!

Gusts of wind send pages that have come loose from some volume or other flying into the sky, where they hang for a moment on the crest of the flames, fluttering like huge black butterflies in the midst of a crackling shower of embers. Also burning on the fire are some papers from the private library of the elderly Don Víctor Rahola, a neighbour and friend of Señor Huguet's. The boy hears Don Víctor himself say this, laughing cheerfully as he does so. He doesn't seem at all bothered if the flies come or not. You're not far wrong, *nano*, because my papers are buzzing through the air like flies! Ringo recalls that the previous summer his mother had been this man's night nurse in his pretty villa up on Paseo del Monte, looking after him as he lay in bed under a big mosquito net, and that she had told him that Don Víctor was a wise, polite old fellow who loved practical jokes, a writer who no longer writes and often asks her to sit by his bed and read him a book.

"Don't take your scarf off, Son."

He sometimes wonders why his mother is never exactly a nurse like all the others. She herself told him one day: I'm not exactly a nurse, I'm more of a care assistant, and a friend of the nuns. She only looks after old people in homes, residences or their own houses, but she is not a qualified nurse. She works at night and is badly paid.

The bonfire's scorching heat forces the books open, and finger-like flames flick through their pages. Just in case the flies come, he hears someone mutter again behind his back. And also if the cockroaches arrive, or the rats, or lice, he thinks. On some street corners in their neighbourhood there are piles of rubbish that also attract flies, but he cannot imagine why they would want to descend on this fire. Let them come, he says to himself, my father can kill them with his rat poison, together with all the mosquitoes, moths and bugs who dare poke their noses in. He has never needed to light a fire to get rid of them before, and yet here he is now, watchful and diligent, stoking the embers with his stick wherever necessary, pushing back into the flames any publications that fall out or scraps of charred paper. Why though is he burning only Catalan books, just in case? Does that mean they're books that attract flies, Mother, infected books and documents with fly droppings on them? Is that why they have to be burned? Because they could infect us all?

But she pays him no attention, or does not hear, and has no idea what he's talking about. Ringo sees her on the arm of a neighbour, Señora Rius. He watches them with their heads close together, exchanging sad glances, both of them wearing tight-fitting coats with the collars raised. His mother's constant tendency for sadness . . . What kind of horrible flies can they be, Mother? Are they tsetse flies, the ones that give you sleeping sickness? Yes, they're a bit like that, my boy, says Señora Ruiz, with a faint, friendly smile: they put you to sleep and your dreams turn into nightmares. Are the books terribly dangerous for children, sinful books, full of illustrations of naked nymphs with transparent fly's wings on their back, or fairies with flowing locks and naked breasts who sleep in the lakes and float though the woods, sweet air and water sprites like in that small book you keep at home, Mother, the one with those lovely drawings you like so much? Are the flies that might come so dangerous? Is that why we're here at night in Señor Huguet's garden to help father and his friends, just in case the flies come? Yes, we're here to help. Keep your scarf on properly. So where are the flies? he insists.

The answer comes in the barely audible rustle of burning pages, the murmur of words turned to ashes, an endless buzzing in the boy's ears. He will hear this again so often that it becomes an insistent whistle.

"Not so close, pumpkinhead, or you'll get burned," his father warns him.

They joke with him, especially his father, and yet he is aware that all those there seem dejected. One of them talks in a low, mournful voice of Don Víctor's brother, who died barely two years ago, and the boy understands that he was killed by blue flies that had previously destroyed his books. Standing close to the flames, he watches fascinated as the volumes open like black flowers, the pages twisting and turning black while sparks like fireflies climb into the starry night sky. He thinks he can see that the fire is separating the words from the pages, which then fly up for a moment before turning into whirling embers, words and embers joined together as they rise into the night. He suddenly feels the need to step back a few paces, grasp his mother's welcoming hand and hear her whisper, this time more to her friend than to him: Your father knows what he's doing. They'll come with a search warrant, and it's better they find nothing, isn't it, María? The eager flames are also reflected in her pinched, sleepy face, as her husband, the irrepressible, merry Capitán of the Rat-catcher Brigade, jokes and curses while he wields his stick: "We're the arsehole of the world, my boy, I've told you many times. So now we're going to warm that arsehole up." His mother's thin, cold left hand with its long fingers and pale, unvarnished nails, squeezes his, trembling slightly in a way that distresses him.

"Stay here with me, Son."

He has seen those fingers sticking a hypodermic needle into the thick, rough skin of an orange, of many oranges, doing the injection over and over again with an unsure, trembling hand, trying and trying until she has perfected it. Why don't you use your right? He has asked her sometimes. She practises for a few minutes every day before she goes off to work, and for a while at night before going to sleep. She sits on the edge of the bed with her shawl wrapped round her, her back to her husband, who has buried his head under the pillow. On the bedside table there's a small image of the Infant Jesus of Prague, and the lamp is covered with a red cloth in order not to disturb the Rat-catcher's sleep, just as it was when Ringo had measles and spent happy hours in the company of *The Jungle Book*. After a few uncertain tests, with the orange in her right hand and the needle in the left, she administers the jab, suddenly but delicately, quickly but as gently as possible. This is her patient way of learning how to give injections, now that the nuns at Las Darderas have taken her on to look after old people in their residence on Calle Sors, or in their home. She will soon also learn to wrap bandages and to wash old people's behinds, put them to bed, feed them and keep them entertained by playing cards or Ludo with them, or reading them a book, but what she finds most difficult is to give injections, because she is frightened of hurting them. She occasionally complains she isn't strong enough to lift some stout, heavy grandmother in and out of the bath, but she is grateful to the nuns for the work, and always finds some reason for being happy.

"Today I learnt how to play three-card *brisca*."

It is on occasions like this that Ringo feels closest to her, when he hears her talking about the good times she has at work, and tells them about the old people's mischief-making and manias, their fears, weaknesses and little whims, and above all when he watches her tirelessly practising with the needle and orange and observes, on tenterhooks, how her shaking hand tries again and again to push the needle in without doing harm. Poor orange! The Rat-catcher laughs from beneath the pillow: Alberta light of my life, you'd learn much quicker if you used a bishop's arse.

The usual ill-timed, foul-mouthed comment from her husband. Why does she put up with it? Why allow him to call her Alberta, when everyone else calls her Berta, and she herself has said that is what she prefers?

Now I'm going to tell you something about our Alberta, his father explains to him one day, glass of brandy in one hand, gesturing dismissively although his voice is firm, so listen carefully and make no mistake: Your mother isn't blind, she's a believer. And remember: to be a believer and to want to be one in spite of everything, to be one for herself and in silence, ignoring our hypocritical and pompous ecclesiastical hierarchy, to be one without having recourse to the ostentation of a corrupted Church and clergy, who pervert the souls of children in catechism classes and the confessional, who offend the memory of the dead at funerals and of the living in their ranting homilies, to be a believer despite all the vileness blessed by bishops and cardinals, and to know as well how to forgive all the fooling around and digs at her expense she faces in her own home, from the mouth of her own husband: all these things are what this modest woman offers as her lesson, one you would do well to remember. It's true that her good-for-nothing husband does not share her faith or her pious practices, it's true he is a blasphemer and a heretic, but it is no less true that she never once, however hurtful his jokes, has reproached him for them or tried to stop him . . .

The whitish smoke, increasingly full of sparks and embers, curls up into the night, and for a brief moment high in the sky forms extraordinary figures that intrigue Ringo. For a moment he imagines he can see the burning bodies of Mowgli and Shere Khan the tiger writhing in the midst of the flames, but they disappear almost immediately. He carries on looking, and it's not long before he gets a fleeting glimpse of a volume whose title *The Conquest of Bread* is burning along with its *girls who become anaemic in the factories of Manchester*, the only words he stumbled across by chance at home one day, when he opened the book out of curiosity, thinking it was a mystery or crime novel. On another collapsed part of the bonfire, a copy from the *Men of Daring* collection, costing 60 cents with bright-red lettering announcing the title *The Wings of Death*, suddenly opens its pages like a hedgehog sensing danger, and rolls to the edge of the pyre. The flames have already consumed half the brightly coloured front cover illustration, a plane emerging from a storm cloud to confront a giant condor, wings spread as it threatens to sweep the airman from the skies. Ringo immediately recognises the pilot in his cockpit:

"Oh, no, please! Nooo!"

It is one of the little novels featuring Bill Barnes, the famous Air Adventurer. His father's lack of attention as he hurriedly emptied their bookcase has condemned the aviation hero to death, burned to a crisp in a makeshift bonfire behind a shed in a hidden garden in a poor neighbourhood in post-war Barcelona. Bill could never have imagined such an abrupt, unheroic end. Shit! Shit! The boy points his trembling finger at the book being so unjustly consumed by the flames, and reproaches his father for this huge mistake. Bill shouldn't be here, Bill and his plane don't deserve to end this way, turned to ashes right in front of his eyes! Seizing the stick from his father, he tries to pull the book out of the fire, but it's too late, the hero and all his derring-do shrivel into a dark rose that crumples and wrinkles in a few seconds, ash printed in double columns that for a brief moment is still bound and resistant.

"It's being burnt to ashes!"

"I'm sorry, Son, I must have picked the comic up without realising it."

"It's not a comic!"

"I told you not to put anything of yours on that shelf . . ."

"Why didn't you look? Why?"

"There's no need to cry over such a small thing. Right now much more important stories are being burnt, but look, nobody is complaining. I've already said I'm sorry."

That's a rotten lie, how could he possibly be sorry when he doesn't have a conscience, only a rat with its stomach full of poison frothing green at the mouth? Ringo glowers spitefully at the charred pages of the book still standing upright, until they finally collapse and completely disintegrate. Bill Barnes curses you from on high, you heartless buzzard! He senses his mother's hand in his once more, but there is no pull, sign or gesture to show she wants to get him away from there. The fire does not crackle, the books do not seem to complain as they are consumed, apart from a faint whistle. Señor Sucre and Señor Casal are circling around it cautiously: they both laugh at his outburst, at how upset he is over such a small thing. Banned books always smell suspicious, says Señor Sucre, with his perpetual mocking laugh, his throat eager for a tot of brandy. Then Ringo sees old Señor Pujol, the smoke-seller, approaching him. He is coming round from the far side of the bonfire, from the shadows stretching beyond the red glow, and walks with his hands cupped in front of his chest. Can you see this smoke, my boy? he says, opening and closing his hands above a flame. He turns towards him with his hands clasped together, not like somebody praying but as though he had caught a butterfly and did not want to harm it, or as though he was carrying a tiny lit lamp. Then, half smiling as he looks Ringo in the eye, he opens his hands and lets out a puff of white smoke.

"What do you say if we hide this book of smoke I've found in a safe, secret place," he says ceremoniously. "And when you're grown up, you can recover it. Ha, ha!"

Don Víctor is walking head down round the shadowy garden, and seems to be talking to himself. I'm walking on the ashes of beloved books, Ringo thinks he hears him mutter in what sounds like a prayer, although it could just be more tomfoolery. Señor Casal, who had been a school-teacher and now works as caretaker in a building on Calle Camelias approaches the bonfire with a bunch of papers in one hand and a member-ship card in the other. He stares at it for a moment, and Ringo can read *A.F.A.R.E., Army of the Interior*. Suddenly, as if it was scorching his fingers, he throws everything into the flames, then steps away and is engulfed by the shadows. When did you get back from Canfranc? somebody asks his father. He was in La Carroña, his mother insists. Where is Canfranc, Mama? These compromising documents, says Señor Roura, trying not to laugh, were until today hidden in a basement in Calle Fahrenheit up in the Clot neighbourhood. Don't you think that's an irony of fate? Señor Falcón is also going round like a sleepwalker. He is very tall, thin and short-sighted, and the flames are reflected in his thick glasses until he takes them off to wipe on his handkerchief, and then the fire shines even more brightly in his sick, doleful eyes, as intensely as if he had a ruby the size of a chickpea burning in each pupil.

"What kind of plane was it that you liked so much?" There's a weary, flat tone to his father's voice, but it rouses Ringo from his thoughts. "A fighter, a seaplane, a bomber? Come on, we'll find another one the same, don't be so upset."

It doesn't matter, I'll make sure Bill's plane takes off again. That's what the boy thinks and is about to tell his father, to say it loud and clear so that he is heard by all those who have been laughing at him in a kindly way, those who have come here tonight ready to burn everything just in case, because of the flies. But no-one hears him say anything, and it is quite likely he never managed to utter a word. Possibly he did no more than think it, without taking his eyes off the flames. He will spend his life thinking things like this, without ever saying them. For example, that he can see the plane escaping the flames yet again, climbing into the starry night, leaving far below the writhing black smoke and that strange ceremony of fire, destruction and death. From the cockpit enveloped in flames, the hero smiles at him and waves a greeting.

Ringo remembers now another argument with his father that took place some time after Bill Barnes had saved himself by flying out above the big bonfire. The Rat-catcher had eventually learnt what had happened with the air rifle in his grandparents' vegetable garden, but he brought up the subject as if he knew nothing.

"By the way, Son, what became of that air rifle Uncle Luis gave you?"

"I don't have it anymore."

"You don't? What happened?"

"I swapped it for *The Mystery of the Laughing Shadow* and *The Red Menace*."

"And what's that?"

"They're novels."

"You exchanged the airgun for a couple of cheap second-hand novels? Your Uncle Luis won't be happy when he hears that."

Uncle Luis isn't his uncle or anything of the kind. He's nothing more

121

than a workmate of his father's, another of the brigade's rat-killers. A starving barfly, a poor devil, a casual council worker who prefers to spend his time knocking back plonk. He and his father have insisted Ringo call him uncle. Just to annoy him.

"That's a shame," his father adds. "It was a good air rifle, comrade."

Calling him "comrade" is just to annoy him as well. He says it in a friendly way, as if it's a joke, but that word is two-faced: the Falangists call themselves comrade too, don't they? And what does it mean when they say it? As time goes by, Ringo is beginning to realise certain things. He hates the fact that his father enjoys upsetting people, he hates that he's such a show-off, when in front of his mother and his colleagues from the pest control brigade he makes out he's more of a red, more of a rebel, more libertarian than the anarchist *Seisdedos* himself – who by the way, Uncle Luis tells him, was killed just three days after you were born, kid, on January 11, 1933. Above all, Ringo detests his father's self-serving, deceitful way of forgetting certain things, and his barefaced contradictions; he would boast to his friends that he had always been a diehard anarchist, and yet at the same time was proud that during the civil war his Alberta was a switchboard operator at the Socialist Party headquarters. Nowadays the anarchists don't bite, says the big show-off, they've been tamed and trained like mice in a circus, like those grateful immigrants up in Campo de la Bota who kiss the priests' hands. He comes out with things like that, the lying Rat-catcher, completely out of the blue.

"So you took a dislike to the airgun, did you?" his father goes on. "Might I know why?"

"Just because. I don't want to see it again, and that's that."

"Alright, so you don't want to see it again. And who did you give it to, who was the lucky fellow?"

"A boy I made friends with. An altar server from Las Ánimas."

"Hmm." His father stares at him, and he lowers his gaze. "So you didn't want to. No way . . ."

"No way what?"

"No way you wanted to kill any more pigeons with that gun."

"I've never shot at pigeons."

"At birds then. You think you should never have shot them, is that right?"

"Yes."

"And that's why you got rid of the air rifle."

"Yes."

"And you thought that was an end of it."

Shit, of course I did, he shouts inwardly.

"Well, there's something you need to know, comrade," his father says. "The priest at Las Ánimas has been spotted firing the air rifle in the parish garden. Taking potshots at the sparrows, would you believe? Your friend the altar boy must have lent it to him, or the reverend took it from him, or bought it, who knows? No, don't look at me like that, he wouldn't be the first son of a bitch priest to go around firing a gun. So as you see, even if it's not you pulling the trigger, your air rifle is still killing birds. If you think about it, you haven't ended anything."

Ringo suddenly feels anger rising in his throat like vomit. He would gladly have strangled the hypocritical, arrogant, busybody of a rat-catcher there and then.

"I'm not to blame for that."

"I didn't say you were, Son."

"I was fed up with the air rifle."

"Fed up with the rifle, or of killing birds?"

"It's the same."

"No, it's not."

"It isn't? What's the point then?"

"Well, perhaps so you learn to be a bit more responsible. And besides, you could have given it to me."

"To kill rats with? Because you make a living killing rats and mice, don't you?"

"Yes, that's my job."

"With an air rifle?"

"Well, there are better and easier ways, but an air rifle, even if it only fires pellets, is also good," he says, ruffling the boy's hair. "Don't be angry, dammit. I'm only telling you all this so you think for yourself a bit, so you understand that to get what you want you have to do more than pick up or not pick up an air rifle."

Ringo also hates having his hair ruffled. Killing rats and mice with an air rifle isn't the same as killing birds, he thinks, it's not something that's going to stay with you for the rest of your life. It's not. A disgusting blue rat is a disgusting blue rat, and a little bird seeking shelter from the rain in a fig tree is quite different. Even if it's a predatory sparrow that's cruelly devouring a worm. Anyway, he can't bear being called comrade or having his hair mussed up.

"Besides, I don't believe you," he retorts. "The parish priest is a good man."

"Do you mean that priest with the crew-cut who was the first one to give you music lessons, that Reverend Amadeo Oller, your mother's friend?"

"He taught me and a lot of other kids at Las Ánimas. Reverend Amadeo would never fire an air rifle."

"He wasn't the one who was shooting. It was a young, good-looking priest, a conceited little rat."

"I couldn't care less. It's not my air rifle anymore."

8

ADVENTURES IN ANOTHER NEIGHBOURHOOD

In the years between thirteen and sixteen, many things happen to him, the importance of which he does not grasp at the time. Shortly after he has turned thirteen, one luminous autumn afternoon, stuffed in the grey coat he hates because it immediately labels him as an apprentice on an errand, he is standing on the corner of Calles Valencia and Bruch, in the select Ensanche district, staring in wonder at the facade of the Conservatorio Municipal de Música. No-one, and still less the music students who pass by to enter or leave the conservatoire, could imagine that at only thirteen, working more than nine hours a day, earning twelve pesetas per week, and obliged to wear his ugly, oversized coat, this youngster has on him an emerald and ruby necklace, and a gold brooch in the shape of a salamander dripping with enamel, pearls, opals and diamonds, two pieces valued at more than thirty thousand pesetas. He has to deliver them to an important jeweller's shop near here, without loitering in the street or getting distracted by anything. To avoid the pieces being stolen on a tram or the metro, he is carrying them in a small canvas bag tied to his belt and dangling inside his underpants, very close to his cock. Every so often he feels with his fingers to make sure the bag is still there beneath his clothes, but right now he isn't even thinking about it,

125

because he's listening to music he believes was always destined for him.

Despondent, hands in the pockets of his overall, he is admiring the philharmonic reliefs on the grand entrance to the conservatoire, the two towers ending in their upturned cones, piano and clarinet music escaping through the tall windows as students practise. From the street he can also see the staircase up to the foyer – ten steps, he's already counted them – and a little higher up the stairs leading to the classrooms. Why am I not climbing those steps as well, he wonders, why does the finger of fate always have to come between the piano and me? He knows the answer – somebody told him you needed the school exam to be able to enrol at the conservatoire, and he doesn't have it – but whenever he passes by here, usually on an errand for the workshop, he comes to a halt in front of this imposing building and asks himself the same painful question. How high and solid the walls look, how impenetrable, he often thinks.

On this occasion he is feeling sorry for himself, and lingers too long, until he senses someone is staring at him. Standing by the door, behind a small group of students who are coming out noisily, a girl in granny glasses and a white raincoat with a hood is openly observing him. To judge by her crestfallen appearance, in spite of the distance and the glasses she is wearing, the boy could swear she's been crying, and could also swear she doesn't care whether anyone notices. She looks to be two or three years older than him, sixteen perhaps. Her pale white forehead is framed with black curls, and she is clutching a violin case and a folder to her chest. Her small snow-white hand on the black case seems to be beckoning him. All of a sudden the folder slips from her grasp and falls open. Some sheet music and a notebook fall to the pavement. He goes over and bends down to help her pick up the scores and the notebook; her smile of thanks sends a shiver down his spine.

"Thank you."

As they straighten up she is peering at him from so close that they bump heads. The dreamy apprentice sees the pitying look she gives his grotesque coat, and thinks: that's done it. But he hears her say in a friendly voice:

"Are you a magician? Where did you spring from, magician?"

"I'm no magician."

"You are to me. What's your name?"

Quick, think of a name, he tells himself as he continues staring at her like a dummy.

"My . . . Mi Minor."

"What's that, are you making fun of me?" The girl's bright smile floods over him. "Alright, Mi Minor. Fine. Would you like to do me another favour? Could you come into the conservatoire with me for a moment?"

"Me? What for?"

"It's a very special favour. I need a magician."

"A magician? But I'm not one."

"But you could be for a few minutes. Would you do that for me?"

Her half-open mouth suggests the anxiety of an asthmatic, and she has a cold sore on her top lip. This red patch serves to accentuate her anxiousness, especially when she licks her lip with the tip of her tongue to stop it itching.

"Just for a minute," he stammers, still holding her notebook. He starts leafing through it with sudden interest, or simply because he is still disconcerted. She lets him do it, without asking for it back.

"You'd be doing me a huge favour, Mi Minor. Will you?"

The sound of a trombone comes through one of the big windows.

"But why? Why me?"

"I'll tell you later. I'm going to present you to somebody as though you were my cousin, and you say to him: 'It was me'. That's all. 'It was me.' And then you can go."

To encourage him, and as a foretaste of her grateful thanks, she holds out her hand. As he takes it in his own it now seems to him as though he is holding a bird's wing, a handful of down that is soft to the touch.

"Would you do it for me?" she whispers. "We don't know each other, but I can see you're a good sort . . . Nobody's going to ask you anything, and you won't have to explain. You only need say: 'It was me'. It's nothing

127

bad, I promise. Then you come out again, wait for me here, and I'll explain everything . . . Are you listening?"

"Yes, I'm listening."

The girl lowers her hood, freeing a dark mass of curly hair. Her smile broadens.

"So, would you do that for me? Please!"

He is already nodding in agreement as he reads the title on the cover of the notebook he still has in his hands: *Barcelona Municipal School of Music. Music Practice And Theory. Elementary Class*.

"If you give me this book, I'll do as you ask."

"It's yours."

For a fleeting moment he considers the risks of carrying such valuable jewels on him and getting involved in something he shouldn't, something that Señor Munté, the workshop owner, is always warning him against, but he dismisses the concern on the spot. It's impossible that this girl, who looks like a diligent student crossed with a snow princess, no doubt destined to become the greatest violin virtuoso of all time, and who seems to have been in tears, could be part of a plan to rob him right there, on the steps of the conservatoire and at the heart of this discreet musical hubbub he has always wanted to be part of. He has several questions about her strange request, but does not ask any of them, for fear of breaking the spell and having to hand back the music book, so he tucks it under his arm, plunges his hands into his coat pockets and, plucking up his courage, follows her into the temple of music that would not admit him as a student.

He climbs the first steps to fame on the staircase to the foyer without taking his eyes off the girl's elegant hair or the violin case propped on her hip, swept along by her enigmatic will, as it pushes her on to who knows where or what. His knees are knocking; his head is a whirl of tunes. They go down a dimly lit corridor, bypassing other students, children's voices singing songs in the background, then cross the piano studio where scales and arpeggios fill the air, and follow another, less crowded corridor until the dark mane of hair comes to a halt. The boy finds himself outside what looks like a small, dark office, its walls lined with posters: Menuhin, Royal Albert Hall. Prokofiev's Second Violin Concerto in G Minor. Sitting behind a desk he sees a young, good-looking man wearing a black roll-neck jersey and an air of authority. His glasses are pushed back on his forehead, and he is rubbing his eyes with a weary gesture.

As soon as she enters, the girl steps to one side, lowers her head, and pulls her hood up again.

"Sir, this is my cousin." Staring at the floor and with a quaver in her voice, she adds: "He has something to say to you."

The young teacher raises his head and stares at her. As he does so, his mouth twists in an angry grimace, and a vein pulses at his temple. He seems to want to say something, but cannot make up his mind. He really is a handsome man, thinks the apprentice. Now the door is going to close behind me and they'll steal my jewels, he thinks. But the music teacher does not even seem to have noticed him: he only has eyes for his hooded pupil. Roughly straightening some scores on his desk, he finally turns his gaze towards Ringo. The bogus cousin is waiting for a signal from the girl, but doesn't dare look at her for fear of giving the game away and getting her into trouble. He can sense her at his side, slightly behind him, standing stiff and expectant by the door she is still holding open.

"It was me," he finally says, loud and clear. And unable to avoid it, driven by a sudden impulse, in a rasping voice that sounds as if it is coming from someone else, he adds: "And I'd do it again!"

Closing his eyes, he rushes to complete the rest of what he has agreed: to turn smartly on his heel and get out of there. He does not dare look at the girl, and lowers his hand to his groin, feeling for the bag with the jewellery beneath his coat and trousers. Almost at once, the door slams shut behind him. This happens so suddenly and violently, it must have been the girl who closed it, but why was she in such a hurry? He stands for a couple of minutes outside in the corridor, listening as hard as he can for the sound of voices on the other side of the door, but all he hears is silence.

As he paces up and down in the street opposite the conservatoire entrance, he wonders why on earth he had to go and say more than he should have. Then he starts to think about the door that almost hit him in the back when it was so quickly and eloquently slammed. It was me. Was that the magic formula? Obviously it was, and behind it there must have been a secret, disturbing settling of scores between the young violinist and her teacher. Once she had got what she wanted, of course she was keen to shut the door and leave him out. He also thinks about the pink cold sore on the girl's lip, her slow, drooping eyelids, the soft down of her hand reaching for his, and all at once everything becomes clear. There's no point waiting for her, she won't come and explain anything to him, she never had any intention of doing so. Even so, he hangs around in front of the building for more than an hour, risking a telling-off from the jeweller because of the late delivery of his order.

He has been back three times on purpose, on different days and at different times, and whenever he goes into the centre of Barcelona with a delivery from the workshop he comes to the corner of Calles Valencia and Bruch and stands for a while outside the conservatoire in the hope of seeing her going in or coming out with her hood up, her violin case, and those hands that feel as soft as down. But he never sees her again.

9

THE ARSEHOLE OF THE WORLD IN 1945

"And the Roxy cinema too?"

"Yes, the Roxy, of course," his father replies.

"And the Bosque?"

"The Bosque as well."

"And Proyecciones, and the Mundial."

"Proyecciones no, the Mundial, yes."

"And father, what about the Capitol and the Metropol?"

"Neither of them."

"What about the Kursaal? And the Fantasio?"

"Not them either, comrade. Nor the Windsor or the Monte Carlo or the Coliseum. No first run cinema, got it?"

"What about the Maryland?"

"The Maryland, of course. But it's a bit far. The Delicias, the Rovira, the Iberia and the Moderno. The ushers are all friends of mine. We'll go and see them so they can get to know you too, then they'll let you in for free whenever you like."

"Really? When can we go?"

"In a few days."

"When do you get back from Canfranc?"

"I've never been to Canfranc. I've never lost anything in Canfranc.

There's no such place as Canfranc, got it?"

What a fib, he thinks. Ringo knows his father goes regularly to Canfranc because that's where, according to his mother, he can get reliable, cheap rat poison for the brigade. But for some mysterious reason he prefers to deny those trips, to deny that Canfranc even exists, and what takes him there. The thing is, there are always lies, distortions and contradictions lurking behind whatever the Rat-catcher says. And also, in the midst of all this bluster and pretence, there is often a stupendous nugget of truth, for example this incredible list of cinemas his father's brigade has disinfected where friendly ushers are willing to let him in for nothing.

This is a real, unexpected present he is given on an extremely cold day at the start of December, a month after he has turned thirteen and is about to leave school to start working in Señor Munté's workshop. From early on this boring Sunday afternoon he has been in two minds whether to ask his mother for money for the cinema, because he senses there's not a peseta in the house. His father has sent him to the bedroom to get a packet of Chesterfields he left in his jacket hanging in the wardrobe, and he has searched in all the pockets, sniffing expectantly at them (he loves the smell of Virginia tobacco impregnated in the linings) but all he has found are a few coins. He has kept them, and now is unsure if it is because his mother saw him committing this small theft, or for some other reason, that she is so silent and depressed as she irons shirts on the dining-room table. His mother's gloomy spells are so well known to him that he can predict them: the thin film of fear on her hard-working, bony hands as she sews buttons, folds shirts and handkerchiefs, jabs oranges or quickly does up her white housecoat, the fear she has of being left without work because she is not a qualified nurse, fear that the stove might go out or she could lose the ration card, or that there'll be a knock at the door in the middle of the night, fear that the priest-baiter could be taken away to a police station, and that the boy could end up in an orphanage if she's not there one day. The red-fringed lamp casts its light on the wallpapered walls, and the shadow of the fringe falls on the far side of the table onto his father's lizard-skinned hands, folded lifeless one on top of the other, and the dim light glows on the wine bottle and glass, on the bronze ashtray with the two golden spikes, and on the smoke rising from the not fully extinguished cigarette butt, before gradually dissipating in the surrounding gloom. A subtle net of domestic repercussions, of mutually agreed and accepted habits, hangs over his father and mother, suggesting conflicts postponed yet again, a possibly violent argument that for a long time now they have kept in check, one that will never burst into the open with him present.

He has been told not to snoop around at home, to go out to play. He could go up to Las Ánimas to see the latest production by the theatre group, or play Ping-Pong with El Quique or the Cazorla brothers, but he prefers to stay at home with Jim Hawkins and poor Ben Gunn, who dreams of eating cheese. He really likes that episode, he finds it very funny. Then, sitting at the table with the heating dish next to the window, he looks at the illustrations in "The Flight of Prince Hassin" and "The Defeat of James Brooke", the last two chapters in Salgari's *The Pirates of Malaysia*.

"We're the arsehole of the world, Alberta light of my life," his father groans, his voice deliberately sorrowful. "You can see that clearly from La Carroña. And even more so from Canfranc . . . well, it looks as if we'd better go out, *nano*." Winking at him to win his support, he gets up from the table with a sudden burst of energy. "Let's go out into the street for some fresh air before your mother decides to hit me over the head with the iron."

"Wear your scarf, Son," she says, still ironing, without even looking up at either of them. "And tell that good-for-nothing father of yours to take an umbrella. It's going to rain."

This is why from that day on, walking through Gràcia to fill a gloomy Sunday afternoon threatening rain, the doors to some of the local cinemas are thrown open for him without his having to pay. His father stops to greet doormen and ushers, and the boy is formally presented. First they show up at the Roxy in Plaza Lesseps. They're showing a silly Spanish film and "Buffalo Bill", with Gary Cooper, but he's already seen it at another cinema.

"See how big this place is. Take a good look," says his father, dropping his heavy hand on the boy's shoulder while he stares at the façade. "It took us more than a week to clean it, but there wasn't a flea or bug left alive. And thanks to who, eh?"

"The light brigade of rat-catchers."

"That's right. Come on, I'll introduce you to the doorman, he's a good friend."

In every cinema, without going beyond the entrance curtain, the same confident request: Do me a favour, if my boy here comes, let him in. He loves films, he'd spend his life watching them if he could. Come whenever you like, lad, they all say. On the screen of the Roxy, at the far end of the immense auditorium, there's the sound of shooting. A magic blink of his eyes, and he can see once again how Wild Bill Hickok is shot in the back, and the last kiss his girl gives him on the lips, only this time Bill Hickok cannot wipe it away with the back of his hand, because he's already dead on the ground.

Later on they go by the Selecto, and his father remembers that until a short time earlier it was a pigsty.

"You could pick up lice and scabies and I don't know what else in the artistes' dressing rooms. But by the time we left, you could eat your dinner off any seat."

"You did a good job, Father."

"But this one is no good. It's not for minors."

"I know."

"On we go then."

He's stopped to look at the display case of photos. "The Four Feathers". He likes June Duprez a lot. On the board announcing the variety shows, Chen-Li Puss in Boots has vanished, and now another pair of glittering legs and another name is engraved on his mind: the *Supervedette* Lina Lamarr, a comic dancer.

134

"Do you think there are any blue rats left in there, Father?"

"Who knows? Keep going."

"With all the blue rats that are around, I've still not seen even one."

"I wouldn't say that."

"Do you think that before your brigade finishes them all off I'll be able to see some?"

"You've come across them lots of times."

"No I haven't, I haven't seen a single one . . ."

"What are you standing there for? Come on, let's go." He examines his fingernails, rubs them on his lapel. "If they gave you five pesetas for every one you've seen, you'd be a millionaire."

"But I haven't, Father."

"And I say you have." Avoiding the boy's inquisitive gaze, he feels with his hand for his shoulder once more. "The thing is, sometimes those rats lose their colour in the rain. It's normal, if you think about it. Brown rats though, who have a very soft skin . . ."

"Hey, you're making fun of me!"

"Don't stop, keep going."

He'll have to show me a blue rat, he thinks, or I'll never believe him.

"Didn't you hear me? Keep walking," his father insists. "And don't imagine that it's only rats that can infect you. Not long ago in some cinemas if you took a piss in the toilets you could catch the clap." He points to an ancient-looking balcony on the far side of the street, next to Fontana metro station. "Look – when you were five we used to live behind that balcony, on the first floor. Your mother's younger brother Francisco died there. He was only seventeen. He was called up at sixteen. He was brought back from the Battle of the Ebro with typhus, covered in lice. He hadn't fired a shot. You won't remember, you were too young, but from that balcony one January day seven years ago now, you and I watched the Nationalist troops march into Barcelona . . . Well, anyway, as I was saying. Do you know what gonorrhea is, Son? Or the clap?"

"It's a venerable disease."

"Venereal."

"That's it."

"But do you know how you catch it?" They cross the road opposite Cuesta's jewellery shop and walk on down the left-hand pavement. "Or syphilis? You're growing up, and it's time you knew these things, isn't it?"

"But I already know all that, Father."

"I bet you do! Look, this is the Smart cinema."

"It's not called the Smart anymore, it's the Proyecciones now."

"It's an infectious disease of the cock that you get if you go whoring in the Barrio Chino." They have halted in front of the cinema, and the boy is staring at the posters. "Whores. Do you know what they are? Of course there are whores everywhere, not just in the Chino . . . Besides," he says, a melancholy note in his voice, "today that district isn't what it used to be, or anything like it. You should have seen it fifteen years ago, when we used to go to La Criolla on Calle Cid . . . Well, I only went once. Dreadful little alleyways lined with bars and prostitutes and queers and the worst sort kind of pimp you can imagine . . . But anyway, there's nowhere like it to go whoring. But it's not to be recommended, do you hear me? And it's as well you know that. I suppose it hasn't yet crossed your mind to go down there for a look with your little friends on a Saturday night, has it?"

"Not me."

"Do you know what whoring means, Son?"

"Of course."

"It's the kind of thing you should know by now. Wrap up well in your scarf. Your mother wants you and me to talk about it, so we have to."

"Alright."

"There's no choice. You need to know certain things."

"Uhuh."

"Better today than tomorrow, your mother says. And she may be right. What do you think?"

"Well, I'm not sure . . ."

He remembers seeing his father standing on the rusty balcony they

136

have now left behind. He can see him there in a thick overcoat with the collar up, weeping silently, an unlit cigar between his lips, as he watches the soldiers marching down from Plaza Lesseps, exhausted under their heavy capes and rolled-up blankets, rifles slung over their shoulders, boots resounding on the cobblestones. Ringo is crouching between two pots of geraniums, his face thrust between the bars of the balcony. Recalling that day, his father always said that the boy, seeing him crying and chewing the cigar, suddenly burst into tears himself. Not because he felt impotent and furious at seeing the Nationalists march past, obviously not, he was too small to understand that a war and untold hopes had been lost, but possibly because he empathetically felt the same sorrow, because this was the first time he had ever seen his father cry. But what he remembers most are the troops marching down the street: that strange, wriggling caterpillar of backs bristling with rifle bayonets, equipment belts and canteens, and above all in the last rank, three dead little birds swinging from a wire stuck in a backpack.

"Let's go on," his father says, nudging him with his elbow. "We've never worked in this cinema, so they don't know me. . . . Careful, here comes a vulture in a cassock." A young, alert-looking priest was coming up the same pavement, the skirts of his cassock billowing out as he strode along carrying a bulging briefcase. After he had passed by them, the Rat-catcher turns to look at him. "He's a poof! You only need look at the way he walks."

"Ha," Ringo agrees, lowering his head.

At that moment he would give anything to be with his friends back in the village in the country, swimming in a green pond among the leaping frogs. He tries to summon up this image at times like these, because this is what he most loves to do, apart from reading books or musical scores: to swim, dive, fill his ears with water and music and nothing else.

"So, tell me something," insists the Rat-catcher. "What's the first thing you look at when you see a girl?"

"Me?"

"Yes, you."

Err . . . I dunno. The eyes."

"The eyes. Very thoughtful of you." He pauses for a few seconds, then adds: "The eyes. That's a very clever answer. Now tell me: what's the first thing you look at when you see a girl?"

"What . . . ?"

"I mean one of those beauties, a stunner as they call them these days. I know it's a silly question. But you must notice what it is you like, I don't know, the arse for example . . . there's nothing bad about that, it's normal. Yes, don't look at me like that, everybody thinks it's normal."

"Yes, but the fact is . . ."

"Girls' arses, dammit! Do you like girls or not? I don't know why you think it's so odd! It's a simple enough question!"

It takes him an age to reply, and when he does so he hides his mouth, nose, and almost his eyes, in the top of his scarf.

"The thing is, I don't really look."

"Come off it! How can you not, a normal boy like you! Remember, it's your mother who's insisting we have this little talk. I reckon it's something we ought to do when you're fifteen or sixteen, but your mother's been going on and on about it . . . Look, here on the right is the Mundial cinema. Let's go in and say hello to Señora Anita in the box office. She's a good woman. She'll let you in for free, and you can bring a friend as well, if you like. Or if you want to bring a girlfriend, eh?" He laughs and slaps him so hard on the back he almost doubles up. "Great, isn't it?"

"Yes, great, just great."

"Well, that's that," his father concludes, lowering his voice. "So now we've had our little talk."

Shortly afterwards he comes to a halt on the pavement, caught up all of a sudden in concerns of his own. Staring down at the glistening road surface, he unhurriedly raises a bent cigarette to his lips and lights it with a flickering, badly aimed match.

It's cold, and it is as if the street prolongs the sadness and smell of the metro corridors. Heavy raincoats and autumnal overcoats that seem to be parading along suspended from their hangers, old women wearing black mantillas, children in mourning with wide-open, inquisitive eyes, chilled pedestrians hurrying by, couples in their Sunday best coming and going from the Monumental bar, all pass them and fade into the greyest hour. His father stands there, the weight of sorrow and regret making him stoop as he watches night fall on the wet cobbles. They're moving like clockwork toys, aren't they, Ringo hears him mutter. He knows these mood swings well: just as when least expected he can play the fool, so equally unexpectedly the wastrel, the merry priest-baiter, the charlatan as his mother calls him, suddenly disappears and in his place remains this embittered and anti-social grouch, this rough, insensitive fellow. At that moment everything connected to him, the surprise absences, the case with poison in it, his colleagues in the pest control brigade, his work tools, all turn into something clandestine, vaguely dangerous. Even now, as he stands on the edge of the pavement engrossed in thoughts of his own, his back turned to the people going up and down the street, his thickset body in the raincoat with raised collar, he creates an atmosphere of secrecy, as does his voice, thickened by cigarette smoke and his own hoarseness, like a belch that turns into a private prayer: We're in the arsehole of the world, Son, we are the arsehole of the world.

His mood lightens half an hour later when he says exactly the same thing at the Maryland cinema in Plaza Urquinaona, the one furthest from their house. He explains that its English-sounding name has been changed to the Plaza, since officially these days they are Germanophile, but that he still calls it the Maryland. This week they are showing "Blood, Sweat, and Tears" and – as at the Roxy – "Buffalo Bill". In the foyer, after he has been presented to Señor Batallé, the doorman and usher, Ringo pokes his head through the curtains into the stalls, and sees that Wild Bill Hickok has not been shot yet. His father's voice grows gruffer as he chokes back his anger and says: "Who cares what happens here in Spain, Batallé? Do you still think that the solution to all our problems will come from abroad?" To which Señor Batallé responds in a cautious whisper: Where else from, Pep? You can start looking for another job, because in case you haven't heard, the war with the Boches is over, and soon Canfranc won't be Europe's rich storeroom any more. They've closed the border and blocked the tunnel, there are at least ten thousand soldiers in the area and they're building bunkers all along the Pyrenees, but it's not like it used to be, when the Gestapo guarded the frontier on the other side, and the Falange on this. Why do you keep going to the British consulate near here when they no longer need to communicate with the border? Nowadays I go by Pont de Rei and sleep in Vilella, his father says. Marcelino sends you greetings. And whatever you might say, there's still a lot to be done . . . I agree, but it's not the same, now we have to wait for things to improve, the doorman insists: Didn't you know that the United Nations has just condemned the regime? So what? Do you think that means they're going to come? How naïve can you get? his father grumbles. Of course they will. And they'll toss the bastard Generalissimo in the same sewer where they pitched the Nazis. And we'll live to see that day, Pep! You think so? You really think we're that important to those gentlemen of the United Nations? You really have become gullible, haven't you, damn and blast it! Have you forgotten that only two years ago we had four thousand men in Valle de Arán just waiting for those sons of bitches, who never arrived? We're living a lie, dammit, so don't pin your hopes on it!

By now both of them are on their high horses. They think they are debating the currents of the great waves of recent history; in fact they are yet again doing nothing more than revealing their deep-seated melancholy, their intimate defeats. It is from repeated conversations and arguments of this kind that the boy becomes accustomed to living in an atmosphere heavy with daily doses of bitterness and a sadness that he sees as a curse. He wants nothing to do with history, he feels no need to settle scores with any of that, and so he prefers to slip into the stalls once more and recover Bill Hickok's black Stetson and silver revolver after he has been treacherously shot in the back, while he hears the Rat-catcher's plaintive voice whispering to his friend Batallé: They'll never come, dammit! Can't you see we don't count, can't you see we're the arsehole of the world?

In his father's mouth, this arsehole of the world always expresses the same sense of loss and lack of self-esteem, however ludicrously and sarcastically he puts it, whatever the different variations he uses: we're the greatest shit that history has ever produced; we're the sewer of the West; we're the greatest scum that ever has been or ever will be on the face of this earth; we're less than nothing of the most absolute nothing there is. Whatever the reasoning behind this well-worn catchphrase, Ringo does not think that this self-incriminating *we are* includes him and his mother, but is more directed at the group of his father's semi-clandestine friends, his colleagues in the pest-control brigade, the filthy, stinking holes where they sometimes have to work during his forced, lengthy absences, whether the commissions he received for his trips to Canfranc – and did this mysterious Canfranc really exist? – or the farmhouse at La Carroña were legal or not. Ringo thought about the poverty and hardships he must have shared with his Alberta light of my life for so many years, the family's past and present misfortunes . . . No, he would never have compared his Alberta light of my life to the arsehole of the world, always supposing the world did have an arsehole. Not directly, at least, because in spite of frequently behaving like a wastrel and scatterbrain, he never avoided what he saw as his main responsibility as father and husband: to bring money home whenever he could, a little or a lot, however he could and whatever the cost.

The arsehole of the world. For a long time the boy took those words as a simple respite, a bar-room quip that had become a habit, the snort of a man sick and tired of his own jokes, blaspheming and lies, but eventually he understood that this so-often-mentioned arse is nothing other than the country he lives in, and that the relation spoken about in such derogatory terms between country and arse reflects a general feeling of exclusion, self-loathing and defeat, a lack of esteem they all recognise and accept, the sad conclusion that we count for nothing in the world. So we are the greatest shit, and even worse than that, as his father says, and so do Señor Sucre and Capitán Blay, who are always ranting as they sit on a bench on Plaza Rovira or at the bar counter. In this grey city, with its penitence and ashes, where nothing interests the rest of the world, when, as he heard Señor Sucre comment, even foreign ambassadors are sent packing, and we are suffering unprecedented international isolation, why on earth should we be listened to anywhere, with that sewer rat we have in the Pardo taking himself for the Moorish guard and the sentinel of the Occident – Señor Sucre is well read, and people listen to him when he speaks – always surrounded by those yokes and arrows like black spiders, those blue prayers and anthems. We are nothing, my boy, even our football team can only play Portugal, we've ended up so badly that the rest of the world doesn't even know we exist, we are their laughing stock, *nano*.

The following Sunday he is sitting in the front row at the Delicias cinema, together with El Quique and El Chato. All he had to tell the doorman was I'm Pep the Rat-catcher's son and all three of them got in for free. He's known El Quique by his nickname *Pegamil* for some time now, and lately all he talks about are girls he is sure would let you grope them if we took them up on Montaña Pelada, and how much Victoria Mir looks like María Montez when she's in a swimsuit with her towel wrapped round her head like a turban, although you won't have noticed, he tells Ringo, because when you watch a film you look for other things, but they really do resemble one another.

"That's because of their arses!" shouts Chato.

El Quique claims to have been the first to think of her when the gang was having a collective wank in the ruins of Can Xirot. They were all doing it imagining María Montez, but he started thinking of Violeta and came almost at once. He said it was like feeling a gentle electric shock go through him. Ringo considers El Quique as his best friend, although he couldn't really say why, and often invites him to the cinema. To keep him quiet during the film, he always promises to make up a tale where Violeta is abducted and is about to be tortured by the dacoits or the Sioux, with El Quique as her only hope. This deference has its origin in one of his first fantasies, which has El Quique as protagonist, which he later turned into a recurring dream: Violeta Mir is living in the jungle in a semi-wild state, threatened by a thousand dangers – she is chased by a panther that pounces on her, tears her clothes, and is on the verge of devouring her. El Quique arrives with his bow, and kills the panther just in the nick of time with an arrow between the eyes. Then he picks Violeta up in his arms, soothes her scratches, and takes her to swim in the lake with Tarzan and Jane. For a long while this was *El Pegamil's* favourite tall tale, which he often asked for. Then one day the narrator added a variant: El Quique misses with his first arrow, and the panther eats one of Violeta's legs. A second, well-aimed arrow kills the beast, and El Quique manages to save the girl, whom we soon see not only swimming in the lake but beating Jane in a race.

"Alright, but later on they meet the wizard Merlin, who restores her leg," Ringo added when he noticed how crestfallen his friend was as he refused to accept the change and demanded he hit the target with his first arrow. Ringo insisted, and so the two friends fell out. Ringo's uneasy conscience advised him to bring back Violeta's thigh and to make his peace with El Quique, but for some time his pride would not let him do so. By the time he finally relented and went back to the first version of the story, this devoured thigh had become an obsession with El Quique: in his own tales, which were always breathless and thrown together any old how, a panther would suddenly appear at the most unlikely moment, about to take a bite out of Violeta's dark thigh; she would scream for help, and he would appear with his bow and arrows . . .

Now, lounging in the stalls in the Delicias, he is silent until midway through the film, but then can contain himself no longer, and whispers in Ringo's ear:

"Don't make it the dacoits, Ringo. This time she is abducted by Yellow Hand and his Cheyenne."

"O.K."

"And I'm an explorer in the jungle, and my name is Alan Baxter. And I save her just as she's about to drown in the lake."

"Alright."

"And she's dressed like María Montez in 'The Thousand and One Nights', with a turban on her head . . ."

"Fine, whatever you like, but now we're watching the film, so be quiet."

Basil Rathbone stabs an orange with his knife, and Tyrone Power watches with an ironic smile as they dine in the house of the crooked mayor of Los Angeles, a flabby, cowardly marionette manipulated by his ambitious captain of the guard. Among the other guests are the stunningly beautiful Linda Darnell, but for the moment the boys only have eyes for Tyrone Power and Basil Rathbone. The latter does not yet realise that his guest Diego Vega is Zorro himself, the masked avenger. The boys know Basil Rathbone very well, they have seen him play the villain in "Captain Blood", in "The Adventures of Robin Hood" and "The Adventures of Marco Polo", and even in "David Copperfield", where he portrayed the evil Mister Murstone, always looking like some sinister bird of prey with that hooked nose of his. His sadistic smile broadens as he tortures the orange with his knife and stares disdainfully at Tyrone Power who, masterfully accentuating the mask of a foppish dandy so that nobody will suspect he is Zorro, says to him:

"*I see you treat that fruit like an enemy.*"

"*Or a rival,*" replies the captain, and then the plump, obsequious mayor comes out with the incredible line:

"*My great Esteban here misses no opportunity to cross swords with someone. Not for nothing was he a fencing master in Barcelona!*"

Stupefied, Ringo springs upright in his seat in the Delicias and, still bemused, digs his friend in the ribs.

"Quique! Did you hear that? Did you hear what he said?"

"I think so."

"He said: in Barcelona! That's right, isn't it?"

"Yes, that's right," confirms El Chato to his left. "I swear I heard it! He said in Barcelona."

Unbelievable, it's unbelievably incredible. What a surprise, boys. How wonderful, how strange to hear the name of their city spoken by famous Hollywood actors, so far away from them, from this parochial, irredeemable Sunday afternoon gloom. Ringo intends to tell all the rest of the gang who haven't seen the film yet, and his mother the moment he gets home, but above all his father, when he returns from Canfranc. They know we exist, we're not so insignificant, Father, they haven't forgotten us! In Hollywood they know our city exists! Basil Rathbone was a fencing master in Barcelona!

His astonishment and joy are not shared in the least by his father, who is amused and surprised at his euphoria, and confesses he has no idea who Basil Rathbone is, and nor has he seen the film. Although Ringo is disappointed his father doesn't remember how often he has complained bitterly for precisely this reason, for being or being in the arsehole of the world, he himself, all of us, our city, and the whole of Spain including its football team, which is also the arsehole of the world because nowadays only Portugal will play them, he forgives him because he knows he has never been the slightest bit interested in the cinema, not even as a pastime; he is so unimpressed it takes a great effort for him to stay awake to the end of a film.

His mother, on the other hand, smiles when she hears him tell the story, turning her face away from him. But he notices her slight nod of pleasure, as if she could hear a distant, pleasing music.

10

CALLIGRAPHY OF DREAMS

On the southern slope of the hill, near the summit, there are three
steps of a staircase cut into the rock.

"Hello there, Paqui, has the letter arrived?"

The greeting and the question thrust into the bar a few seconds before the opulent curves bursting out of the white uniform. She has only left home for a moment to have a small glass of brandy and to ask if there's any news. The tavern is empty as usual in mid-afternoon, so there is no danger of being indiscreet, although everyone knows she is not afraid of gossip. The therapist is wearing her normal domestic work clothes, with slippers, curlers in her hair, eyebrows plucked and the familiar smell of embrocation wafting from her hands as she waves them in the air, making her bracelets clink. Almost immediately she notices Berta's son sitting still by the window, camouflaged by the greenish light filtering in through the blinds. When he hears the hoarse, annoying voice invading the bar, he drops his head still lower over his book.

"Didn't you hear me, Paqui?" says Señora Mir, making a beeline for the counter. "Has it arrived, or shall I throw myself under a tram, for real this time?"

"You do like to exaggerate, don't you, Vicky?" the other woman replies.

"Well, has it or hasn't it?"

Standing on a stool to clean the dusty bottles on the highest shelf, Señora Paqui stops and turns to her friend.

"Do you know something, sweetheart? You're taking this far too seriously . . ."

"Do you mind just giving me an answer, Paqui? What about that business of mine? The letter should be here by now! Didn't he say he was going to bring it the next day?"

"No, my treasure, that's not what he said. He had to write it first. Besides, as you know, love letters always take ages to arrive . . ." Shaking the dust off the cloth she has been using, she adds with a scornful twist of the mouth: "Well, so they say."

"You're not here all day. Your brother serves in the mornings. Perhaps he knows something. Ask him."

"He would have told me."

"Have you asked him?"

"Of course."

"Where is he now?"

Without waiting for a reply, Señora Mir strides to the back of the bar. As she passes the boy, she raises a plump arm and tousles his hair.

"How's that hand of yours doing, mister pianist?" she says without stopping. "Writing to your girlfriend?"

He gives a start, and in a rapid reflex action hides his bandaged hand and pencil inside his sling, as though stung by an insect. With the other hand he covers the small squared-off school notebook he has placed on top of the novel he is reading. How distant he is from these whispered confidences and simpering, from the plump, perfumed hand in his hair, from those dreamy blue eyes. Hunched over the pages of *Beware of Pity* he struggles to clasp the yellow pencil between thumb and middle finger. To be seen with the pencil in his fingers makes him feel self-conscious and ridiculous: he thinks he's been found out, caught out in a deception, trying to catch smoke in his hand or something similar. As long as this nosy woman is around, he prefers to keep his hand and pencil hidden, with his head down over the novel, and the novel covering the school notebook, where he is concealing what he has just written with his other hand.

"Agustín! Come out a moment!" Señora Paqui shouts from the bar counter. "Is there anything for Vicky?"

The tavern keeper, with a belly as heavy as he is world-weary, is an affable, red-faced man in his fifties, with bulging eyes and a bushy, greying moustache. He appears at the kitchen door in his black and grey striped apron, holding a bottle of oil. He calls out: "Here!" in a tired, mocking voice. Before Señora Mir has even reached him, he says no, that nobody came with any letter the whole morning.

"I'm frying some little birds that'll make you lick your fingers, Señora Mir," he adds with a smile. "Like to try one?"

"Not on your life!" And swinging round her ample bulk, a look of reproach on her face, she heads back to the bar, where her glass of brandy is waiting. "That's disgusting, Paqui. Where does he get those poor little sparrows?"

"I know, I know, I'm furious about it. The wine wholesaler is the one, he buys them from a grower in the Panadés. I told my brother that next time I'll feed them to the cat." She adds in a resigned voice: "Well, you heard him. Nothing yet. And we're keeping an eye out, I promise you. It might come through the post . . ."

"No chance! Why do you think he prefers to leave it here? Don't you remember I told you that letter mustn't get into the hands of the girl?" She downs the brandy in two quick gulps, and stares blankly in front of her. She seems very upset. "Do you know what, sweetheart? Pour me another one."

Those poor little sparrows, she said! Can you imagine anything more corny? In order not to have to see her so close to, or no more than necessary, because it's impossible not to hear her, Ringo turns his head and looks out into the street. On the edge of the far pavement a little boy of about six, in a short-sleeved shirt and with unkempt hair, is pedalling furiously on a small yellow bicycle. Two small stabilising wheels help him keep his balance. Ringo knows him: it's Tito, the hairdresser Rufina's youngest. The boy dismounts, and crossly examines the poorly fixed stabilisers, which are preventing him going any faster.

Even though he is looking out into the street, Ringo cannot help noticing out of the corner of his eye that Señora Mir is fluffing up her hair with her podgy fingers, biting her fleshy bottom lip, and staring at the wall behind the bar counter. She says despairingly:

"He'd be better kneeling down."

She is staring at a calendar advertising a soft drink. In the centre is a blown-up, hand-tinted old photograph which shows eleven tough football players posing before they play a historic game. This museum piece of muscular legs is what has caught her attention. It is the previous year's calendar, with the month of December still attached thanks to Agustín's enthusiasm for the historic football team that used to be the neighbourhood's local club. The photograph is something of a relic: underneath, in bold letters, it reads: C.D. EUROPA, 1924–25 SEASON. Five sturdy players are posing shoulder to shoulder with one knee on the ground, the centre-half holding the ball. Behind them, arms folded and grim-faced, stand six more, including the goalkeeper in his cap and kneepads. They are all wearing baggy shorts down to the knees, and tight-fitting shirts, with the blue V on the chest. These battle-hardened players are staring fiercely at the camera, ready for a fight, as if they were facing a blizzard. The left-winger, with a handkerchief round his forehead and hair sticking up like a feather duster, is so bow-legged you could drive a tram between his legs.

"Don't be so pig-headed," says Señora Paqui. "It's not him."

Señora Mir tosses down the second glass of brandy and leaves it on the counter, saying sadly, "Put it on the slate, my love," and immediately heading for the door. But before she leaves she turns round again, hands on hips.

"I could swear it is. What would you do, Paqui? Tell me the truth."

"What would I do about what . . . ?"

"Would you wait?"

"I would. Of course I would."

"How long?"

Paqui takes her time before responding, and does so in a whisper.

"He's crazy about you, Vicky. Or haven't you realised that yet?"

"Did he give you that impression? Really?" Señora Mir wants to know, eyes gleaming.

"You should have seen him sitting there, writing away. He found it so hard! And he promised he would get that letter to you. You're the one he wants, you're his beloved!"

"Yes, but how long would you wait?"

"Tell me something first. What happened that day you lay down in the street? Was it bad news from France? You told me your brother was ill . . ."

"No. That was when he was in the concentration camp . . . It's over now, he's fine. No, it was me, I lost my rag . . . I don't know how to explain it."

"So what happened to make you go out into the street like that?"

"I don't know, Paqui! I'll tell you some day." Pensive as she lifts her left breast to fit into the bra more comfortably, she slyly half-closes her eyes and whispers: "That filthy towel wrapped round her head, to pretend . . . If only I'd believed him, if only."

"Believed what, Vicky? What did you mean?"

"Nothing. O.K., don't change the subject. I asked you how long you would wait."

"However long it takes, of course!" She stares at her friend, annoyed that she has not managed to get anything clear, then says more gently: "Don't get him wrong, Vicky. He's not like other men. He doesn't say things just for the sake of it."

"Ah, no? And what would you know?"

"I've never seen anyone so determined to keep a promise. He's mad about you, Vicky."

"Do you really think so? Or are you just saying it to encourage me?"

Without waiting for her reply, Señora Mir purses her pine-cone mouth thoughtfully, pats her haunches and says goodbye with a vague wave of the hand that could mean either I don't care, or God be with you.

Yet again, Ringo cannot help viewing all this as ridiculous. Oh the heartaches of Doña Floripondio! He simply finds it hard to believe that this caricature of a woman is capable of living a real love story, and hard to believe that Señora Paquita, who has so often made fun of her, is now egging her on, encouraging her to wait for that letter. How could she, an old maid, say that an old wreck like her friend could be anyone's beloved? What did Señora Paquita mean by beloved anyway? Has she seen her slobbering over any of her previous pick-ups in Parque Güell or letting them fondle her in some cave on Montaña Pelada?

Weighed in the balance of the boy's daily arguments with himself, what he imagines is far more important than what he has lived, and although the frontier between what he sees and what he struggles to make out is very imprecise, he usually has no doubt when it comes to the moment of choice: even if he is unsure whether his voluptuous neighbour warrants compassion or laughter, in this case he feels disinclined to feel sorry for her. However fascinating the prospects of her amorous misadventures might seem, for him they will always represent the lowest level of the grotesque and farcical.

With Señora Mir gone, the unwilling witness no longer pays any attention to the bar, but instead allows his gaze to wander to the quiet, sunny street through the slats of the blind. A while ago he saw Señor Sucre and Capitán Blay walk past, chatting on their way to Plaza Rovira. They took it in turns every two metres or so to emphasise a point in their interminable argument, but without shouting or gesticulating, their heads close together, hands behind their backs, staring down at the ground. At the far side of the street, on the peeling wall without doors or windows, a large patch of damp looks like a tornado whirling ominously towards the little boy pedalling on the pavement edge. As he goes up and down on his tiny bike, head straining as he hunches over the handlebars, he seems to be carrying out some boring task or punishment. The bicycle is an old piece of junk with a fixed wheel and no brakes. The two stabilisers help him keep his balance and stop him falling over, but slow him down and cancel out all his efforts, preventing him from sprinting across the imaginary finishing line as the winner. The boy gets off the bike and starts kicking it.

Ringo's eyes stray from the street to his writing. He is still clumsily holding the pencil in his bandaged hand, while with the other he is shyly concealing his first effort. All at once, sensitive to other echoes, another rhythm, other readings, he decides to correct it and to be more precise.

On its southern slope, cut from a rock, there are three lonely steps of a staircase that was never finished, which no-one knows where it was leading to.

He thinks that it is only in this unknown, abrupt territory of writing and its resonances that he will be able to discover the luminous passage between words and deeds, a propitious place where he can keep his hostile surroundings at bay and reinvent himself. He would like to be able to proclaim that for the best part of the day his spirit is not where he is in his body, whether he is sitting in the undulating grounds of Parque Güell, book in hand, or at a table next to the window in this gloomy bar, but that it is roaming far from his neighbourhood and city across very different landscapes and often in a delicate sentimental balance, nourishing his sense of exile on long, lonely walks on the crunching snow of the Nevksy Prospect, for example, or travelling by carriage along the paths of Yarmouth, or perhaps strolling along the foggy alleyways of Blackfriars on the banks of the Thames, or among the desolate heights of Yorkshire where the wind always howls, or entering Pension Vauquer on rue Neuve-Sainte-Geneviève, or on his stomach on the plains of Kenya near Mount Kilimanjaro, under the shady trees at Thornfield or even wandering the hills of Balaclava among the shrapnel and slaughtered cavalrymen. Because everything beyond these walls, outside the tavern, has been robbed of meaning, beauty and future. There is nothing beyond a routine of downtrodden beings and trivial desires: because who can be happy day after day with this monotonous, endless succession of grey, cowering facades, these streets with potholed or still not asphalted pavements, beaten earth tracks on which the local kids draw the skull and crossbones with their penknives, empty waste lots and crumbling, filthy corners with the black spider stencilled on them. What little keeps him here is all that he is missing. Every time he lifts his gaze from his book he feels lost, displaced by an unexpected twist of fate, and this sense of not belonging becomes even keener whenever he thinks about his fortuitous family origin; if he stops to consider it, he also is a fraud perpetrated by destiny, a huge fraud, because he appears to be the son of somebody who is not in reality his mother, not to mention his father, the king of deception. And it does not take long to discover a whole lot of things that might have been different, because perhaps his biological father is still alive somewhere, and who knows how many half-brothers and sisters, cousins and nephews and uncles and aunts he might have, although he is never likely to meet any of them, and the most reasonable thing is to accept he has four parents and eight grandparents, a network of ghostly blood relations as well as another equally ghostly network of fictional creations, and that everything is naturally strange, accidental and deceitful. For example, this sunny gently sloping street that he is looking at through the bar window without really seeing as a boy struggles along on his little bike, this street also hides a fraud, a mystification that few people know about, because its name is not what it seems, as Señor Sucre explained in great detail to Capitán Blay one summer evening when they were sitting outside the bar with a porrón of wine cooling in an ice bucket. Known as Torrente de las Flores, said Señor Sucre, our beloved street, which runs straight down from Travesera de Dalt to Travesera de Gràcia, coming out directly opposite the Delicias cinema, is popularly thought long ago to have been a rushing stream of crystalline waters bordered by flowers, hence the name. But this belief is based on a misconception, as Señor Sucre explained that night to anyone who would listen – that is, to nobody apart from Capitán Blay, smoking pensively next to him, and Berta's boy, all ears as usual, fascinated by the two old men's eccentric memory – this district of La Salud of which today we are so proud, must effectively have originally, thousands of years ago, been a virgin, extraordinary orchard, a flowery, splendid Eden, but out of respect for the truth it has to be said that the street takes its name from the family names of a gentleman from El Ferrol called Manuel Torrent Flores, the owner of the land and the stream here that he sold for development at the end of the nineteenth century.

"So any idea of flowers and torrents is completely wrong. Nowadays, as with so many things in this rat-ridden city," Señor Sucre craftily concludes, "even the name of our street is nothing but a damn lie."

"And what do you say, young man?" Capitán Blay teases him when he sees Ringo listening to them open-mouthed. "Would you say the street goes from the mountains to the sea, or from the sea to the mountains?"

Laughter mixed with coughing from the two cranky old pensioners. Although he realised they were making fun of him yet again, he still chose a reply based on logic. He always wanted to keep on their good side.

"From the mountains to the sea, Capitán, because the street runs downhill."

"This part of the street is where you're most likely to see optical illusions," Capitán Blay had said on one occasion, studying the old lengths of rail. Perhaps that's what the kid on the bike is experiencing now, thinks Ringo: he just has to set off down the street to gain his balance and win his bet. This is a very common experience, something lots of children his age have been through – if of course by luck or thanks to their parents they own a bike, which was not his case – and something that on this occasion, although he doesn't know why, seems to him significant. Recently, lots of things have begun to seem significant to him, but today it takes him some time to discover that the tiny, furious cyclist is not intent on destroying his bicycle but only the part that is denying him victory and preventing him from enjoying the wind in his face, frustrating the great adventure of learning how to balance on his own without help or advice from anybody else. Sitting on the edge of the pavement near the drain, the boy is angrily shaking the struts holding on the supporting wheels, trying to loosen the screws. He has a determined expression on his face: he is going to get rid of the stupid little wheels if he has to tear them off with his teeth. But after quite some time he has got almost nowhere. When he sees somebody he knows going past, a house-painter with a ladder over his shoulder, he asks him for help. Please, have you got a hammer? The man is in a hurry, and smiles without stopping, although he ruffles his hair affectionately and continues on his way. Over the next half hour, the boy asks several passers-by for help, whether he knows them or not. Some of them don't even look at him; others do not stop, merely listen with a smile and give different excuses. A spanner? I'm sorry, I've run out of them. And another: Why don't you go home and tell your mother what you're trying to do, my little man? The boy stands up, slips his little penis out of the side of his shorts and pees against the wall where the tornado appears to be whirling towards him. The last person to stop when he hears his appeal is a lock-smith from Calle Martí. He explains that these little stabilisers that he wants to get rid of are there to help him balance and to prevent him coming a cropper. The boy also hates the bike's fixed wheel, and asks him if it's possible to change it, but the man doesn't respond. I don't want to ride with a fixed wheel! he complains when he is on his own again. Every so often he gets up to kick and thump the bike, and then sits down again.

Ringo stops looking at him for a moment when he realises his numbed fingers are still holding the pencil. He lets go of it finally and examines what he has written. He notes down a correction, but he doesn't like it, so he rejects it, then passes the time doodling a winged *gruppetto* on an imaginary stave. When he raises his head again, Tito is shaking the stabilisers even more furiously and stubbornly, now on the verge of tears. His insistence, the interminable argument between boy and bike as to who should be in control of the balancing and can claim victory, holds Ringo's attention for some considerable time. Finally, Tito manages to unscrew the metal supports. He throws them and the stabiliser wheels into the open drain. Then he stands the bike at the edge of the pavement and climbs on. With one foot on the pedal and the other on the ground, he shoots a triumphant glance over his shoulder in the direction of the tavern window before he launches himself down the street, well aware he is being watched.

He is bound to crash many times before he succeeds, and will return home with scraped knees and a few bruises. Ringo looks away from the street and drops the blind. He raises it again quickly when he hears the sound of crashing metal. No, he hasn't been hit by a car, and nobody seems to have seen him – apart from Ringo. The boy gets to his feet in the gutter, casts a defiant glance towards the bar, licks a scrape on his hand, shakes the dust off his shorts, and wheels his bike back up the hill. As he goes past the tavern, he gives another sideways, challenging glance in the direction of the only witness to his feat. And this time the witness has understood. Dropping the pencil on to the scrawled-on sheet of paper, he watches with an intense, unwavering attention, surprisingly focused on capturing the details, as the little boy launches himself at full tilt down the street, determined and fast despite the lurches and crashes, his chin to the handle-bar, eyes fixed ahead of him with a manic intensity, a powerful tension created in equal measure by optimism and frustration plain on his face, until he falls yet again in a tangle of wheels, arms, and legs, only to spring up at once, knees scraped bare and blood on his cheeks, walk back up the street, sit on the saddle and set off again from the pavement edge, pushing off with one foot and a determination that negates all fear of crashing. From the bar, with his maimed hand raised in the air, and feeling the lack of the pencil between his fingers, Ringo cannot help but observe this persistent, desperate pedalling that ends time and again in a fall, the repeated mental pressure on the pedals, the enraged lowered head charging at the air and everything else in its way. Some passers-by advise him to stop, but the kid won't listen to anybody, there is no way he is going to get off his bike. He is in a race against time, because he knows someone is bound to tell his mother. His worst crash comes when he hits the disused tram tracks: without meaning to, he gets one of the wheels stuck in a rail, the bicycle stops and Tito is flung over the handlebars. He gets up again and rides on, and a short while later, when he has lost count of the falls – the last few increasingly controlled – all of a sudden he steadies himself and begins to ride round in circles, a broad grin on his face as he glances back at Ringo. Still looking at him and smiling, Tito turns the corner into Calle Martí and disappears in the direction of Plaza del Norte with a victory whoop.

All this time, ideas for his writing have been germinating, and something leads Ringo to tear out the page he has been scribbling on and use a clean one. He picks up the pencil with his painful fingers and listens to the music of the words as they come back to him. It's not a banal tune like the ones he often hums, unconsciously falling back on the imaginary four-four rhythm he has learnt from the music scores; from the start, from his first timid attempt, it was like a well-known melody he had heard a thousand times but never completed, a mutilated succession of notes that his auditive memory had stored away and was now converting into words; a musical phrase with echoes that could not be traced back this time to the lines of any musical stave (there was no room for any mistake in this, the echoes were clear and consciously assumed) but to the heights of a mountain covered in perpetual snows. And so the bandaged hand which a short while before had been immobile now picks up the pencil and, with renewed energy despite occasional stabbing pains in his sacrificed finger, he corrects and concludes what will turn out to be (although as yet he does not know it) a seminal paragraph.

Montaña Pelada is a bare, arid hill some two hundred and sixty-six metres high, and the origin of its name is confused. On its eastern flank fossils of prehistoric tortoises and mammoth bones have been found. Near the summit stands a large, flat rock with three steps of a staircase that was never finished. No-one has ever been able to explain where a staircase was intended to lead in such a barren, desolate place.

11

A NOT VERY CLEAN, POORLY LIT PLACE

"Ringo, are you coming to Barrio Chino?"

This is the third Saturday running that El Quique has come into Bar Rosales after supper with the same suggestion. If you've never set foot in a whorehouse in Barrio Chino, *nano*, you've never lived. There are three in Calle Robadors almost next to each other: El Recreo, El Jardín and La Gaucha, it's easy to slip inside. And although El Quique is not allowed in because he's too young, and usually ends up in the gutter outside with a slapped face or a kick up the backside, nosing around in brothels has become his favourite pastime.

"You should see the fat cows in El Jardín, they look like they're from before the war! But there's one, La Manoli . . . Wow, I get a hard-on just looking at her."

"Alright, you don't have to be crude about it."

"Well, are you coming or not?"

Ringo is enjoying the cool of evening on the pavement outside the bar, sitting with his chair pushed up against the wall, his jacket over his shoulders, a beer in his undamaged hand, watching the world go by. He doesn't seem to want to do anything. A while ago he was reading his very dog-eared but favourite book of short stories, and now he stuffs it into the baggiest pocket of his jacket.

"Not if you're going in a gang," he says. "Too much fuss."

"Just you and me."

It's a misty, muggy evening towards the end of September. El Quique has burst into the bar dressed up in a stifling, brown double-breasted suit, with a polka-dot tie, a litre of brilliantine on his hair and extravagantly framed sunglasses, because sunglasses make you look older, *nano*, so it's easier to sneak in. Four Lucky Strike cigarettes snitched from his father are poking out of the top pocket of his jacket. Very pleased with himself, hot but all smiles, he pushes his round, greasy face close to his friend's and awaits his response. When he saw Ringo so caught up in his book, he stared at him in astonishment, wondering how on earth he could spend Saturday night sitting out here or inside the bar reading or listening to the old-timers' boring conversations or the slap of dominoes on the marble tabletops. He sometimes thinks Ringo isn't growing up normally like the rest of them, like him and Roger for example, as if he is still fantasising with his outlandish stories, lying flat on a stagecoach roof firing at the Apaches chasing him across the prairie. He feels like telling him: Ringo, those horses are cardboard cutouts!

"Jesus, don't be such a dummy. Come on, let's do it!"

"Find somebody else," he says. "I haven't even got enough for the tram."

Before he left home, after his mother went to La Esperanza to do her night shift, he had looked in a small coffee cup on the sideboard where on some Saturdays she leaves him two or three pesetas. This time there is only small change. The sight of his mother fiddling with this money always makes him sad; whenever he saw her pale, skinny hand fumbling for a few coins in the bottom of her small purse just for him, he felt selfish, useless and a spendthrift. There was a five-peseta note under a small plate, but that was for the bread and milk and a kilo of sweet potatoes that he himself had to buy early next morning before she got up, and, if there was enough, for a pot of cream sprinkled with sugar.

"It won't cost you a thing," El Quique insists brightly. "I'll pay. I'm flush, kid, I won at dominoes this afternoon. Come on! We'll go for a stroll to El Jardín to see what's going on."

"What will that be? Nothing."

"Well, we can only look, but ..."

"Yeah, like wallflowers."

"What else can we do? They don't let you touch them. And as for a fuck, for now don't even dream of it . . . In El Recreo it's fifteen pesetas a time. But you can see the girls close up. Then at home you have a toss, and that's that."

"They won't let us in."

"Of course they will! What do you bet? We'll get in whenever you like, kid, I swear. On Saturday nights it's crowded with guys and they don't pay much attention, you just have to get in the queue and slip through. The only place where they wouldn't let me in was at La Carola, oh, and in La Madame Petit, the women there cost the earth . . . Look, I'll show you things you've never seen, Ringo. In a shop window on Calle San Ramón there's a dildo that looks like a donkey's donger, you'll split your sides laughing when you see it . . . but first we'll have a few beers in Los Cabales, to get in the mood. I'll pay. What do you say?"

Ringo excuses himself by raising his bandaged hand.

"I can't even put my hand in my pocket to buy a round."

"Like I said, I'm paying. Come on, man!"

You can see from his dull, bulging eyes that all he thinks about is naked women. Out of the gang from four years earlier, El Quique, Roger and Rafa Cazorla are the only ones who still go to Bar Rosales, at first for the table football more than anything else, then to play dominoes, and to go together to a dance every Sunday. El Quique, who doesn't hide his soft spot for Ringo and claims to be his best friend, and to understand and respect his love of pianos and novels – and not just thrillers or cowboy books – has often tried to get him to the Verdi or the Cooperativa La Lealtad, the two dancehalls where Violeta goes, with her mother as chaperone, but he has always refused.

Tonight though, he lets himself be dragged along out of curiosity. And after he has seen what was to be seen, it occurs to him that to some extent the fantasies El Quique demanded in the tales he used to invent, fantasies of tits and arses, wherever possible glimpsed through Oriental veils, odalisques in brilliant Technicolor concealed beneath gauzes and tulles like Yvonne de Carlo or María Montez, have finally become real in his Saturday night forays into the roughest brothels, especially in the crowded, poorly lit salon at El Jardín where eight or ten women parade round the centre like in an Arab slave market. They display themselves in their slips or nothing more than bras and suspender belts, flushed and bumping into each other because of the lack of room. They walk round as if in their sleep, rolls of flesh rippling as they fan themselves, their greasy, thick hair falling in waves onto bare shoulders; one of them has a towel wrapped round her head like a turban. On their feet they wear threadbare satin slippers or green and red very high-heeled shoes; another has black stockings and a suspender belt, and bruises all over her body; the youngest is wearing white socks and rubber sandals. They sway their fat buttocks in a bored fashion, and smile at the men peering at them with mocking looks of desire or submissive melancholy. Most of the men are standing, although some occupy the bench that runs round walls painted a greeny-yellow colour, as lumpy as a pool of vomit. A small door leads to a darkened staircase, and in the corners spittoons are overflowing with cigarette butts and gobs of spit. A thin layer of bluish cigarette smoke floats in air saturated with bursts of sour sweat and talcum powder, murmuring and occasional laughter can be heard between long silences laden with all kinds of coughs, the insidious clearing of throats, and the uneasy move-ment of feet in an inhibited, reverent shuffle that for an instant reminds Ringo of Good Fridays in the Las Ánimas church packed with the faithful advancing like sleepwalkers towards the altar. A few of the whores are singing softly to themselves as they turn and turn, apparently oblivious to the charms they are displaying. One of them has her hands busy doing some crochet-work, while the youngest and least ugly (although she is still ugly) with bushy eyebrows and dimples like slits in her doll's face, catches his attention by glancing at him over her shoulder with a sorrowful look, as if saying: What are you doing here, child, how old are you?

Some years earlier he had imagined in great detail a tall tale he has never dared tell the rest of the gang. It featured a pretty young prostitute battered and bruised by her experiences, ruined by a tragic destiny, while he was her pampered lover, a pariah living the life of a vice-filled libertine, redeemed by her love. That lurid, lowlife story in which he saw himself as an adventurer and a louse, but also a misunderstood genius of the piano who had sunk into perversion and failure, now seems to him ridiculous as it floods back into his memory in this filthy brothel amongst idle, inert gawkers who only want to pass the time, and makes him feel utterly naïve. This is no place for fantasy, kid, this is a whorehouse, and men come here to fuck. He feels for the book of short stories in his pocket and is already thinking of making his escape, when behind his back he hears a familiar voice.

"Don't turn round," whispers El Quique. "Guess who's behind you."

"It was too awful to be true, Señor Anselmo," the voice is saying. "You can see for yourself, she doesn't work in a place like this. I've asked and they don't even know her. We're wasting our time. For the love of God, forget that woman; don't torment yourself any more."

It is a hollow, sombre voice that suddenly takes on a note of patient commiseration. Yes, it's his, there's no other voice like it. Ringo waits a few seconds then turns cautiously round to confirm out of the corner of his eye that scarcely two metres away, among the group of standing onlookers, he can make out the familiar reverential attitude, the furtive, predatory look of the slender figure leaning his splendid snow-white locks towards the squat little fellow he is towering above as he talks to him, so considerate and enveloping that is it almost as though he is manoeuvring to steal his wallet: the same thoughtful deference, the same lofty kindness that he demonstrated in Bar Rosales. His companion, a well-dressed middle-aged man, is bald and chubby and is listening to him with a hang-dog expression, his neck stretched as he tries not to miss any of the prostitutes' twirls on the floor. Señor Alonso, on the other hand, shows no interest in the spectacle; twisting his body as lame people do, and lifting his foot from the ground with some difficulty, he seems anxious to leave.

Ringo would not have paid him the slightest attention anywhere but here. More than three months have gone by since the last time he was seen in Bar Rosales, and his unseemly affair with Señora Mir only survives in the secrets she shares with Señora Paquita, the two chatterboxes at the bar. Unless Señora Mir revives their interest with another public performance, the neighbourhood will soon forget the lame man who once prowled its streets. Yet, although Ringo would never admit as much, this character has never ceased secretly to intrigue him. Tall, broad-shouldered and with a thin, hooked nose that reminds Ringo of the sinister Fagin, he now sports a bushy moustache as thick as his head of hair, and a weary grimace on his full lips. His long, olive-skinned face with its deep, strangely symmetrical lines, still exudes its magnetism and flinty harmony, and yet something – possibly the novelty of the moustache or the hooded, mournful lids over his grey eyes – is starting to make him look his age. A man with a vigorous old age, as he remembers Señor Sucre once remarking. He is dressed with his customary care and formality, that of a veteran sportsman from a poor suburb, a faded blue unbuttoned polo shirt, a tobacco-coloured, loose-fitting linen jacket with ample pockets and the collar raised, with a black scarf round his neck.

"What, you're surprised?" whispers El Quique. "I'm not. You can meet anyone here, including your own father. One day I saw Señora Rufina's husband come in, and another night it was the owner of the store on Calle Argentona."

"O.K., so we've seen all there is to see. Shall we go?"

"What are you talking about? We've only just got here! Did you see Manoli? Yum!"

"No, I didn't see her. It's very dark in here, and it stinks. I'm off."

"Shit, *nano*, but what did you expect? I know what's wrong with you. You're afraid someone you know will see you and mention it in the neighbourhood, and your mother will get to hear of it . . ."

"Are you coming or not?"

All this time he has been concealing his injured hand in his pocket, wearing the scarf round his neck. Before he leaves he wants to put his arm back in the sling, and with it recuperate, or so he hopes, his secret, most authentic identity. While he is asking El Quique to tie the scarf for the sling, he sees La Manoli staring at him over her shoulder. She is a voluptuous, dark-haired woman, her breasts bare; her stern gaze tells him she knows he is little more than fifteen.

"Shit, what's your hurry?" El Quique reproaches him. "I'm staying until I get thrown out. Then I'll take a look in Bar Cádiz or the Kentucky, which will be full of tarts . . ."

"In that case, good luck to you," says Ringo, and as he slips towards the exit he casts a last glance at Señor Alonso, who is still trying to convince his companion that the woman he is looking for isn't there.

Out in the street he has to force his way through the stream of men walking slowly in both directions, crowded together but not looking at each other, pretending they are somewhere else. El Quique had already told him that on Saturday nights there are so many men in Calle Robadors that it's almost impossible to move, and every so often the police have to come and disperse them with their batons. Whenever they do this, the strollers seek refuge in the doorways and bars, and come out again once the police have passed, to renew their visits to the three brothels. As Ringo forces his way through, leaving behind the silent crowds of men entering and leaving the packed bars, purulent words like syphilis, blennorrahgia, chancre, gonorrhea, which have so worried him since he first heard them from his father, press in on him now and slide along the glistening cobbles, where the neon lights are reflected: *Urinary tract, Beds, Rubbers.* Soon afterwards he finds himself in dark, less busy side streets, treading on rubble and in foul-smelling water along a route he hopes will take him back to Las Ramblas.

He is in no hurry, and besides, he would not mind getting lost, although he is well aware of the stigma and bad reputation attached to this legendary neighbourhood. At a certain point his excitement grows when he thinks someone is following him. He turns round, but sees nothing unusual; a drunk's wavering shadow, an empty bottle rolling across the cobbles, a dog scavenging in the rubbish. Curiosity leads him to prolong his exploration with a detour: first he takes Calle San José Oriol, then plunges into Calle de las Tapias, where according to the older men in the workshop a trick with a whore up against the wall in the darkest part of the street would only cost him a peseta . . . Or were they talking about somewhere even more infamous, a hole known as Terra Negra at the foot of Montjuich hill? Two women with enormous backsides are chatting on the pavement to a weedy-looking guy in a vest, while another woman stands in a doorway looking at herself in a hand mirror. Ringo carries on quickly without pausing, avoiding the light from the streetlamps and hearing the tinkle of laughter behind him, then turns left into Calle San Pablo. His intention is to reach Conde del Asalto via Calle San Ramón, with its strange offers and low dives. He comes to a halt on the corner and by the light of a streetlamp confirms he has no money left either for a last beer or for the tram home. A few metres away on the same corner a tavern is open, with the sound of clapping and music coming from within. He is staring at the sign – Bar Los Joseles – when he hears the sombre voice behind him once more:

"My, my, who's this I see? I know this lad."

It could be a coincidence, but that would make it the second of the night. Ringo slowly turns round, annoyed, not knowing what to expect, and finds himself confronted with the familiar twisted smile, the grey gaze beneath the hooded lids.

"Do you mean me?"

"Your name is . . ." the man pauses for a moment. "Let's think, something that sounds like a bell . . . Oh, yes, I remember! Ringo. That's what the boys in Bar Rosales call you, isn't it?"

"Yes, you're right, but that's not my real name."

He would never have imagined that one day he would renounce being called Ringo, and he wonders why he has done such a thing.

"What brings you here, so far from home? You're not lost, are you?"

"No, Señor."

"Well, well. You do remember me, don't you?"

"Of course. Señor Alonso."

"That's right. And how are you, lad?"

It is only now that he realises the man is holding out his hand, with an elaborately carved bone ring on his middle finger. His skin is silky and warm, his handshake firm. So formal – as if they were meeting for the first time.

"I saw you go by and said to myself, why, it's that boy who studies music and spends his days sitting in the Rosales, always on his own and so polite, always reading, studying, or discreetly listening in when the grown-ups are talking." He speaks slowly, in a friendly singsong that is slightly mocking but encourages his complicity. His tired eyes smile as he takes a pack of Luckies from his pocket. "Well, well. Do you smoke?"

Ringo shakes his head, and watches as the man transfers the cigarette to his mouth without touching it: he taps a couple of times on the back of the hand holding the packet, the cigarette pops out, and his lips catch it almost in mid-air, smiling all the while. Not bad, thinks the youngster, although he's seen William Powell do it much more stylishly. Yet he cannot deny he feels a certain curiosity. Perhaps he should have accepted the cigarette and been friendlier and more receptive, to discover his intentions, whatever they might be; it could be that the man is sorry he was seen in such a notorious whorehouse and wants to justify himself. He stares at Ringo, strokes his moustache with his knuckle, and then notices the bandaged hand peeping out of the sling.

"What's this? Did you trap it in the piano lid?"

Ringo takes the joke on board reluctantly. He explains briefly what happened in the workshop, without admitting to any regret for having to give up his music studies. He does not look the older man in the eye, and stays facing the opposite corner of Conde del Asalto, making it plain he intends to continue on his way. Hesitating over how harsh he should be, he is surprised to hear himself saying in a cold, cutting voice:

"I walked a girl home, she lives close to here. Her mother works at night in Calle Arco del Teatro, in Madame Petit's, but the rest of her family don't know that . . . she used to work in La Emilia, but now that she's old . . . Well, they're quite poor. Her grandfather has a Steinway piano and she told me they were selling it, so tonight I wanted to see it, because my mother promised to buy me one, but it's very old and out of tune, and there are three keys missing, so I'm not sure . . ." Pausing for breath he goes on: "Do you live near here too, Señor Alonso?"

Señor Alonso shakes his head. He tugs and shifts the position of his bad leg on the pavement, so he is now facing the bar on the corner.

"I was with a friend. Listen, are you in a hurry? Can I buy you a soft drink or a beer?"

"The thing is, it's very late . . ."

"Just five minutes. Right here." He points to the Los Joseles sign. "What about it?" And, seeing him still unsure, he adds: "I know, you're asking yourself what I came looking for at night in this godforsaken place . . . It's not what you think. I came for a friend who's having a hard time. A sad story." He falls silent for a moment, looks down at the cigarette smoking between his fingers as if surprised by it, and adds: "He was married to a young woman who left him, and he still hasn't got over it. Every so often he takes it into his head to go looking for her, wherever it may be, especially if somebody tells him he thinks he's seen her. One day I had to fetch him off the women's beach at La Barceloneta. You should have seen the row that caused. He's a good man, you know, a benefactor. Not long ago he gave a proper football, boots and new shirts to the lads I train in my neighbourhood . . . He's been unlucky."

He's lying, thinks Ringo. Chinese whispers in the Barrio Chino. A load of nonsense. He wants something from me. He feels Señor Alonso's hand lightly touching his elbow, encouraging him to come with him to the bar, while he goes on in his smooth, even voice:

"Although you have to make your own luck in this life. Or so I reckon. What do you think?" He shrugs. "So what?" 'My good friend made a mistake. He doesn't want to admit it, but he made a mistake. Firstly, he should never have married such a young woman, don't you agree? Secondly, once he'd done that, he should never have behaved like an old man who can't bear to be reminded that he married a woman too young for him. I don't know if you follow me . . ."

"Is it true what Señor Agustín says, that you played as a forward for Europa? And that you had to give up because you injured your leg?"

"A bear bit me. One of Jupiter's defenders." Then, with a sly smile: "The bastard really did bite. One day he made a vicious tackle, and that was that."

He is limping more than before, and is just as slippery and enigmatic. Ringo's mind fills with dark conjectures: seeing him so much at ease in the Calle Robadors brothel, so at home in that atmosphere and with the clients, so much part of the raw desires of that rancid market, yet at the same time so indifferent to it, dealing with his own business without showing the slightest interest in the prostitutes, makes Ringo think he could well live close to here. This man has never wanted to reveal where he lived, so these wretched, foul-smelling streets could well be his secret field of operations, whatever they might consist of.

And yet, when they got inside the tavern, and he trod with obvious distaste on the filthy carpet of sawdust, prawn shells and olive pits beneath the counter, breathing in an atmosphere heavy with the smell of sour wine and rubbish, the lame man suddenly does not seem at all in tune with either the neighbourhood or its inhabitants. Despite his lameness and the way one foot is twisted slightly inwards, he enters the bar with smooth, elastic steps, like a prowling feline.

"Take a look at this," he says dismissively. "Ali Baba's cave."

Los Joseles is a small tavern that tonight has been taken over by a gypsy clan dressed to the nines, determined to enjoy a family celebration. They are sitting at the only two tables beneath a ceiling of hams and sausages hanging from the beams together with strings of garlic, bunches of herbs and sticky flypaper. The men sport frilly white shirts, chunky rings on their fingers and have alcohol-soaked voices. The women wear large hoops in their ears and flowers in their hair. A girl who seems to be asleep in a chair propped against a barrel is breastfeeding a baby whose bald head is peeping out of the shawl wrapped round it. There is no-one serving behind the bar, but as soon as the two of them come in, a dark-complexioned young man with plastered-down hair smothered in brilliantine gets up quickly from one of the tables and positions himself behind the array of tapas on the counter. When they are both sitting at the bar, Señor Alonso examines the food and orders two beers and some skewered meat.

"Or do you prefer something else, Ringo?" he asks in a friendly voice. "Some anchovies, perhaps?"

On display are baby squid, Russian salad, prawns, tripe, snails, mussels in tomato sauce. For a moment Ringo thinks he can see fried little birds on one of the plates with their legs sticking up, but they turn out to be sweet peppers with toothpicks in them.

"I don't know, it's all the same to me."

"Those spicy potatoes look good."

"Let's have some then."

He has just realised how hungry he is. Señor Alonso orders a plate of prawns as well. Behind the counter, above the shelves and rows of bottles, an ancient mirror hangs from the wall, tilting downwards. It reflects the image of the young woman dozing as she breastfeeds her baby, deaf to the racket her family is making as they guzzle beer and sangria and rowdily clap their hands and sing. She is very young: no more than a girl, with her flowery blouse and black curly hair, a sprig of jasmine woven through it.

The smiling barman pours more beer outside the glass than in it, and excuses himself halfheartedly. He says he's only been doing this for a few days, because his uncle, who owns the place, is ill. His face is pleasant, but pockmarked; he is wearing a black shirt with a white waistcoat, and is constantly smiling and showing his rotten teeth. Señor Alonso changes his mind.

"Listen, make mine a brandy with aniseed instead." He turns and slaps Ringo on the back. "Well, well, how are things? What's new in your neighbourhood?"

"Everything's the same . . . more or less."

"What about the tavern? How is Señora Paquita getting on?"

"Fine."

"And that fat lump of a brother of hers, Agustín?"

"Señor Agustín has bought a new radio for the bar."

"Really? Fantastic." He is still smiling thoughtfully. "And what about Violeta, eh? You like that girl, don't you?"

"Me? Not a bit of it!"

"I can tell from the way you used to look at her. You had your eye on her, don't tell me you didn't."

Ringo shrugs. He's already pestering me, he thinks. He keeps his distance, suspicious. Señor Alonso says nothing for a while, then goes on:

"And how is her mother? How is the healer doing?"

"Oh, her. I don't know . . . Fine."

"Didn't she and her daughter go to live in Badalona?" Ringo shakes his head. "No? She was always talking of leaving, she never felt happy in your neighbourhood. Her mother-in-law, Señora Aurora, has a flower stall in a Badalona market, and lives on her own . . ."

"Does she? I didn't know that."

"So they didn't leave, and everything's still the same."

"No, Señor. Something did happen." Ringo adds in a solemn tone: "Señora Mir tried to kill herself."

"For heaven's sake, kid, what are you saying!"

"She threw herself under a tram. Yes, Señor, she really did. Didn't you hear about it?" he enquires, peeling a prawn. "Everyone saw it, in the street . . ."

"When did it happen? Where?"

"They say the wheel braked a few inches from her head. Seriously. Less than that, Señor." Then, in a relieved voice: "Well, in the end it was nothing more than a dreadful scare. Don't ask me, I don't know anything more. You hear so many things; some people have nothing better to do. And it seems as if Señora Mir likes to have people talking about her . . . the whole day long there are comments and gossip about what she is or isn't doing. She talks of nothing else herself, but I really don't get to hear anything. And besides, I don't care. I don't believe a word of it."

Señor Alonso is staring down at the floor, a troubled look on his face.

"Did she really do that?"

"She did; well, more or less." He feels compelled to glance away, then clears his throat and changes the subject. "We haven't seen you in the neighbourhood for ages, Señor Alonso."

The older man reacts, taking a deep breath and running his hands slowly across the top of the counter.

"Oh, I don't stay up late now like I used to!" he says with a faint smile. "That's a thing of the past. At my age you don't always feel like it. As you can see, I've gone quite rusty."

What he says doesn't make sense, thinks Ringo, because neither in Bar Rosales nor at Señora Mir's when they were together was he known for staying up late. Ringo studies the long, bony hands with their prominent blue veins between the knuckles as they rest calmly on the bleach-scoured wooden counter, and beyond them the man as he lowers his head again, lost in gloomy thoughts. But this only lasts a moment. He straightens up, and says brightly, if in a slightly strained voice:

"Do you know what's what, lad? What has to happen, happens, and that's all there is to it. And it so happens that recently I've decided I don't want any more bad news, or nastiness, or whatever. Yes, damn and blast it, that's enough sadness, I told myself, quite enough of that, kid. I like to call myself kid, you know, even though I'm not of an age for it. Perhaps it's because I spend whole days among a crowd of kids," he

171

concludes, his voice tailing off, then falls silent for a while. All at once he slaps himself on the forehead and exclaims: "Caramba, I was forgetting! Do you mind waiting here a few minutes? I've got to sort something out, but I'll be right back . . . Order another beer, or anything you like, it's on me. Listen, my friend," he says, searching for the barman, "serve the boy whatever he wants." He limps off towards the door: "I won't be five minutes!"

Half an hour and three beers later, Ringo wonders how he can have been so naïve, and his mind is filled with all kinds of suspicions. But the mirror's spell is more powerful than all the rest, and keeps him tied to the bar counter facing five small empty plates: he's wolfed down one of prawns, another of cockles, two spicy potatoes and a Russian salad. He does a mental calculation and realizes that altogether tonight he has drunk five beers – three here and two with El Quique, plus two small glasses of wine he sneaked in Los Cabales, not counting the beer in the doorway at Bar Rosales before setting out on this adventure. He feels more than tipsy, secretly transgressive, almost euphoric; he thinks he must already have been drunk when Señor Alonso accosted him outside, pretending it was by accident. What was behind it? Possibly nothing. The fact is, if he doesn't come back, Ringo has no idea how he's going to be able to pay for what he's had. But why would that lame, rusty fellow leave him in the lurch; where would that get him? To restore a sense of normality, he asks the barman for another beer and a plate of Russian salad.

"Oh, and would you have a bit of bread too?"

The barman's easy way of dealing with the gypsy clan, serving them and joining in the fun from time to time, occasionally paying close attention to the breastfeeding mother, suggests he must in some way be related to them. The mirror, weaver of shadows and blotches of quicksilver, encloses an arcane, dark atmosphere that seems to have nothing to do with the tavern or to reflect what is in it, apart from the sleeping girl with the baby clamped to her breast. It reminds him of a strange, disturbing film in which a bedroom mirror (a larger, cleaner mirror than this one) suddenly no longer reflected the room where it was hanging, but a very different one, with a different atmosphere and decor, another marriage bed and furniture from another era, a silent bedroom lost in time, where a crime had apparently been committed.

The more he stares at it, the more incredibly beautiful and sensual the girl appears, the more confused everything around her; the dark barrel the chair back is resting against is not clear in the mirror, nor is the old bullfight poster pinned to the wall, only her and the child at her breast, and the maternal tenderness of her hands rocking him in his sleep. But the mirror offers only a partial view of them, and so Ringo moves along the bar slightly to frame the image properly, to fix it and record in his memory something he knows he will never forget: the chance transfiguration of the beauty of the girl's face, her head to one side with the lips half-open and her purple, drooping eyelids closed, her child-like arms enfolding the baby, the persistent gentle grip of her hands rocking him, the precariously balanced chair. All around her, the rest of her family go on talking incessantly, and their nasal voices are like the buzz of a swarm of bees. The baby must have finished suckling by now and be asleep as well, he thinks, he doesn't seem to be so tightly fixed to the nipple, and now he can see a bit of the tip of the breast behind the bald head lolling to one side. All this is in the mirror and seems stable and real, far from the deceitful quicksilver blotches and the phantom world of the tavern and its unexpected gypsy atmosphere. It all seems far removed from the contingent, blurred remainder of the scene, and he can sense in his blood the fascination of the future, something impossible to define but more tangible, intense and lived than real life, an internal exaltation that gains sustenance from good omens and unknown opportunities. He has often imagined how exciting life could be thanks to his lucky star, but he has never felt it to be so naturally possible as it is tonight, so certain and clear. Here he can glimpse all the signs that one day are destined to mark his desires and achievements; not only does he firmly believe this, but he can see and assume it so intensely and nervously that he even starts to be wary of his surroundings, as if somebody might be lurking in the shadows, ready to snatch these prospects from him.

All of a sudden the girl in the mirror opens her big, intensely black eyes, fixes them on him with a smile, and sticks out her tongue. Almost simultaneously, Señor Alonso's dark, bony hand clasps his shoulder.

"I'm sorry, lad, I was kept longer than I expected." He looks askance at the noisy flamenco revelry. "I can see you haven't been bored."

"No chance of that."

"My God, what a pain. And no-one can stop them."

"Don't you like gypsies, Señor Alonso?"

The older man stares at him for a moment, eyes twinkling.

"My dear boy, gypsies have been my lifelong friends. I live surrounded by gypsies and illiterate migrants from the south who are as quick to use their fists as they are to kick a ball, kids like you who dream of becoming someone in life and escaping from their wretched surroundings as quickly as they can." His voice is not the same as before he left, the words sound thick with saliva and he gives off a strong smell of aniseed and brandy. "But what I can't stand is the way they get together to celebrate. I know what I'm talking about . . . Well, as you can see, it's nothing like the Rosales in here, is it?"

"You're right there."

"We can leave whenever you say the word. Or would you like something more?" He looks him up and down, judging his condition. "It's late, and they're about to close. I'll go with you to the tram stop."

"There's no need."

"I think there is. Look, if you miss the last tram you're going to have to walk home, and it's a good stretch up to Gràcia. I'm in the same boat, but first I have to go back to my friend's place."

"I thought you lived around here . . . Do you know something? I'd like to live in this district."

"Don't say that. Nobody likes to live in shit. Well, tomorrow we have to get up early. Hey, barman!" he clicks his fingers to attract the waiter's attention. As he does so, a blue ink stain becomes visible between his thumb and first finger. "Give me a packet of Virginia tobacco and tell me what's owing."

"Well, I'd like to," Ringo insists despondently, staring at the hand opening the wallet. That stain wasn't there when he left, he thinks, and then all at once he starts to feel sick. His head hurts and his hands are sweaty. He finishes the beer and mumbles: "Anyway, thanks for the invitation, Señor Alonso."

"Are you feeling alright?"

"Fantastic. Fantastic."

In the mirror, the girl with the flowery blouse rocks the baby, her eyes closed once more. Again, the light around her grows dim, the tavern fades, so do the barrels and the two tables with the carousing gypsies, the bullfight poster and the food hanging from the ceiling, everything around her becomes dark and hidden, and then vanishes completely. As Ringo peels away from the counter, he glances at her one last time.

A short while later he finds himself in Las Ramblas waiting for the number 30 opposite the terrace outside the Cosmos café. Señor Alonso is still alongside him, offering him constant, incisive support: lost in the shadows, his austere face has somehow taken on a vaguely Faustian outline, with a deceptive gaze and a cardboard nose. The tram stop is deserted, and the café is shut. Ringo excuses himself at the entrance to the public lavatories and rushes down into them on his own, because he knows he is about to be sick. He hardly has time to rest his hands on the scaly lavatory wall of the lavatory before his stomach starts to churn and he brings up the first mouthful of vomit, which splashes his shoes. Afterwards, he rinses his mouth with tap water and cleans the tips of his shoes with toilet paper. Back up in the street he still feels giddy, and is convinced that his flies are open and one of his shoelaces is undone, and yet he doesn't dare lower his gaze to look because he's frightened his head might start to spin. It is obvious that the lame ex-footballer will not leave him alone until the tram arrives. And he keeps on talking to him.

"What happened to your hand? I guess it won't stop you making rings and earrings."

He shrugs and peers down at the sling. He moves his fingers, but can't feel them. The blood's gone to sleep, he thinks.

"My mother's looking for a job for me," he says, as if dreaming.

"That's good." The thick, dark lips broaden in a smile. "You'll have to learn another trade, but I'm sure you'll make a go of it."

"Of course."

"What would you like to do?"

Ringo shrugs again.

"The other day I saw a sign in a music shop: they wanted an assistant. I'm not sure, I might try that. I could be a piano-tuner . . ."

Two municipal street cleaners cross the central promenade carrying a hosepipe over their shoulders as if it was – he thinks he must write this down in his black oilskin notebook – a huge dead snake. Bending slightly at the waist as if trying to sell a dummy on the pitch, the ex-footballer lifts his foot from the pavement and comes closer, hand in his jacket pocket.

"Now you go straight home, and tomorrow's another day, alright?" He appears to hesitate for a second, then says: "Look, seeing that I bumped into you . . . Could I ask you to do me a favour? Could you leave something from me in Bar Rosales?" He keeps his hand in his pocket as he questions him with his eyes. "You told me you still went there, didn't you?"

"That's right."

"I've got something for Señora Paquita. Could you give it her from me? She knows what it's about. Would you do me that favour?"

Aaagh! His stomach churns again, and he is on the point of throwing up once more.

"A message for Señora Paquita? Of course."

"Could you give it her tomorrow morning, as discreetly as possible? She's been expecting it for ages . . ."

"Well, she's hardly ever there in the mornings. But her brother Señor Agustín is."

"No, not to Señor Agustín. It's something you need to hand personally to his sister. I'd go myself, but I can't: I have to go on a trip first thing tomorrow." He takes a pale-pink envelope out of his pocket. It's sealed and has a name written in the top corner, a name beginning with a capital V, which Ringo cannot completely make out, although he knows full well to whom it's addressed. "Try to give it to her without anyone seeing you, right? When there aren't many people in the bar." He is suddenly anxious, doubtful, and so he adds with a smile, seeking his support: "That way we'll avoid any gossip, won't we? I was even thinking . . . You know the address . . ." he pauses again, hesitates. "No, there would be too many questions. Better for Señora Paquita to take care of that. As I said, she'll know what needs to be done. Here it is."

Aha, so that's what this was all about, he thinks. So it seems the famous affair is not over yet. Still feeling sick, afraid he might black out, and choking back bittersweet saliva, Ringo takes the envelope in his bandaged hand, because with the other one he is feeling for change in the left pocket of his jacket: a couple of coins have fallen through a hole in the lining, but he can't reach them and is worried he won't have the forty cents he needs for the tram. All at once, with the letter in his anesthetised hand, pinned gently in his numb fingers, he feels downhearted and annoyed. In the alternative world that is being created in complete opposition to what is real (except possibly what he can see in the mirror) there can be no place for such sordid, depressing tales of woe like those of the voluptuous blonde and her crippled lover. You try to be friendly and polite, to always be ready to do someone a favour, and look where it gets you, dammit. He can feel how thin the envelope is: it must contain a single folded sheet, most likely an extremely short letter. But together with the envelope, there's a five peseta note!

"Got it. And five pesetas!"

"They're yours. So you can take your girl to the cinema."

"Oh, thanks! But you shouldn't have . . ."

"Don't answer back. And be careful you don't lose it." He takes the

177

envelope and the banknote from him, puts them both in Ringo's jacket pocket, then nervously does it up. "Better in there. The truth is, I don't know if it will be of any use, that letter should have reached its destination long ago . . . I asked Señora Paquita to be discreet, and I'm asking the same of you. It's a private matter, you understand."

"Of course, of course. I'll t . . . take it."

"Are you feeling alright?"

"Fantastic," he mumbles, though his head is whirling.

Once again in his mind's eye he is confronting the shadowy mirror in the tavern, where now the quicksilver is like a leprous sore devouring the young girl's face; at the same time he nods, head down, staring at his feet, accepting the loss and the disenchantment, and finally notices that yes, one of his shoelaces is completely undone. He is feeling for somewhere to hold on to, thinking if I bend down I'll fall flat on my face when he realises that Señor Alonso's long, bony fingers are already busily at work, just like his mother's nimble fingers when she ties his bandage or buttons up his shirt, with an incredible, tender agility, so that in the blink of an eye the laces are tied again. But it is not the diligently attentive fingers that surprise and disturb him, nor the evidence of how drunk he is, which obliges him to accept help if he wants to get home safe and sound, but the fact of seeing this man on his knees before him as if he is trying to embrace his feet for a favour granted.

"It's what I do best," the man says, straightening up. "I'm an expert at tying footballers' boots and boxers' gloves. Here comes your tram . . . Ah, and one last thing. Señora Paquita is bound to ask where you saw me. You needn't mention this district that you like so much," he adds with a knowing smile. "Neither Calle Robadors or Calle San Ramón, get it?"

"Of course not, Señor."

Ringo's throat feels rough and full of bile; his head is spinning, and his feet are someone else's. He jumps on to the rear platform before the tram has even come to a halt. Goodbye and good luck, Señor Alonso. He turns round, holding out a hand that hangs in mid-air because the tram has set off again. He stands on the platform for some distance, letting himself be seen by the man standing under the bleary light from the streetlamp, hands in his pockets and looking very correct, tall despite his limp, or perhaps because of it, the bad leg slightly behind the other as if unsure whether it can lift off the ground, while all around him the night closes in, leaving him increasingly small, solitary and hemmed in, until finally Ringo sees him turn and go limping off down Las Ramblas.

Five pesetas! Before they reach Calle Santa Ana, Ringo stealthily steps down from the moving tram and runs across the central promenade to the other side of the road. He gets caught up in a group of revellers outside the Poliorama theatre. He feels for the banknote and envelope in his pocket, and as he quickens his pace tries to work out where he is. He doesn't need to see the envelope again, but wants to reassure himself about the money; he takes it out to look at it, then stows it in his pocket once more. Five pesetas is not enough to get him into El Jardín, or La Gaucha, although possibly if some young whore took pity on him and offered him a reduction . . . But no, no whoring. He calculates that the best way to get back to Los Joseles without bumping into Señor Alonso (by now he has no doubt that he lives in the Barrio Chino, probably in some dark side street, in an attic at the top of a narrow, slimy flight of stairs) is to take Calle Pintor Fortuny, make a detour round the inner streets and come out into Calle Hospital, cross it and then go down as far as Calle San Pablo until he reaches the corner with Calle San Ramón.

The pockmarked barman tells him he is about to close, but welcomes him with a smile and serves him the night's last glass of beer. Making an effort to appear stiffly erect, stubborn and befuddled, Ringo returns to his post at the bar as a solitary, fanciful dreamer. All of a sudden he is engulfed in a sweet aroma of jasmine. It takes him a while to realise what is going on. She has climbed down from the mirror and its enchantment and is washing up glasses behind the bar, her sleeves rolled and her thick black hair covering her face. Muttering under her breath, and obviously in a very bad mood, she keeps casting sideways glances at the barman, who is coming and going from the table to the counter with jugs, glasses and dirty plates. In one of his journeys, the waiter bends forward to whisper something in her ear, but she avoids him, muttering confused insults: a curse on your dead folk, I've had it to here shedding tears . . At the same time, the group of gypsies has come to the end of its merrymaking, and is about to leave. They have all got up and are gathering their things; the baby is wailing in the arms of an old woman standing by the door, and the two oldest men are settling the bill at the bar. Ringo gulps down his beer, and from that moment on, time becomes strangely retractable. When he pushes his glass towards her with a cautious, beseeching hand, she takes it quickly without looking at him, but their fingers brush against each other, and through the mass of dark hair he glimpses a fleeting smile on her disdainful lips. By then though he has gone through the suddenly misty mirror and finds himself on the floor, one side of his face pressed against the sawdust strewn with prawn shells, gobs of spit, and toothpicks. As if in a dream, he hears gypsy voices trying to wake him by tapping him on the cheek, it's nothing, my boy, come back, get up. She is also close by, looking him in the face in a friendly way for the first time, offering him a glass of cold, bitter coffee. As she brings it up to his mouth and he takes slow, obedient sips, her small, dark hands give off the acrid smell of bleach. What happened to me? he stutters, and feels to see if the envelope and the money are still in his pocket, but at that moment a black cat comes walking towards them with elastic steps, she strokes it and the animal arches its back lazily, and all this distracts his attention. Now it's home for you, my boy, he hears from the sweetest cold-ridden voice he has ever heard, while her agile, caressing hands slide his arm back in the sling, shake the sawdust from his hair, and slip the jacket over his shoulders. The young waiter refuses to charge him for the drink, and accompanies him to the door in a friendly, concerned manner. When he is ten metres further up the same pavement as the tavern, he hears the metal shutter clattering down behind him, with a crash that mingles with a thunderclap down towards the port. The cobbles of Calle San Ramón gleam like dirty silver.

The first raindrops start to fall before he reaches Las Ramblas. At this time of the morning there are no trams or metro. So much the better, Ringo, you can go back home on foot, with the threat of rain in the air. First up Las Ramblas, then across the deserted, spectral Plaza de Cataluña, up the empty Paseo de Gràcia, turn onto El Diagonal until you reach Paseo de San Juan, from there up to Travesera and right again into Calle Escorial. Out of the deep shadows in some doorways he sees the girl in the mirror beckoning to him, undoing her blouse. Rain in his shoes. The pink message in his pocket. Why should I care about that damned letter? Up Calle Escorial and straight on, don't get distracted, on the right avoid the shadows of Avenida General Mola-Mulo-Mola, as the Rat-catcher calls him, carry on uphill, making sure you keep your balance on the edge of the pavement by the gutter that by now is almost overflowing with water until you reach the blasted La Salud neighbourhood, until you have passed your future, wonderful life as a famous pianist, that's what you should do, kid, that's what you're going to do, so stop feeling sorry for yourself. All of a sudden, as he is crossing Plaza Joanich, the rain starts to come down more heavily. He takes his jacket off and covers his soaked head with it, and while I'm at it, I'll cover that shadowy mirror hanging in front of my eyes.

Leaving the square behind, he falls over three times because he insists on walking along the edge of the pavement in a state of high euphoria. Even the rain seems to him like a blessing. Aren't those two shiny dots the red eyes of a rat staring at him from the black opening of a sewer? Greetings, comrade rat, let's be friends, soon we'll be swimming together in the shadows! Shortly afterwards he stops to urinate against the wall of the empty lot of Can Compte, in the darkest part of Calle Escorial, but before his hands reach his flies he realises they have been unbuttoned all this time, possibly all night, since long before he went down into the public lavatory on the Ramblas, perhaps ever since he left home to go and sit outside the entrance to Bar Rosales . . . Well, and so what, enjoying the rain on his face, eyes closed and his mouth open, you've lived your first night of whoring in the Barrio Chino, and by chance you've experienced more surprises and emotions than you bargained for. He still feels nauseous and disorientated, but the future is where it should be, everything is where it should be, including the book of short stories he instinct-ively gropes for in the baggy jacket pocket: yet again he can hear thunder crashing over the endless savannah, the horizon lit by distant flashes of lightning, he can hear the roar of the leopard lost on the summit, sniffing at its own solitary, frozen death, the crunch of its paws in the snow . . . A tune is rattling around his head, but again he cannot identify it. Hooded and hunched in the rain, he tries to make out the golden stream of urine as it mixes with the rain, and beneath his muddy feet he catches again a glimpse of a subterranean world full of rats and slimy tunnels, of regurgitated, pestilent waters, and he tries to find himself in an image of himself watching over the disturbing girl sleeping forever in future time. He is thinking that perhaps this image holds the answer to every-thing, an explanation for the world, when he suddenly feels an empty sensation in the pit of his stomach, and from out of the shadows he has a sense of foreboding that sends his hand shooting to his inside pocket.

A split second later, he turns his head and thinks he sees the pink envelope floating in the rush of filthy water sweeping along the gutter. Ghost-like and fleeting, the letter comes to a halt for a moment by the open drain, then spins round on itself as it is about to be swallowed up. Face down, then face up, the water has almost completely erased the name of the person to whom it was addressed. The swirling torrent holds it up for a moment, long enough for him to be able to bend down and save it, but without knowing why, he does not move as the rain lashes down, and watches as it spins like a carousel, round and round, shrouded by the cloudy water, until all at once the drain finally swallows it and it disappears into the abyss.

"Farewell, Señora Mir."

12

MARIA MONTEZ'S TURBAN

"Halt, bullet!" declares the solemn but kindly looking Sacred Heart of Jesus that peers out at visitors from its plaque on the front door of the apartment. It was nailed there six years earlier by the ex-Blue Division combatant Ramón Mir in a gesture of thanks for his having returned from the Eastern Front miraculously safe and sound. That day, using the butt of his pistol, and with a mixture of patriotic fervour and wounded manhood, muttering prayers of gratitude for having been spared a Bolshevik bullet, he hammered in the nails of an inadmissible, secret and vengeful rancour, and then polished the plaque with a cloth until it shone. Nowadays the life-saving image is somewhat dented and chipped at the edges, and the finger pointing to the flaming red heart shows signs of rust. The bright colours have faded, and the divine finger's rusty tip contaminates not only the radiant organ but also the kind eyes that seem to be saying to Ringo now: Don't worry, my boy, nobody in this house will call you to account for what happened, because nobody will ever know, least of all the person the letter was meant for, who would most likely die of heartbreak if she ever found out.

Straightening the sling round his arm, Ringo prepares to ring the bell. He could never have imagined that one day he would call at this door and put himself in the hands of Señora Mir, the last person in the world he wants to see. Despite the fact that there is no reason she should find out about his night-time encounter with Señor Alonso, and still less about the stupid errand he had given him, because he hasn't mentioned that even to El Quique, and even though he thinks that what happened could easily be remedied (he could go the very next day to look for the lame ex-footballer, who would be bound to understand and forgive him, and possibly might even write another letter and entrust that to him) he cannot rid himself of a vague sense of unease, an enervating melancholy. This is why, when he comments to his mother that his shoulder and back are hurting more and more, and she recommends he has a good back rub with alcohol, he is immediately on his guard.

"I don't need any back rub! I'll soon be completely fine!"

In his opinion, the persistent pain is down to his habit of sleeping on his right side. His mother does not agree. She says the pain is due, among other things, to the fact that he stubbornly continues to wear his arm in a sling far longer than necessary, because he enjoys going out with it like that, doubtless because he wants to show off to some girl or other. Why is he still playing games? The wound has healed, the hand is no longer swollen, and the scruffy bandage which he himself has been changing in recent days is also unnecessary. He retorts that it's precisely now that he most needs the support of the sling, because his shoulder aches terribly, and so does his back.

"On the contrary," his mother scolds him. "It hurts terribly because you keep your arm up from the moment you get up to when you go back to bed. That's not a normal posture, Son. I ran into Victoria yesterday as I was leaving the clinic, I told her about it and we agreed you'd go and see her."

"Oh, no!"

"Oh, yes! And don't play any more games. A good back rub and you'll no longer feel like going around showing off in my pretty scarf. Victoria is delighted. In fact, she told me she wanted to talk to you."

"To me? What for?"

"I've no idea."

She can't want anything from me, he thinks quickly, and yet again reassures himself: there's no way she can know we came across that lame guy in the Barrio Chino . . . not unless that sex-mad El Quique started bragging in the bar.

"She wouldn't say," his mother goes on, "but she winked at me while she was powdering her nose, and I could guess . . ."

"Whatever it is, I don't want to go!"

"My goodness, she isn't going to eat you!" She smiles as she adds: "Do you know something? I could swear she was thinking of her daughter. I bet she wants to find her a boyfriend, so you should be flattered."

"What are you talking about? Is that why you're forcing me to go to her place? Look, my shoulder hardly hurts at all! See how well I can move my arm!"

"I don't want to hear any more complaints." Her voice hardens. "Victoria has generously offered her services, and you should be grateful. A good back rub isn't going to hurt you; quite the opposite. Besides," she adds in a weary tone, "I've heard she's losing clients. They haven't called on her at all at the residence for ages now, they say she isn't as good as she used to be. The poor woman is going through a bad patch, and I don't want her to think we've lost faith. So you're going to see her . . . Come on, Son, be reasonable for once."

Be reasonable. How is he supposed to be reasonable? Three days after his nocturnal adventure in the seedy part of the city and his eventful return in the rain and lightning, he still cannot get things straight. Apart from the enchantment provided by the beer, the quicksilver and other shadows in the ever-present mirror, and that ill-defined promise of the longed-for sexual adventure, all he retains of that night is a confused memory he cannot disentangle however hard he tries, and which left him feeling cheated and stupid. Your first night whoring, and you fall in love! How dumb can you get! Struggling with hazy thoughts of exoneration, blaming what happened on his being drunk for the first time in his life, which left him senseless and groggy by the end of the night, he finds it hard to admit that he really saw the drain swallowing the letter in the rainstorm, that he realised what was going on and did nothing to save the envelope from ending up in the sewer. Sometimes he prefers to believe it was taken from his pocket together with the banknote; the girl's small hands fluttering like wings round his face, hands smelling of bleach enveloping him with movements that were both urgent and affectionate . . . But why would they steal a letter without an address from his pocket? Who could possibly be interested in that? Could they have thought it had money in it? Or perhaps what happened was that the quick, stealthy hand, whoever it belonged to (but not hers, please, not hers) felt the five-peseta note and an envelope instead of a wallet, and decided that was better than nothing? In any case, he finds it hard to imagine who could have tried to pick his pocket, and where.

And yet whether the envelope and the money were stolen or lost, and despite the persistent sensation that all this happened in the recurrent ambit of shadowy mirrors and dreams, places only inhabited in novels and films, and although he tries over and over again to dismiss the matter as unimportant, he still feels disquiet. The mistake of doing nothing to stop the letter going down the drain (even though he is not entirely convinced he really lived the episode, and sometimes thinks he dreamt it), that simple, unfortunate mistake, which can only be put down to his calculated indifference, has taken root in his mind. However much he tries to convince himself it was not important, that if the blasted letter is lost for ever, then goodbye and good riddance, and to hell with the silly lovers from Montaña Pelada; however much he wants to forget it, he cannot. Of course, he could have stuffed the envelope under his vest or in his underpants, and made sure it was still there by the way it rubbed against his cock. Why on earth didn't he check he still had it with him when he left the tavern? In his mind's eye he can still see the black cat, an arrogant, arched reminder of that night, stealing into the bar for the girl to gently stroke it, and yet he has no idea if he was awake or saw it in his sleep. Often this feeling of guilt is nothing more than a sheet of paper crumpling next to his heart, as if he was still carrying the envelope in his inside pocket, and at these moments he asks himself what it would have cost him to have concealed it better, as he had always done with the jewels whenever he had to deliver them and travelled in packed metro and trams, or walked through the dark back streets of the Barrio Gótico to the tiny workshop of an engraver or stone-setter, or along the soft, empty corridors of the Ritz Hotel to knock on the door of a suite and surprise some high-class kept woman by giving her an emerald and aquamarine necklace. On all those occasions he had carried and protected with body and mind (always alert and responsible) objects that were much more valuable than a ridiculous love letter (or its exact opposite) – treasures of platinum and diamond whose loss would have carried serious conse-quences for him, although perhaps only bringing a fleeting sense of disappointment to the woman they were meant for at the delay in receiving the longed-for gift – but would never have caused, prolonged or aggravated Señora Mir's pathetic vigil, as she waddled every other day into Bar Rosales to ask if the letter had arrived, whether or not it contained a conciliatory message or a definitive goodbye.

The previous day's hangover, as he ran errands for his mother half-asleep – going to collect the staples and bread on the ration card, then to buy a lettuce, two green peppers, and a kilo of salad tomatoes (which made him remember Grandma Tecla's last visit to Barcelona, her basket filled with tomatoes and aubergines from her vegetable garden, apricots and peaches from the vine, as well as eggs and a skinned rabbit, and led him to wonder why on earth he had refused to go back with her to her village while his mother was looked for a job for him, a job he already knows he is not going to like) – had momentarily excused him from having to analyse what had happened and evaluate the consequences. It was only during the following weeks, when his sense of unease persisted, that he began to ask himself questions and to invent excuses: why worry when it was more than likely that the blasted letter didn't contain the good news Señora Mir was hoping for? Besides, what if it were not exactly what could be called a love letter? What if it was a cowardly goodbye, and not the apology she so desired, nor a wish for another meeting, a passionate re-encounter? He recalls what Señor Alonso had said, and the resigned expression on his face when he gave him the envelope: A strictly private matter. What if he wrote that he never wanted to see her again, that he no longer loved her, that for him the relationship was definitely over, there's no future in it, sweetheart, it was good and nice while it lasted, don't take this badly, but farewell, etc? Wasn't that what really suited such a rancid, absurd affair between two old, discredited lovers, stale leftovers from a past of God knows what mismatches and failures, that the two of them doubtless had conspired to forget? Weren't those words – there's no future in it – precisely the most appropriate in this case? As with so many people Ringo knows, it was written on their faces: like his father's friends in the Rat-catcher Brigade, like Señor Sucre and Capitán Blay, like the old card or dominoes players in the tavern on those interminable Sunday afternoons, like his own mother, and occasionally, when he stands there staring into space, at home or elsewhere, thinking no-one can see him, like the Rat-catcher himself, the man who is always so mocking and foul-mouthed.

Ringo even tried to convince himself that at some point during that eventful night (lived or dreamed, by now it was the same) when he stuck his hand into his pocket to make sure the letter was still there, his rain-soaked fingers had somehow felt the ill-omened message, the unwanted, dreaded news and the pain it was bound to cause Señora Mir. And when he thought of her wish to be quickly forgiven and reconciled with her man, a feeling she had so often expressed in public, and which she nourished day after day, a sentiment which seemed so deep-seated and persistent, so shameless, so oblivious to wagging tongues or even ridicule – if he thought of this, and that perhaps the message was the final rupture, the death of the hope she had kept alive until now, a cruel farewell rather than a renewed vow of love, then he almost managed to convince himself that she would have preferred the letter never to have reached her, and so she had been spared a fatal disenchantment.

He was sure this is what it must have been. Otherwise, if what was in the message was forgiveness and renewed affection, why did Señor Alonso have to hide behind a go-between, why didn't he hand her the envelope himself? Why didn't he want to show his face, why didn't he want to go anywhere near Bar Rosales? So that he didn't have to explain himself to anybody, not even Señora Paquita. Ringo could see clearly now why he left him on his own for so long in that dive in the Barrio Chino: so he could go and write his shameful farewell, no doubt in his own home (if not, where could he have got the paper and the envelope? It was impossible that he had them on him) and put an end to the affair without having to be seen in the neighbourhood, taking advantage of their casual (or perhaps not so casual) encounter . . . Because it must have been true that he still felt sorry for Señora Mir. Nothing that man said or did that night was by accident; nothing except perhaps when he bent down to tie Ringo's shoelaces and wipe off any traces of vomit while he was at it: and it is this, precisely the memory of this, his deft hands discreetly rubbing his shoe, that most upsets Ringo and occasionally makes him feel really bad. Why would a mature, experienced man like him, an ex-footballer from a historic club whom they say knew years of glory, somebody who always won respect in the tavern for both his authority and his discretion, whether he was talking about women or games of chance or whatever, why would a man like that suddenly show himself as so needy, so anxious to please a boy he hardly knew? Was he so desperate for a go-between, was it so difficult and complicated for him to free himself from a miserable little love affair with his bargain-basement lover?

Three days before his mother forces him to go and visit Señora Mir, one evening when he is returning home after exchanging a book in the Calle Asturias store, as he is walking up from Plaza Rovira he sees El Quique, Roger and the Cazorla brothers standing on the corner of Calle Argentona, about thirty metres from Bar Rosales. Doubled up with laughter, El Quique signals him to come over quickly, because something hilarious is about to happen. Also with them is Tito, the hairdresser's son. He is on his bike, chewing on a sweet, one foot on the edge of the pavement and the other on the raised pedal. There's a gleam in his eyes as he stares at the bar, poised to sprint off towards it. He has one hand on the handlebar; in the other he is clutching a crumpled envelope.

"Wait, Tito," says Roger. "Don't attack until you see her come out."

"Give it to her and race off as fast as you can," says Rafa. "And you'll have earned yourself another sweet."

Ringo tries to snatch the letter, but Roger stops him, pretending to punch him in the stomach. Ringo takes the blows on his body, keeping his hand in his sling.

"Let me see that, Tito," he says to the boy.

"There's no time, she's going to come out any second."

"No time for what?"

"We've got a little present for her!" says El Quique triumphantly. "She's in there snivelling to Señora Paquita, asking her about the letter for the hundredth time . . . It's a hoot, *nano*! When she comes out, Tito's going to give her our little present and we'll split our sides laughing!"

"Why didn't you tell me before?" says Ringo, shoving Roger away to stop him punching. "Be careful with my arm, you animal!"

"I never touched you!"

"What's wrong with you, *nano*?" El Quique looks at him wide-eyed, but the gap-toothed, fun-loving smile between the bushy sideburns that now adorn his round face is no longer that of a young boy obsessed with fantasies about tits and arses. He's been working for three months as an apprentice lathe operator, and the others have also started going their own way: Roger is cleaning trams in the Plaza Lesseps depot, *Chato* Morales is an apprentice mechanic in a garage over in Vallcarca and is hardly ever seen in the neighbourhood any more, Rafa Cazorla works in a locksmith's on Calle Torrijos, and his brother is a bell-boy in a hotel on Las Ramblas. Ringo suddenly feels like sending them all to hell, these stupid apprentices of nothing, El Quique above all.

"Come on, you idiots, what are you plotting?"

"Nothing!" protests Rafa. "We just want to see how she reacts."

"What's that Tito is holding?"

"It's a joke, dammit," El Quique says. "It's just a bit of fun with Violeta's mother. What's wrong, have you got something against it?" He doubles up with laughter again: "Ha, ha ha! Besides, it was your idea!"

"Yes, don't you remember?" says Roger. "One day when she was knocking it back in Bar Rosales you drew a big flying prick on a piece of paper and wanted to put it in her coat pocket . . ."

"I don't remember. Give me that, Tito. I want to see it."

He doesn't have time. Tito, who hasn't taken his eyes off the bar doorway for a second, pushes off from the edge of the pavement and hurtles as far as the next corner. Señora Mir has just left the bar and is crossing the street in her white coat and slippers, patting her hair and swaying her hips in her usual nonchalant manner. The tiny cyclist catches up with her in the middle of the road, loops round her a couple of times, pedalling frantically, and she comes to a halt and smiles at him, until she notices the envelope in his hand. The boy stretches out his arm and hands it to her, head down, still pedalling, then races off down the street towards Plaza Rovira. Señora Mir reaches the far pavement with the envelope in her hand, opens it and takes out the piece of paper. She stands there staring at it, wary and startled. Her face falls, and she glances up almost at once. She puts a hand out to the wall for support, and looks all round her with piteous eyes, without seeing anyone or understanding why somebody has played this trick on her. Ringo meanwhile has hidden behind El Quique and Roger, who are writhing with laughter on the street corner, together with Rafa. Still motionless on the pavement, Señora Mir reaches out to the wall again, glancing down at the paper and shaking her head. Almost immediately, Ringo finds himself trying to throttle El Quique by the shirt collar.

"What have you done?"

"'Hey, let go of me! What's wrong with you? It's only a drawing . . ."

"A winged prick, Ringo," says Rafa Cazorla. "With hair and everything!"

"And balls like hard-boiled eggs!" Sito Cazorla guffaws.

"And what d'you think we wrote underneath? I'm coming flying, my love!"

"For Chrissake, Ringo, what's got into you?" says El Quique. "We drew winged pricks like that until we were sick of them, don't you remember?"

"This isn't the same, you idiot. You really are an idiot."

"Thanks a lot, friend," El Quique says, laughing. "But look at the expression on her fat face, just look!"

Peeping round the corner, they see her crumpling the paper with her fist across her stomach, then with her face down on her chest, turn to look where the laughter is coming from. They dart back quickly, but she has seen them, although Ringo thinks he might have escaped because he was hidden behind the others. Slowly, pushing her feet into the pink slippers and shaking her head in a sad, resigned gesture, she starts walking up the pavement once more until she reaches the doorway to her building.

Tito reappears on his bike to claim his second sweet, and the three friends smile at Ringo, pleased with the effect of their dirty trick and awaiting his approval.

"You're a lot of bastards," he grunts, turning his back on them and walking off.

"You're the bastard!" shouts El Quique. Then he mutters to himself, bewildered: "What's got into him?"

Now, face to face with the dented plaque of the Sacred Heart, he settles his arm in the sling and finally makes up his mind to ring the bell. A few seconds' wait, the sound of shuffling feet inside, and Violeta opens the door with the same suspicious sloth evident in her downcast, languid eyes, with faint purple lines beneath them. She has a towel wrapped round her head like a turban; it was once blue and is torn in several places;

she has on a pair of backless sandals and a sleeveless grey cotton housecoat that is so threadbare it looks like a cobweb sticking to her body.

"What do you want?"

"Your mother's expecting me."

"Now?"

"Yes, now."

The girl blinks slowly at him, bends her head forward slightly, and touches some strands of hair on the back of her neck that have escaped the towel. Ringo is not at all surprised at her sly glance or furtive movements.

"What's wrong, don't you believe me? Your mother told me to come at seven."

The line of her thigh is accentuated as she leans again the doorjamb. She looks at him in a bored but not hostile way. She takes her time and finally says, "It's not seven yet," her voice almost inaudible.

Narrowing her eyes, and in such an offhand tone he can barely follow her, she tells him that her mother is busy attending to Señora Elvira, the butcher's mother. The poor woman is half-paralysed, she has to be given leg-stretching exercises, and these take time. It would be better if he came back in half or three-quarters of an hour, but if he wants to wait in the dining-room and keep the butcher company . . .

Chat with Señor Samsó? No way. He's a complete numbskull. Ringo has never been in the dining-room that also functions as a waiting area, but he can picture the butcher sitting there, alone and bored, looking after his ancient mother's crutches, and delighted to have someone to pass the time with. No way.

"I'll wait out here."

Violeta shrugs, but doesn't close the door. She stares at him for a few moments, and then says in the same apathetic voice:

"We'll find something. Come on in."

Wearily, she opens the door wide, and when he is in the hall suddenly closes it behind him. She pulls the collar of her housecoat up and turns her back on him, her body moving as if it was a burden, a heavy weight or a

193

tedious responsibility, as if its striking attractions had nothing to do with her. She walks down the corridor with reluctant steps; a radio somewhere in the apartment is playing music. Beneath the pale ivory of her bare heels, the sandals clack across the mosaic tiles. "And you, where can you be, who knows what adventure you're living, how far you are from me," say words of the song. It's a big apartment full of old-fashioned furniture, with a sugary, stale smell to it; the dark corridor ends in an explosion of light flooding into the dining-room from the rear veranda with its faded coloured-glass panes. But instead of taking him there, Violeta leads him into a small room halfway down the corridor.

It looks like a laundry room, but is obviously something more than that. There is hardly enough space for the ironing board laden with a pile of washing, the narrow iron bed pushed against the wall and covered in a green eiderdown, two wicker chairs, and a table with a heating dish under it and empty glass jars on top. There's a faint smell of roast almonds in the air. It's not a radio that's playing the music, but a small record player perched precariously on a folding chair. On the bed are different-coloured cushions, a naked china doll with no hair, two cinema magazines, a few old copies of *Flechas y Pelayos*, an open sewing basket, and a fan. Pinned on the wall, Errol Flynn, his arm in a sling just like Ringo, smiles encouragingly at him in a photograph from "The Charge of the Light Brigade". Alongside it are two programmes from the Salón Cibeles advertising the orchestras of Mario Visconti and Gene Kim.

"You can wait here," says Violeta, switching off the record player and picking up several sleeves and records from the bed.

"Is this your room?" There's no response. "You're lucky to have a room of your own. I sleep in the corridor, in a truckle bed like yours. There's only one bedroom in our flat; we sublet, you know." Silence. "What were you listening to?"

"I wasn't."

"That's a lie. It's a song I know you like a lot."

"You can sit on the bed if you like. You're going to have to wait a while."

"Last year, at the saint's day fiesta, you danced it with me."

"Did I? I don't remember."

"A rotten lie." As he flops on to the bed, he drops his good hand to his hip, as if he is drawing a gun from its holster. "Got you bang to rights, sister. 'Perfidy', the song is called."

As ever, he has mixed feelings as he observes her. Since she has looked several times at the arm in a sling across his chest, even if her deep, dark eyes are still cold and distant, he is expecting her to ask about it – he's hoping she will. But Violeta doesn't say a word. She stands by the door, arms folded, every so often casting him a sideways glance, disdainful but conscious she is attracting furtive scrutiny of her legs and the triangle formed in the material between her thighs and stomach, a confluence of slight creases curving in towards her pelvis. Ringo's eyes narrow beneath the imaginary shade of a cowboy hat. He is secretly annoyed at himself for not being able to avoid the images that this-girl-he-does-not-like-at-all conjures up, and so, in an automatic gesture of self-defence, he hastens to remind himself yet again of the strident mismatch of shapes – these rounded hips are completely out of kilter with such tiny tits and with the girl's narrow, weak chest – but this disharmony (he cannot help but realise yet again, whether he wants to or not) this dissonance between childish and adult forms that will soon be voluptuous, is precisely what attracts him.

"What about that lame fellow?" says Ringo at last, as if casually. "Doesn't he come round anymore: is his leg better then?"

"How should I know?"

"Is it true someone took a bite out of him in a football game, and that's why it's shorter, and with the foot turned in . . . ?"

"Why should that interest me?"

She stares fixedly down at her fingernails, as if to close the matter. But he needs to insist, to goad her; he has come here full of trepidation, fearful of having to face Señora Mir, and he has no wish to be intimidated by her daughter.

195

"A strange guy. But I became a friend of his at the bar. Well, almost a friend. And your mother thinks a lot of him, everyone knows that. Until recently they were more than friends, they were a couple, weren't they . . . he was her boyfriend, wasn't he? What do you say, Violeta?"

"I say shit."

"They also say – and please don't be angry – they also say it won't take her long to find someone else, and that it would be the best thing for her . . ." He falls silent, waiting expectantly for her answer: he would like her to agree with him, and say that yes, her mother is looking for another man. "What do you think?"

"I think shit." She quickly reaches up to the blue towel, making sure it is tied tightly round her head, and continues staring at him. She plays with the wet strands on the back of her neck, but doesn't seem nervous. Finally she adds: "Is what my mother does or doesn't do that important to you?"

"I couldn't give a damn, as you well know. It's just what I hear. That if she found a new boyfriend she'd quickly forget the lame guy, and that it would be better for her. Of course it would. Mind you, it's not me saying this, it's what I heard in the bar. What do you think?"

Violeta looks at him with an aggrieved expression.

"Why are you telling me all this gossip? Why are you talking about couples and boyfriends, and asking all these . . . I don't know . . . smutty questions?"

"I'm sorry, I didn't think you'd take it like that."

"Will you please shut up about it?" She closes her eyes as if they were stinging. When she opens them again she notices the loose bandage hanging out of the sling. "Who made such a messy bandage? It looks a sight. I bet it wasn't your mother."

"I put a safety pin in, but it came undone . . ."

"I heard what happened to your hand in the workshop. You must have been daydreaming. As usual."

"Perhaps."

Violeta folds her arms again, and leans back against the door. She raises her knee to press a naked foot against the frame, letting the housecoat fall slightly open.

"So what are you going to do now? You'll have to learn another trade."

"I'm not sure." The triangle of tanned skin the open coat allows him to see above the knee suggests a pair of well-rounded thighs. "I'd like to work in a circus . . . I could be a magician, or a ventriloquist. I can do all kinds of voices. I'd wear evening dress and a bow tie and a top hat and do impressions of animals or people . . . it's easy. But in fact, it's most likely I'll be a piano tuner."

"Ha, a piano tuner. And while you're waiting, what are you up to? Nothing, loafing around. It's a shame, but that's what you like doing. Loafing around."

"It's not true. I study music. I don't have a piano yet, but I study on my own. And I also give my mother a hand, buying things, helping her in the kitchen . . ."

"Ah, so you're a hard-working boy, are you? Where did you learn, in the courses run by the Falange's Female Section, like me?" She smiles spitefully. "You're a good-for-nothing, that's what you are. A shame. Why do they call you Ringo? Isn't your name Mingo?"

"No!"

Denying his real name has always been something more than a game or a joke. If she weren't such a strange creature and almost two years older than him, he would have been happy to explain. My name is Domingo, doll, but as a child they took away the doh, the first note on the musical scale, and what was left was Mingo, which I hate. It's a mutilated name, like my finger. They took away the musical note, but I changed just one more letter, and since then, if you want me you'll have to come and look for me on the prairies of Arizona, far away from this shitty neighbourhood.

"It sounds almost the same, but it's not," he says, his gaze alternating between the shameless thigh and the lines beneath the girl's insolent eyes, disparate elements reconciled by desire. Out of politeness, he focuses on her eyes, but not for long.

"It's a shame," insists Violeta.

"Why is that?"

"Because a girl I know likes you a lot."

"Ah yes? Who might that be?"

Violeta says nothing, but meets his gaze until he is forced to lower his eyes. They fix instead on her knee and everything near it, openly and despite himself. He is sure he has more than enough energy to achieve any goal he may set himself in life, even that of becoming a celebrated pianist with only nine fingers, but at this very moment he finds himself unable to do something as simple as looking away from her raised thigh and the fold of her housecoat over her crotch.

"I'm no layabout," he insists. "They're trying to find me work. It could be in an important piano store . . ." He points to the photograph of Errol Flynn. "Look, he's got his arm like mine, and the scarf is very similar . . . 'Into the Valley of Death rode the six hundred!' Do you remember? Have you seen the movie?"

Violeta has turned her right ear towards him so she can hear more clearly, and Ringo suddenly recalls that the year before, dancing with her in the street on the same night she was crowned Princess of the Fiesta, every time he thought of something to say, that small, perfumed ear would immediately be brought close to his lips. At first he thought she was pretending to be hard of hearing so that she could come closer, but when he realised she really did have difficulty, he was the one who took advantage: every so often he spoke in a low whisper so that her ear would be near him, and sometimes he even brushed the lobe with his lips. Soon afterwards, in a disconcertingly spontaneous and generous gesture, she pressed her stomach and thighs against him. And it was dancing to "Perfidy" in the darkest, highest part of the street, under a ceiling of coloured bunting rustling like leaves in the breeze, that he responded to her furtive pressure with that night's first erection. She must remember this, even if now she pretends to be interested in something different:

"How is your wound? Does it hurt?"

"Yes, it does sometimes . . . Does it really interest you?"

He clenches his fist and rolls his eyes, trying to summon up a stab of pain in his phantom finger. Her mouth half-open as if she finds it hard to breathe, Violeta watches him, smiling coldly.

"Can I see it?"

"What for?" Ringo's untamed eyes grow suspicious beneath the tilted brim of his hat. His left hand hovers over the butt of the revolver at his waist. "Why do you want to look at it, Frenchie?"

"Because I understand a bit about these things, stupid. I'm doing a course in nursing at the Santa Madrona School on Calle Escorial." She keeps staring at him. "And what did you call me?"

"It doesn't matter, it's just a name I like. Have you learnt how to do injections? And can you heal with your hands, like your mother?"

"No way. I want to be a real nurse. I've been doing a course with the nuns at the Remedio clinic for a month now. Hadn't you heard? So, are you going to let me have a look then?"

Ringo is still sitting on the bed, with his bandaged hand in his lap. He smiles, unwraps the bandage and shows her the missing finger.

"Look. Do you like it?"

Violeta bends down, examines it closely, then shrugs.

"So-so. It's quite an ugly wound."

"That's because it hasn't healed yet. Come closer and take a good look."

She obeys, to get a better view of the folded centre of the stump, the small, livid scar like a little star surrounded by tiny lumps. As she does so, she carelessly rests her hand on Ringo's knee. He stares down at the nails painted the colour of tainted silver on a warm, calm hand that is suddenly adult.

"It still hurts, you know?" he says. "And I get strange sensations. Sometimes I start picking my nose with the finger that no longer exists, or scratching my ear . . ."

"Ha, what a fibber!"

"Bah, you don't deserve to know." While he is reluctantly doing up the bandage again, hoping in vain that Violeta will offer to do it for him, an imaginary muscular spasm in his arm twists his mouth in a fake grimace of pain. "It's nothing. Problems with my shoulder, I must have put it out . . . Bad luck follows me everywhere. And to top it all, the other day my mother and yours met by chance outside the clinic, and they have nothing better to do than to talk about my back pains. And what do they decide? That I need a back rub! That's why I came here, just for that, don't imagine there's anything else behind it . . ."

"Huh."

"Yes, some evil spell has brought me here."

"What nonsense you talk, you're such a show-off."

"I didn't even expect to find you here. I know they don't close until eight in the stationer's where you work."

"I don't work there some afternoons. I already told you, I'm doing a few courses. O.K., I'll tell my mother you're here."

She goes out, leaving the door ajar, and before long he hears her mother's gravelly voice from the glassed-in verandah, muffled as if it came from the depths of a cave:

"The boy can wait," and then, almost without transition, she shouts furiously: "And will you take that towel off, Violeta, do me a damn favour and throw it in the bin! Can't you see it's completely useless? How often do I have to tell you? I don't ever want to see it in this house again! I've had it up to here with your insolence! Take it off at once or I'll give you a good slap . . . ! And bring another cushion here for Señora Elvira!"

And immediately afterwards, in an unctuous tone:

"I'm so sorry, Señora Elvira. But I've got a thing about that towel. I dislike it so much that if it wasn't for the fact that I don't even want to touch it, I'd have torn it to shreds myself."

"It's a question of age, Vicky. I've taken a dislike to cannelloni, when I always used to love them."

"It belonged to her father, he always used that towel," says Señora Mir. Then her voice takes on a scolding tone again: "Violeta, how long is it since you've been to Badalona to see your grandmother? And what about your father? Have you been to see your father?"

"I haven't had time, Mama. And I have a headache."

"Nonsense! And that melon must be ready to throw away . . ."

"I'll go tomorrow."

"Tomorrow you'll say the same thing."

"But he doesn't even recognise me, Mama! He spends the whole day doing crochet, and he doesn't want melons or chocolate, all he asks for are balls of wool . . ."

"That doesn't matter, I want you to go and see him once a week! What do you think, Señora Elvira? Is it asking too much of a daughter that she goes and visits her sick father once a week at least? He doesn't recognise me either, the poor man . . ."

The sound of a door slamming silences the grating voice. Ringo leans back and looks round the small room. On the far wall there are three shelves of unpainted pine; holding more jars and tins, a few dark-coloured stones with smooth, polished surfaces, and bunches of dried herbs and stalks arranged by size and tied with blue and red ribbons that have been very carefully knotted. This effort goes beyond the strictly necessary, and seems more to do with having them look good for anyone considering them. Each of the bunches has a small piece of paper attached, labelled with green ink in a delicate hand. Tarragon, lavender, elderberry, mint, chamomile, belladonna, broom, eucalyptus, thyme, olive leaves, liquorice. On the wall is a framed photograph of Violeta at the saint's day fiesta. She is posing very seriously with her father on the orchestra platform, only a few seconds before she burst into tears. She is about to turn sixteen, and still has pigtails and white ankle socks. She is not very attractive, and is wearing a white dress with a frilly skirt, with the Princess of the Fiesta sash across her chest, and is clutching a bunch of white roses. She is trying to smile, but can only manage a grimace. The music has been interrupted, she has just been crowned princess, and all round the platform there is an air of expectation among the couples standing with their arms round each other, waiting for the dance to continue, and among the neighbours looking on from their balconies. All of a sudden there is the sound of loud whistling, and Violeta's face contorts with horror and sadness (although this is not in the photograph), and Ringo remembers that he and Roger, hidden somewhere among the crowd, also whistled as loud as they could, joining in the general disapproval, because the chosen princess was by no means the prettiest girl in the neighbourhood. Everybody thinks that other better-looking, more popular and friendly contestants deserved the title and crown much more than she did. They know she was chosen princess thanks to her father's manoeuvring: not only is he the local councillor, but he is chair of the fiesta committee as well. He is a self-important braggart, always in a temper. Faced by the boos and whistles of the crowd, Violeta jumps down from the platform in tears. She buries her face in the bunch of roses, with a cloud of confetti still floating round her, and runs to seek the safety of the doorway to her home.

A door opening somewhere allows Ringo to hear the gruff voice once more:

" . . . and is he sleeping O.K. now, at least? Can't you hear me? I'm asking you if your father is sleeping well at least . . . Can you hear me, Violeta?"

"He says that every day he wakes up tired with dirty fingernails."

"Dirty fingernails?"

"He says he cleans them every night before he goes to bed, but that when he wakes up they're dirty, and he can't bear it . . . That's what he says."

"There you are then: go and clean his fingernails! Now go into the kitchen and put the eucalyptus on to boil. And get rid of that rag of a towel if you don't want me to do something worse than your father did!"

"Ugh! And whose fault would it be if you did that, Mama, whose fault?"

"Get out of here, I said! Shameless hussy! And clean the shelves and tell me what we need!"

Shortly afterwards, her voice takes on a wheedling tone, with a self-pitying edge to it. Even so, Ringo can always sense an unhealthy vibration, a perverse strand to her deep, growling, almost masculine voice that seems so unsuited to a fat, empty-headed and flighty woman like Señora Mir.

" . . . it was a pistol he brought from over there, Señora Elvira, from those distant, godforsaken lands. The doctor said he'd removed the bullet from his head cleanly . . . Stuff and nonsense! I've always thought the damned bullet is still stuck in his noddle, and is spinning round and round so much it won't let him sleep. Prussia is to blame! they say he shouts at night. The poor fellow no longer knows what he's saying, because he was never in Prussia, he was in Russia. No, I could swear they never took that bullet out . . ."

"Don't be so silly, woman. If they hadn't taken it out, he'd be dead by now."

"I've been wrong so often in my life, Señora Elvira! God forgive me, but sometimes I think it would have been better if Ramón had died right there, outside the church . . . The man in the sanatorium isn't my husband. And he wasn't for the last few days he lived in this house."

As if he has heard her and wants to say something, Señor Mir suddenly emerges from the shadows of the corridor, finger raised as if demanding attention because he has something important to say. He advances trembling towards the two women in his underpants, limping the way Señor Alonso does, with a bloody bandage round his head, the big service pistol in his hand and his field glasses hanging across his chest . . . This is how Ringo imagines him, killing time as he sits on the bed, listening closely. He stares at a big jar full of eucalyptus leaves, and knows they are from a tree in Parque Güell; he can still see Señora Mir collecting them from the lower branches, her chubby bare arms raised, surrounded by leaves like curved daggers; then he hears voices from the verandah once more:

" . . . the thing is, my veins are a disaster, Vicky. I don't know what to do, I daren't even look at my legs. Nothing is any use: elastic stockings, nylons, crutches or no crutches . . ."

"What you have, Señora Elvira, are varicose and thread veins; nothing serious. I'll give you a cream. If you'd seen Señor Alonso's leg the first time he came, and especially his foot . . ."

"How strange that someone as lame as him doesn't use a stick, don't you think?"

"He doesn't need one. It's only a slight limp, and besides, it favours him. It looks very distinguished, don't you think?"

"No, I don't think so."

"Seeing as he's so tall and handsome, with such good taste in clothes and that proud head of white hair of his . . ."

"Goodness, you can be so naive, Vicky! And you talk such rubbish! All that sort of thing has brought you nothing but disappointment. How have you let so many men ruin your life?"

"Ay, Señora Elvira, what am I to do? Look, I've always been a passionate woman. No-one can live without a bit of affection, can they?"

"Ten more minutes and it's your turn," announces Violeta as she comes in, eyes lowered, her hair loose and the towel in her hands. She folds it carefully. She bends at the foot of the bed and, crouching there for a few moments in a slow, self-absorbed gesture, slides her hand with its shiny nails over the blue, frayed surface of the neatly folded towel and then tucks it under the mattress and sits on it. Taking a brush out of her housecoat pocket, she smiles an enigmatic smile and starts furiously brushing her tangled, damp hair.

"Didn't she just tell you to throw that towel in the bin? Why don't you obey your mother?" Ringo asks jokingly, although he adds something unexpected: "We all have something to hide, don't we?"

"I don't hide anything that isn't mine."

"Want to know something? One night I was coming home, and it was pouring with rain, with thunder and lightning, and I saw a dead bird being swept away down a drain . . ."

"So what?"

"So nothing. My stuff. Stuff and nonsense."

"You talk just for the sake of it, don't you? You're not all there some-times, are you, kid?"

"And what about you? Do you keep any other secrets under the mattress? Lipstick? A photograph of Coletes . . . ?"

Once again he bites his tongue, although she doesn't appear to have heard him. He remembers that the year before Violeta was meant to be crazy about a boy from Calle Legalidad, who for some reason he never discovered was known as El Coletes. After smooching with her for almost two months, he had dropped her like a stone. According to El Quique, who had seen the two of them at it in a dark alleyway, the boy had done every-thing with her apart from sticking it in. Now Violeta doesn't even blink when she hears his name, and so Ringo turns his attention to the shelves with the herbs and jars on them, and pretends he is suddenly interested:

"Wow, take a look at that lot! What are those stones for?"

"They're hot stones. Mama will put some on your back, and you've no idea what it's like. They burn, you know, smart guy."

"Yeah, I believe you. There are heaps of stones like them on Montaña Pelada . . . And I think there's a lot of nonsense about all this. Señora Paquita thinks your mother doesn't use oil to prepare the herbs anymore even if she says she does, because olive oil is very expensive, and so she makes her potions with heaven knows what."

"Yes, of course. With billy-goat tails probably. Smart, aren't you? Such a smart guy."

She throws the brush onto the bed and stands up, takes a small notebook and a pencil stub out of her pocket, examines the glass jars on the stands, and writes something down. The pencil has got coloured ink in it, and whenever she sucks it before making a new note, it leaves her lips purple. Ringo watches her silently. She soon finishes and sits on the bed again, picks up the brush and goes on brushing her hair furiously, her purple lips half open. She stands up when she hears her mother calling from the corridor as she accompanies Señora Elvira and her son to the front door. Violeta! That daughter of mine is never there when I need her. Her patient recommendations to the old woman mingle with the tapping of the crutches and her son's observations on how useless her footwear is. There is the sound of the door closing, then of another opening and closing.

"The torture is awaiting you in the dispensary, kid," says Violeta. "You can go in now."

"Where?"

"To the verandah. Sit there and wait."

"And your mother?"

"She'll be there straightaway." She opens the door and stands aside to let him through, her eyes lowered, her hip thrust forward. "You can go now."

"Are you coming with me?"

Violeta shakes her head and returns slowly to the bed, her back straight above her enticing buttocks, fluffing her reddish locks with her hand. She explains in a bored voice that she has to work in the kitchen, where she has to mix the herbs, pound them in the mortar, then boil them over a low flame. She also prepares peppers for dyes, peels potatoes and sweet potatoes, grinds grains, and cleans lentils.

"I also make jam. Do you like blackberry jam?"

"No. But come with me, please."

The girl smiles vaguely as she looks at him and says nothing. She has sat down again on the corner of the bed where she's hidden the towel, and carries on energetically brushing her hair. As she does so, she reveals the fuzz under her arm. It looks like a black flower, or a small hedgehog hiding there. Yet again Ringo confirms that she is not pretty. She isn't. Why then do even the most trivial of her gestures attract him? What is there beneath her docile eyelids, why are her silences and her gaze so disturbing?

Oblivious now to everything that doesn't involve looking after her hair, Violeta lowers her eyes and starts to sing softly – "The sea, mirror of my heart . . ." – while he relives the moment when everyone was booing and whistling on the night of the saint's day fiesta, and sees her running home, the cloud of confetti bursting round her head.

He had thought it would be a more or less private atmosphere, protected from any indiscreet glances, rather than this brightly lit end of the verandah, with its coloured-glass panes (some of them broken), and with a view of the backs of other buildings, all of them with similar rusty verandahs with broken panes and moth-eaten blinds. From some of these galleries baking in the noonday sun comes the clucking of tame hens. There's a trolley on wheels like the ones he has seen in the corridors at the Nuestra Señora del Remedio clinic, a white cupboard, and unpainted shelves holding towels, pillows, clay bowls and jars with creams and potions in them. There is also a rack with a white coat hanging from it, and a battered wicker chair in which he has now been sitting for several minutes, surrounded by the smell of hot leather and herbs treated with alcohol, listening to Señora Mir arguing with her daughter somewhere in the apartment. Then there is the sound of a door slamming once more.

"So here we have this polite, well-brought up young boy, so spoilt by his mother," says Señora Mir seconds before she appears on the verandah, wrapped in her white coat, wearing the slippers with the pink pompoms, her hair drawn up in an untidy bun. Her eyelashes are thick with blue mascara, but her full, pale, pine-cone lips have no lipstick on them. They look strangely youthful, and traces of rouge at the corners of her mouth lend her smile a weary look. "So let's see, what's wrong with you?"

"Hello, Señora Mir."

"You've got your mother into a state, haven't you? Well anyway, first let's deal with that sling. We don't want to see it any more. Get rid of it, O.K.?"

"I don't know, I think it helps . . ."

"Not a bit of it, my dear. Put the scarf away in your pocket, and take off your jacket, shirt, and sandals. Let me see your hand." She takes hold of it, removes the bandage roughly but efficiently, then examines the scar. "Don't worry. We'll put some corn oil on it and it'll look a lot better. Fancy ruining such a pretty headscarf to make a sling! And what for? You think

207

it helps the arm to stay still and rest, don't you? Well, it doesn't, because the arms drops anyway without you realising it, it hangs down and becomes lazy, and in the end the muscles contract. Sit here on the trolley. That's right. Now lift your right arm on your own, little by little . . . No, not like that," she laughs hoarsely, "not like my Ramón's salute, my boy, we've already had enough of that in this house. Raise your arm straight above your head, as if you were lifting a weight, and tell me if it hurts here when you do so, here in your shoulder. Does it?"

"No."

"Now do the same, but with your elbow in the air, and your hand facing downwards . . . That's right. How does that feel?"

"That hurts."

"O.K., so there we have another problem. Undo your belt and lie face down. Rest your chin on the pillow, with your arms down by your sides. That's right."

The pillow greets him with a stale reminder of heavy, faded smells. Face down on the trolley, his eyes discover a glass vase almost hidden behind the white coat hanging from the rack. Inside, a slender blue rose amid a bunch of lavender. Too slender, too perfect, and too blue not to be made of paper. The blue rose of forgetfulness in Señora Mir's apartment! But it's not the perfume of roses that his nostrils can now detect, rather the intense odour of camphorated alcohol. Gradually, the arcane air in the verandah starts to distil denser, more disturbing essences, closer to the secrets of adult sex than to aromatic herbs, oils and potions. Out of the corner of his eye he can see Señora Mir lubricating her small, podgy hands with the yellowish contents of a glass pot, and then, for a brief moment, he sees them approaching, hanging by her sides like the talons of a bird of prey. To ward off the ill omens Ringo closes his eyes and amuses himself with a rapid re-run of his personal collection of risible images of the plump Señora Mir having sex with the lame ex-footballer . . . Where could they have done it? Right here, on this trolley? On the floor in a great hurry and laughing all the time, with stifled caresses and groans, her on top and him underneath? Don't miss it, my boy. She strips off and gives her man a sweet smile. She kneels down willingly and raises her arse. Rolls of fat on her thighs and bulbous pink buttocks. But where? In Violeta's room or in the marriage bed itself, with the photograph of the local councillor, the ex-combatant, smiling at them from the bedside table? The bare, kissable mouth is now suspended only a few inches from his defenceless back. He can sense her breath on him.

"Loosen your belt, sweetheart," Señora Mir orders, and he can feel her sticky fingers probing the tendons round the nape of his neck. "You're tense, little one. Relax or I'll be annoyed." She taps him on the behind, and recites: "Just a little scratch, you'll hardly notice it . . . I bet that's what they said to you when you were small and they were giving you an injection, wasn't it? Well, don't be frightened, Vicky's not going to hurt you either."

"I'm not frightened."

At any rate, it's not the fear or nervousness that this hopeless, corny romantic imagines, forever caught up in the web of her own feelings; no, it's something very confused that is worming into his consciousness, a bitter, intermittent but crushing melancholy. Beneath the constant pressure of her perfumed fingers, fingers that now are incisive and surprisingly strong, he himself wants, and yet doesn't want, to feel guilty. It occurs to him that such an awkward situation, where all of a sudden he finds himself at the mercy of these hands and potions, is the result of his cowardice the other afternoon when he hid round the corner, and above all, is the punishment he deserves for his irresponsible, delirious fantasy the other night in the rain . . . He wasn't able to shake off this nervousness as he flopped onto the trolley, the fear of the conversation he is bound to have to listen and reply to, similar to the way he feels when he is having his hair cut: there's no way of escaping the traditional chat with the barber, which is always a boring waste of time, a torture. But here it could be a lot worse. Even though he thinks she knows, or ought to know, that a boy scarcely more than fifteen is not an appropriate audience for the secrets of a woman of over forty, he can't help remembering how little she has ever cared about scandalising either adults or children in the neighbourhood, turning her ridiculous romances into a source of great hilarity. Humorous variations, usually quite rude if not downright smutty, of the same story. What Señora Mir calls "a bit of extra affection" could be the reason behind her current frayed temper while she desperately awaits the longed-for letter and possible reconciliation with the last man to take to his heels and leave her: so be ready with your lies, kid, or, if you prefer, be prepared to withhold the truth.

"Tell me if I'm hurting you."

"No, no . . ."

He can feel her sticky hands pressing insistently on his back. They glide from his tailbone up along his spine, stopping and forcing down each vertebra, and then suddenly speeding up and pressing more heavily as she reaches the back of his neck. After working there for a while, her fingers return to the bottom of his spine, where she plunges them into the top of his buttocks.

"That feels good, doesn't it? Now turn on your side. On your left side."

Thick, plump wrists like a big cardboard doll's; small, fleshy hands that couldn't stretch an octave (he knows this just from feeling them spread open on his back); podgy fingers that possess unexpected strength and which for several minutes seem determined to dismantle or displace his right shoulder blade. Then she tells him to lie on his front again, and this time her oiled hands travel over all his back, out from his spine to his sides, and from the nape almost down to his buttocks, pressuring with her thumbs as if she is trying to split his flesh open. Like steel pincers, her fingers massage the knots and tendons round his neck. Occasionally he can feel her plump lips close to the back of his head, her warm, rapid breath.

"Does it hurt here?"

"No, no . . ."

"And here, this shoulder?"

"A bit . . ."

Some quick pinches, like a spider crawling over his skin, and a new smell in the air, this time of roast almonds. He remembers his mother commenting that Señora Mir sincerely believed in the emotional treatment of muscles, and so applied very personal criteria to her work. For example, she would smile all the time as she rubbed the most painful area. Why does she do that? Because the good woman is convinced that her smile, a polite smile, even though you don't see it because you're face down on the trolley, has beneficial effects which are transmitted to your body through her hands . . . To hell with that woman's magic powers! said the Rat-catcher one day. At any rate, she hasn't transmitted anything special to him so far, thinks Ringo. Her fingers press down increasingly hard, especially her thumbs, but their slow, calm progress creates an expectant silence, probably leading up to what has terrified him from the start: the heart-to-heart chat, revelations. His worst fears are about to come true.

"That boy who's a friend of yours, what's his name? The one who plays dominoes with the old men in Bar Rosales, he's small, a big, round head, yes, you know who I mean, one of those who goes up to Parque Güell to spy on courting couples . . . I feel very sorry for those peeping toms, I really do. Well anyway, that boy said that by chance he had seen Señor Alonso not long ago, in a garden . . . Do you know anything about that, Ringo? No? You didn't hear him say that? Last Sunday that poor wretch told everyone in the bar that he saw Señor Alonso with a hosepipe, watering a garden. Apparently they all laughed, as if it was a joke. Of course, standing there waving a hosepipe . . . Paqui, who heard him, asked him where and when he had seen him, and she says the boy was embarrassed and pretended he didn't know what she was talking about: first he said he didn't remember, then that it was a joke . . . To tell you the truth, that lad has always seemed a bit slow to me, not to mention dirty-minded. That's why I prefer to talk to you. You're such a polite, responsible boy. Can I ask you, just out of curiosity, if you've heard anything about that, if they've told you . . . ? No? Do you think the lad invented it? You knew Señor Abel Alonso, didn't you? You must have often seen him in the bar . . . Do you know he had a soft spot for you?" Her skilful hands continue working at a deliberate pace that her voice falls in with. Every now and then he can sense her thick lips almost brushing his back. "He had noticed you, you made a good impression, he liked you. Do you know what he told me one day? He told me: That boy will go far. Yes, that's what he said. He had a good eye for some things, the rogue . . . my, did he have a good eye . . ."

Ringo would give anything not to have to go on listening to her. He flattens his right ear into the pillow for a while, and then the left one, alternating the eye with which he has a partial view of the woman bent over him, her round, shiny face with curls sticking to her forehead, the wrinkled skin in her cleavage, her breasts swinging to the rhythm of her hands. Her powerful thumbs are still digging into his defenceless spine when he feels several drops of sweat hitting his back; thick, warm drops that fall infrequently but regularly, and his stomach clenches every time.

"What was that, my love?" says Señora Mir with her guttural, fleshy laugh. "Did you let off a little fart? Well, that doesn't matter, does it? You don't have to be embarrassed or go red over that . . . I let one off in the bar the other day, although it was so soft it was almost inaudible. But let's talk about higher things, shall we? Your mother told me you're not going back to the jeweller's. Too bad. What does your father say? I must say, Pep is always out and about with his cleansing brigade, your mother works herself to death day and night at the residence or the clinic, and you're always on your own . . . A boy your age, spending so many hours in that tavern, and always alone, that can't be good, sweetheart. However much you like reading and all that. You ought to be at home more, child, and your father should pay you more attention."

"There's no-one at home," he grunts, face down in the pillow. "My father is never there."

"From the way you talk about him, it seems to me you don't have a proper respect for him . . . Yes, he's a good-for-nothing and a heretic, we all know that. He must have led your mother a merry dance, poor woman, and then he's always going around claiming to be such a Red and a blasphemer . . . Everybody thinks he's a hopeless case, but do you know how I see him? I see him as a peeled chestnut. Have you seen what the shell of a chestnut looks like inside? Of course you have. It's got a soft down all over it, just like a jewel box. You make jewels, so you know what I mean. Well, your father is like a chestnut shell, tough on the outside but soft as velvet inside . . . Yes, you heard me. And it's thanks to him I get news of my poor brother, God save him, the fellow had to go into exile. Listen, I'm going to tell you something very few people know. Do you remember when my Ramón started to lose his memory after his operation, and how sometimes he got lost in the street and didn't know his way home? Well, one night as he was leaving Bar Rosales, he fell flat on his face on the pavement and started bleeding. He was pretty drunk at the time. And do you know who saw him and went to help? That good-for-nothing father of yours! I don't know how to get home, and I've got nowhere to go, they say my husband said, and that rogue Pep said to him: Of course you've got somewhere to go, councillor, you can go to hell! And then he helped him up and took him home. I bet you didn't know that! So you see, some people can be friendly and generous even though they don't look it, and come to think of it, I remember that Señor Alonso, that he too . . . well, haven't you got anything to say?"

He grunts, pushing his face as far as he can into the pillow to muffle his voice:

"I'm . . . I'm moved, Señora Mir."

"You see, child?" she nods with satisfaction, and adds: "Goodness gracious me! I reckon your mother is right, and that all you care about is studying music and going around showing off with that sling of yours . . . Don't you ever go dancing? Let's see, let me tell you something, sweetheart. But it's a secret, eh, you have to swear to me you won't say a word to Violeta. The thing is, she quite likes you . . . Yes, don't be surprised that I know, we mothers are aware of these things. It's not for me to say, but don't you think she's a sweet, affectionate girl with everybody? If you could only see how she respects her father. But she has no luck with boyfriends."

She breaks off, moistens her fingers again in the glass pot, and starts gently massaging his back once more. "Don't you ever go dancing at the Verdi or the Cooperativa La Lealtad? Your friends do, they never miss a Sunday, and you should see how they swarm round my Violeta . . . But lately she prefers La Lealtad. We never see you there. Why is that, sweetheart?"

"I don't like dancing . . ."

"Nonsense!" She taps his buttock again. "Don't start again with your fibs, eh! You danced with Violeta at the street fiesta last year, and I could swear the two of you were quite . . . you know what I mean."

"The thing is, I can't dance very well," he manages to mutter in a faint voice.

"Mind you, I'm not saying it as a reproach. We women don't really care if a man can dance or not. What we really appreciate is a polite, affectionate partner. But sometimes you have that so near to you, you don't even see it . . . Why do I say that? Because a sweet, romantic girl should immediately be able to spot the attentive, discreet young man who has been waiting for her all along. And my Violeta is that sort of girl. Listen, in La Lealtad she has to fight off the pests who bother her all the time, you know what I mean, she gets bored always saying no, I won't dance with him, Mama, nor with him, he clings like a leech. The thing is, they're so vulgar when they approach her, if you know what I mean . . . and the end result is that she spends the whole afternoon just sitting there, poor thing. As if they had all taken a dislike to her. But I know she'd be different with you . . . Go on, promise me you'll come to the dance one of these Sundays. As a special favour, to see if we can encourage her a bit. Will you promise? Pull your trousers down a bit, or I'll get oil on them . . . Can't you hear me?"

"Yes, Señora Mir," he says, burying his mouth still deeper into the pillow.

"But a proper promise, I mean. You have to really mean it!"

"Well, okay, I . . . I promise."

Why did you do that, you dummy? Soon she'll be asking you to take your trousers and pants off altogether, she'll run her vengeful claws all the way down to your arsehole and stick her nails in you. Unable to prevent himself hearing her, the only thing he can do is to stubbornly persist in pressing his mouth and nose up against the pillow, where the stale smells mingle with his attacks of bad conscience. Meanwhile, she is now pummelling his back with the edge of her hands, alternating them quickly and with astonishing precision in a warm, relaxing drumming up and down from the nape of his neck almost to his buttocks. And there is a sudden fresh shower of sweat cascading from her moon-shaped face: big, hot drops that her hands quickly burst and wipe away on his skin.

"And when I think how wonderful it is to be in love when you're young!" says Señora Mir, a quiver in her voice. "I sometimes see you in the bar, always on your own, and frankly I'm really impressed by your enthusiasm for books . . . it's truly wonderful. Sitting there all afternoon, without lifting your eyes, page after page, it's really something! It's wonderful to see such enthusiasm in someone so young, isn't it? I bought a novel by Vargas Vila called . . . *Aura or the Violets*, I don't know if you know it, it's very strong stuff, very dramatic, I bought it for Violeta because of the title, but I haven't let her read it yet, she's too young." Another sigh: no knowing, he thinks, if it's provoked by the continued efforts of her hands, or by something else. "And before I forget, just out of curiosity . . . have you heard of anyone who by coincidence has run into him lately, over in El Carmelo or El Guinardó . . . ? Señor Alonso, I mean. Perhaps, sweetheart, if you chanced, and I'm not saying you ought to do it, of course, or that it is absolutely necessary, but if you should happen to see him one day, and would like to come running to tell me . . . or if you heard of someone who had done so. A while ago I was told he lived over that way, where the anti-aircraft batteries used to be on El Carmelo, but he always denied it . . . Do you think it's normal he never told me where he lives?"

More drops of sweat falling onto his back, one after the other, heavy and warm, swept away at once by her vigorous hands as they spread the ointment.

"I'm so glad you're coming to La Lealtad! Your friends from Bar

Rosales will be there too, causing trouble, but you needn't pay them any attention ... oh, and do you still go up to Montaña Pelada with them?" she asks, a melancholy note in her voice. "Have you been blackberrying in Can Xirot, or to Turó de la Rovira ... ? No, of course not, you're all too old for that. Now you go on your own, to read, study, think of your own things. It's better that way, quieter. It does you good being up there, doesn't it? Just by Parque Güell, it's such a wonderful view ... Goodness gracious me, sweetheart, do you know what's just occurred to me? We could go up there with Violeta for a picnic, just the three of us, would you like that? You're growing up, child, you're a man now, you've even got a bit of a moustache! Do you know something: if I was a man I'd grow a moustache. Ah, and before I forget there's a favour I wanted to ask you ... I know, you must be thinking what is this, this boring woman asking me for things all the time, but there's no-one else I can ask ... Would you be so kind as to bring me a bit of rosemary and fennel the next time you walk up Montaña Pelada? I go there sometimes, but the climb tires me out, and my collection of herbs here is running low ... the tarragon has already flowered. And by the way, if when you're up there or at Can Xirot, you should happen to see Señor Alonso out for a walk, the way he used to, could you please tell him I've got some important news for him ... ? His foot needs attention, you know."

He agrees, burying himself still deeper wherever he can, incapable of reacting. He feels her strong hands gripping the tendons round his neck, and treating them as if she wanted to turn them inside out, twist them, rearrange them. It seems as though her fingers are armed with metal thimbles. Then she moves to the top of the trolley and bends over his back, sliding her hands time and again from shoulders to buttocks, so that her midriff gently bumps against Ringo's head, which is projecting slightly over the end of the bed, and the generosity and warmth accumulated in the well-rounded shapes hidden beneath her coat welcome his befuddled brow.

"Tell me if I hurt you, sweetheart," he hears her purr, as fresh drops of sweat regularly splash onto his skin on the nape of his neck, his shoulder blades, the groove of his spine. "It's an old injury from playing football, a very nasty fracture. He's got poor circulation and is in pain day and night, you know. He needs attention, lots of attention." Her thick, choking voice echoes in the back of her throat in a way he finds obscene. "Oh, how he enjoyed me massaging that foot of his, the rogue! If you only knew, my boy! Poor Señora Paytubi has got big, misshapen feet, with dreadful corns, she's always asking me to give her strong massages. The poor woman's a pain, always moaning, but I put up with her just for that, because of the big, ugly footballer's feet she has . . . because . . . they're like . . . they remind me of . . ."

All at once his skin is moist, as though her hands had become hot all of a sudden, and he shudders as he realises what is going on. They're not drops of sweat dripping onto his back, of course they're not. She's been whimpering for some time now, and you weren't even aware of it, because her laments and little laughs sound so alike. His muscles and tendons contract beneath hands that have lost all their strength and life, although they keep moving with a crazy insistence, as her increasingly frequent and warm tears drop onto his skin, and he hears her first, restrained sobs. When did this melodrama start, when did the tears take over? Or was it never sweat, and were they tears right from the beginning, stealthily released and camouflaged by her constant chatter, and immediately mingling with the essence of turpentine or whatever other muck she was spreading across his back? He doesn't want to open his eyes, and keeps his mouth pressed to the pillow until he feels her burning hands skittering down from his shoulders to his dorsal muscles, trembling like wounded little animals, abandoning his back altogether and seizing his bare, stiff left foot that is cold and bloodless, massaging it, her thumbs digging into the sole, the instep, and then the toes, one by one. Taken so completely by surprise that he surrenders his foot to her without the slightest resistance, his face and his thoughts sunk into the battered pillow, with her stifled sobs reaching him as if from another world, Ringo wonders what on earth to do now, and whether it wouldn't be a good idea to call Violeta.

The hands treat his foot with a vengeful mixture of brutality and possessiveness, rough and tender, squeezing and twisting it so insistently and energetically that in the end the pain becomes unbearable. For a while he refuses to admit that Señora Mir can be obsessed by a foot in such a possessive, unhealthy manner. He prefers to think she is working in her own way, and that he has to put up with it, that possibly there is a real connection between the nerves of the foot and those in his painful back, that his foot is like Señor Alonso's injured one. Soon though, when he feels a new, sharp twist, this time as if the hands really mean him harm, he pulls his leg up and is about to protest, when a stifled cry and the sound of glass smashing on the floor makes him raise his head and open his eyes.

He sees her lying on the floor by the head of the trolley, curled up in a foetal position, weeping copiously, her fists screwed up round her eyes like those of an angry, disconsolate little girl trying to attract attention to her unhappiness, to the amorous mess, the scaly romantic infection that is her life. There's a trace of blood on her knee, and he is still sitting up on the trolley staring at her, uncertain what to do, when the door bursts open and Violeta comes rushing in. Carefully avoiding the shards of glass, she bends over her mother and, without asking what has happened, without offering any words of comfort or telling her to stop crying, she rapidly helps her to her feet. She glances coldly at Ringo.

"Get dressed and go."

Sitting on the trolley, he moves his leg, rotating his reddened, painful foot. Beneath it he sees that the sharpest fragment of glass still has a half torn-off label that reads: *Essence of Eucalyptus*.

"I didn't do or say anything . . . she just fell."

Violeta looks at him again. This time her eyes narrow as if they were burning, as if gusts of wind were making it hard for her to see, and were tensing her mouth and nostrils.

"Go away, please! Go!"

"I've no idea what happened to her . . . All of a sudden she was on the floor. Look what she did to my foot . . ."

218

It's ruined, he is on the point of saying. Sobbing, her face buried in her hands, Señora Mir lets herself be led out by her daughter. Once they have left the verandah, Ringo sits staring at the shattered glass on the floor. While he is putting on his shirt and sandals he decides that before he leaves he'll pick up every single piece, and not leave even the tiniest shard behind. But he soon cuts himself on his sound left hand, and opts instead to sweep them all together in a little pile, pushing them with the tip of his sandal. Leaving the verandah, he limps across the dining-room and heads down the corridor to the front door. Smeared with essence of eucalyptus ointment, his foot slides on the sole of his sandal. He has cramp all up his leg, his toes are aching, and it feels as though he has needles sticking out of his ankle: you deserve to have it broken, for being such an imbecile, you deserve to be stuck with a turned-in foot, like the ex-footballer . . . From one of the rooms comes the sound of discreet reproaches between mother and daughter, the occasional moan. Every time he moves his left foot he feels an excruciating pain, and he can hardly put any weight on it. I couldn't give a damn about that woman's problems, he tells himself, and all of a sudden something induces him to exaggerate the limp until he is dragging the foot along, producing a mocking, sinister sound that will bring back memories when it is heard by mother and daughter, wherever they have taken refuge. He has almost reached the hallway when a door leading onto the corridor opens and Violeta pokes her head out.

"Please don't do that!"

"What?"

"Don't drag your foot like that. Don't do it."

"Why not?" he says, without stopping. Over the girl's shoulder through the half-open door he can make out an untidy bedroom, deep in a warm darkness that must be ideal for rolling around in. "What's the matter? Didn't you tell me to go?"

"But not limping like that, please."

"Well, I'm going to! Who could it upset, who does it matter to?"

Although he knows he is being unfair and feels bad about it, before he reaches the front door he further accentuates his limp and gives Violeta a sideways glance full of spite and sadness, as if to say I know the crap that went on in here, don't think I don't, the things your mother and her lover got up to. And yet he cannot prevent the sudden appearance in his mind of the rain-soaked letter swirling round in the overflowing drain, caught between the rushing waters and his own lack of decision. For a split second, as the letter sinks yet again in the whirlpool that never stops spinning, he senses for the first time that a catastrophe is imminent, that something is silently being hatched that will cause irreparable damage.

"It's not for me," he hears Violeta whisper as he crosses the threshold. "Please don't do it any more . . . I beg you . . . It's not for me."

It's getting dark when he steps out into the street. The days are growing shorter, the light is more diffuse and deceptive, there is a cold edge to the air. Mist dims the yellowish light from the streetlamps. The squeal of a tram turning in the nearby square, a bicycle bell in the distance, the clatter of a metal shutter being lowered. He comes to a halt for a moment opposite the two rails at the street corner, obstinately persisting in their truncated curve to nowhere. Further down, a weak, bluish glow emanates from the glass entrance to Bar Rosales, barely enough to outline the stooped back of a man standing on the edge of the pavement, hands in his pockets, swaying a little as he stares down at his shoes with the bewildered air of someone who does not recognise them as his. Calle Martí is deserted. Shiny green weeds are growing in the cracks between the ruined tiles of the old pavement. As Ringo walks home, his disquiet returns, the almost physical sensation of having left something more than his tortured foot behind on Señora Mir's trolley. Why are you still limping, dummy, when it doesn't hurt anymore? The four-fingered hand touches the headscarf in his jacket pocket, feeling for its silky caress. For a few moments, the soft texture of the material imparts the gentle, warm feeling of a bunch of feathers to his tiny scar, until finally he resolves to undo the knot of this fine sling.

13

THE SMELL OF ROAST COFFEE

One Sunday mid-morning, at a time when he should already be in the kitchen warming milk and toasting bread for his mother's breakfast, he is still flat out with the sheet pulled up to his nose, unsure where he is, when he hears his father's imperious voice calling to him as if in a dream. He jumps out of bed, rapidly pulling on trousers and shirt.

Sitting at the dining-room table with a bottle of the Martell brandy he usually brings from Canfranc, pencil in hand, the Rat-catcher is busily noting something in the top corner of the back of three unstamped, crumpled letters. On one of them he writes an A, on the second a P, and on the third a V. With the other hand he scratches his pensive brow with green-tinged fingernails, all the while clutching a balloon brandy glass as if it is a natural appendage, adroitly manipulating it without it getting in the way at all.

"Good morning, sleepyhead."

Ringo replies with a grunt, struggling to get his jersey on. His father puts the letters and pencil to one side, swirls the brandy round in the glass, takes a sip, and picks his old work case off the floor and examines its well-worn clasps. Then he rubs his chin, again with the hand holding the glass. He arrived from another whirlwind trip only the day before, and this morning, fresh out of the shower but still unshaven, in his grey roll-neck goalkeeper's jersey and with his leather jacket round his shoulders, he is ready for the off again. With his bulky body leaning forward, and his backside perched on the edge of the chair, it looks as if he could set out at any moment. Things never change, thinks Ringo: however much he says how good it is to be home, the Rat-catcher always seems about to leave again.

"I need you to run an errand for me."

"Right now?"

"Right now."

"I need to get mother's breakfast . . ."

"I'll do that. We'll let her sleep in a while this morning."

"The electric ring isn't working. And she likes her coffee very strong and hot. She also likes toast with honey . . ."

"I know what she likes."

"Yes, but you never remember."

His father stares at him for an instant.

"Alright, Son, get it off your chest. Any more complaints? Hurry up, I don't have much time." He takes another sip of brandy and turns his attention back to the clasps on his case. "Well, let's leave it for now. I want you to go to the Mirasol bar as fast as you can. Do you know where that is?"

"I think so."

"It's in Plaza Gala Placidia, opposite Atracciones Caspolino. You went there once with me and Uncle Luis." He stares at him again, then adds more gently: "Now listen carefully, Son. You're to take this case to the bar, and do exactly as I tell you. There's nothing inside that might interest you, so don't bother opening it. When you reach the Mirasol, you'll see Uncle Luis sitting out on the terrace, but you're not to say hello to him. Act as if you didn't know him. He'll not show any sign he knows you either, or say a word to you. Go straight into the bar and order a soft drink at the counter. Make sure you don't let go of the case at any time. While you're drinking your drink, Uncle Luis will come in to go to the toilet, but you're to pretend you haven't seen him. When he's back sitting out on the terrace, ask the waiter where the toilet is, pay for your drink, and go for a pee. You'll see another case the same as this under the washbasin; take it and leave this one in its place. When you come out of the toilet, don't pause at the bar, but go straight into the street and come running home. Give your mother the case, and help her with whatever she asks you to do. Got all that?"

"Of course."

"Okay, take this, and be very careful. Wash your face and comb your hair before you go."

Contrary to his expectation, the case is not heavy. He is on the verge of asking what's in it, but intuits that he should not. His father looks at him as if he has read his mind. He has another errand for him, and further instructions:

"Let's see how you get on. Then I want you to deliver these letters."

He fans himself with them, still holding the brandy glass in the same hand. He looks at his son uncertainly.

"I don't like having to ask you this, and your mother will be annoyed when she finds out. But the way things are, it's better she stays at home."

He hands Ringo the letters. None of them has a name or address on it.

"Where do I have to take them?"

"Your mother will tell you when the time comes. For now, just remember: what you don't know, you can't tell if you're asked."

"What would that be?"

"Whatever."

That errand is for later, he explains; first comes the Mirasol bar, where he has to behave completely naturally at all times, without attracting any attention.

"Will you be able to do that, Son? Can I count on you?"

"Of course."

"By the time you're back, I'll be gone." He stands up at last, and goes through the contents of the pockets of his trousers, jacket and raincoat, emptying them all out onto the table: cigarettes, tin lighter, handkerchief, keys, purse and loose change. Then he quickly puts it all back in the

223

pockets. "I suppose your mother will tell you some things, if she thinks it's advisable...You'll get instructions about delivering these letters and anything else that's necessary. I probably won't be back for a long while, so you'll have to look after our Alberta. I know you will, and that you'll behave . . . Later on we can talk about your future, about a job that will suit you, and so on. Alright?"

Ringo nods, head on his chest. He still thinks his father is not really concerned about whatever the future may hold for him, whatever his aspirations might be, and that only his mother cares. At the same time, he suspects that this might be a real goodbye, and is worried it might mean an embarrassing hug, and even, God forbid, a kiss. He cannot recall his father ever giving him one, or that he ever wanted or expected to receive one on any occasion. He has never missed any disgusting kiss, and has no wish to get one now: he has grown used to the tap on the cheek, the slap on his back, or just a wink. But the Rat-catcher surprises him with a sort of affectionate shuffle, suddenly flinging an arm round his shoulders, without looking at him, so quickly he only has time to notice once more the faint lingering smell of roast coffee on his jersey.

"I know I can rely on you, pumpkinhead. Take this for the drink and the tram." He gives him three pesetas. "Will you remember to do everything the way I told you?"

"Of course."

"Off you go then. Get off at the Rambla del Prat, and the Mirasol's a stone's throw away."

Everything goes according to plan, apart from taking the tram. Ringo decides to go there and back on foot, running part of the way, spending money only on the soft drink. It's a sunny autumn day, almost hot. Everything seems normal and unchanging: the trams screech as they cross Plaza Lesseps, there's not much traffic, two beggars are dozing on the steps of the church; in Calle Salmerón and the Rambla del Prat people go about their own business either eagerly or reluctantly, grey shoulders and lowered heads sharing the same weight of silence.

Uncle Luis is reading a newspaper on the terrace of the Mirasol bar, accompanied by an older man who has a dog tied to the leg of his chair. Ringo puts so much effort into pretending he hasn't seen him that he collides with a chair, and as he falls he bangs into the edge of a table, but he never lets go of the case. Even before he reaches the bar counter his lip is swelling up, and he curses his bad luck. When he has done as instructed, asking for a soft drink and paying for it, he sees Uncle Luis come into the bar and head for the back; and soon afterwards sees him coming out. He asks the waiter where the toilet is. He finishes his drink, goes into the toilet and, still clutching the case, pees so quickly and nervously he wets the front of his trousers. Cursing yet again, he pulls the chain, leaves the case and picks up the other one, which is identical and weighs more or less the same, although there's a slight metallic rattle from inside – perhaps this is the case with the torch and some other tools, he thinks, maybe even a tin of poison – pulls the chain again because the sound of the flushing water calms him, comes out and walks straight out into the street, conceal-ing the wet patch on his flies with his free hand. Out of the corner of his eye he sees Uncle Luis move away from the counter and stride hurriedly into the toilet again.

DO NOT KICK THE CARS, he reads on the sign on the dodgem car rink as he passes by Atracciones Caspolino. Do not piss your pants, dammit.

The case he takes home doesn't contain the torch or any other rat-catching equipment. All that's inside are a ball of green wool with two crochet hooks stuck in it, a tin of peas, and a thick bundle of magazines and newspapers rolled up to bulk it out. His mother throws all the papers into the bin, and keeps the wool and the peas.

"Luis always adds a little something, poor fellow," he hears her say sadly. And a short while later: "Where have you put the letters? Give them to me, I'll take care of them."

"He said you shouldn't."

"Give me them this minute! Your father must have gone crazy. Fancy sending you to the Mirasol. And the letters too."

"Why do they have a letter written on them?"

"For no reason that matters to you. They're news from friends to their families . . . Work things and favours that your father coordinates, a chain of friendly hands stretching back to Gràcia."

At dusk the next day he learns that the police have arrested Uncle Luis, and that others in the rat-catching brigade could meet the same fate, including his father. He hears the news when he gets back from a long, solitary ramble round Montaña Pelada with a copy of *Amok* under his arm, a walk as uncertain in its direction as it is disturbing to find his mother at home when she should be in the clinic. She doesn't seem particularly anxious or nervous when she breaks the news of the arrest to him; she is checking the contents of her handbag and hurriedly putting on her coat, and merely adds that she has spent the afternoon trying to find Uncle Luis' brother-in-law, a taxi driver who has friends in the police headquarters, without any success, and that she is leaving his supper in the kitchen, tuna pasties with lentils or boiled rice, it's for him to choose, all he has to do is heat the meal on the stove.

In bed that night he abandons *Amok* because he can't help thinking about the Rat-catcher. Even then he can't get to sleep; he keeps tossing and turning, and at one particular moment, his head drooping for the umpteenth time on the pillow, he suddenly feels as if he were peering over the edge of the abyss, plunging headlong into his own vertigo. Waking in different surroundings, he becomes aware that it's the end of a phase of his life. Let's face facts, Ringo, fumigate those doubts and accept the truth: your father is a smuggler, or something worse. In the first mists of sleep, he recalls a hot August day some two or three years earlier, when he was still employed as an apprentice. Before returning to work after lunch, he had gone to the newspaper kiosk in Plaza Rovira to look at the new supply of comics, when behind him he heard those two hoarse, mocking voices that so often bewildered him, the verbal ribaldry of the outrageous pair of gossipy clowns, those kings of tall tales who roam the neighbourhood at all hours. On this occasion they are chatting next to the kiosk, under the shade of a leafy plane tree.

"No two ways about it, Blay!" exclaims Señor Sucre. "If you're a smuggler or a black-marketeer and they catch you, you'll be tried as a black-marketeer and a smuggler, in other words, as a criminal, a wrong-doer, not for anything else."

"But he is something else," says old man Blay.

"Ha. But that something else is usually up to the people at the border. And he isn't someone at the border. He's a travelling salesman, shall we say. In other words, in inverted commas."

"Here it's a question of fumigating well without being seen. And Pep knows how to fumigate."

"It doesn't matter if he's fumigating or plotting. Call it what you will. If they catch him, he'll be a criminal."

"I know what I'm talking about. Fumigate is the word, Sucre, my friend. We have to fumigate as much as we can. That's what."

They fall silent for a while. Then Señor Sucre's throaty rattle starts up once more:

"What do you think, Blay? I'm thinking of showing work again at the October Salon this year. It's been so long since I've shown anything that many of my friends must think I don't paint anymore, that I'm doing something else."

"Aha, is that so? It's just as I was telling you. That's right."

They are sitting shoulder to shoulder on the stone bench. Capitán Blay has his glass of coffee laced with aniseed from the Comulada bar, and Señor Sucre is fanning himself with an oriental metal fan. Standing at the side of the kiosk where the comics are displayed, Ringo can see them out of the corner of his eye. They say more than they know, and on top of that they make a joke of it, he thinks, and yet he can't stop listening to them while he pretends to be interested in the weekly delivery of new adventures, the brightly coloured display of comics, cheap novels, and annuals pegged to the sides of the kiosk.

"It's true, Pep is a man of many facets," says Señor Sucre. "And invisibility is one of them. Sometimes it seems to me he is no longer with us, as if he were already dead . . . Blay, have you heard of the asphodel, the plant that makes the dead visible?"

"No; 'Neither God, nor master'. That's my motto."

"It's a plant that grows straight out of a rock."

"Strewth! How can a plant grow out of a rock?"

When he hears this, Ringo recalls the flat rock up on Montaña Pelada.

"Pep is a rare kind of asphodel," says Señor Sucre. "He's what's needed in Bar Rosales or any other tavern. I think I know him well, though he never ceases to surprise me. One night, in the Comulada bar, he bought a drink for that dolt Ramón Mir, and was laughing and joking with him . . . By the way, they say our dear councillor is getting worse every day. Apparently he lost his left ball fighting with the Blue Division."

"He did? Well, 'we lost more in Cuba'."

"A lot more, friend, there's no comparison! Oh, those imperial glories are a thing of the past, Blay, and the misfortunes of the present will soon pass too, and who knows what a dismal future awaits us! I think I'll have a coffee and aniseed as well. Aha, look over there. Isn't that Pep's son standing by the kiosk, about to take a comic?"

"Yes, you're right. Do you think he's going to pinch a comic? He's a bit old for them, isn't he?"

"Hmmm. I know forty-year-old men who read comics. But look, he's been standing there a long time, pretending to read."

Ringo feels the man's little eyes crawling like insects over the back of his neck. The screech of a tram braking at a stop, the cooing of pigeons as they hop across the square, Rip Kirby punching a hoodlum, a rabbit and a pistol appearing out of Merlin the Magician's hat on the cover of his annual.

"So then," he hears Señor Sucre's jerky voice once more, "you reckon there's something important behind all those trips to the border?"

"Important? I wouldn't know," says Capitán Blay. "Nothing's been important to me for a long while now."

"No? Really? How old are you, Blay?"

"Too old. A lot older than you, dammit!"

"You've nothing to complain about. You'll bury the lot of us, I'm sure. Do you know something, Blay? Have you ever stopped to think that at the start of the century the average life expectancy for men was only thirty-five?"

At this time of day, the August sun is fierce on Ringo's bare neck. He doesn't flinch, and continues listening intently.

"Be that as it may," says Señor Sucre, "with Spain the way it is, thirty-five is more than enough, don't you reckon? Well, I'm going to get my drink. But I want it with rum in it, it's healthier . . . I was thinking I haven't seen much of that Pep in the Comulada recently. A shame, isn't it?"

"I've already told you, he spends the whole time fumigating. Have some aniseed in your coffee, dammit, you'll thank me for it . . . . I'm not sure whether you know it or not, but at the border post at Canfranc you can get a French rat poison that's more powerful than any they sell here, and cheaper. They allow it through the customs on the quiet. Everyone knows we don't have good rat poison here in Spain. Of course, a lot more things get through as well. I know of someone called Massana who used to manage to avoid the Gestapo and the Civil Guard and brought in nylon stockings and kilos of saccharine, and at the same time used the journey to smuggle in Jews, spies and airmen . . . But nowadays things have changed. Now they smuggle in that infallible rat poison."

"Goodness! To call what Pep brings in rat poison! You're quite something, my dear Blay!"

"Yes, you can laugh. But ask Gaspar Huguet, the coffee roaster. He'll tell you that all that's missing is the signal."

"What signal?"

"One day you'll get a postcard from the Valley of the Fallen and the stamp with Franco's head on it will be upside down. That'll be the signal."

"The signal for what, Blay?"

"Ah, nobody knows as yet. But it will be the signal, you can be sure of that."

The clink of the spoon against the glass as he stirs the coffee, the rhythmic rustle of the fan through the hot air, and then Señor Sucre calling to him:

"Hey you, boy!"

He stuffs his hands in his trouser pockets, sinks his head between his shoulders, and turns round towards them. He narrows his eyes, suspicious and bristling with premonitions like a cat.

"Yes, you," says Señor Sucre. "Come here a moment . . . Could you do me a favour? Go to the Comulada bar and ask for a coffee laced with rum for me. Tell them I'll come by later to pay."

Ringo does as he's asked, dragging his feet, hoping to hear more. The drink passes to Señor Sucre's thin hands, with their pastel-coloured patches of orange, blue and mauve. Ringo stares at them, intrigued, and tries to formulate a question about where exactly his father is now – and then finds himself awake, face down on the pillow.

Please don't think about it anymore, Son, don't insist, don't keep going over it in your mind, his mother advises him the next day. He's not always involved in what you imagine, really he isn't, either on his own or with others, still less with a knapsack on his back and wearing a balaclava, where on earth did you get that idea, and even less carrying weapons, My God, he'd never do that, there's never been anything like that. That's not how you should see him, not now or before, when there were still Germans up there . . . and we don't know anything about the brigade, or about Manuel.

"It's better if we lie low for a while, that's all," she adds. "We have to wait. Then we'll see. Let that be enough for you for now. Because the fact is, everything is still the same. Your father's away because of his work, and here at home we don't know when he'll be back. That's what you're to say if they ask you."

She doesn't know how long this is going to last either. If they're lucky, only a few months. As for what was in the case he took to the Mirasol bar, he's not to worry about it. The only thing he needs to know is that his father and some friends have been helping a lot of people, inside Spain and outside, and running risks.

"Nothing we should feel ashamed of, Son," she says. "On the contrary. Even though you might find it hard to believe, almost everything your father has done has been to help other people. You mustn't forget that. And please, don't ask me anything more."

"Yes, I know. He's forbidden you to tell me anything."

"You're wrong. You'll know what you ought to know when the time comes. But before he left, he asked me to explain a few things to you . . ."

"There's no need," he cuts in. "I know all about it. Contraband, that's what it is, isn't it? Him and Uncle Luis, and Manuel as well, and probably others in the brigade. On the border or close to it, I looked on the map. They smuggle in coffee for Señor Huguet, and roast it together in secret. And that's why they're going to arrest him as a smuggler, isn't it?"

"I wish that was all there was to it, Son, I really do."

She seems very tired. She is doing day shifts now, looking after an old woman in a traditional villa on Plaza Lesseps, and she goes to bed early. But today she will not go to sleep until she has reassured her son. I really wish that was all he did, she repeats, although your father wouldn't like to hear me say so. He only does it to earn a few pesetas because he's travelling anyway. Virginia tobacco, sheer nylon stockings, French cognac, expensive perfumes . . . not exactly worth running the risk of going to prison for.

"What is worth it," she adds, "and what many people really thank him for, is the other thing he does, his work as a postman."

"A postman?"

"A delivery man, if you prefer. He takes and brings news from comrades to their families. Parcels, letters, money . . . He's a messenger, let's say."

But she doesn't tell him everything, not by a long chalk, because the time isn't ripe yet. She doesn't mention Ramiro López, Señora Mir's much loved and missed brother, who is an old friend of his father and Uncle Luis.

She doesn't tell him that Ramiro had been a member of an escape network on the French border, an employee at Canfranc station and close collaborator with the Customs chief there, when he was linked to a Resistance group working with Allied agents operating in Spain. She makes no mention at all of the relation between the Rat-catcher and people at the border; she doesn't tell him that what he gets up to now is nothing like what he was doing six years earlier, well before they closed the railway tunnel, when the world was at war. Nor does she recall the incursions that in those days really were dangerous, when the train linked Canfranc with Zaragoza, Madrid and Lisbon, and his father and Uncle Luis collected clandestine correspondence at the border and handed it over in Zaragoza for it to be sent to the British embassy in Madrid, or brought it to the consulate in Barcelona. Nor does she tell him they passed themselves off as busy travelling salesmen with false documents, carrying perfumes and nylons but also photographs and letters hidden among the underwear, or mention the messages and visas the British consulate in Barcelona gave them to pass on to Ramiro López's group and the Customs chief, counterfeit visas allowing Allied combatants and civilians to go through Spain to Portugal or Gibraltar, and does not reveal that many of them were Jews fleeing the German occupation of France. She does not mention any of this because it's all in the past, and she does not now want to see the fear of those days in her son's face; he'll learn about it someday, if his father decides to tell him. All she says is that this is how he and Uncle Luis began, taking and bringing messages and money for the relatives of friends who could not return, and that they did this using contacts at the border who were linked to Señora Mir's brother, and that they are still doing this, doing people favours, even though the tunnel at Canfranc is closed now, and the war finished more than three years ago. And that yes, it's true, they had dealt in contraband goods, in fact that was their only reason for starting, and she of course had never approved of that, it was something that had been and still was the source of many stifled arguments and bones of contention. And anyway, Son, don't go thinking they bring anything that valuable home, just a few things to help us get by, nothing that means we'll no longer be poor . . .

A week later, two policemen turn up with a search warrant, which they enforce in a halfhearted, routine way. Ringo is not at home that day. His mother tells him about it that night without seeming the least bit worried. All this was predictable, Son, I've been expecting it for a long while. The next day she is summoned to police headquarters on Vía Layetana and interrogated, although to her this also seems equally routine, and even considerate. They didn't behave like men from the Social Brigade, she says later. In answer to questions about the whereabouts and illegal activities of her husband and other members of the Municipal Cleansing and Pest Control Service, she gives the same response: the team went to do some work in Gerona, in a textile factory on the banks of the river Oñar, and since then she has had no news of her husband and has no idea when he will be back. It's better not to lie to us, Señora, I'm telling you for your own good. Look, sir, that's how my husband usually behaves, he's pretty inconsiderate, a wastrel, but I can't believe he's ever hurt anyone, I really can't. I don't know anything about any trips to Zaragoza or Canfranc, and nor does my son, still less any links he may have with black-marketeers or exiles.

"And you are to say the same if they ask you, Son. You don't know anything," she warns him while she is darning socks sitting on her bed next to the bedside table with the lamp giving off a faint red light next to the image of the Infant Jesus of Prague. As usual, the dignity and good sense of what she says help ward off fear and despair from the house's precarious orderliness, this fragile imitation of hearth and home, protecting it from the harshness of a night like this one when, too tired to go out, she asks her son to drop by Señora Mir's and take a bag of used clothes for her.

"Victoria collects clothing each winter and takes it to the church or the Social Assistance, where she has nurse friends who distribute it. It's for needy people. The nuns at the Residence have given me several things that are in good condition. Wear your scarf and take care, Son. It's after dark, and the weather's cold."

It's a canvas bag with white and blue fringes, and handles like hoop earrings. It's stuffed full and is quite heavy; he's never seen it in the house before. He sets off and halfway there, near Calle Sors and the corner with Calle Martí, close to the open drain, a battered, empty tin can is just waiting for him to kick it. He has always liked kicking tins, but this time he walks on by in the shadows, with a vague feeling of clandestinity and danger. So much so that a little further on he comes to a halt under a streetlight and stealthily opens the bag to examine its contents. Two pairs of trousers and an old jersey, a scarf, blouses and a pleated skirt, clothes that have been mended and are in need of an iron, but are at least clean. And underneath everything else, three ironed shirts neatly folded and buttoned up, three vests and three pairs of underpants, also folded, four pairs of socks and a pair of striped pyjamas. As he feels in the bottom of the bag, he comes across a bottle of Floïd liniment, a small box of razor blades, a carton of Chesterfields and a crunchy packet of roast coffee, one of the ones the Rat-catcher always brings home from Señor Huguet's.

He's been praying it will be Violeta who opens the door. Instead it's her mother, in housecoat and slippers, with rollers in her hair, and her round, unmade-up face floating in the darkness of the hallway like a pale, phantasmal moon. At first she is taken aback to see the boy, but soon puts on a smile. She does not switch on the light. She has been peeling a mandarin, and is wearing a huge cheap golden bracelet.

"Where are you going out in the cold at this time of night, child?"

"I've brought you this from my mother."

"Oh, O.K., that's fine, Darling." She quickly takes charge of the bag and stands there for a few seconds waiting for him to say something more, staring at him with that plastic-doll smile of hers. "And how is our dear Berta?"

"She wanted to come herself, but she's not feeling very well." He leans forward to inspect the hall and the darkened corridor. "Isn't Violeta in?"

"She's just this minute gone to bed. She was bored, the poor thing." She keeps her hand on the door, without opening it any further. "We were here together on our own, listening to the radio . . . Was there something you wanted to say to her, sweetheart?"

Her plump hand chucks him under the chin. The fragrance of mandarin on her fingers. Why does she have a voice like a wounded cat today, much gentler than usual? From the back of the apartment, next to the verandah, comes the sound of exultant voices on the radio.

"No, it doesn't matter."

"I'll tell her you asked after her. She'll be pleased." As she puts the bag on the floor, the bottle of Floïd liniment clinks. Her smiling, alert face does not alter. "I won't ask you in, because she must be asleep already. But if you want to leave her a message . . . As you know, I go with her every Sunday to the dance at La Lealtad. You promised you'd come some day, sweetheart, didn't you? Or have you forgotten already?"

"No, I remember. Well, I have to be going."

Yet he doesn't move, though he is not quite sure why. He stares at her, as if expecting her to say something more. He suddenly brings up his right leg and, covering the front of his trousers as if he is embarrassingly caught short, he lowers his gaze and says pleadingly:

"Oh, Señora Mir, oh, please!" He groans, improvising a grotesque fantasy act, hiding behind a mask of pain: "I'm so sorry, but would you let me in to go to the toilet a moment? I can't hold it in any longer . . . !"

"Of course, sweetheart, of course! Follow me."

The bathroom is at the end of a recess to the right of the corridor, before Violeta's bedroom. Señora Mir switches the light on in the corridor, and shuts the front door. The bathroom is clean and tidy with a few homely touches obviously meant for guests. The toilet lid is lined with goatskin. A small towelling rug in front of the bidet. A spotless mirror edged with transfers of brightly coloured flowers. The showerhead in place over the shiny clean bathtub. A white wardrobe full of folded towels, and two bathrobes behind the door – one white, the other pink –

bath caps, a cardboard box full of curlers, and a mass of female toiletries lined up on a glass shelf. And in a glass, a small razor . . . which could well be hers, to shave her legs with. But there is something more suspicious: when Ringo lifts the toilet lid (because all at once he really does need to pee, and remembers that the same thing happened to him during the play-acting in the Mirasol bar) he sees a cigarette butt floating in the stagnant water, coming apart and ringed with a slight yellowish stain. He can't imagine Violeta locked in here, smoking cigarettes in secret, but who knows if her mother . . . He pulls the chain and wonders whether he ought to wash his hands. He does so, and hears Señora Mir's voice from the other side of the door: Take a clean towel! When he emerges, he bumps straight into her: she has a concerned smile on her face, and is holding the bag. She has not moved.

"Everything alright?"

"Yes, Señora Mir . . . Well, I'll be going."

He did not notice it when he had rushed into the apartment, pretending he was desperate, but now, as he reaches the hall again and is about to leave, his nostrils catch the faint smell of roast coffee coming from the clothes hanging on the rack very close to the front door: several over-coats he cannot make out properly in the darkness. He comes to a halt, his nostrils dilated, then feels her hand on his arm.

"Wait, my boy." She keeps him on the threshold, looking him up and down with her smiling, perspicacious eyes. "You look a bit wild to me." She winds the scarf round his neck, pushes a lock of hair off his forehead. "I wanted to ask you something, if you don't mind . . . Your mother tells me you still like to go up to Parque Güell and Montaña Pelada. That's nice . . . Well, the fact is I wanted to ask you if by any chance you had seen Señor Alonso up there? You remember him, don't you? The thing is, I have to give him a message. I forgot to tell him something important . . ."

"No, Señora Mir, I haven't seen him. Besides, I've hardly been up there recently . . ."

"Hmm. It's just in case you run into him some day. You might do, who knows . . . And now, get along home. And don't worry, sweetheart, I'll tell Violeta you asked after her."

"Yes, thanks. Bye."

"Be very careful on the stairs, there's not much light. And remember, you promised!"

He starts down, but turns back to look up at her. Señora Mir is still standing with a smile on her face by the half-open door, but then slowly closes it completely. The unexpected smell of coffee and the suggestion of a mystery stay with him in the darkness as he feels his way down to the last step on the ground floor, and he has time to imagine Señora Mir going back to the dining-room carrying the bag. He can see her emptying it out on the table, and separating the ironed shirts from the second-hand, mended clothing, putting the carton of Chesterfields and the jar of Floïd liniment and the razor blades to one side, opening the small bag of roast coffee to sniff it, and finally smiling at the man playing Patience at a corner of the table, doubtless in a vest and wrapped in a blanket. He also sees her with the coffee grinder on her lap, smiling as she turns the handle, happy to be able to help her unfortunate friend Berta, and to offer her clandestine guest another cup of authentic, perfumed real coffee . . . Yes, in the home of a Falangist, why not? He can see him at the table shuffling the cards over and over again, lost in thought, the smoke from his cigarette curling round his exhausted head, unshaven, his hair uncombed, sullen, blasphemous, and more clandestine than ever. Now we really are the arsehole of the world, Father! Brandy from the keg in a glass, Chesterfield butts in an overflowing ashtray. I'll only be here a couple of days, Vicky my love. At times friendly, at others full of resentment. The good woman snores all night long and only has this cheap keg brandy. He helps her in the kitchen. Sometimes he falls asleep, head in hands, on the table where the ex-councillor used to eat. Listening to the radio. Glancing at Violeta's shapely backside when she walks down the corridor, pulling her housecoat more tightly round her. Hiding in the bedroom when a patient comes either for a back rub, a herbal recipe or some relief for their bunions.

A profile portrait of José Antonio Primo de Rivera in a silver frame. Just for a couple of days, my hospitable friend . . . Yes, all things considered, what better place than this? Who would think of looking for him in the house of a local councillor, an ex-combatant, a home blessed by the Sacred Heart?

"What are you talking about?" His mother laughs heartily, but with her back to him. "That's a good one! What weird ideas you get, Son!"

She's not in bed yet, although she is in her nightdress. She is in the bedroom, sorting out the wardrobe.

"I saw what was in the bag, Mother . . ."

"You did? It's all for a charity."

" . . . and the whole flat smelled of roast coffee, the sort Father brings home."

"So what? It's not the first time I've given Victoria a bit of coffee. What's so strange about that?" She closes the wardrobe and turns towards him, slightly annoyed. "Listen, you and I cannot know where your father is. I've already told you, all we know is that he went on a trip and isn't back yet."

"I know that, there's no need to tell me . . ."

"It would be best if you didn't even know he is away on a trip." She smiles at him with a lively, teasing glint in her eyes, as she gathers her hair on the back of her neck. "I don't know if you understand me, Son . . . You'll see, the first days are the worst. You have to leave home as quickly as possible. Anywhere will do . . . just as long as you can count on the friendship and loyalty of the person you are staying with. But not at Victoria's! It's only for a few days, until a safer place can be found . . . and poor Victoria, if the word got round! That's all she needs, with the reputation she has! Do you understand me, Son?"

And yet later on she admits that perhaps it's true, his father might have stayed for a while at Señora Mir's. Two days and a night, no more. After that he left and found refuge somewhere unknown, and from that moment on, she refuses to answer his questions and won't tell him anything else.

And yet, in the course of the following month, a gloomy, unpleasant November, as he observes his mother's behaviour and interprets her stubborn silences and lapses into sadness, Ringo comes to the conclusion that she and the Rat-catcher have arranged secret meetings in Señora Mir's apartment after he has left it, on at least a couple of occasions, both of them falling on Sunday night.

It all began the day his mother, while stuffing things into a bag behind his back – he managed to see a carton of Virginia tobacco and some envelopes – complained of a bad headache and neck pains, and announced she would go and visit her friend Victoria that evening. I need one of those miracle potions she prepares, she told him. She repeats the visit a fortnight later, also late on Sunday evening, and on both occasions, to judge by her state of mind when she returns home – even more disheartened and anxious than when she left – Ringo deduces that she has seen him. When he gives her to understand that he knows, he immediately senses her scrutinising him affectionately, although she denies any such meetings and, eyes moist, expressly forbids him from mentioning his father at home or anywhere else, for everyone's good, for the good of a lot of people. She even tells him it would be best for him not to think of his father anymore, or to think of him as if he were dead or had gone away, never to return. Ringo interprets this as wanting to free him from feeling he has to justify or protect the Rat-catcher, or to pry into his secret activities or his current whereabouts.

And yet, as if contradicting her own fears and precautions, she is quick to tell him about other urgent tasks. First and foremost, they have to safeguard his father's job as coffee roaster several nights a week with Señor Huguet, a good friend who has protected their family. Foreseeing what might happen, some time earlier his father had agreed with Señor Huguet that if he had to be away for longer than usual, he would allow his son to take over until he returned.

"I don't like the idea of you going there, Son, but we need the money. It's fifty pesetas a week, which come in very handy. It's a special rate that Señor Huguet pays. You'll be a good assistant, I'm sure Señor Huguet won't have any reason to complain."

"Of course. Don't worry."

He knows what awaits him, even though he has no idea for how long. His father has already mentioned this extra job, thanks to the generosity and trust Señor Huguet has in him. A widower with two unmarried daughters, Señor Huguet had worked for R.E.N.F.E. at Sants station until he lost his job after he was denounced for his anarcho-syndicalist past. One of his brothers-in-law, who has an important grocery store on Calle Aragón, set him up in the coffee-roasting business. Assembling the roasting equipment and looking after it doesn't take much, the Rat-catcher had told him, just a bit of skill. A few years ago, Señor Huguet used to do everything himself, but he's getting on now and needs help. Four times a week, on Mondays, Wednesdays, Saturdays and Sundays, you have to get up at two in the morning and make sure you wrap up warm, even though Señor Huguet's house is nearby, a three-minute walk to Oliveras Passage, a hidden alleyway near the Europa football ground. Señor Huguet will open the garden gate swathed in an old bathrobe and wearing a thick scarf. Holding a torch and stumbling as he goes, he'll lead you over to the shed, where he'll already have lit the lamp, which gives off a wheezing hiss the whole time. You have to get the wood for the fire and assemble the iron struts that hold the drum where the mixture of coffee beans and sugar goes. Huguet prepares the mixture, carefully weighing each part on scales, while I start the fire. Don't expect Señor Huguet to say much, he's a man of few words. Then, making sure the flames stay the same so that the heat is constant, all you have to do is keep turning the handle that spins the metal sphere where the sugared beans are slowly roasting. They turn and turn inside the drum with a sound like pebbles on a beach, and, would you believe it, that's the only sound you hear in all the three hours you're in that shack, Ringo tells El Quique. But it's not an exhausting job. You can do it sitting on a stool or on the floor, while Señor Huguet gets out the sieve where we pour the still smoking roasted beans. We leave them there to cool off for a while, then all that's left is to scoop them up in a little shovel and fill the glossy paper packets – a quarter of a kilo in each one –and that's that. When I leave, Señor Huguet always gives me one for my mother.

His scarf covering nose and ears, Ringo walks home along deserted streets, stealthy and resentful in the feeble glow from the streetlamps, under the bare branches of the lime trees along the Paseo del Monte, fingers perfumed with the smell of roast coffee furiously pounding the keyboard in the clear early morning air.

In mid-December, without warning, the cold becomes so intense that in the evening the interior of Bar Rosales is little more than a patch of pale yellow light. The window where Ringo sits to read occasionally frames hurried, stooped figures passing by in the street, blurred silhouettes that mingle with the persistent phantoms of his imagination. Because in the past few days, in addition to the arrival of the cold and his night-time job roasting coffee beans, several things have happened that have acquired a special resonance in the bar. The first is that, thanks to his improved health and good behaviour in the San Andrés asylum, ex-councillor Ramón Mir has been given a fortnight's leave to spend the Christmas and New Year holidays at home with his wife and daughter. For some time now it's been said he doesn't recognise either of them, that he's completely nuts, beyond all recovery, but this does not seem to be the case; not entirely, at least. One rainy afternoon he is seen getting out of a taxi leaning on Violeta's arm. He is pale, much thinner, with lifeless eyes, but he still has the same air of a bellicose bird of prey, and his hair is combed impeccably, with more brilliantine and dark stickiness than ever. Señora Paqui says he felt dizzy in the taxi, and that was why he looked ill, but that his head is a whole lot better, that the treatment is working wonders, and this is why he has been allowed to spend these precious holidays with his family. That and because of his good behaviour.

"It's not true," says Agustín, who is so fat it's never clear whether he is standing or sitting behind the counter. "No dangerous madman is let loose for good behaviour."

"He's been let out with the permission of the military authorities," comments Señor Carmona from the card-players' table. "Or of the Falangists. His own people, at any rate."

"That's not true either," says the tavern-keeper, setting up three thick glasses for their coffee and aniseed. "Who can guess the real reason?"

"His own private mental nurse will have done it," says Señor Rius, dealing the cards slowly and carefully. "As a councillor and cook with the Blue Division, I bet he has his own nurse, and he's the only one who can give his consent . . ."

"No, wrong again! The permission and consent came from his wife! That's obvious!" insists Señor Agustín, serving the card-players their drinks. "And why? Because she thinks her husband is so loopy he no longer has any idea of what's going on. If not, why would she bring him home, when she's still hoping her lover boy will put in another appearance . . . Have you ever seen a family as crazy as that one, and all because the husband went off to Russia to fight?"

"That's enough, Agustín, please!" his sister protests. "Poor Vicky. It was her daughter who got him out of there. And you can say what you like, but they have cured him. He doesn't look the same."

"I never thought he was completely mad, Paqui," says Señor Carmona. "But it's true, he looks a different person."

"A different person, my eye!" Señor Agustín explodes. "He's the same old troublemaker as ever. It's true he doesn't go round boasting, or shouting and arguing with people, but he comes in here twice a day demanding his glass of Tío Pepe and pretending he's somewhere else when it comes to paying. He always used to leave without so much as a thank you, and he wants to do the same now, because of his pretty face and his blue shirt, the scoundrel. He may be another person, but whenever he can he tries to take advantage . . . Yesterday he came in with the idea he could carry on charging his quota for Social Assistance, and wanted a donation for his youth camps in return for not reporting me for selling Virginia tobacco. The same dirty tricks as when he was a councillor. And I've heard he's been doing the same in other taverns in the neighbourhood."

Señor Agustín insists that when Mir is speaking directly to you he shows glimpses of the abusive, bossy fellow who was such a pain in the arse, the vestiges of the arrogant attitude many people happily thought was a thing of the past following that pistol shot on the steps of San José de la Montaña, but it seems they were wrong.

"There are still those who look down at the ground when he passes, friends, if you hadn't noticed. Because crazy or in his right mind, he's just the same as ever."

Seeing him walk along the street, slowly and in a pensive mood, or standing at the counter in Bar Rosales, staring at his glass of sherry without showing the slightest interest in the other customers or any desire to talk to anybody, not even to scold the youths rowdily playing table football, he does indeed seem like a new man. His gaze is more troubled, he is much thinner, and he wears loose clothes that aren't his, a corduroy jacket that looks as if it belongs to somebody else, sometimes with a black beret pulled down over his ears; but what is really new about him is his self-absorbed manner, his slow, unspontaneous gestures, as if he was deciphering what he should do or say in the air. However, as it doesn't take long to discover, this apparent formality does not prevent him enjoying the fortnight of freedom he has been given, or to surprise everyone with several forays outside his home. He attends services at Las Ánimas, and midnight Mass with his daughter, even the solemn ceremony of the Nativity of the Poor, standing erect at the foot of the altar surrounded by the Congregation of Pious Ladies, and also turns up for the nativity play put on by the church theatre group. But in spite of these regular pious appearances, commented on and celebrated by the faithful, other reports and rumours, even if they are scurrilous bar-room gossip, claim that while the ex-councillor has always been a hypocrite and a Holy Joe he is also a rogue and a womaniser, or to put it more precisely, a shameless whoremonger. A few days before Twelfth Night, there are ribald comments in Bar Rosales to the effect that he was seen in the Quimet on the Rambla del Prat in the company of a tart, with a guitar in his hands, catching the peanuts she was launching towards his mouth. Roger and the eldest of the Cazorla brothers confirm this: they were there and split their sides laughing at his behaviour. The gossip also is that he was seen in Panam's, a low dive on Las Ramblas, and El Quique – well, El Quique swears he can't be that off his head, because he has two or three condoms in his pocket, and he's seen them.

After the Christmas festivities are over, one rainy afternoon Violeta and her father set off down the street under an umbrella to Plaza Rovira, where they wait for a taxi. That day the ex-councillor really does look like a different person: sad and downcast beneath the umbrella his daughter is holding, with the beret over his eyes and staring obsessively at his hands, he lets her adjust his scarf and do up a button on his raincoat. Shortly afterwards they take a taxi and disappear in the rain towards San Andrés. Three days later, suffering from acute liver pains, Señor Mir is rushed to the Hospital del Mar.

More or less around the same date, exactly three days after he has turned sixteen, one 11 January as night is drawing in, Ringo is reading at his table in Bar Rosales when Roger comes in saying that a woman has been killed in the Delicias cinema. But not in the stalls, the toilets or the foyer: in the projection room. A strange story, the intrigue increasing the more they learn about it. The victim is a prostitute, and was found strangled with a tie on a pile of reels in their cans next to the projector. They say the murderer is the projectionist, and that the police found him in the back row of seats even before the film had finished. Nothing further is known for the moment. The cinema was cleared and sealed off by order of the authorities. El Quique and a kid from his street, who had sneaked into the first afternoon performance, say there was a break in the film that lasted longer than usual. They were showing "La calle sin sol" and "Gilda", which was interrupted during the scene in the casino when she starts to undo the zip on her dress and says I can never get the hang of zips, but if somebody would like to help me . . . at which an admirer in the audience shouted that he would be delighted. That was when the film went off, El Quique explained, and added he was already expecting it to, because of course they would cut a film like that, with a gorgeous woman about to be shown stark naked . . .

Over the next few days more details emerge; the streetwalker was a beautiful Chinese woman, an ex-acrobat and variety artiste, who had once been something more than a friend to ex-councillor Mir, and she wasn't strangled with a tie but a black stocking.

"With a length of film," Señor Agustín asserts. "The cashier saw her when she was being carried out. They say it was the murderer himself who called the police, but that after that he had nothing to say, he was in a daze."

"It seems the victim was wearing her coat, but with nothing underneath," suggests El Quique.

For a while this is the only subject of conversation in the bar, as everyone speculates about who the victim was, and on the murderer's motive; whether he killed her out of jealousy, if she lived at the top of Calle Verdi and had a son, that she wasn't a Chinese tart but was from Aragón, and also that she had often been seen entering or leaving the police station on Calle Travesera. Finally the topic is exhausted, and the lively conversation among the customers turns elsewhere. The same occurs with the gossip about Ramón Mir's recovered mental health, which is put down to his recent enthusiastic addiction to whoring and living it up. Soon enough, everything slides back into the slime of winter that the days seem to slither along, into the uniform grey that the neighbourhood and the city bear like a stigma, so that it seems yet again that the things that really matter in life must be different, and must take place far from here, far from us. For example, lads: Larry Darrell renounces the beautiful Isabel and heads for the Himalayas in search of the fount of wisdom on a razor's edge; the young Nick Adams stares at the trout's fins moving as they struggle against the current of the river with two hearts, Jay Gatsby rows

245

eagerly in his small rowing boat out to a gangster's luxury yacht, towards a dream that will be his downfall, and Ringo installs himself yet again at his table by the tavern window and watches night close in on the street which, the same as every Sunday at this time, appears suddenly inhospitable and abandoned.

Shortly afterwards, Señora Mir and Violeta leave their building and walk arm-in-arm down the centre of the street, fresh from the hair salon and dressed to the nines. They walk quickly and nervously, whispering and leaning against one another. Yet again, the mother is accompanying her daughter to the dance at the Verdi, or possibly the Cooperativa La Lealtad. According to the gang, it is the mother who chooses the venue, and that always depends on the expectations roused the previous Sunday by the attention and behaviour some young man has shown to Violeta; how often he had asked her to dance, if he had offered her a drink or not, if he spoke politely and chatted to her or only wanted to get close and rub himself against her. Her mother's got eyes in the back of her head, El Quique used to say, before you can try anything she's spotted you.

As on every Sunday, when the two of them are passing Bar Rosales, Señora Mir relinquishes Violeta's arm and comes in to say hello to Señora Paquita. Sometimes, after the usual question, she stays talking to her for a few minutes while she has a small glass of brandy. Violeta waits for her in the street, pacing up and down and looking thoughtful, with her hair in surprising tight curls round her pale face, wearing a short grey cloth coat with velvet collar and cuffs, red woollen gloves and lilac medium-heeled shoes. Yet again her mother has said she'll be right out, that she will only be a minute, but Violeta knows this isn't the case. She knows that if her mother tosses down the first drink, she'll ask for another one and sip it slowly, losing all sense of time.

"Pour me another one, Paqui," says Señora Mir, leaning on the bar. "I'm ruining my liver, but don't worry, Princess, it can take it. And it warms the cockles of my heart. It's a long walk to Calle Montseny, and it's really cold out there."

"Why don't you go to Salón Verdi? It's much closer?"

"Because the Mario Visconti Orchestra is on at La Lealtad. Their singer is fantastic, very melodious . . . Well, my daughter likes him."

She coughs as she says this, and looks away. Today she has no wish to see herself reflected in her carping eyes. She is dressed and made up so strikingly she seems to have more on her than can possibly be taken in at first glance. She is spilling out of a short grey woollen coat with a rabbit-fur collar, allowing glimpses of a cherry-red blouse that matches the fierce scarlet of her lips. She appears on edge, suffering from the cold, and vulnerable, her voice hoarse and weak. She has tried to bring everything together with an elaborate toilette that must have taken hours to apply, but has been unable to camouflage the deep lines round her eyes or the sour grimace at the corners of her mouth, or to rekindle the liveliness of her eyes, the cheerful, unexpected glint that has always been her most eloquent response to the world. Her face is no longer capable of that radical transformation that gave rise to all the ribaldry, and beneath the laboriously applied cosmetics there is no disguising the face of a woman worn down by the daily grind and by a broken marriage. The coat smells of wet sheep, and hanging from her shoulder is a big leather bag with a lacy fringe. The heavy bracelets tinkle as she anxiously tugs off her gloves and raises the glass to her lips with trembling fingers, cupping her other hand to conceal it as if she was shielding it from the wind or from prying eyes.

"Have you looked at yourself in the mirror, Vicky?"

"More than I would have liked, sweetie. Don't get at me."

"You don't look well," says her friend. "You ought to stay in bed. Why don't you let Violeta go on her own?"

"Huh, on her own! How many years is it since you've been dancing, my love? There are so many louts around! It sends a shiver down my spine just looking at them." She rolls her eyes, lined with mascara and a sense of the injustice of life, and adds: "Young people today are so cruel, Paqui."

She raises her shoulder and rubs it against her ear in a stroking gesture that conjures up luxurious furs caressing her neck, then sighs and searches desperately in her bag until she pulls out a packet of Chesterfield. She stands with the cigarette pinched between her fingers, but doesn't light it. Instead, she skilfully rolls it to and fro, lost in her thoughts.

"Your daughter is freezing out there in the street," says Señora Paqui. "Why don't you tell her to come in?"

"She prefers it out there."

"I can't understand why you don't let her in."

"I would let her, but she doesn't want to."

"Go on, tell her I'll give her a coffee."

"Me? You do it. Go out and tell her, see what she says."

"Why? What's her problem?"

"I think it's because of those boys at the table football. She says they make fun of her, that they're filthy pigs. She can't even bear to see them, and she's right. Kids today are a worthless bunch."

"But they aren't here. They left a while ago."

"It doesn't matter. You know how stubborn she is."

"I reckon she doesn't like seeing you in here, Vicky." She fills her glass of soda water to the brim. "Here. This is the only thing you should be drinking."

"Oh no, you can pour that away." She giggles nervously: "I've cut soda out of my diet, sweetie. It gives me heartburn."

"I don't think that's funny."

"Oh, Paqui, how boring you can be! Yours truly here has got her responsibilities, hasn't she? My husband in hospital, unsure whether or not they'll have to operate, and me running up and down all the blessed day. And if you knew how little I want to go dancing in this cold. But I have to bring a little happiness into her life, don't I? What else can I do? She's so strange, poor thing. How are we going to find her a boyfriend if she never goes out?" she observes her daughter in the street through the steamed-up glass of the door. "Look at her. She's pretty when she makes an effort, don't you think, Paqui?"

This scene is repeated every Sunday, with very few variations, with or without permed hair, with or without fake-luxurious furs on her shoulders, but always with Violeta waiting out in the street for her, the habitual prelude to dancing. Also during the week, at any time of day. Whenever Señora Mir is coming or going past the bar, she stops and enters, and asks the eternal question, the real and only reason for appearing, the question she doesn't appear to want to give up on, however often she is disappointed. It frequently precedes a greeting or any other kind of polite formula, even her urgent desire for a drink:

"Any news, Paqui?"

For the first time, Señora Paquita allows a hint of hostility to appear in her reply, despite her friendly tone:

"News, what news, darling?"

"Goodness gracious! My letter: what other news could there be?"

"There you go again! No, I haven't had any letter."

"What's the matter, princess? Are you annoyed at me?"

"I'm . . . .weary, Vicky."

"I only asked a question. Won't I even be to be able to ask you now?"

"I warned you, I told you not to get your hopes up . . ."

"Oh my, that's a good one! What you told me is that I had to wait, don't you remember? That's what you told me . . . Or do you know something more you're not telling me?"

"Of course not, Vicky. But if I were you I'd forget that letter for good . . . I mean, I wouldn't keep on waiting for it. Not now."

"Ah, but I'm not you, sweetie!"

She says this with a defiant smile, the unlit cigarette rolling between her red, shiny fingernails, but her friend knows that behind the smile lies deep distress, a persistent anguish that she finds hard to explain after such a long, useless wait, when disillusionment and resignation would be more natural. Nothing has changed in her obstinate attitude over the past six months, apart from her appearance, which is rapidly deteriorating. Despite all the make-up and the wide variety of hairdos. Stiffly erect on her stiletto heels, she controls a slight shiver at the back of her neck. She

249

has one hand on the edge of the bar, and the other on her waist, like a bird about to take flight, and looks over her shoulder at the regulars playing cards under a gently rippling cloud of blue mist floating above their bent heads as they concentrate on the vagaries of the pack. Glancing in their direction, she catches the occasional mocking grin that possibly makes her think they are gossiping about her again, but there is no ill-feeling or bitterness or resentment in her gaze, nothing more than a mixture of disappointment and smiling bewilderment. The wide-open blue eyes are those of a woman who has suffered a kind of hallucination, somehow agreeable, but basically inexplicable.

A little beyond the domino players, sitting at another table with a book open in front of him, Berta's boy deliberately turns away from her to stare fixedly out into the street, and for a moment Señora Mir's gaze falters. Oh my lad, my lad, where's your manners, he might read in her face if he dared glance at her, aren't you ever going to keep your promise? Is that why you're refusing to look at me?

"What a lovely song, Paqui!" she suddenly exclaims, listening hard. "I like it because . . . because . . . I've no idea why!"

"What song?"

"Are you deaf? The one on the radio."

She smiles at nothing for a moment, her heart and memory connected to a musical thread only she perceives. The radio is silent at the far end of the bar, with a napkin and a toothpick holder on it.

"What nonsense you talk, Vicky. The radio's switched off."

"You're the one who's switched off!"

The gaudy cockatoo can hear the song because she carries the tune the whole time in her swinging hips: this no doubt is what the domino players near the bar would think if they still paid her any attention, if they were still trying to outdo one another with the crude jokes and vulgar gossip they indulged in so frequently at her expense the previous summer. Today the scatterbrain's hair is a mass of blonde curls like a young girl's. Take a good look at her, look at her shiny poppy red lips, at the rouge on her flabby cheeks, at the mascara daubed on her eyelashes. Like a wedding cake.

"All I want is that someday my daughter will be able to look after herself," she says after another sip of brandy. "That's all I want, Paqui. That to be happy she doesn't have to wait for some heartless rascal to decide he wants to sleep with her, if you follow me. Nowadays girls don't know what they want, they have no values." She wets her lips with the brandy again, then goes on: "I know what I'm talking about, because I've been through it too . . . Do you remember Ricardo, Paqui? That handsome Ricardo Taltavull, the one who used to click his tongue so disgustingly. How could I fall for a man who rummages in his ears with a matchstick and makes strange noises with his mouth, as if he always had phlegm in his throat? Too disgusting for words, don't you think? I must have been blind not to see it! And even so, I was crazy about him for almost a year. There's no explaining that sort of thing, but it does happen."

"Only to you, Vicky," sighs Señora Paquita. "These things only happen to you."

"Oh my girl, who hasn't been in love with someone completely unsuitable at some time or other?" Another pause, another sip. "And on top of all that, there's a lot less work, I don't know why. It must be because nobody has any aches and pains anymore. It's been ages since I've worked at the clinic, they never call me . . . Of course, nowadays they reckon penicillin cures everything. Do you know what I reckon, Paqui? That this damned penicillin is taking all my patients."

"Rubbish. It's just snake oil. You'll see, things will pick up this winter and you'll get more people . . ."

"Men don't get hernias anymore, Paqui. As many women with backache as you like. But not a single man with a hernia. I had a good number of them before . . . As for the letter, perhaps your brother knows something . . ."

Señora Paqui tries changing the subject:

"Listen, I think I could do with a back-rub myself, Vicky."

"Have you asked Agustín?"

"My problem is I don't stop all day long, so I don't have time for anything."

"Do you mind being quiet while I'm talking, Paqui, please?"

She closes her eyes for a moment, then casts a doleful glance at the handsome knock-kneed football player on the calendar, the one who she thinks should have kneeled down for the photograph. Despite this, she can't help but admire the impressive musculature above his sturdy knees, as well as the proud lift of his bandaged head, the wild defiance of the future. She finishes her drink, pays, and says goodbye to her friend, who insists she should go home. On the threshold, with the door open, she turns and her eyes once more seek out Berta's son crouching by the window with his sleepy face: what happened to your promise, my boy?

Beneath his heavy lids he can sense her silent reproach. I'm sorry, not this Sunday either, Señora. Since he's started working at night he feels tired all day long, and the smell of roast coffee on his jacket and scarf acts like a sleeping draught to make him sleepier still. His eyes are closing now over the pages of his book, and so he rubs the misted-up window to pick out the figure of Violeta in the street again. Now she is standing on the edge of the pavement on the far side of the road, motionless, with her feet close together. Her gloved hands are pressing a cheap yellow Perspex purse against her stomach, and she is staring down at the ground to avoid meeting the eyes of any passers-by. When she sees her mother coming out of the bar she crosses to meet her, and meekly hangs on her arm. The two of them walk down the street in the middle of the road, huddled together to warm each other, like two young friends off to a dance in search of excitement. The mother teeters on her high heels as she whispers something in her daughter's ear; Violeta listens, head down and silent, with that sensual incongruity that Ringo discerns yet again, even though she is some distance away and has her back to him: really pretty legs and an ugly face, wary gait but a pert behind.

Only half an hour later is he able to concentrate on young Michael

Furey standing in a remote Galway garden, freezing in the rain as he peers up at his beloved's window. The fateful atmosphere of the scene keeps him awake for a good while, until once again tiredness and an uneasy conscience numb his brain and he decides to close the book. He gets up and leaves the bar, standing on the pavement outside. It's gone five, and night is falling. But why are you doing this? he wonders, who is forcing you to keep a stupid promise you made to a half-crazy woman who is desperate to find her ugly daughter a boyfriend? He goes back into the bar, asks Señora Paquita if she will please keep the book for him, then goes out once more, wrapping the scarf round his neck and glancing up at the balcony to Señora Mir's already darkened flat on the opposite side of the road. He comes to a halt for a moment and thinks: it's the least I can do, and yet he can't bring himself to take the first step. On the balcony, the ragged Easter palm attached to the rusty ironwork for almost two years now, dried out and battered from being in all weathers for so long, has come loose and threatens to fall to pieces in the street below. Ringo thinks he sees a light being lit behind the balcony windows, and a shadow flitting across the dining-room. And something that is not so much a feeling, more of a slight twinge of conscience, finally sets him in motion as he tells himself for the umpteenth time, it's the least you can do, kid, turn up there simply to warn them.

He has never been in the Cooperativa La Lealtad before, but when he has climbed the stairs and finds himself confronted with the dance floor everything looks very familiar because he has heard so often from El Quique and Roger what the place is like and how easy it is to pick up a girl, especially on hot summer nights when the balcony onto Calle Montseny is open and couples go out for a bit of fresh air and a quick grapple. The orchestra is playing a rumba; the singer is wearing a sky-blue jacket with sparkly silver lapels and is shaking maracas. The dance floor is packed with couples, and all round Ringo little groups of youngsters are talking and shouting, standing or sitting on folding chairs. Flashy ties, quiffs, jackets with padded shoulders, girls in cardigans, nylons and ankle socks. He can't see El Quique or the others: they must have gone to the Verdi. It takes him a while to locate Violeta. She is not one of those girls who stand by the side of the floor waiting to be asked to dance, shyly or staring openly at the boys, hips jutting. She seems to know that she stands little chance against them, and to judge from where he finally discovers her, she has given up all hope. She is on a chair by the far wall, near one of the exits to the balcony that runs the length of the building, but is shut now. She is saying no to a thin boy with big ears who is standing cheekily in front of her, arms akimbo. Hands resting on the gloves and purse in her lap, she shakes her head time and again, without even looking up at him. The confused lighting in the dance hall does her no favours. Without her coat, she is wearing a fairly short pleated orange skirt and a mauve satin blouse with a black belt and a tight collar. Before she is left alone again, she sees Ringo pushing his way towards her, his jacket unbuttoned and hands in pockets, his hair spilling down his forehead and the scarf crossed over his chest like a pair of cartridge belts.

"Hello there, Violeta."

"Hello."

"Where's your mother?"

"What . . . ?" she tilts her head to hear him better.

"Your mother. Didn't she come with you?"

"Is it that important to you?"

"I came to tell her something . . . I saw something very strange."

"You did?"

"Yes. I need to tell your mother at once . . . Seriously, where is she?"

The orchestra is playing so loudly his words are drowned out. He surveys his surroundings, without success. He remembers the gang's jokes in Bar Rosales: the mother clings to the bar, and the daughter lets herself be pawed on the balcony or in the toilets: It's as easy as pie, kid. Violeta crosses her legs very slowly, and studiously straightens one of the pleats in her skirt. She gives him a hard look.

"Take your scarf off, will you? It makes me feel hot just looking at it. What do you have to say to my mother?"

"That there's someone in your house. There's a light on in the dining-room, you can see it from the street. I swear! I noticed it as I was leaving the bar. There's somebody inside – it must be a burglar . . . Where is your mother?"

She stares at him, silent and thoughtful, apparently not the slightest bit alarmed.

"A light in the dining-room?"

"I swear!"

"When did you see it?"

"Just now, about a quarter of an hour ago. The time it took me to walk here."

"Is that so?" Once again she looks thoughtful but unperturbed, with a faint smile playing across her face. She straightens another pleat on her skirt. "That's why you came, because you think there's a burglar in our flat?"

"Well, let's see, I knew you two were here, didn't I? I saw you leave home, you and your mother . . . What do you expect me to think, if I see a light and there's nobody in?"

"Mama must have forgotten to switch it off."

Ringo takes off his scarf, fetches a chair, and sits down beside her.

"Are you sure? Someone could have got in by the balcony, grabbing the rail . . . the Easter palm has come loose, it's about to fall off."

"It is?"

"He might have come back, and if he doesn't have a key . . ."

"Who might have come back?"

"That man with the limp, your mother's friend."

"Don't talk to me about him! I wish he were dead!"

"Well, there's a light on in the dining-room, Violeta, I swear. We have to warn your mother. Where is she?"

"Where do you think? At the bar." She looks at him maliciously. "I

255

get it. You want Mama to see you, don't you? So that she'll know you've come . . . even if it's only with the excuse that you've seen a burglar."

"Me?"

"Yes, you. Because she made you promise you'd come. Do you think I didn't know? I know all the tricks my mother gets up to."

"What are you saying? I came because I wanted to. Nobody makes me do anything. This afternoon I intended to go to the Verdi cinema, so you see . . . They're showing 'The Nine-Fingered Beast', have you seen it? It's about a pianist who has his finger cut off, and he becomes a murderer to avenge himself, but he's still the greatest pianist in the world . . . He's Peter Lorre. I was about to buy the ticket when I said to myself, this isn't right, *nano*, you ought to go and warn Violeta and her mother there's somebody in their flat."

"You don't say. Alright, so now you've warned us. But tell me this: why did you promise my mother you'd come and dance with me, when as far as I know you don't even like dancing?"

There is no way he is going to tell her the reason. He's not even sure of it himself. Violeta smiles mockingly and adds:

"Don't worry, you idiot. You don't have to dance with me if you don't want to."

"Of course I do. I came because of what I told you," he insists, scrutinising her unconvinced profile, while the orchestra launches into a mambo that produces an explosion of joy and feminine squeals on the dance floor. "Aren't you worried that a stranger has sneaked into your flat?"

Violeta turns slowly and looks him in the eye.

"Do you really not know?"

"Know what?"

"Have you really not been told?" she asks witheringly, staring at him intently, as though trying to hypnotise him. "Really and truly, you know nothing? I can't believe it . . ."

"I'm telling you again, I saw a light on in your flat! Cross my heart and hope to die!"

"Alright, so there was a light. Now tell me something . . . What's your father up to? What news do you have of him?"

"My father's in France," he says rapidly. "What's that got to do . . . ?"

"Well actually, it's got a lot to do with it. If I told you he might have switched that light on, would you believe me? He has a key to the flat. Mama gave it him, and recently he's met your mother there more than once, always after dark. Don't tell me you didn't know. You're so smart." She uncrosses her legs, then crosses them again brusquely and conclusively, and for a moment the suggestiveness of her gesture is more powerful than his poorly concealed surprise at what he has just heard. He immediately reacts as if he has been caught out, and shifts his gaze to the hands on her lap. Her long, delicate fingers, with their deliberate, enveloping movements, are fiddling with her purse. "Why did they meet in my house and in secret? I've no idea. Ask your mother."

"My father's in France, I tell you. Most likely with your uncle. And I know why . . ."

"I don't want you to explain anything," Violeta interrupts him, "I don't want to know anything more. Thank God it was only a few days, and I hardly even noticed. He was shut up in his room the whole time and only came out at night, so don't ask me anything, because I know nothing."

Her eyelids flutter disagreeably: they are heavy, with thick, reddish lashes. Ringo meanwhile, still taken aback by what he has just heard, is thinking about the light on the balcony. So from time to time the Rat-catcher is to be seen around here . . . At any rate what matters now is that the light he saw – although he is starting to wonder whether he really did see it – is the justification for him being here, and not his blasted uneasy conscience. What on earth does anything else matter to me? Then, on the strength of a sudden impulse, he reveals an intimate wish of his, a fantasy he has been elaborating.

"One day I'm going to France. One day my father will send for my mother and me, and we'll leave this arsehole of the world for good."

Violeta stares at him in disbelief.

"You will? That's good. And when is this going to happen?"

"I don't know, it depends on a lot of things." He lowers his voice, and adds mysteriously: "We'll have to wait and see, and above all not go round saying anything about it, alright? Be very careful. Well anyway, since I'm here . . ."

Since he has come, he means to say, since he has kept his promise and she is alone and so obviously available, with her hard little breasts beneath her blouse and her apple-like knees, seated so upright on her chair and nodding her head to the music . . .

"Do you want to dance?"

"Ugh! I'm tired. Besides, you don't like dancing."

"That depends."

He's taken off his scarf, and doesn't know what to do with it. After the mambo, the crooner conducts the first bars of a slow tune and tilts his head at the microphone, singing in a low, syrupy voice.

"The singer is crap," says Ringo.

"He's very handsome."

"He's got the face of a goat."

"Well, I like him."

"And the pianist plays with a pole stuck up his arse, he thinks he's José Iturbí or someone . . . and just look at the drummer. This orchestra is useless."

"It's the best. Last month they were playing at the Salón Cibeles."

They fall silent for a while, watching the couples slowly gyrating round the edge of the dance floor. A boy with a huge conk and a tightly combed zeppelin head plants himself in front of Violeta, hands in pockets, and asks her to dance. He's even uglier than the one before, thinks Ringo. She says no, and the boy turns round and walks off dejectedly. Violeta takes Ringo's scarf from him and puts it on the back of the chair.

"Your scarf smells really nice," she says. "Roast coffee, isn't it?"

Ringo shrugs. The scarf is a perfumed reminder of his secret nights. Less than twelve hours ago it was hanging from a hook in a corner of Señor

Huguet's shed while he turned the handle by the fire. But he doesn't want to talk about the fire or those nights with Violeta.

"Come on, let's go," says Violeta, standing up. "Mama ought to see you've come. She's in the bar. Come on, what are you waiting for?"

"No, dammit, that's not why I came!"

"It isn't?"

"No. But you . . . can I tell you something? You shouldn't leave your mother on her own, least of all in the bar. You shouldn't do that."

Applause for the orchestra. Violeta stares at him, then drops into her seat and sighs.

"I know," she says, suddenly overwhelmed. "But there's no way . . . We had another argument as soon as we got here, just for a change. She stays in the bar, and nobody can get her out of there. She burnt herself on the hand with her cigarette, but she insists it was a boy next to her, that of course it wasn't her . . . that she almost fell because the boy was laughing at her and me. I bet her head was spinning. Something always happens to her. She's so accident-prone. But the fact is she's not well, not well at all . . . And you know why? She's still waiting for news from that footballer! How stupid can you get?"

"What footballer?"

"The lame one, who else? That old man who says he broke his leg years ago, Señor Alonso," she says harshly. "Always talking about that leg of his. And then there was that letter that Señora Paquita told Mama about, another of his lies. I bet he never thought of even writing her a postcard."

"A letter?"

"Don't tell me you don't know about it. The story's going round the entire neighbourhood!"

The orchestra strikes up a bolero. Ringo looks pensively down at his hands.

"Well, yes, I did hear something . . . What do you think Señor Alonso would say to her in that letter?"

"Heaven knows. Lies to make it up with her, to see her again . . . God forbid. Mama is getting worse all the time. I don't know what to do. It's like . . . like an illness. The other day she had an argument with Señora Grau; she called her an old busybody and insulted her. Mama said she was sticking her nose in where it was none of her business, and she got dressed and stormed out without paying. I'm sure she won't be back. And it wasn't the first time something like that has happened . . . Really, something needs to be done. Someone ought to tell her that he's married, for example . . . because I'm sure he is, and with children. Eight of them at least. And that he's been in jail . . . Did you know he's been in jail?"

"No."

"Well, he has. He was out on the street when he met Mama. He had just come out of Modelo prison or a concentration camp . . ."

"How do you know?"

"He gave Mama a very nice ring he himself had made out of a sheep bone or whatever. All prisoners make them. Before he went to France, Uncle Ramiro used to make bone rings with a file when he was in prison. I reminded Mama of that, but she didn't want to listen. She never listens to me. But somebody ought to convince her that he's a jailbird . . ."

"But why was he in jail?"

"What does that matter? For being a thief, a con man, or a black-marketeer. Who knows? Most likely for being a Red."

"That's not the same."

"Well, it is more or less." Violeta shrugs. "The fact is that he's a liar, a scrounger, a good-for-nothing. To think she could get involved with someone like that! Exactly what Papa hated! A jailbird, a criminal, a damned Red . . ."

"But he's not a bad person, Violeta. He isn't."

"What do you know?"

"If you tell your mother that, it'll really hurt her."

"So what? Let her suffer. Because who is he anyway, where did he spring from, why did he have to come into the flat . . . ? I bet he's from a shanty town. I could swear he lives in a shack on Montjuich, up near Can

Tunis or worse still, in Campo de la Bota. A lady who gives catechism classes in Las Ánimas and goes a lot to Somorrostro doing charity work saw him one day with a gang of kids playing football on the beach, down by the shanties of Pequin. I didn't tell Mama that, she's capable of going to try to find him in that rubbish dump . . . Have you ever been there? There's nothing but rats and shit! But of course, the fraud would never admit it . . . how does the saying go: 'Easier to catch a liar than a lame man'. Well, it's not true."

"So what are you thinking of doing?"

"I'd like to convince her that he's never coming back, and that he's not going to write or anything. That he's gone to Brazil to work, for example, a long way away, and has no intention of returning . . . You could tell her. Tell her how you saw him one day saying farewell to everybody in the bar."

"But that's a lie. Why don't you tell her?"

"She wouldn't believe me. Ever since the day they had an argument and she threw him out, Mama doesn't believe a word I say."

"Why's that?"

Violeta falls silent, and stares cold-eyed at the couples crowding the dance floor, their heads turning submissively to the slow rhythm of the melodious bolero.

"Aaagh!" she spits in disgust. "Because that's how she is!"

Here, as she waits on her chair to be asked to dance, in this harsh light and rocked by the suggestive music, the imbalance between her pretty legs and ugly face is more shocking and disconcerting than ever. And yet the more striking the contrast, the greater the attraction. Perhaps this is why he tries again:

"Well, shall we dance?"

Violeta makes a vague gesture with her head that could just as well be a yes as a no, then thinks for a few moments before saying:

"No."

She busies herself once more with her purse and straightening the pleats of her skirt. Her fingers move rapidly and delicately. All at once she stands up.

"Alright then," she concedes. "That's why you came, isn't it?"

Just by putting his arm round her waist, fingers brushing against the ridge of her back under the blouse, his hand can sense the lively spring in her buttocks as she steps out. Even his amputated finger can feel a slight tautening that lifts the heart. She holds up her moist, hot right hand and as they take the first steps he folds it in his and brings it down to his chest, encouraging a more or less casual touching. Her other hand is resting on his shoulder close to the back of his head, but she is still clutching her small gloves and purse, so there is no chance of any effusive response. Even so, as she stretches her neck and turns her face away from him, he can feel the docility of her body as she lets him pull her to him. Violeta's left thigh slips between his legs, imprisoned as if by accident and always slightly behind his movements, and he summons a warm rush to his groin: he needs to believe that this is why he is here, for this bumping and grinding, that this is the only reason for coming, what else, Quique, Roger, Rafa, lads, what else could bring me here, what other emotion could lead me to want to please an old bat who's searching for a boyfriend for her daughter? Why could he have come if not to press his tool up against those thighs, even if only to confirm yet again that it means nothing to Violeta, that she doesn't respond to any prompting, that she seems unaware of your hard-on, and with complete indifference starts to hum the song along with the orchestra, apparently oblivious to the ritual of stealthy movements between her thighs, her body as unresponsive as it was during the saint's day fiesta the year before.

After a while, annoyed at the lack of response, he brings his mouth to her deaf ear:

"Listen, Violeta, there's something I want you to explain. Last summer, when your mother made that scene in the middle of the street, you were at home, weren't you? I heard your mother say so to Señora Paquita . . . Why didn't you come down to help her?"

262

"Why do you ask? Is it that important?"

"I couldn't give a damn. But your mother was lying out there in the street and you didn't even come out on to your balcony."

"I didn't know anything about it. I was in bed with a bump on my head."

"A bump?"

"I'd had a fall in the bathroom. Just as well I had the towel wrapped round my head, because otherwise . . ."

"Well, somebody wanted to go and fetch you, but your mother said you weren't at home, that you'd gone to the beach with a girlfriend. Why did she lie?"

"I don't know . . . I guess she didn't want me to see her in a state like that."

The crooner sings with his fish lips pressed up against the microphone; the loudspeaker converts his nasal drawl into crashing scrap metal. *Cabaretera, mi dulce arrabalera.* Every so often as Ringo takes a forward step he misses the beat in his haste to press himself against her and treads on her foot. Think of my poor feet occasionally, she murmurs jokingly. But the clumsy Ringo cannot think of her feet, because in his mind's eye he is seeing her in the bathroom, towel wrapped round her head like a turban, staring at herself naked in the mirror before she slips; because he is seeing her on the floor and considering the rising groin that he is now pressing gently with his thigh without getting any reaction, without any sign of acceptance from her. It's like rubbing yourself lovingly against a sack of potatoes.

"So you were the little innocent," he mutters. "And that day, when your mother and the lame footballer had their fight, you were there . . . What happened? Why did they argue?"

She says nothing, but lets her forehead droop on to his shoulder. Over a stupid little thing, she says after some time; it had to happen, and I was glad it did. She presses herself against him, flinging her arm round his neck, her mouth tight against the lapel of his jacket, and stammers something he doesn't understand, but which sounds like a swear word, followed by a garbled string of reproaches: it was a misunderstanding, some nonsense of her mother's, a misapprehension she still hasn't got over, but which I'm glad of. She describes all this in a flat monotone, as if she were reading it with great difficulty on his lapel, pausing and hesitating the whole time: if she had gone to the beach that Sunday with her friend Merche as planned, if Señora Terol had not had cellulite and her mother gone to visit her, if that man had not stayed at home to wait for her, if I had only taken a shower half an hour later . . . A brief account of facts linked by a fateful outcome. A strange voice with a murmur of rain. Ringo closes his eyes in order to see her more clearly: beyond the emotionless words there is a pretty bathroom, and she is looking at herself naked in the mirror as she wraps the towel round her head. Barefoot and still damp, she leans forward, then straightens up with the towel in place. Her small breasts and ample thighs push forward, but as she turns to reach for the bathrobe she slips and falls backwards, hitting the back of her head on the edge of the bath. It could have been worse, she says, the turban softened the blow, but even so I saw stars and could hardly speak. At that moment, the ex-footballer was in the dining-room laying the table, he liked to help, he always set the places when he stayed for a free meal, and he must have heard her cry out. He rushed in, lifted her in his arms, covered her with the bathrobe, took her to her room and laid her out on her camp bed – but she only learned all this sometime later.

"I'm not saying he touched me, eh? But who knows . . ."

"Oh yes? Why do you say that?"

"Touched me in a certain way, I mean. You know . . . If he did, I wasn't aware of it, I didn't realise."

"Huh! A girl always realises something like that."

How long has passed? she asked herself when she came to. And she cannot say for certain if he touched her, but all of a sudden she finds herself stretched out on the bed, half-covered and still groggy, completely defenceless, with the towel wrapped round her head like a turban. How long had she been like that? And he's bending over her trying to revive her by tapping her on the cheek and calling to her, Violeta, my child, his voice and hands leave a scalding sensation, and what could she do, she was unable to react, she had no idea what was going on, and neither of them heard the front door or the footsteps along the corridor, until they saw her standing in the doorway in her white coat and holding the vanity case with her creams and potions . . .

Ringo would like to see her face while she is talking, because her voice sounds so strange and muffled with her mouth pressed against his chest that it conveys no emotion. Almost at once, she loosens the arm round his neck and raises her head, as if she had been unburdening herself of a secret and had needed to bury herself in him to do so, hiding her face and adopting another voice.

"He tried to explain," she goes on. "But without making much effort. Mama didn't listen anyway, she said some terrible things to him. Terrible. That he was to get out of the house and never come back. She slapped him and threw everything on the table at him – plates and glasses and a bottle, everything he had laid out for the three of us. She was sobbing all the while, and suddenly rushed out into the corridor and downstairs . . . And he gathered his things and left as well. I thought he had gone after her to bring her back and explain, but not a bit of it: he vanished completely and never came back."

"And what did you do?"

"Nothing. I shut myself in the bathroom again, and kept quiet."

"You kept quiet? Why?"

"Because deep down I was pleased he was gone. Because he would have left her anyway. That's why."

"How do you know?"

"Because he didn't love her anymore. She didn't realise it, but I did. He managed to say to her: I promise to forgive you, and I'll write to you, or something of the sort, but he took advantage of what had happened to leave her for good." She falls silent for a while, then adds: "I've told you all this so you'll see I'm not making it up. It was all so terrible for Mama."

And she refuses to understand, adds Violeta reluctantly, her voice thick with a spiteful delight. That woman cannot or will not understand; she's always been like that, she trusts other people too much, and when they deceive her she never learns, she's so damned stupid and naive, she'll always be looking for someone to look after her and protect her, someone who's kind and attentive. She's always needed that, and that's precisely why she's ended up losing all her self-esteem. For some time now, Papa has been nothing more than a distant memory for her, and an unpleasant one at that, and so that man is all she thinks about. The days after that rogue left her, she said some unbearable things.

"Do you know what she said one day? She said that the worst thing of all, what had hurt her most, was not that I was half-naked in bed with him almost on top of me, but to see me with his towel on my head – because that was the towel he used! See how unhinged she was? That towel was mine, it always had been!"

The next tune is a slow one, but Ringo isn't listening or following the rhythm, simply turning very slowly, pushing his pelvis forward, getting aroused every so often. That girl already does it, Roger told him one day as they watched Violeta leaving the bar carrying a bottle of wine and the soda siphon. How can you tell if a girl's already done it? he had asked, and quick as a flash El Quique had replied on Roger's behalf: It's easy, kid, you can tell by the dark lines under her eyes and by the way she walks so stiffly, as if she's swallowed a broom.

"Mind my feet," whispers Violeta. She can feel his hand slowly sliding down her back until, as if without meaning to, the four fingers are touching the rounded top of her buttock. "And keep your hand up, please. Don't think it's because you've got a finger missing that I don't like it. It's not that . . ."

"Alright. Shall we go out to the balcony?"

"In this cold? No, thanks. Let me see it." She takes his hand and raises it level with her chest. She carries on dancing while she examines the stump: "Can you button up your shirt with it? Can you hold a spoon properly, comb your hair?"

"This hand can do anything. It can even do this, look."

The four fingers slip out of Violeta's grasp and crawl like a tarantula up the buttons on her blouse, then creep to one side and delicately cup her left breast. She glances at him expectantly, a sudden warm gleam in her eyes, and moves back gently. Taking hold of the mutilated hand once more, she tugs on it and turns round, trying to force a way through the dancing couples lost in the music. Ringo lets her drag him off, but the dance floor is packed, so he decides to push ahead of her and take the initiative. He struggles to force a way through, and soon feels Violeta clinging to his shoulders, like a drowning woman. Although they still haven't emerged from the crush, he can see himself out on the balcony with her, in spite of the cold, alone in the darkest corner, kissing . . .

"Let's go and see Mama for a moment," says Violeta when they finally manage to get clear of the dancing throng.

She isn't in the bar anymore. The manager, a middle-aged, slow but amiable fellow says she left over half an hour earlier, shortly after she had an argument at the bar with a lad who was wearing a pair of football boots instead of shoes, the lout. Why did they argue? He doesn't know how it started, he wasn't there, but apparently she made some remark about the boots that the lad didn't like. I'm sure she only wanted to be friendly, to have a bit of a joke, but that kid is an oaf, I know him, he's always looking for a fight. He said he had won a football and the pair of boots in some church tombola, and that he'd made a bet with a friend that he would come to dance with them on. He was making fun of her, but she didn't realise, all she seemed interested in was which church he had won the boots at. She seemed obsessed. She insisted so much and begged and begged so much that in the end to add to the fun the boy gave her confused directions to the church down by La Barceloneta. It was unbelievable, but she seemed to believe him.

"And after that, she left. She told me she'd see you at home, and that she wasn't worried about you because she saw you were in good company . . ."

"Did she leave owing anything, Señor Pedro?" asks Violeta.

"Nothing."

"She must have been bored," says Ringo. "That's why she left."

"She's never done that before. I'll give her what for."

"Bah. You'll see, she'll be at home waiting when you get back . . ."

"She can't get in. The key's in my bag." She feels for his hand with hers, squeezes it. "Will you come with me?"

It is only just after seven o'clock when they leave, but it's already completely dark and has started to drizzle. They walk shoulder to shoulder down the narrow, poorly lit streets of Gràcia. Ringo suggests her mother is bound to be waiting for her in the tavern, chatting to Señora Paquita; or perhaps she took it into her head to visit one of her friends or clients. In any case, she can't be far and will soon be home, where else would she go? But Violeta is silent for a long while. Then she says, as if thinking out loud: She doesn't have much work now, but she doesn't need much anyway, we're getting a good pension because of what's happened to Papa, and besides, I'll have a job soon, next month. Suddenly carefree, she starts to zigzag in front of him, almost dancing, sheltering under the balconies to avoid the drizzle, stopping every so often and allowing him to cuddle her. In a dark doorway on Calle de la Perla she offers no resistance when he kisses her: it's as if she is asleep. Five minutes later, her back against the wall of the Salesian school in Plaza del Norte, under the soaking wet branches of a bougainvillea, she lets him lift her skirt. He prematurely undoes his flies, but at no moment receives anything more in response to his desperate fumbling than passive consent. His hands persist with her breasts for a while, until he feels once more that he is humping a sack of potatoes, and when he feels her gloved hand pressing on his shoulder to dissuade him, he gives up. She is not even breathing heavily. She's never done that before, he hears her whisper, but she might be referring to her mother again.

As they approach Bar Rosales, Ringo walks ahead of her and goes in. All the Sunday evening regulars are there, and the atmosphere is warm and inviting. Señora Mir has not been back. Over by the table football, Señor Agustín seems very busy fixing one of the players onto its rod. No, they haven't seen Vicky since she left for the dance, says Señora Paquita. Is something wrong? No, nothing, Señora Paquita. He recovers the book he left with her and says thank you. He slips to the door and turns round, about to add something more, when he sees her smiling mischievously at him, trying to contain a laugh:

"Try to be more careful, love, or your little birdie will fly away."

Oh, shit! He turns and rapidly does up his flies before going out into the street. He could have sworn he had done so as quickly and discreetly as possible the moment Violeta, back against the wall, suddenly turned her cold eyes on him, closed her legs and pushed him away with a gentle but firm hand. Ringo is having such bad luck with his flies that he is starting to believe there's a gypsy curse on them. Why does this kind of thing always have to happen to me?

"She's not there," he tells Violeta, who has been waiting for him on the pavement. "And they haven't seen her. But don't worry, she'll be back before long, you'll see. I'm sure of it."

He tries to take her hand, but she pretends not to notice. As he walks up the street to her house with her, he stealthily uses his phantom finger to make sure that every single one of the buttons on his flies are properly done up, because he is suddenly wary that they are undone again, and even senses that the cold night air has crept inside. There is no interior light visible from Señora Mir's apartment anymore. When they have almost reached the doorway to her building, the rain starts coming down more heavily. Violeta runs on ahead of him, opens the street door and ducks inside the courtyard. Taken aback, he stands out on the pavement, peering into the shadows at the foot of the stairs. She gives him a sad, fleeting smile as she searches for the key, then dashes up as fast as she can.

Even if the smile had meant something else, he would not have followed her. And now he knows for certain why he is standing there, in the middle of the street in the pouring rain until he sees a light go on behind the balcony, and ducks into the doorway, determined to wait. She's left the street door open for her mother, he thinks, not for me. The street is deserted, and the lights are like yellow-stained cotton balls hanging in the darkness. For almost an hour the only traffic is a taxi that makes the sound of torn silk as it splashes along the road, a single headlight picking out both the lashing rain and, all of a sudden, a distant corner of his memory as cold and inhospitable as this doorway itself. Frustrated, and with his feet squelching in his shoes, he is unwilling to accept any other mysterious sign that claims to give his life direction, and yet only a few minutes later, when he decides to transfer his vigil to the Rosales bar and runs there, covering his head with his scarf, he is forced to admit the obstinate persistence of these signs, because the smell of the rain on his face as he runs seems to be a promise of the future, just like when he was a child.

He sits at his table and rubs the misted-up window with his hand. At the next table, Señor Agustín is eating a wild asparagus tortilla, playing draughts with one of the customers. While he is drying the rain off his scarf, Señora Paquita comes out of the kitchen carrying a bowl of Russian salad. She stops beside him: So who's this dreamy Romeo who stands out in the rain staring like a dummy at a girl? Yours truly here, Señora Paquita. You've got wet ears and you're tired out, you ought to go home and change your clothes. He listens to her, half asleep. I'm fine, Señora Paquita. I saw you standing out there like a booby. Were you expecting Violeta to come out on to the balcony, or did you want to catch pneumonia? That's it, I wanted to catch pneumonia, Señora Paqui. Your mother must be waiting for you to have supper. My mother is working night shifts until the end of the month, there's nobody at home waiting for me. She turns her back on him and goes to leave the Russian salad on her brother's table. Then she returns, hands on hips, you'll have a glass of hot milk, won't you? I don't want milk, thank you. Then a cup of cocoa.

I'd prefer a double brandy, Señora Paquita, so that I can get drunk more quickly. Hey, don't you try to be funny with me! What a disaster you are, just look at the state of you, look at your scarf, and your shoes. He replies, in a weak, dull voice, I'm fine, Señora Paqui, but she is already behind the bar, where she opens a cocoa drink, pours out a glass, heats it in the steam from the coffee machine, adds a tot of brandy, and comes back over.

"I've cheered it up a little." She leaves the glass on the table. "Drink it down and get straight off home," she orders, before returning to the kitchen.

He drinks it sleepily and thinks things over. What kind of idiot dances with a sack of potatoes simply because her mother asks him to do her a favour? Your servant here, the dummy's dummy. Every so often he rubs the steamed-up window with his hand, keeping an eye on Señora Mir's doorway. The rain has eased off to a drizzle. At last, around half past nine, he sees her toiling up the middle of the street, carefully stepping between fleeting glints of light and reflections as sharp as broken glass on the wet asphalt. She is hunched over, staggering on her high heels, her wet skirt stuck to her sturdy thighs, covering her head with the jacket, its fur collar flattened by the rain and beaded with droplets of light as she passes beneath the streetlamp, as if it were sheltering fireflies. When she reaches her doorway she halts and seems to hesitate. She looks from side to side and stands motionless for some time, head down. She looks like a huge, ugly paper bird, deflated and streaming with water. Her chin on her chest, she takes one step forward and two back, shakes her jacket and then stands still again. When at last she decides to go in, Ringo closes his book, gets up from the table, and goes over to the bar kitchen to announce, loudly and firmly:

"I'm going, Señora Paqui. Thanks, and goodnight."

"Bye, you ninny."

14

RESCUED WORDS

Señor Carmona says he found her lying on the second-floor landing in her wet clothes, head resting on the step closest to her front door. This was at dawn, and there wasn't much light, so I stumbled over her and nearly fell down the stairs, he explained in the tavern. It was horrible seeing her like stretched out like that, I thought she was dead. She had taken her shoes off, there were holes in the knees of her stockings, and her face was white as a sheet apart from a few smears of make-up. Señor Carmona works as a stevedore down at the docks, and leaves home very early each morning. He says he rang the bell until he woke Violeta, who was startled, then angry with her mother. Between the two of them they tried to rouse her and get her into the flat.

So, Ringo deduces, she didn't ring the bell, she spent the night out on the landing. She must have been drunk and unable to find the doorbell, or perhaps she felt so ashamed of herself she didn't want Violeta to see her in such a state; or perhaps she did ring, but her daughter was already asleep and didn't hear. Why didn't she stay awake to wait for her, knowing she didn't have the key? Ringo doesn't want to ask himself any more questions, he prefers to think about something else or to doze over his music scores and his book. The clandestine job he has at night in the coffee-roasting shed makes him drowsy every morning as he kills time in Bar Rosales.

A fortnight later he learns that Señora Mir's night-time wandering is just the first of a litany of shocks for Violeta, the first in a series of madcap escapades outside the neighbourhood. At the same time, her mother's lack of care for her appearance and for the flat, her desire to be left alone and her helplessness, as well as the neglect of her clients that set in some weeks earlier, now seems to have become an irreversible decline. One sunny Sunday morning in February, she left her home early in the morning, and did not come back for lunch. That afternoon, after searching for her in several local taverns, and even in the bar at the Salón Cibeles and La Lealtad, Violeta heard from Rufina the hairdresser that she had been seen mid-morning wandering like a sleepwalker up the highway to El Carmelo. Night was falling by the time her daughter found her on the eastern slope of Montaña Pelada, sitting on the three steps of the unfinished stairway cut into the rock. Hugging her basket of dried lavender to her chest, she was gazing intently at black smoke curling upwards into the sky from the miserable roofs of the shacks of El Carmelo. She refused to stand up, but seemed lucid and calm, explaining that she'd climbed up there to pick elderflowers.

"She's promised me she won't escape again, Señora Paqui," says Violeta as she drinks a milky coffee at the counter in Bar Rosales. "She's in bed now. Grandma Aurora is coming to visit her this afternoon or tomorrow . . . I don't think she'll get up, but if you or Señor Agustín see her coming out of the building, please let me know at the hospital." She glances over at Ringo, as if including him in her request.

To come across Violeta in the bar, and see her talking in a friendly way with Señora Paquita, is a novelty for him. She is wearing a white turtleneck jumper and a coat that is too short for her. Her hair is done up in a bun, her shoes and stockings are white, and she is carrying a new nurse's uniform over her arm. Señora Paquita listens with a worried look on her face. She sees the poor girl's life as an endless succession of calamities: her only family are her mother and father and her paternal grandmother – who has not wanted anything to do with her son Ramón for many years now – and she is bound to feel very lonely.

Ringo on the other hand does not know what to think. He is hypnotised yet again by the sight of Violeta. He stares and stares at her, but cannot recognise the girl who only a fortnight earlier had let him lift her skirt and caress her buttocks beneath a bougainvillea dripping with rain. Crouching behind his book, shielded yet again from a fickle, ungraspable reality, he thinks her profile is suddenly that of an adult, as if her new job and all the worries of the past few days had accelerated the transition from adolescence to womanhood. With a vague sense of loss, his eyes travel down to her legs in their white stockings. He surveys her placid, mature calves calmly pressed together, and wonders why the scent of her wet hair should linger more stubbornly in his memory than anything else, and why that scent is even sharper than desire, why now as she talks briefly to Señora Paquita in a low voice, struggling to overcome a hostility that is even more pointed than usual, listening to her words of advice with her head tilted towards her good ear, why all of a sudden this girl seems older than her eighteen years. She has scarcely paid him any attention: he looks like a shadow against the wall tiles, simply one of many in the gloomy tavern, so ever-present and familiar it is like a state of mind.

"If you'll only be patient, Violeta, you'll see that everything will work out," says Señora Paquita. "And don't forget, we're here if you need us for anything."

Drily, as if to make it clear that she's not here out of pleasure, Violeta informs Señora Paquita that for three days now she has been working as a nurse in the Hospital del Mar, thanks to a recommendation from Mother Josefina, a nun who is a friend of her mother's. She has a renewable six-month contract and is pleased because in her free moments between patients she will be able to attend her father, who is still interned in the hospital. Also, in spite of all the difficulties, she is continuing with her studies, in the hope of becoming a theatre nurse.

Only too aware of what is in store for the young girl, Señora Paquita repeats her offer of support.

"We'll keep an eye out, you can leave without worrying. Do you want me to bring you anything from the market?"

"I don't need anything today. But tonight I'll leave you the ration cards, and if you'd be so kind . . ."

"Of course. The less your mother goes out, the better. Do you want me to call in on her later, to see if she needs . . . ?"

"She doesn't want to see anyone at the moment," Violeta cuts her off. She finishes her coffee and rummages in her purse. "Well, I have to be going."

"Poor Vicky, what's happening to her is terrible. I've been trying to warn her. The number of times I've argued with her over that stupid business . . ."

"She'll get over it." And then, in the same peremptory tone as before: "But if she escapes again, now I'll know where to find her. I'll be late for work. Bye."

Early every morning from then on, as she leaves home to catch the number 39 tram to the Hospital del Mar, Violeta drops in at Bar Rosales to tell Señora Paquita the latest news and to ask her to buy something or other. Ringo is always there, invariably on his own and bent over a book, the smell of roast coffee on his clothes, with his incurable sleepiness and his feelings of resentment, ready to embark on he still has no idea what. Some days Violeta says hello and little more to him; on others, she doesn't even seem to see him. She drinks her milky coffee quickly, answers Señora Paquita's questions almost in a whisper, and then leaves. If it's Señor Agustín who is behind the bar, she is more discreet. Her coldness and self-control come increasingly to the fore as the days go by and her mother becomes increasingly self-destructive, sinking deeper and deeper into a heartbreak she has still not accepted or exhausted.

From that first night when Señora Mir fell asleep drunk on the staircase, Violeta seems to have understood very clearly what is going on:

a whole series of shocks has turned her mother's life upside down, and robbed her of her will, but now she knows their coordinates, and thanks to a secret network of associations can guess where her wandering is likely to take her, and where she is to be found: the side entrance to Parque Güell and the waste land opposite, the southern slope of Montaña Pelada, the streets around the Cottolengo and the winding road up to El Carmelo, especially in the last, highest stretch, when it goes from Calle Pasteur to Gran Vista and takes in her favourite Delicias bar, where she can spend hours joking with old Andalusians, knocking back brandy from the keg and hoping to meet someone who might perhaps know of someone who might know . . . Her paranoia and fantasies sometimes lead her to go up to strangers or to make friendly enquiries at sporting reunions and parish clubs in the hope of hearing something about the ex-footballer or ex-tram driver Abel Alonso, the generous mentor and enthusiastic trainer of youth groups in the shanty neighbourhoods, slightly lame but still well turned out, who apparently lived or still lives in the area. Her extravagant way of dressing and increasingly outlandish make-up, allied to a cheerful amiability that often ends up in an alcoholic jumble of words, means that some people either feel sorry for her or make fun of her, but she doesn't seem to care much. She always carries her basket full of herbs with her. If Violeta appears, she takes her by the arm and lets herself be led home without complaining.

On the morning of Saturday, 23 February, Señora Mir was being looked after by her mother-in-law, a small, sour-faced old woman who was seen in the tavern buying a flask of brandy. She showed no desire to inform Señora Paquita about her daughter-in-law's state of mind, or who the brandy was for. She departed before midday, leaving word at the bar that she was going back home to Badalona. A short time later, Señora Mir was patiently trimming some geraniums on her balcony, in a housecoat and slippers, without make-up, her face wrapped in a thick scarf. But early that same afternoon, freshly dressed up and rouged, wearing her sunglasses with the white frames, her clinking bracelets and her palm basket for collecting herbs, she is seen leaving her building and struggling up the street. She comes face to face with Señora Grau, who later explains that when she saw her she felt so upset and sorry that she tried without success to convince her to go back home. Señora Mir did not even look at her, but continued on her way up the hill until she disappeared in Traversera de Dalt.

As night is falling, Violeta comes into the tavern to ask if they have seen her mother. She stands in the doorway, holding the glass door open, her indolent eyes searching for Señora Paquita, who isn't there. Señor Agustín is kneeling by a barrel filling bottles of wine with a funnel, and at the back table four very talkative old men are playing cards. No, we haven't seen your mother in here all day, says the tavern keeper. Almost at once, Ringo notices the girl looking in his direction, and shakes his head sadly. He's sitting at his table, jacket round his shoulders, his head leaning against the wall, struggling to keep his eyes open. He soon closes them, but a while later he realises she is still there, holding the door and staring at him. Then he hears her slightly croaking voice:

"Are you asleep over there?"

"Me?" He straightens his head. "Of course not. I was thinking of you."

"Yes, like I believe that."

She can't make up her mind to come in, still toying with the door.

"My mother's escaped again."

"Do you want me to help look for her?"

Violeta bites her lip, and thinks it over.

"It's not six yet, but it's night already. It gets dark quickly at this time of year."

Ringo is slow to react:

"It does. Are you frightened of going on your own . . . . ? Where will you go, all alone?"

"I don't know, round the neighbourhood."

"Well, do you want me to go with you or not?"

Their glances collide.

"No, thanks."

"O.K., fine. My mother is on night shift again and I have to go with her, and then I have some errands to run . . . so the truth is, I couldn't really go." He stands up slowly, hair falling over his eyes, and puts on his jacket and scarf. "She must have gone to see your grandma. She'll be back, don't worry. She always comes back."

He hasn't even finished when he hears the sound of the bar door slamming. Slamming on his lies. And yet it's true he already had a plan that did not include Violeta. He lets a few minutes pass before going out into the street so that he won't run into her, then enters the stationer's on Calle Providencia where she once worked. He is served by the new assistant, Merche, a dark, chubby-cheeked girl in glasses who lives on Calle de Sors and the year before was Violeta's inseparable friend. She's become very odd, she says, she's not friends with me anymore. No, she doesn't have any pink envelopes. Doesn't he like purple ones, or pale green, or light blue, with silk paper lining? No, thanks. He goes to another stationer's shop, with the same result, until he finally discovers what he is looking for at the kiosk in Plaza Rovira.

Later that night, alone at home and sitting at the dining-room table in the same position and in the same chair as his father the last time he saw him, the paper appears before his eyes in all its pink nakedness, and nothing that occurs to him seems convincing. After an hour he gets up, wraps the scarf round his neck, and rushes off to Señor Huguet's coffee-roasting shed beneath a clear, starry sky with a full moon. While he is turning the handle, the dirty rainwater swirls yet again round the open drain, and when he reaches out his hand half-heartedly at the last minute, he burns his fingers. He soothes his hand in a bucket, and Señor Huguet takes him to task: if he wants to pull a piece of wood out because the fire's too hot, he should use the tongs or put on gloves.

Returning home in the early hours, he puts the bag of coffee on the sideboard and then, without taking off his scarf, he sits down again at the table and picks up the pen, his fingertips still smarting. In his mind's eye he can picture everything he was thinking as he knelt in front of the fire, one hand turning the drum filled with coffee and sugar, the other plunged into the bucket of water. Painstakingly, he writes the name on the envelope, giving the capital V a joyous flourish to the right, just as he remembers having caught a glimpse of on that fateful night of drunken nausea on Las Ramblas.

He sleeps for three hours, head down on the table. At eight in the morning his mother returns from the Residence. She's brought half a puff-pastry cream cake the nuns have given her from the kitchen. He's already prepared coffee, warmed the milk, and toasted the bread on the electric burner. While they are having breakfast together, his mother scolds him yet again for getting up so early.

"You should be asleep. You're working now."

"I'm not sleepy."

"I can make the coffee. Besides, I drink enough of it during the night."

"But the coffee the nuns give you isn't as good as this, is it, Mama?"

She looks so pensive, sitting there with her hands round the bowl of coffee, that he stares at her for a while without saying anything. Eventually he asks: "What are we going to do, Mama?"

"What do you mean?" She studies his face and understands. "Wait. There's nothing else we can do."

As ever, she has come home tired and wanting to go straight to bed, and yet she does all she can to prolong this impromptu early morning conversation. It's the time of day when sleep is calling that she feels her son is at his closest and most distant. Another five or ten minutes to raise his spirits.

"This bad luck won't last for ever," she says. "Don't worry, you're not going to spend your life roasting coffee . . ."

"No, I don't mind, really."

"Señor Huguet is looking for something better for you. One of his brothers-in-law has a grocery store on Calle Aragón. It's a very important place, they deliver to people's homes, and he says that before long they're going to need another assistant, or delivery boy . . . I know it's not perfect, Son, but at least it will be less tiring than working at night."

"It's all the same to me."

"Well, we can think it over, can't we? Go on, talk to me. What's the news in the neighbourhood . . . ? Do you know, the other day I met Violeta in the street? She looks pretty in her nurse's uniform and cap, don't you think?"

She says she thinks Violeta has high hopes of her job, in spite of the worries her mother gives her: according to her, she has lost control of her drinking and is deteriorating day by day. She feels sorry for her friend Victoria, and her behaviour confuses her. She finds it hard to believe that losing the love of any man can lead a woman to such a terrible lack of self-awareness and despair, especially a woman who had not previously shown any sign of weakness when faced with adversity. Of course everything she had been forced to put up with from that idiot of a husband of hers over the years must have something to do with it . . . She intends to go and see her one of these days, she adds as she gets up from the table and collects the dishes, I'll take her some second-hand clothes and a packet of coffee as a gift. She suggests they both go.

"Why should I go, Mama?" he asks anxiously. "What could I say to her . . . ? Leave that, it's my turn today."

He carries the bowls and the rest of the things into the kitchen. Shortly afterwards, while he is having a shower, he glances down at the plughole, where the soapy water round his feet slows its whirling for a second, and this time the spinning envelope seems to let itself be plucked out and rescued before it vanishes for the umpteenth time into the dark drain. Ringo dresses, recovering the smell of the night in his jersey and scarf. Before going out he approaches his mother's bedroom door, listening hard. Two sneezes tell him she isn't asleep yet. She must be praying to the Infant Jesus of Prague on the bedside table, asking him to protect the Rat-catcher, wherever he may be now. Has her Infant ever listened to her?

"I'm going, Mama. Do you need anything?"

"No."

He falls silent for a while before his next question:

"When are we going to France, Mama?"

"What did you say?"

"I said, when are we leaving here . . ."

This time she is the one who takes time to respond:

"Leaving here? Why should we be leaving, Son?" Then another, longer silence. "Why do you ask?"

"No reason. Get some rest."

He's been thinking it over carefully, and for three days he hasn't been back to Bar Rosales so as not to run into Violeta. When he does return to his daily routine, he does something he has never done before: he asks Señor Agustín for a pack of cards and starts playing Patience while waiting for Señora Paquita to come back from the market in Calle Camelias and take over from her brother at the bar. He thinks it would be better to do what he is planning in the early afternoon, when she spends more time in the kitchen than serving, but he doesn't want to wait any longer. Señor Frías has just opened his barber shop next door, and has come into the bar for his early morning coffee. Señor Agustín, leafing through a newspaper on the counter, satisfies his customer's curiosity without much enthusiasm: Yes, indeed, Señora Mir was committed to the Hospital San Pablo late yesterday afternoon. Some boys in El Guinardó found her curled up behind some bushes near the highway up to El Carmelo, and told the staff at the nearby Padre Alegre Cottolengo. They stole her bag, earrings, bracelets, and a basket with herbs in it. Or she lost them, who knows? So she slept there like a log all night until those boys found her? Señor Agustín doesn't know much more, and still can't quite believe what happened, he can't imagine her sleeping out all night, in this cold . . . Ringo can see it, it's not hard to imagine: lying on her side demurely, ready to accept whatever came her way, her pink knees pressed together, her cheek resting on her plump hands, the eyelids with their long, greasy lashes closed over her fantasy. Taken in as an emergency to the San Pablo, says Señor Agustín. A nun who knows her informed her daughter and her mother-in-law. A wound to her head and bruising on her legs, fortunately nothing serious, apparently they're bringing her home tomorrow, and the Badalona grandmother is already here to lend a hand. When she came round she was as right as rain, and guess what she asked for, the cheeky devil? That's right, a little brandy! She didn't want to talk to anybody. When she did explain what had happened, she did so in a rambling, confused manner, but according to her daughter what she said made sense: that afternoon she had been visiting her husband in the asylum. She took him Virginia tobacco and a new pair of pyjamas, cleaned his nails, and then went to Badalona to see her mother-in-law in the market, at the flower stall she has there, and finally visited the Cottolengo, where she had promised to take some children's clothes. And that when she left there it was already dark, and she can't remember anything more. And guess what she said when she finished, bursting into tears? Señor Agustín concludes slyly: that she wasn't at all bothered her bag or her bracelets had been stolen, that the only thing she regretted losing was a ring made from a chicken or pig bone, would you believe?

"Well I never," the barber shakes his head thoughtfully.

"Yes. What a woman, eh?"

Ringo lifts his hand to his chest to feel the slight rustle of the envelope underneath his shirt and jersey. The barber says goodbye and Señor Agustín goes on reading *El Mundo Deportivo*, elbows on the bar. A short while before he gave a loud belch and apologised, saying he has had terrible toothache for a week now. He made a joke about his contented belly, and served himself a small glass of mint liqueur, savouring it and smiling at Ringo with his tiny rat's eyes concealed behind his high, ruddy cheekbones.

When Señor Agustín sees his sister come in with the shopping, he leaves the newspaper open on the counter and carries the basket into the

282

kitchen. Señora Paquita stays on her feet, passes by Ringo without looking at him, and as she is taking off her coat announces that she's going upstairs to change her shoes.

"Put the fish in the fridge and get along to the dentist, I'll sort out everything else," she says, raising her voice so that her brother will hear her. "The cod is for Violeta and her grandmother."

While she is upstairs, Señor Agustín appears in a raincoat and beret. I'm off, Paqui! he shouts from the street door, and makes the usual gesture to Ringo: *keep an eye out for anyone coming in*. As soon as he is on his own, Ringo gets up from the stool, lifts the hem of his jersey, and undoes his shirt. It takes only three quick strides to leave the envelope on the open newspaper. Shortly afterwards, it is the first thing Señora Paquita sees when she moves behind the counter, putting on her apron. She picks it up and turns it over and over, as if she does not know what it is. The envelope is sealed; on the front is written the letter V, on the back there is nothing.

"Who brought this?" she asks Ringo. "Why didn't you call me . . . ? Was Señor Alonso just here?"

"No, it was a boy, Señora Paqui," Ringo says rapidly, not raising his eyes from his game of Patience. "He left a minute ago. He's not from the neighbourhood, I've never seen him around here . . . He asked for you, and seemed in a great hurry. I told him you'd be down straightaway, but he didn't want to wait. He told me the message was from Señor Alonso, and that you would know what to do with it . . ."

"Goodness." She doesn't know whether to be pleased or not. She sketches a smile that reveals her small, dark teeth, and there is a bright gleam in her black eyes. "Is that what he told you?"

"Yes, Señora. He told me: I've brought this letter for the lady who runs the bar. And he showed me the envelope before leaving it there. For Señora Paquita from Señor Alonso, she's expecting it, he said. Then he left."

He is holding a jack of hearts that he can't place in the game.

"So we'll have to tell Violeta," Señora Paquita says to herself, then stands there thinking, still staring at the envelope. "Though I don't know

283

. . . He's got a nerve. But now she has to know about it. Yes, she can decide what to do . . ."

"Is it something important, Señora Paquita?" There's no reply. "Do you want me to go and tell Violeta?"

"She's not at home," she says vaguely. "She's dropping by later for her shopping."

Violeta arrives a few minutes later, tired and in a hurry. She's spent the night by her mother's bedside in the hospital, and Grandma Aurora is waiting for her at home. She is carrying a large envelope with X-rays and test results. Her mother is not well at all, she has very high blood pressure and they have found first-stage diabetes. Taking the cod, she says she probably won't need anything more from the market because her grandmother wants her to go and live with her in Badalona, at least until her mother gets out of hospital.

"I think that's for the best," says Señora Paquita. She hesitates a moment, then goes on: "Do you want to make your mother happy? Give her this. She didn't want you to see it, but . . ." She takes the letter from beneath her apron. "But you must give it to her. It's bound to cheer her up."

"A pleasure." Before taking the letter, she stares at it suspiciously in Señora Paquita's hand. "Oh, that. About time too." Looking disdainfully at the big letter V in blue ink: "And he didn't even have the guts to write her name."

Tearing the envelope open, she takes out the two sheets of pink paper, and slowly unfolds them, as if she were touching some infected material.

"Perhaps you shouldn't read it, my girl . . ." Señora Paquita hesitates.

But Violeta has moved slightly away from her, and is already reading. With a sullen look on her face, and obviously put out. Her stern, distrustful eyes read the lines of writing quickly, while the impostor sits in his favourite refuge next to the window shuffling the pack for a new game of Patience. He watches her closely, in his mind reading the letter at the same time as her, accompanying her word by word, not forgetting a single one, so carefully chosen and so urgently endowed with meaning, but now all of a sudden so vacuous, so empty and fragile in Violeta's interior voice:

Canfranc, 7th December 1948

Dear Vicky,

I hope this letter finds you well. Forgive me, because I ought to have written to you long ago. I'll explain the reason for the delay, but first you need to know that I have never stopped thinking of you.

I'm writing to you from France, from a remote spot lost high in the Pyrenees. It's a starry night, and I'm sitting on the ground with my knapsack beside me. Cold, ice, and silence. The snowy mountains are shining in the moonlight. Snowstorms on the highest peaks, and tracks in the snow along the path. I'm giving this letter to messengers I can trust, a chain of friendly hands, but I have no idea when it will reach you.

I've been told that you are looking for me, that you've been seen wandering on Montaña Pelada, or on the loneliest slopes of Parque Güell and up on Monte Carmelo; that you ask after me day and night, that you've been seen waiting for me where we used to meet, sitting for hours under the blossoming lime tree in the ruins of Can Xirot. You shouldn't do that, Vicky. Out of the love I have for you, I beg you not to. Because I no longer go where I used to go, light of my life, because I'm not what you think I am, because nothing is exactly the same any more, pumpkinhead; because, although my love is still the same, I am not the man I was and am not where I once was. Think of me as an impostor, that we are all living an illusion, and that nobody knows when we will be free of it, but that our love is real.

An unexpected dirty trick of fate, which is always against me and all my plans, has obliged me to absent myself for a time from this city I hate, full of blue rats and broken promises, but I am sure you will forgive me. Urgent matters of the greatest importance, that I should not explain for your own safety, because what you don't know you can't tell, have brought me to France fleeing from justice and I don't know when I'll be able to return. But you have been and continue to be my lucky star, and I know I shall not get lost. I'd like to live in words, because in them I shall be faithful to you for ever, to the far side of death.

It is possible that this letter is not what you were hoping for, the one announcing our rapid, so greatly desired reunion. Possibly I should ask you to forget me, perhaps it would be best for us to say farewell, I don't know, I have never lived a love as strong as this, and have never felt so confused . . . What would a woman as generous as you think if she knew that the man she loved so much, who always made so much of his ideals, is now no more than a charlatan, a good-for-nothing, a restless soul, a cheap smuggler who one day could end up in prison? Don't you think that there's no longer any place for our love in Barcelona? All I can say to you is this: Don't wait for me, but let me wait for you everywhere, in everything. The land I'm going to is called Shangri-la, and they say it's a land of fantasy. But what does that matter if we have dreamed it, what does it matter if it is a lie?

Listen: Don't go out alone at night; don't stray into neighbourhoods you don't know. You won't find me in any tavern or sports centre, don't search for me in the choking city of children with no home or parents, the accursed city of blue rats.

I'm sorry to have to tell you all this, but closing my eyes and shrugging my shoulders again, as I have done until now, is something I feel I can no longer do. I've already hurt you enough that way. I'm overwhelmed by a strange sense of guilt for the pain I caused you without meaning to . . . I don't know whether I'll be able to explain it to you some day. No matter. Tomorrow I am leaving here for distant snow-capped mountains and valleys of shadow, and I have no notion, my love, of when I'll be able to return, and so I cannot and should not ask you to wait for me. I want you to take care of yourself, don't drink so much, don't ruin your life, don't give them any reason to gossip about you in the neighbourhood. Listen to your daughter, and you'll see how everything works out. Up there, near the summit of Montaña Pelada, among the bushes of lavender and thyme where the wind blows, we will be happy again someday. I'll pick herbs again for you. In spring the brightly coloured kites will dance in the blue sky once more, and you and I will see it all, we'll climb hand-in-hand up hillsides filled with broom.

With this thought I leave you. Good luck, Vicky my love. I send you a million kisses, and may the angels watch over you as you sleep.

From someone who loves and will never forget you,

Abel Alonso

She reads all this in one go, without a single incredulous or disapproving twist of the mouth, without showing any surprise or satisfaction, without blinking even once at any paragraph or word. Two sheets covered in a rushed, crude and pointed calligraphy, leaning dramatically over to the right as though caught in a gale or as if trying to escape beyond the edges of the paper. Two sheets of a pale, pure pink that he rescued from oblivion and that Violeta finishes reading, then folds once more and hastily replaces in the envelope. She doesn't look at Ringo once, not even out of the corner of her eye. And then, with a faint, spiky and vengeful smile she takes the envelope in both hands, closes her eyes, and for a few interminable seconds seems determined to tear it to pieces.

"You mother didn't want you to read it," says Señora Paquita. "But of course, after all that's happened . . ." Then, unable to contain her curiosity: "I hope it's not bad news."

Violeta shrugs.

"It's arrived too late, Señora Paqui. Mama doesn't need anything like this anymore."

But her hands don't move, and in the end she doesn't tear the letter up. She undoes her coat roughly and stows the envelope in the deep pocket of her nurse's uniform. She's not sure whether she will let her mother read it, we'll see, she says, getting ready to leave. She reckons that what her mother needs now is to forget, and besides, she adds in a scornful tone, in the end the famous letter is nothing but a pack of lies, disgusting memories and false promises. What else was there to expect from the penniless fraud who wrote it?

"Goodbye and thank you, Señora Paquita. In a few days we're going to live with grandmother. Mama is going to need a lot of looking after from now on, and I can't manage on my own. I'll be very sorry when we have to go . . ."

"That's fine, sweetheart. Be strong. Everything will work out."

Señora Paquita herself opens the door for her. As Violeta is crossing the threshold, she glances fleetingly at Ringo.

Three days later, from early in the morning, a bucket and two old wooden crates overflowing with bunches of dried herbs tied up with ribbons, jars of leaves and roots, and pots containing creams and oils, stood out on the pavement awaiting the rubbish truck. Later on, two men came to load furniture and possessions into a van and Violeta went into Bar Rosales to bid farewell to Señora Paquita and her brother. Ringo wasn't there to see or listen, but he learnt she was accompanied by a young porter from the Hospital del Mar who helped her with the move, and to whom Señora Paquita offered vermouth and olives. Less hostile and evasive than on previous occasions, Violeta reported that her mother had been transferred directly from the San Pablo hospital to her mother-in-law's house in Badalona, that she was still in bed there, but well looked after, although she was still very ill, and that she had asked her to tell Señora Paqui how sorry she was to leave the neighbourhood, that she would miss the tavern and the nice chats she had with her, and that well, what could you do, she had thought her liver could stand it, but she had no luck there either, that's life, isn't it?

At eight o'clock that same day, wearing for the first time a striped overall and grey woollen gloves, Ringo starts work in Ultramarinos J. Casadeus and Brothers, a century-old establishment in Calle Aragón on the corner of Calle Bruch. Balanced on his shoulder is a big basket of foodstuffs and drinks for him to deliver to a select clientele living in the Ensanche, known for their generous tips.

It'll only be for a while, his mother has told him, nothing bad lasts for ever. For a short while, yes, how often has he heard those well-intentioned words, at home, in the tavern, in so many places, but the truth is that in the end everything lasts until you're ready for the knackers' yard. More than anything else, more than the daily burden of desires and needs, even more than his fear or uncertainty over the future, he is oppressed by a vague sense of disquiet that he didn't do what he should have, what was most appropriate and best, even though he is well aware that the best and most appropriate course of action would not have made the slightest bit of difference.

Since then the impostor has on more than one occasion imagined those flashing eyes reading the longed-for letter, the frantic movement of her eyelashes and the pursing of her fleshy lips as she paused over some sentence or other, or held her breath at this or that phrase or word that perhaps succeeded in offering her a taste of all that her passionate heart had so eagerly pursued, whether or not it was the best and most appropriate for her. Sometimes it has occurred to him it is better not to know if the letter eventually reached her, if it pleased or disappointed her, if it eased her heart and left it indifferent, if at the very least it brought her the comfort of forgetting.

EPILOGUE

Everything that grew took a long time to grow.
And everything that disappeared took a long time to be forgotten.

JOSEPH ROTH

15

THE MESSENGER'S ERRATIC FOOTSTEPS

One Sunday morning in August 1958, the young man still known to some of his friends as Ringo entered the Club Natación Cataluña to enquire about the benefits of membership. The club was situated on the ground floor of a building next door to the Delicias cinema, at number 218 on Travesera de Gràcia, and used the installations and pool that belonged to the Baños Populares de Barcelona. The young man was considering going for a swim there three or four times a week, at times when the swimming pool wasn't very crowded. He had turned twenty-five, and could permit himself this small outlay. He had a steady job in a bookshop, two of his short stories had recently been published in a literary magazine, and he was planning to write his first novel. His mother was still looking after old people in the Residence on Calle Sors, at more reasonable hours these days. His father, after spending three years in Modelo prison and returning home very thin, with pulmonary emphysema and physically diminished – although just as loudmouthed and unreliable as ever, as to her great relief Alberta light of my life was able to confirm – had, thanks to the efforts of the Mother Superior at the Las Darderas convent, obtained the post of supervisor in a school run by the Sisters of Mary. During the breaks he was there to keep an eye on both the youngsters and on any strangers trying to sneak into the school.

The first thing Ringo did was to take a look at the pool from the balcony, where a group of local boys were playing noisily among the wooden benches. A game of water polo between two youth teams had just finished, and some of the players were still fooling around with the ball in front of one of the goals. Their cheerful splashes and shouts echoed round the enclosed space of the club. On the edge of the pool, just about to dive in with their hands together and knees bent, a gaggle of girls were trying to attract someone's attention. Three boys were competing to dive for something at the bottom of the pool, a coin perhaps. On the far side, a suntanned man in a brief pair of trunks was instructing a group of small children swimming in single file, all of them wearing rubber rings. From the balcony, a few married couples in their Sunday best were admiring their offsprings' prowess while they guzzled drinks and packets of crisps. Behind them, an old man in a white overalls and a cyclist's cap was pushing his broom beneath the seats to sweep up what they had thrown away.

Ringo sat on the bench, draped his arms over the railing, and stared down at the bottom of the pool three or four metres below him. It reminded him of the muddy water and leaping frogs in the irrigation ponds that marked the childhood summers he spent in El Panadés, and for an instant the recollection made him feel as if he had somehow been caught out, as though somebody had read his thoughts and was reproaching him for his secret love of frogs and dirty water. It was then that he noticed the old man: he had stopped sweeping and was staring at him, raising the peak of his cap with one finger to see more clearly. Ringo did not recognise him until he saw him suddenly lurch towards him as if unscrewing his foot from the floor, and come over smiling, hand outstretched.

"My, my, look who's here."

Ringo stood up feeling uneasy, pretending not to see the hand.

"How are you?"

The yellowish, still abundant head of hair that the cap could barely cover, the greying stubble, the voice weakened by asthma, his profile more angular, but the same weary grey of the eyes, the same handsome symmetry of the deep wrinkles on his face. He also still retained something of his former energy in the high shoulders and neck, and a friendly air that suggested a constant readiness to help.

"So-so, my lad. No more than so-so. Sit down, don't stand on ceremony." He sat down beside him slowly, leaning on the broom. Before speaking he took a deep breath and cleared his throat nervously. "What a surprise seeing you here at the club."

"I might join. To swim a bit."

"Good idea. Are you interested in water polo?"

"I was just looking . . . I didn't know you worked here."

"I'll soon have been here two years." Ringo did not know what to say, so Señor Alonso added: "Would you like a drink? A beer? I could bring it you in a jiffy, there's a bar downstairs . . ."

"Thanks, I don't want anything."

It was hot, so Ringo took his coat off and hung it over the railing. Abel Alonso sat very still, his mouth wide open as he drew breath before he spoke again.

"Life became hard, you know? The club lent me a hand. Maintenance and things like that. Just think, my best goalie, from way back, a kid who lived in the shacks at Can Tunis and was always looking for trouble, is now the hundred metres butterfly champion here." He smiled, giving slow, feeble nods of the head. "He's the one who got me the job. As you see, there's always some grateful kid."

Ringo felt confused. He looked around.

"It's very noisy, isn't it?"

"Everything echoes in here."

"It seems like a nice atmosphere."

"A family atmosphere, especially on Sundays. And they scream like little devils. It's a sign of the kids' good mental health. I've always believed that. Would you like one?"

He had taken a sweet out of his pocket and began carefully unwrapping it. Ringo said no. Then he said, just to break the silence that troubled him more than the conversation:

"Well anyway, it wasn't that long ago."

"Ten years. Too long for me." He rolled the sweet around in his mouth noisily but without any fuss, covering it with saliva and the bitterness of his words. Yes, now he really was an old man, inside and out, thought Ringo. "You must have done your national service."

"Yes."

"That's good. Well, what's new? How are things down there, what are people saying?" He cleared his throat again, then said more darkly: "What news of Violeta, that girl you didn't like . . . ?"

"I haven't seen her since she left the neighbourhood with her mother."

"Oh, so they went in the end, did they? She wanted to be an operating-theatre nurse, didn't she?" He nodded his head slowly and thoughtfully again, as if confirming something to himself. "Yes, that was what she was studying. So you haven't seen her again. Well, well. Nor her mother either?"

Ringo paused for a few moments before replying.

"Señora Mir died some time ago."

"She did? Victoria died? When was that?"

"It must have been about five years back. I heard Agustín say so in the tavern. It seems she was very ill."

"I'm sorry to hear it. Poor Victoria was an alcoholic."

"It wasn't just the drink," Ringo snorted. "She never recovered from a night when she went out looking for you and got lost. She caught pneumonia and had a very hard time of it."

"I didn't know any of that. Where did she get lost . . . ?"

"You'd already washed your hands of the situation."

The note of reproach took the old man aback. Nodding resignedly once more, he smiled wryly:

"If I remember rightly, my lad, the last time we met you were quite merry."

"I was drunk. There was no way you should have trusted me that night."

Señor Alonso took his time replying.

"Oh, well, I suppose you're right. I was irresponsible, see, and at my age that kind of stupidity is unforgiveable . . . Besides, it was cowardly of me, I should have sorted things out myself . . . By the way, I never had a chance to thank you. It's true, we faced that difficult situation shoulder to shoulder." The frantic chorus of childish cries from down in the pool caught his attention. A string of corks floating on the surface marked off the area where the youngest children were swimming, closely watched by their instructor. Ringo looked down as well. Little frogs doing the breaststroke in their rings. "Anyway, you weren't so drunk that night, no sir. But you were very excited at exploring the seamy side of the city, you felt like a real man. So serious, wanting so much to fall in love . . ." His face crumpled as he smiled at the pleasant memory. "Do you remember, in that dive on Calle San Ramón? You do remember, don't you?"

"Of course," Ringo admitted reluctantly, preferring to concentrate on what was going on in the pool, the scuffles between the water polo players and the little splashing frogs.

"It's true you were a bit tipsy, but you knew what you were doing, otherwise I wouldn't have entrusted you with that errand. I always appreciated you, you know, and always trusted you – don't ask me why. Such an observant, polite and responsible lad . . . I suppose you got home safely, and the next day took the letter to Bar Rosales. I suppose you must have, although the fact is I never heard anything more . . ."

"Yes, I got home safely."

"Well then," he nodded, satisfied, "everything turned out as intended. And when you handed Señora Paquita the letter, you knew who it was for, didn't you? Because you looked at the envelope . . ."

"There was no need, Señor Alonso."

"Don't tell me you weren't the tiniest bit curious . . ." he paused as Ringo gestured impatiently. "What's wrong? Was there some problem?"

"No problem, no," Ringo retorted. Why on earth does this fellow want to rake up that ghastly business again now? "Look, don't get me wrong, but I wasn't in the least bit interested in your love affairs . . . besides, it wasn't hard to guess what the message was, it was predictable."

"Oh, it was, was it?" Señor Alonso's eyes searched his face. "You mean to say you knew beforehand who the letter was for?"

"Of course I did," said Ringo, picking up his jacket and putting it on again. "Time had gone by, and you had no wish to see her again, so the message was clear . . ."

"What are you doing? Leaving already?"

"It's late."

"Hang on a moment, will you? There's something I wanted to explain . . ."

Señor Alonso hesitated. His head sank between his shoulders in a sudden gesture of contrition. Ringo sat down again to listen to his stammered, confused excuses. He made so many false starts, coughs, and clearings of the throat that he sounded just like the engine of a Biscuter scooter. He admitted it had been a mistake, and beyond that a crazy move, I must have been mad, he said, just think, a desperate plea from someone who doesn't even dare show his face, a cry for help that had to pass through the hands of a fifteen-year-old boy, and then those of an old maid running a bar . . . It was crucial Señora Paqui didn't discover where he was living, he added, not her or anyone else, so the details of the rendezvous were inside the envelope, together with the insane proposal. That they should run away together, no less! It had been the greatest, most unforgivable mistake he had ever made, and it had taken him less than two days to regret taking advantage of such a level-headed and reliable boy like him, and he had felt really bad, because he couldn't shake off his crazy passion for that young girl. He had tried to forget her, spending a lot of time and effort to do so without success, and anyway in the end he never got any reply from her, and had not heard anything more about it. He never knew if she hadn't wanted to respond to his call, or if she'd been prevented from doing so, and besides, it was all for the best . . . Yes indeed, because when a man plays such a dirty trick as he had, he didn't deserve anything more than scorn and to be forgotten. He recalled Victoria's generous hospitality, and its unfortunate consequences, the coming into close contact with that strangest of creatures, someone so unhappy, so withdrawn and sullen, and yet at the same time so full of life, with a furtive sensuality that was so intense it could have led them both to perdition . . .

"I bet she laughed at me and tore the letter up," Señor Alonso concluded, puffing out his cheeks. "So much the better. She really was unbelievable. The last time I saw her she pretended she had fallen in the bathroom, just to keep me from leaving."

"But . . ."

At first, Ringo had been only half-listening to this tortuous outpouring of guilt, regrets, and self-justification, until the old man's dark voice began to trail off. Doubts had already been growing in his mind, but at that moment the truth struck home in both his heart and his brain. He sat staring at him like somebody who has seen a ghost but still can't quite believe what he is seeing. He got to his feet slowly without knowing why, staring into space as though trying to interpret the flood of images overwhelming him.

"What are you saying?" he murmured, collapsing back onto the bench.

"Believe me, I was desperate to avoid it."

"That's impossible. Señora Paquita was expecting a letter for Señora Mir. Right from the start she said it was for her . . . the letter was for Señora Mir!"

"I never told her anything of the sort. No way. What a gossip she was! I can understand she must have been really surprised when she got the letter, but naturally . . . Are you listening?"

But naturally, he explained, he couldn't tell Señora Paquita who the letter was for, because she would have gone straight round to inform Violeta's mother, and then there would have been hell to pay;

all he could ask her to do was to be patient and discreet.

"But you . . ." Ringo could not get the words out. "You knew what great friends Señora Mir and Señora Paquita were, you knew they liked to gossip, to fantasise . . ."

"Yes, that's true too," Señor Alonso admitted, a light-hearted note stealing into his voice. "They were as alike as two peas. Well, I made so many mistakes . . . What can I say, I was bedazzled, I had no idea what was going on, I could only think of one thing . . . Anyway, you shouldn't have paid any attention to the ramblings of an old goat like her, should you? That woman was all talk. Well, none of that matters now."

Ringo could not get over his astonishment. Among the many dismal questions whirling round his brain, what was uppermost was the feeling that he had been caught in a trap. The mouse finally took the cheese.

"So that's it. It was pretty disgusting of you, wasn't it? She was little more than a child . . ."

Señor Alonso wagged his forefinger to deny this. He smiled vaguely and said:

"No, it was her mother who was the child. Oh yes, she really was, I can tell you. She really was," he said, closing his eyes. Then almost at once, sensing Ringo's reaction, he opened them again. "What's wrong, are you leaving already?"

"Goodbye, Señor Alonso."

Ringo had got to his feet once more, and this time seemed determined to leave. The other man stood up as well.

"Well, I hope to see you again . . . it would be good if you joined the club. Membership is twenty-five pesetas a month. Cheap, isn't it? You could ask your girlfriend to come along . . ." He decided to offer him his hand, with an imperceptible knowing wink, a timid plea for him to understand and forget. "I wish you all the best, my lad."

Ringo accepted his outstretched hand coldly, as though mortally offended. An adolescent's natural disposition towards pretence and imposture that years earlier had created a gratifying to-and-fro between truth and lies, and which now was starting to weave invention and memory together in his attempts to write (but as yet without any feelings of guilt), led him to utter a few conventional words of farewell, then he headed for the stairs leading down to the foyer. As he descended the first steps he could still feel the old faun's affable, condescending gaze on the back of his neck, and before he reached the exit, when the hubbub of voices and cries from the pool began to die down, he began to reflect on good intentions and how useless they were. It was true he had nothing to reproach himself for, but in that case, why did the sense of disquiet persist?

Stepping outside, the harsh August light flooding the streets of Gràcia blinded him momentarily. Abel Alonso's description was still ringing in his ears, although by now it had acquired an appropriately sarcastic overtone.

Such an observant, polite and responsible lad.

JUAN MARSÉ, born in Barcelona in 1933, is a Spanish novelist and screen-writer. Following the publication of his first novel in 1960, he has gone on to become one of the most respected living authors in Spain. He has been honoured with many literary awards, including the European Literature Prize and the Cervantes Prize.

NICK CAISTOR is a translator, journalist and author. He has translated more than forty books from Spanish and Portuguese, including works by Paulo Coelho and Eduardo Mendoza. He has twice been awarded the Premio Valle-Inclán for Spanish translation.